THE MINSTREL BOY

THE MINSTREL BOY

A NOVEL

by

A. J. CRONIN

LONDON
VICTOR GOLLANCZ LTD
1975

© A. J. Cronin 1975
ISBN 0 575 01972 7

Printed in Great Britain by
The Camelot Press Ltd, Southampton

THE MINSTREL BOY

ONE

I

On a windy March day in the mid-twenties I was seated in the office of the Prefect of Studies, awaiting admission to the Jesuit Day School of St. Ignatius and, after seven rough years in the free council schools of the city of Winton, rather glad to be there. At my birth, my father, in the first flush of paternity —filled, too, with sanguine expectations of his own future—had entered me for Stonyhurst. When he died, six years later, after a painful and protracted illness, his laudable ambition remained unfulfilled: he left barely enough to pay the doctors and the undertaker.

Yet St. Ignatius was not a bad substitute for the parent Lancashire institution. Built, with its adjacent church, on an eminence not far from the city centre, dedicated to the education of sons of the Catholic bourgeoisie and indeed, since the fees were moderate, of the working class, all the masters were Jesuit priests, for the most part men of birth and breeding, aloof, after the manner of the Order, and to me so intimidating that I sprang to my feet as the door opened behind me.

But it was another boy who strolled in, quite unperturbed, indeed completely at ease. I sat down again and, with a half smile, he seated himself beside me. Infinitely better dressed than I, he had on a dark flannel suit of distinguished cut, fine socks and shining shoes and a spotless soft white shirt set off by a striped green and black tie which I judged, correctly, to be his prep school colours. A linen handkerchief peeped from his breast pocket, and, as if this were not enough, a small cornflower was tucked, and worn with an air of scornful detachment, in his buttonhole. He was, moreover, so devastatingly good looking, with his pale complexion, soft blond hair and flax blue eyes, that I became more and more conscious, not only of my flaming crop of red hair, freckles, long nose, but of my painfully poor attire, old flannel bags, blue jersey knitted by my mother, and a crack in the toe cap of my right, worn-out shoe which I had just acquired by a reckless punt at a ball that bounced from the school yard as I came up the hill. In fact, I hated him, and decided to pick a fight with him at the first opportunity.

Suddenly he stunned me by breaking the silence of that august book-lined chamber.

"Boring, isn't it? Punctuality is not the politeness of Jesuits." He began to sing.

"They left us in the lurch, waitin' at the church."

Then, "I bet Beauchamp's in the pantry having his elevenses. Frightful guzzler, I believe. But terribly cultured. Old Etonian. Convert, of course."

He began again, rather more loudly: "They left me in the lurch, waiting at the church . . ."

At that moment the door swung open and there swept in a fine, massive, imperious figure, well banded by his soutane which, however, failed to conceal a pronounced and advancing corpulence. In his right hand he was carrying a plate on which reposed a large double cheese sandwich. This he placed on his desk, deftly covered with a napkin taken from his drawer. He then sat down rather heavily, with the words, half excusatory, half an apostrophe:

"Edere oportet ut vivas."

"Non vivere ut edas," murmured the little snob beside me.

"Good," said the prelate who was, indeed, the redoubtable Fr. Beauchamp. "But, though you know your Cicero, uncalled for." He paused, looking from one to the other. "As I approached the sanctuary of my study I was greeted by most unlydian strains . . ."

"I am the culprit, reverend sir," my companion acknowledged very fairly. "I have the absurd habit, almost unconscious, when I am nervous or waiting on someone who is late, of erupting into song . . ."

"Indeed!" said Beauchamp grimly. "Then stand up and erupt now. But nothing vulgar, I beg of you."

I suppressed a gleeful chuckle. Now the little prig must really make an ass of himself. He got slowly to his feet. There was a pause. The pause lengthened. Then, fixing his gaze far above Beauchamp's head, he began to sing.

It was the Panus Angelicus, that most lovely and difficult Latin hymn. And as the sweet and moving words filled the room, ascending, as it were, to heaven, the stupid smile faded from my face. Never, never had I heard it sung so beautifully

as now, clear, true, entrancing. Compelled, I gave myself to it.
When it was over, a profound momentous silence followed.

I was stunned, dumbfounded. Although my knowledge of
music was then extremely limited, I had enough good taste
to recognize that the little dressed-up prodigy had a truly
beautiful, an exceptional, a spectacular voice! Beauchamp too
was obviously deeply impressed.

"Ha. Hum," he said, and again, "Ha. Hum. We must
certainly speak of you to our choirmaster, the good Father
Roberts." He paused. "You must be the Fitzgerald boy."

"I am Desmonde Fitzgerald. The Desmonde written with
a final 'e'."

"It shall be so inscribed," Fr. Beauchamp answered with
unexpected mildness. "I have had in fact much correspondence
with your father over the years. A most erudite and distinguished scholar. It was from him that I got my Trinity College
Apocalypse, the Roxburgh Club's rare and much prized
edition." He paused. "But when he wrote me some months
before his death, he said you were to go to Downside."

"Maternal fondness has kept me at home, sir. And inflicted
me upon you. Rather to the relief of the Benedictines."

"So you are now living in Winton?"

"My mother, who is Scottish, wished to return to her native
land. She has taken a house in Overtown Crescent."

"A delightful situation, overlooking the park. I shall
certainly call upon her . . . perhaps she will give me tea." A
reflective look came over his face, he moistened his lips. "As a
Scot she will know of these delicious little iced French cakes, a
speciality of the town. A survival, indeed, of the Old Alliance."

"I shall ensure, sir," Desmonde answered gravely, "that a
generous supply is on hand for your visit."

"Good. Good. Ha. Hum." He turned, inspecting me from
beneath his enormous eyebrows. "And now you?"

Thoroughly embittered by this glowing and intimate
interchange which had made me feel more than ever an out-
sider, I muttered from between clenched teeth:

"I am merely Shannon."

He seemed rather to like this. He beamed, almost
benignantly.

"Ah, yes. You are coming to us on the Kelvin Scholarship."
He leaned forward to inspect an open folder on his desk. "As,

despite your length, you seem rather a 'modest crimson-tippit' youth, would it help your self-esteem to know that your papers were quite exceptional? Father Jaeger, who corrected for the examination, so regarded them. Does that please you?"

"It will please my mother when I tell her."

"What a good answer! Now you are no longer 'merely' but most admirably Shannon." He looked me up and down, kindly, not missing my burst shoe. "And at your convenience you may call on the Bursar for the first instalment of your scholarship. The office is open from two till five."

The rich aroma of new baked bread had now penetrated the napkin and was deliciously permeating the room. I was already drooling and it became clear that the good Prefect of Studies was anxious to get on with his sandwich. Briefly, therefore, he informed us that we were both allocated to the Upper Fourth Form, instructed us as to how we might reach the class room and dismissed us.

But as we passed his desk on the way out he reached out a huge hand and deftly picked the flower from Fitzgerald's buttonhole.

"During school hours, no floral decorations, if you please."

Desmonde flushed but said nothing, merely inclined his head.

But as we came out of the study into the corridor my companion smiled.

"That's Beauchamp for you. Wonderful brain. Insatiable stomach! I'll bet he makes a salad of my cornflower. And what an idiot I was to sing for him. Now I am stuck with another choir. After three years as the bleeding prima donna of my prep school."

"Perhaps your voice will break?" I suggested consolingly.

"It has done, very early. Now I am a beastly, confirmed Don Ottavio, a Cavaradossi, a blasted Pinkerton." Taking my arm, "I hope you'll like me, as we're to be together. I think I might like you. That 'merely' was very pretty. Do you play chess?"

"I play football," I said. "Do you?"

"Never kicked a ball in my life. But I'll come and watch you. I say, why don't we nip over for a quiet ginger beer before we start the toil of the day? There's a good-looking bun shop across the way."

"I'm stony," I said coldly.

"Haven't I asked you? Do come."

He guided me across the street to what was, in fact, a baker's shop which had come to be regarded as the tuck shop of the school. Inside, it was pleasantly cosy. We sat down.

"Two Schweppes' stone gingers, please, as cool as possible, and each with a slice of lemon, if you happen to have such a thing."

The woman behind the counter gave him an odd look but a few moments later two full foaming glasses appeared each with a slice of lemon swimming on top.

"Thank you, madam. May I pay you?"

He paid. It was a long time since I had enjoyed a ginger beer. The first long cool draught was mellowing.

"Good, isn't it?" He smiled. "The citron does improve it. Now tell me about yourself. Apart from scoring goals, what do you want to do?"

I told him I hoped to try for a university scholarship and if lucky to go in for medicine. "What about you?"

He immediately became serious.

"I want very much to become a priest. And it would please my mother too. She is a very dear, pious person." He smiled. "So when you are in Harley Street I shall be a Cardinal in Rome. Those Red Hats are terribly becoming!"

We both burst out laughing. Impossible to resist him. Half an hour ago I was itching to knock his block off. Now he had won me over. I liked him immensely. He drained his glass.

"Shall we have another foaming tankard?"

I felt my face getting very red. But I said very firmly:

"I'm sorry, Fitzgerald, I can't stand you one back. And as I don't intend sponging upon you in future I must tell you that we, my mother and I, are frightfully hard up."

He made sympathetic mutterings. I saw he was dying to ask me, but I had no wish to enlighten him further. And, indeed, he had the good taste not to press me. He said:

"All the best saints were poor, and loved poverty."

"They can have it," I said.

He smiled. "Anyway . . . for heaven's sake don't let it interfere with our friendship."

Five minutes later when we left the shop I made no objection when he took my arm and said:

"It's rather early, but would it bore you if we first-named each other? I do hate being called Fitzgerald. All we Fitzes are almost certainly descended from Charles II's bastards. He threw Fitzes at them with the *bâton sinistre*. It's a repulsive thought. I much prefer Desmonde provided you never, never call me Des. What's yours?"

"I have a perfectly horrible name. I was called Alexander as a vain propitiation, quite useless, to my grandfather. And Joseph in honour of the saint. But my friends usually call me Alec."

We entered the class room. He gave me a pleased look when we saw that our desks were together.

II

DESMONDE'S FATHER HAD been a bookseller. But no modern novel had ever been seen to enter the precincts of the dusty little diamond-paned shop tucked away in a corner of the Dublin Quays, and known throughout Europe and beyond as a storehouse of rare old volumes, special editions of the fine arts, historical pamphlets, the transactions of learned societies and suchlike treasures, sought after by intelligent collectors with an eye for something special at rather less than the outrageous price demanded in London or New York.

Although he had not made a fortune—as he often told his clients when making a deal—Fitzgerald was comfortably situated, and, twelve years older than his wife, he had prudently secured her fortune by a double life endowment policy, which would afford her a substantial annual income on his death—an event which had in fact recently occurred.

His widow, Elizabeth, was Scottish, a Lanarkshire woman who had never been quite at home by the turgid waters of the Liffey. After a decent interval which had enabled her to sell the house and to secure a reasonable sum for the stock and goodwill of the business, she had come to Winton, where, with the facility of a returned native, she had quickly found the small delightful terrace house to which Desmonde had referred when the good Fr. Beauchamp invited himself to tea. With a doting mother, Desmonde had everything he might desire: fine clothes, pocket money ad libitum, a new bicycle to spin down to school. . . .

How different was my situation. My mother, daughter of a
prosperous Ayrshire farmer, had been disowned by her
family when she ran off with my Irish father and, the greater
crime, became a Roman Catholic. After his death, persistence
in this faith had killed all chance of reconciliation. But my brave
little mother was not easily defeated. After a brief course of
instruction she secured a post as a health visitor to the Winton
Corporation. Her work took her to the notorious Anderson
district of the city, slum areas riddled with poverty and destitu-
tion, where so many of the children were blighted and deformed
by rickets. This splendid though exacting work suited my
mother's cheerful and energetic temperament. The pay,
scarcely commensurate with the effort and the results obtained,
was precisely two pounds a week. After deduction of two shillings and sixpence for superannuation tax and a further seven
and sixpence as weekly rental for our two-room 'flat', precisely
thirty shillings remained to feed, clothe, and maintain my
mother and myself until the next twice blessed pay day came
along. But let it not be imagined that we were miserable and
starved in our sparsely furnished 'room and kitchen' four
flights up, interminable steps which I climbed at the trot,
knowing that I was going home, and that always there would be
something to eat there for a hungry boy. Porridge in the morning and, if necessary, in the evening, varied by that inimitable
Scottish dish, pease brose and buttermilk, Scots broth made
from marrow bones, and stiff with vegetables, home baked
scones or bannocks, and at the weekend a joint of beef which
after Sunday manifested itself on succeeding days as hot pot or
shepherd's pie. Nor must I forget the sack of potatoes which
arrived unfailingly every August, sent surreptitiously by an
old worker on the parental farm. These were pilfered goods and
how sweet they were, big floury King Edwards, baked in the
oven and served with a pat of butter. I ate even the skin.

Nevertheless, my style and condition of life differed so
markedly from the ease and comfort of Desmonde's existence
that our continued and growing friendship became all the more
remarkable. We met always with such a sense of joy and
renewal, never a trace of superiority on his side or envy upon
mine, though he had spun down on his new Raleigh bicycle
while I had walked the two miles to school because I had not
a halfpenny for the tram.

Close friendships are usually frowned upon, if not discouraged, in most Jesuit institutions. But as Desmonde and I were later to move up through the various forms, increasingly devoted to each other, there was never a hint of anything suspect in our relationship. I was obviously not the type for a love match—I had gone almost immediately into the football team where, as centre half, my genius for rough play had been observed and commended, while Desmonde, under his light hearted charm, had revealed himself as a postulant, seriously intent upon his vocation. Every morning, before classes began, he was in church for Mass and Holy Communion. He persuaded me to join the Sodality, towards which I had only the slightest leanings. And as the school went down for various services at such times as Easter and Holy Week, kneeling beside him, I would see tears stream from his eyes fixed upon the Crucifix above the altar.

Desmonde was generally liked by the fathers and with Fr. Roberts he was an especial favourite, regarded indeed as a gift from Heaven. With his fellow students he was too exceptional to be popular, being regarded by some as a snob and by others as something of a freak. I am obliged to confess that but for me he might have suffered many indignities from the tougher element in our little community.

But for all his sensitivity, he was not a coward. On one occasion, when cornered by a group of rowdies, scurrilously taunted, and invited to defend himself, he put his hands in his pockets and, with a smile, advanced his face invitingly.

"I can't fight you. But if you want to give me a bloody nose, just go ahead."

For a moment, a petrifying surprise held the group motionless, an open-mouthed still-life, then mutterings broke out in the horrendous Doric of Winton which could be construed as follows:

"He's no feart . . . don't him hit, Wullie . . . lee him alane . . ." remarks suddenly giving way to wild shouts of laughter, less derisory than flattering to Desmonde, who bowed politely, and, his hands still in his pockets, walked quietly away. But I felt sure that his heart was beating like mad as he seated himself on the low stone boundary wall with his back to the playground. This was his favourite seat during recreation. He never took part in our rough and tumble games since he had never learned to kick or control a football. But on this perch, disdainfully he read the office of the day or something from Livy, his favourite author. His main preoccupation, however, was to watch the ebb and flow of life in the narrow little street, to drop a coin in the hand of any beggar, deemed legitimate, who importuned him, and above all, especially when the wind blew hard, as it frequently did on the steep hill, to keep an alert weather eye open for the straw-hatted, blue-uniformed girls who made their way, up and down, to the adjacent convent school.

These girls, all from good-class homes, were naturally regarded by the College as chattering intruders to be ignored with lowered or averted eyes. Desmonde, however, had no such inhibitions; he studied them with curious, impartial detachment, as one might regard a strange, aboriginal race, and his comments, derisory, often amusing, were certainly devoid of amorous yearning.

"Here comes little tubby. I say, doesn't she waddle! And there's mother's darling, note the curly curls. Ribbons too, bless her. Oh, la la! Here's the tall blonde effort. Rather a smasher, but for those enormous feet!"

This was merely school-boy nonsense, but on days of real turbulence when sudden gusts swirled downhill sending hats skimming and tempestuous petticoats ballooning to expose chaste blue serge knickers, I felt that perhaps he was carrying the game too far and that it evinced, perhaps, an unrealized attraction towards the other sex. Whether or not, it did become apparent, from bright-eyed side glances and suppressed giggles, that this frieze of young girls had become emotionally aware of the neat, nonchalant young Apollo perched upon the wall, who often produced, from a side pocket, the forbidden cornflower and tucked it in his buttonhole.

Only one person in the school seemed actively to dislike Desmonde: Fr. Jaeger, who took the fifth form, sponsored and trained the football team, a short, tough, ruddy, perennially active little man to whom I soon became devoted and who in his turn seemed to have some interest in me. One day, as I came into his study he suddenly remarked:

"You're rather intimate with Fitzgerald."

"Yes, we are good friends."

"I don't like soft boys. Have you seen how he sits on the wall staring at the Convent girls, on their way up to school?"

I checked my reply. No one but an idiot argued with Jaeger.
I merely said:

"That wall game is all fun. He's terribly good. Daily communicant . . ."

"That makes it all the more dangerous. A soft spot in that
apple. I foresee great trouble ahead for your pretty, pious
friend."

There the matter ended. Using the sleeve of his old soutane he
began to polish his little briar pipe—his one indulgence—and,
clenching it between his teeth, unlit, since it was Lent, he
launched into his favourite topic: the necessity of a man to keep
himself clean, hard, and fit.

A passionate believer in physical fitness, he perennially
greeted the dawn with an ice cold bath, followed by a series of
Sandow exercises, and so influenced me that I adopted the
habit and followed it faithfully. In his youth, rumour had it,
Jaeger had played for Preston North End. Certainly he was
madly keen on the game, worked hard with the team, came to
all our matches, and nourished the wild ambition that St.
Ignatius might one day win that most coveted trophy, the
Scottish Schools' Shield.

III

YET FR. JAEGER must surely have been mollified, surely
Desmonde redeemed himself, when, quite out of character, he
suddenly became a regular supporter of the school team. On
Saturday mornings he would meet me at the corner of Radnor
Street for the tram that bore us to Annesland on the outskirts of
the city where the playing field was situated. During the game
he posted himself behind the goal of our opponents and when
that citadel was pierced, particularly by a shot from my
ruthless boot, he broke into an excited variation of the Irish jig.

Fr. Jaeger used to have me to his little study upstairs in the
presbytery to discuss tactics before, and after, each game.
Long before it became standard practice in the Professional
Leagues he insisted that the centre half—myself—should not
only act as a defender but should go forward with the ball
well into enemy territory and have a shot at goal. And it was

indeed this advice which enabled me, not only to delight my friend, but to win games that might otherwise have been lost.

After the game, whether triumphant or despondent, Desmonde took me back to his house for lunch, where quite often I would find my mother. Desmonde, with his tact and sensitive fine feeling, had brought our surviving parents together, not a difficult matter since both attended the Sunday High Mass at St. Ignatius, and it was at once evident that the two women liked each other. I had reason to believe, too, without being presumptuous, that Mrs. Fitzgerald approved of my friendship with her son.

What pleasant occasions these were—always a delicious meal, nicely served in that delightful, beautifully furnished sunny room overlooking the park. And what a treat, especially for my dear mother, who had known such things in the past and lacked them for so many years. After coffee the two women went to the window seat to chat, or to take up some sewing which Mrs. Fitzgerald, who worked for the church, could always provide, while Desmonde and I took off on our weekly pilgrimage across the park to the municipal Art Gallery, a fine modern building of red sandstone not far from the Winton University. Already we knew it well and, as a concession to me, we went immediately to the room of the French Impressionists, sat down, and gave ourselves once again to the splendour of some twenty examples of this period. Best of all I loved the Gauguin: two native women seated on the beach against a gorgeous complex of tropic jungle.

"Painted during his first visit to Tahiti," Desmonde murmured.

But my gaze was now on the delicious little Sisley, the Seine at Passy, moving slowly to the equally delicious Vuillard, all lemon and deep purple, then to the Utrillo, a simple street of a Paris faubourg, empty of people but full, oh, so full of Utrillo.

"His best period," whispered my mentor. "Early, when he mixed plaster with his paint."

But I wasn't listening, absorbing the atmosphere of canvases I now knew so well and coveted so avidly.

Desmonde then stood up, deciding I'd had enough of the Impressionists, and moved into the corridor. I followed him to the end room given over to Italian paintings of the early and high Renaissance. These Florentine and Sienese religious compositions did not greatly interest me. I sat on the central settee while he made his way slowly round the circular room, stopping now at some particular favourite, peering close, breathing ecstatically, casting his eyes up to heaven.

"You're being dramatic, Desmonde," I said.

"No, Alec. These lovely old treasures, with their spiritual force, their simple grandeur of conception, they induce in me a heavenly state of being. Look at this Piero della Francesca, and this heavenly Madonna, obviously the centre of a three part altar piece, Florentine school about 1500, and this Pietà. Ah, this is my most ecstatic: the Annunciation by Bartolommeo della Porta."

"Why della Porta?"

"He lived near the Porta Romana. In 1475. A friend of Raphael. I love it so much I managed to get a little reproduction."

I waited with exemplary patience while he continued to rhapsodize, until I heard the strains of the orchestra tuning up in the concert hall below. I then stood up.

"Music, maestro, please."

He smiled, nodded, and took my arm as we went down the wide stone staircase to the splendid theatre which a benignant corporation had provided for the citizens of Winton, and where on many Saturday afternoons the Scottish orchestra might be heard, free of charge, in programmes of good music.

As we entered, Desmonde took one of the typewritten sheets at the door.

"Dash!" he exclaimed as we seated ourselves at the back of the poorly filled hall. "No Vivaldi. No Scarlatti. No Cherubini."

"But glorious Tchaikovsky and heavenly Rimsky-Korsakov."

"Your beastly Russians."

"They induce in me a state of heavenly being!"

He laughed, then was silent. The conductor had appeared, greeted by mild hand clapping, and the first strains of the ballet, Swan Lake, swept towards us.

This orchestra, then beginning to be known in Europe and the United States, was of remarkable quality for a provincial city. The Tchaikovsky was beautifully played and, after the interval, Scheherazade was magnificent.

When the last notes had died we sat for a moment, recovering, silent, until Desmonde said moodily:

"Nothing for us at the Kings this week, I'm afraid."

"What's on?"

"One of these idiotic musical comedies: *Maid of the Mountains*, I believe. What mountains? Everest, Kanchenjungha or Pook's Hill? However," he added, "Mother had word from Dublin that the Carl Rosa will be here quite soon."

"Good!" This was another of our passions, secret, and never to be divulged at school where undoubtedly we should be mocked. We both loved opera, and when it was in town would go on Saturday nights to the sixpenny gallery seats in the Kings Theatre. I insisted on this sixpenny outlay, all I could afford, but occasionally Desmonde, who detested the gallery, would produce two tickets for the stalls which he tried to persuade me were complimentary, obtained by his mother.

"The Carl Rosa was jolly good last month," I said. "I did love the Donizetti."

"*Lucia di Lammermoor.*" Desmonde smiled. "Being a Scot, you would!"

"That girl was really superb. The bridal aria is jolly difficult."

"I'm glad you say bridal, Alec. Crude to call it Mad Song. Yes, she's Geraldine Moore. Quite the toast of the town in Dublin."

"She's a darling, so young and beautiful."

"I shall certainly tell her that, Alec," Desmonde said gravely, "when I meet her."

We both laughed. How could we foresee that this lovely and talented woman would play a major part in Desmonde's future, admittedly hectic, career?

Most of the audience had now filed out—we usually waited, since Desmonde hated to 'crush out with the mob'—so I now glanced at him.

"Tea?"

He smiled. "Delighted, Alec."

My mother, from the beginning of our friendship with the Fitzgeralds, had said: "We must not sponge. We must return, as best we can, the hospitality we receive."

"But surely . . . we're not quite . . ."

"Yes, we are poor," she interrupted quite fiercely, "but we must never, never be ashamed of it."

Desmonde now enjoyed his Saturday tea with me, but his first visit to my home had positively startled him. As we came out of the park and crossed into the mean district of Yorkhill, he viewed the cheap shops therein with ill-concealed distaste, his nostrils dilating as we passed the fish and chip establishment of Antonio Moseno who, already aproned and in his doorway, hailed me across the street.

"Howdya, Meester Shannon. Green pea ready. Chip-a-potata ready twenty meenutes."

"A friend?" remarked Desmonde, casually.

"And a jolly good one. He almost gives me double when I go in for a pennyworth of chips."

As we passed the little butcher's at the end of the row, the blue-striped, belted figure within gave me a wave of his arm in greeting.

"That's another friend," I remarked, forestalling my companion. "He's a Scot. And when my mother goes in just before he closes on Saturday night, she gets a first rate bargain."

Desmonde was silent, and as we were now climbing the steep hill on which the tenement stood, the reason became obvious. Indeed, when we reached our entrance and climbed the four flights of stairs to the top flat, he steadied himself against me, groping for breath, speechless.

"I say, Alec," he wheezed at last, "don't you find this rather too much for you?"

"Nonsense, Desmonde!" I rather laid it on. "When I've had my morning cold bath and run round the building three times—that's a mile—I absolutely spring up these stairs."

"You do?" he said flatly.

I took out my key, opened the door, and led the way into the kitchen where, before tactfully departing, my mother had spread a clean white cover on the little table and laid out the tea things, with a large plate of newly baked shortbread.

Desmonde collapsed into one of the two chairs, watching me in silence while I lit the gas ring, boiled the kettle, expertly brewed tea, and filled the two big cups.

He took a long deep swallow and sighed.

"Terribly good, Alec. Most refreshing."

I refilled his cup and passed the shortbread. He took a piece, bit into it experimentally, then his face lit up.

"I say, Alec, this is delicious."

"Home made, Desmonde. Have another."

We set to work on the tea together. Indeed, with some slight assistance from me, Desmonde practically demolished the plate-ful.

"I'm worse than old Beauchamp with the French cakes," he apologized, hesitating before taking the ninth and final piece.

In reply I gave him his third cup of tea.

Thoroughly revived now, Desmonde looked around, his eye dwelling upon the curtained alcove behind me.

"Is that where you study, Alec?"

I drew the curtain aside with my foot, revealing a narrow iron bedstead, neatly made up and spread with a grey counterpane.

"My mother's bedroom," I said. "You want to see mine?"

He nodded, silently. I took him across the miniature hall and threw open the door of the other room.

"This is my domain." I smiled. "Where I sleep, work, and take my exercise."

He followed me, in a state of total wonder. The room was completely empty, except for a narrow truckle bed at one end and at the window a little dilapidated fold-down deal bureau, deemed not worth putting in the auction when our home was broken up.

As he remained still and completely silent, I took an india-rubber from the mantelpiece, threw it against the wall, and as it came back at a sharp angle, caught it.

"My wall game. When I catch fifty, without a fault, I've won."

Still he did not speak, but came towards me, still with that strange, emotional expression and, to my acute embarrassment, took my hand and went down on one knee.

"Alec," he exclaimed, raising his eyes to me, "you are noble, truly noble, as also is your dear mother. To live like this, spartan lives, nobly and cheerfully, is truly saintly. You shame me. Dear Alec." His voice broke. "Sign me with the cross and give me your blessing."

Dreadfully uncomfortable, I was about to say: "For Heaven's sake, don't be an ass," but for some strange unknown reason I checked myself, murmured the names of the Trinity and marked his upturned forehead with the sign of the cross.

Instantly he relaxed, got to his feet, and vigorously shook my hand.

"Now I feel I have the strength, the courage to emulate you. I must be hard on myself. And I shall begin now." He reflected. "It's a couple of miles from here to my house, uphill most of the way if I cross the park."

"Slightly more than two miles."

"Good! I'm going to start now, walking fast, and I promise you I'll be home in twenty minutes."

"That would be a fine effort, Desmonde."

"I'm off then." He took his cap from the peg in the hall and went to the door. "Thank you for a delicious tea . . . and for yourself."

I waited a moment while he went clattering down the stone steps, then went to the window of my room. True to his word, Desmonde was on his way, arms swinging, head thrust forward. So he continued, until gradually his pace slackened, he seemed suddenly to flag. He had, after all, eaten a considerable quantity of shortbread. And now, indeed, he paused, removed his immaculate handkerchief from his breast pocket and applied it to his brow, resuming thereafter at a slower, a much slower pace. He was now at the end of the hill road, facing the main street. He paused, stood considering the flow of traffic and, as a cab ambled past, looking for a fare, his right arm shot up. The cab stopped, the door opened and Desmonde flung himself inside.

"Home, James," I murmured to myself, "and don't spare the horses." But he had tried.

The sun was now setting over the distant hills of Dumbarton, lighting the rooftops and furnishing my empty room with a magic splendour. As I gazed into the rosy glow of the sunset I wondered what the future held for Desmonde . . . and for me.

IV

DESMONDE, WHO NEVER seemed to overtax himself with work, was naturally clever, and, due to his father, he had the incomparable advantage of three languages. Completely fluent in French and Spanish he could even converse, though more slowly, in Latin. Almost apologetically he explained to me how his father of an evening would take him for a stroll in Phoenix Park, stating firmly at the outset the language in which their converse must be conducted. To relapse into English was an offence, not punishable, but frowned upon by his accomplished parent, a scholar who was often called upon to arrange and catalogue the libraries of great houses in Europe.

As we came into our final school year it was a foregone conclusion that Desmonde would take all the language prizes while I, by intensive study, might succeed in mathematics, science and, with luck, English. It was already settled that Desmonde would go on to the Seminary at Torrijos, in Spain, while I would try for the Marshall Scholarship, sole passport to Winton University and a medical career.

My chances of scholarship were impaired by the fact that our football team was having an unprecedented run of success in the competition for the Scottish Schools' Shield. This coveted trophy had never been won by St. Ignatius and as we came through to the quarter finals, leaving a trail of vanquished schools behind, Fr. Jaeger, who had made me captain of the team the year before, was beside himself with ardour and excitement. Every other evening long training sessions were held in the gymnasium and before every game I had a detailed briefing in Jaeger's study.

"I think we might just do it, Alec." Unable to be still, he pranced up and down the little study. "We are a young, a very young team, but keen, yes, keen. And we have you, Alec, taking the ball forward. Now remember . . ."

Desmonde came with me to all the matches, returning jubilant to our customary Saturday luncheon at Overton Crescent, where he delighted my mother by exaggerated reports of my prowess.

Now that his admission to the Seminary was settled he was amusing himself, and the school, in his own fashion. He had first ascertained the date of Fr. Beauchamp's birthday by consulting *Who's Who*, and as the day drew near, he composed and typed a marvellous letter purporting to come from the Mother Superior of the adjacent Convent School, a venerable old lady who rarely exposed herself to public view.

The letter, widely circulated amongst the school, ran as follows:

'My dear, very dear Fr. Beauchamp,

If I had courage I would address you by your delightful name of Harold, for I must now confess that I have long cherished a deep and passionate reverence for you. Yes, I watch you often, from my window, striding down the causeway, a noble, magnificent, corpulent figure, and with beating heart I long to have known you when we were both younger. When you had just left Eton, laden with honours, and I was a simple maiden, student at the nearby Borstal Reformatory. What joys might have then been in store for us. Alas, Heaven willed otherwise. But now, cloistered though I am, I may, purely and without sin, declare my secret passion. And in celebration of your auspicious name day I venture to send you a birthday cake. Intuition, or perhaps rumour, tells me that, despite the rigorous diet of your Order, you enjoy and are permitted to indulge yourself excessively in sweetmeats.

Heaven bless you, my darling.

I pray for you always—a solace to my love.

Yours adoringly,

Claribel.'

Roars of laughter greeted this masterpiece as it was passed from hand to hand and thereafter enclosed with a huge chocolate cake in a beribboned box.

This box was then secretly conveyed to the jolly, stumpy schoolgirl whom Desmonde had inveigled into the plot. It was she who had actually provided the sheet of Convent notepaper on which the letter was typed, and she who on the appointed day rang the College doorbell and personally presented the gift to Beauchamp. Almost the entire school saw the box delivered and all awaited the outcome with ill-repressed anticipation.

All day long there was no reaction, but at five o'clock, when the school had assembled for evening prayers, Beauchamp made his appearance to conduct the service. Before he began, almost absently, he said:

"Fitzgerald, would you oblige me by standing up?"

Gracefully, Desmonde obeyed.

"You are Desmonde Fitzgerald."

"I have always been led to believe so, sir. If I am in error perhaps you will correct me."

"Enough! Fitzgerald, do you consider me 'corpulent'?"

"Corpulent, sir? That is a word, sir, which comprises a

variety of meanings, from a gross obesity to a benign and grace-
ful embonpoint, eminently becoming to a prelate of your
dignity and stature."

"Ah! I assume you know, or at least know of, the venerable
Mother Superior of our neighbouring Convent School?"

"Who does not, sir?"

"Would you ever, for a moment, believe that she had passed
her early life in a Borstal Reformatory?"

"Sir, you yourself must be aware that many of our greatest
saints, eventually models of piety and devotion, were in their
early years reprobates and malefactors, which did not prevent
their ultimate canonization. Thus, should our Reverend Mother
have been by chance to Borstal, would you wish deliberately to
cast the first stone?"

A ripple ran through the school. We were all enjoying this
immensely.

"Enough, Desmonde!" From the mildness of Beauchamp's
tone it seemed almost as if he were himself enjoying the
exchanges. "Enough, sir. Borstal or not, would you consider it
possible that this venerable and saintly lady would conceive a
secret passion for any man?"

"I would consider it eminently possible, sir!"

"What!"

"The word passion, sir, like your corpulence," here the
school did indeed laugh outright, "has many meanings.
There is the passion, sir, that you might feel if, God forbid, I
should ever annoy you. I would then return to my beloved
mother in tears, exclaiming brokenly: 'Darling Mother, dear
Father Beauchamp, our beloved Prefect of Studies, was in a
raging passion with me!'" Desmonde had to pause until he could
be heard. We were all in hysterics. "Then, sir, there is that very
frequent use of the word when a charming woman might say
casually to her friend, as she came from her garden proudly
bearing a trug loaded with blooms: 'I have a passion for roses,
darling'. Or again, a hen-pecked husband might say to his wife:
'You have a passion for clothes, confound you. Just look at this
milliner's bill . . .' Then, again . . ."

"Enough, Desmonde." We were getting out of control.
Beauchamp held up his hand. "Tell me, did you write that
birthday letter that came with the birthday cake?"

"Sir, that is a leading question. Even in a court of law I would be given time to reflect and consider and if necessary to consult my legal advisers . . ." Desmonde broke off suddenly. He sensed that enough amusement had been extracted from the situation and that to go further would spoil the admirable effect he had created. So he bowed his head and said simply: "I did send the cake, sir. And I did compose the letter. It was all done in fun, sir. If it annoyed you, I am sorry and I will accept my punishment. And I am sure every one of us, who had a part in this silly joke, is equally contrite. I only hope that you enjoyed the cake."

There was a long silence. One might have heard a pin drop. Then Beauchamp spoke.

"Desmonde, I predict, without the slightest hesitation and with complete assurance, that it you do not fall by the wayside, you will end your days as a Cardinal in the inner circle of the Vatican. You have the exact quality of diplomatic equivocation which is highly regarded in that august body. However, you are a pupil under my authority who must be punished. So your punishment will be this." He held us breathless for a long moment. "Next time, send me a cherry cake. I prefer it to chocolate."

It was a master stroke. Beauchamp knew how to handle boys. We rose in a body and, led by Desmonde, cheered him to the echo.

With the vacation drawing near the school was now in high good humour. We had just won our semi-final match against Allan Glens, a famous Scottish school with a strong team we had greatly feared. And how well and with what pleasure do I remember the game, played on the ground of the famous Celtic Club, in perfect weather, a sunny late afternoon, the cropped green turf, lawn smooth, so suited to our passing game, every member of the team in top form, the joy of victory and the cheers that greeted us as we streamed into the pavilion where Fr. Jaeger threw his arms round me in a triumphant hug.

Our greatest hurdle cleared, we were now in the final where our opponents would be a little known team from a small elementary school and, with good reason, it was generally acknowledged that the Shield would at last be ours. I was in high favour; even Fr. Beauchamp, not precisely a sporting man, would beam me a radiant smile as we passed in the corridor.

All our examinations were now over, the results already on the notice board. As anticipated, Desmonde had done superlatively well, taking half of the prizes, while I, a modest plodder, took the other half. However, also on the board was a communiqué from the university, briefly indicating, but with immense joy to myself, and to my dear mother, that I had won the Marshall Bursary. Finally on the board was the annual invitation to the boys of the Upper Sixth, inviting them to the Convent Dance given by the senior girls under the supervision of Mother Superior. This was an established custom between the two schools, doubtless to arrange a meeting between Catholic boys and girls of good education and high morals which might prove salutary, or even fruitful, now that they must face the liberty and temptations of unsheltered life. Naturally, we all regarded it as an immense joke.

The day of the momentous final was now upon us, the match fixed for five o'clock at Hampden Park, the famous international ground, and, for a schoolboys' event, the crowd was exceptionally large. Even now it pains me to write of the event, of which the memory has so often recurred to sting me. We began in great style, swinging the ball about with precision and complete confidence, and for seven minutes we were obviously the masters, almost scoring twice. Then the incident occurred.

Our left back, a boy of no more than fifteen years, had the habit of running, even of walking, with his arms akimbo and in this fashion he tackled one of the opposing forwards. His elbow barely touched the other boy who, alas, slipped and fell. Instantly the whistle of the referee sounded. A penalty!

The kick was taken, a goal was scored, and immediately our young team went to pieces. Then the rain began, drenching us in heavy sheets, driven into our faces by gusts of wind, a pitiless downfall that persisted through the second half into a premature early darkness, almost a black-out with the pitch markings and the ball barely discernible. It was of course equally bad for our opponents, but they had their goal. The seconds were ticking away. In the last minutes of the game, the ball came to me on the touchline, outside the penalty area. I took one desperate blinding shot at the enemy goal. It was a good effort, sailing hard and true for the top corner of the net, when a fierce gust caught and diverted the ball, which struck the junction of the bar and the post, sailed high in the air, and went over.

Instantly the final whistle sounded, we were beaten, one to nothing. In the pavilion poor Fr. Jaeger, ash grey from strain and suspense, immediately quelled our curses against the referee.

"You did your best, boys. We were handicapped by the storm and," he added bitterly, "by the fact that you were wearing green jerseys. Now hurry and change, our bus is waiting."

I could not face the dinner that had been arranged for us. I hid myself in one of the wash rooms, emerging only when the rumble of the bus had died. Then I took my bag and went out into the rain, faced with a long walk to the tram stop and a longer bumpy journey home.

Suddenly in the darkness a hand was on my shoulder.

"I've a taxi waiting, dear Alec. I managed to get it through the gates. Give me your bag. I won't say a word about the game and I'll get you safely home."

He led me to the cab, and into it. This was Desmonde, Desmonde at his best. Thankfully I lay back, utterly spent, and closed my eyes.

After we had cleared the gates and were on our way Desmonde whispered:

"Are you asleep, Alec?"

"Unfortunately, no."

"I'm not going to talk about the match, Alec, but I'd like you to know that I prayed like mad all the time and when your shot just missed being a goal I nearly died."

"I'm glad you survived."

He was silent for some minutes, then:

"I'm leaving for Torrijos, for the Seminary, the day after tomorrow."

"So soon?"

"Yes. Mother is terribly upset. She'll come with me to Madrid, then I may not see her till I'm ordained."

"That's very severe."

"Yes, I understand they're formidably strict."

Again silence, then leaning towards me he murmured:

"You know I love you, Alec."

"Like is the imperative word, Desmonde."

"Well, then I like you immensely and I want you to promise
to keep in touch with me. There's no ban on letters out there so
I mean to write you often. Do you mind?"

"Not at all, and I'll reply, when I'm not tied up with Quain's
anatomy."

"Thank you, thank you, dear Alec."

So the pact was made. And that is why I may continue this
narrative with absolute accuracy despite the fact that we were
often apart for many years.

The taxi drew up. We were now outside my home.

"Thank you sincerely, Desmonde, for being so decent.
It would have taken me more than an hour."

I gave him my hand. I have a vague idea that he tried to
kiss me on the cheek as I got out of the cab, but it was not
successful.

"Good night, Desmonde, and thank you again."

"Good night, my dear Alec."

V

I slept late next morning, from sheer exhaustion, and had
to forgo my usual run in the park. Although the school prizegiving was not until late afternoon, my mother had taken the
whole day off from work. She brought me my breakfast in bed,
a special treat, and on the tray, in addition to my porridge, there
was hot buttered toast and a plate of bacon and egg. Not a word
did she speak of the game although I read in her face maternal
compassion tempered by a determined brightness.

She sat with me while I cleared the tray, then:

"I have a surprise for you, dear." And from the hall she
brought a flat cardboard box, took off the lid and exposed a
new, extremely good looking dark blue suit.

I gazed, enraptured, amazed.

"How did you get it?"

"Never mind, dear. You know that you must have a decent
suit for the university. Hurry and try it on."

"How did you get it?" I repeated, seriously.

"Well . . . you know that silly old silver brooch . . ."

"The one with the ring of pearls."

"I didn't want it, I was tired of it, a useless old thing . . . I sold it . . . to a decent little Jew who knows me in my district."

"You loved that brooch. You said it was your mother's."

She looked at me in silence, then:

"Please don't make a fuss, dear. You had to have a suit for the prizegiving, and especially for the dance afterwards."

"I don't want to go to the dance. I'll hate it."

"You must, you must . . . you never have any amusement or social life." She added: "I had a letter about you this morning, delivered by one of the College servants. From Father Jaeger."

"Do let me see it."

"Certainly not. It's my letter and I shall prize it. Besides, I don't want you to get a swelled head."

She paused, while we confronted each other on the verge of laughter.

"He did mention that he hoped you weren't laid out, as you didn't turn up for dinner. And if you've time he'd like you to come up and see him, before he goes off on Monday."

"He's going away?"

"So it appears."

I pondered, puzzled. At least I would have the answer tonight.

"Do try the suit, dear."

I got up, horribly stiff, and got into my cold bath with some difficulty. A clean white shirt and a new light blue tie had been set out beside the suit. I dressed with care, enjoying myself for inspection, fully aware that I had not been as well turned out for at least five years.

My dear little mother looked me up and down, walked slowly round me, then looked again. No burst of admiration, no superlatives, no lovey-dovey 'oh, my darling', but it was pleasant to read her eyes as she embraced me and said, quietly:

"It is a perfect fit. Now you look *yourself*."

All that day I lazed around, easing my bruises, and getting in the way of my mother, but at five o'clock we were both seated in the school hall where most of the boys were already present with their parents and friends. Desmonde was much in evidence but, as he explained, his mother, busy with arrangements for their departure, was enforcedly absent. However, it was he who started the proceedings by leading us into the school song, the new version composed by Fr. Roberts. The effect was

rather spoiled by the noise of latecomers looking for seats and
dragging chairs, and almost at once Fr. Beauchamp appeared
on the platform. After a short prayer, when everyone stood, he
read an account of the school's progress during the past year,
then began to distribute the prizes. Parents of sons so rewarded
beamed, others less fortunate did not conceal their chagrin. A
woman behind us was heard to remark rancorously to her
neighbour:

"Oor Wullie was fifth in Religious Knowledge. Whet wey
did he no' get a prize."

Finally, speaking more slowly, Beauchamp came to the
upper group and presently Desmonde was called to the platform to accept his books, receiving some applause as he gracefully bowed and retreated. Then it was my turn. And how
relieved and pleased I was, for my mother's sake, at the roar
that greeted my appearance and continued until Beauchamp
raised his hand. He began to speak, presumably about me,
since there were more cheers, but although I caught the
phrase 'our admirable Shannon' my attention, and indeed my
eyes, were fixed on an envelope which lay on top of the pile of
books.

At last the ordeal was over, Beauchamp awkwardly shook
hands with me and I had hobbled back to my seat, where my
mother, crimson with pride, pressed my hand and gave me a
look I shall never forget, a look that sustained me during the
hard years that followed.

Another prayer and we were all dismissed and crowding
towards the doors. I saw my mother down College Hill to the
tramway stop and before I put her on the tram I handed
her the envelope.

"This is five guineas in cash, my prize for the English essay
competition. Will you kindly go to your Jewish friend and get
back your brooch?"

Before she could answer she was in the tram and moving off,
while I, feeling horrendously sentimental and dramatic,
turned up the hill again.

At the school, the tower clock showed twenty minutes past
six. I went immediately to Fr. Jaeger's study. He was there,
seated in his usual chair, not busy in any way and looking, I
thought, rather more than usually pensive.

"I hoped you would come, Alec. Your mother got my letter?"

B

"Yes, she did, sir, and sternly refused to disclose its contents."

"Good!" he said, and smiled. "I did want to see you, Alec, not to talk about the game—that's all dead history, but because I may be . . . going away, fairly soon." He glanced at his wristwatch. "But aren't you supposed to be at the dance?"

"The more of that I miss, sir, the better. And I did want to thank you for giving me the essay prize. You knew I needed the money."

"What nonsense is this? Your essay was miles ahead of the others. You have a bit of a gift in that direction."

"Well, sir," I laughed, "I shall employ it in writing prescriptions. But please tell me, are you going on holiday?"

"Not exactly, but I shall be away."

A silence fell. I saw that he was not smoking. I said:

"Shall I fill you a pipeful, sir?"

This I often did for him, when we were talking football. However, he shook his head.

"I'm rather off my pipe, Alec." He paused. "I seem to have a ridiculous spot on my tongue which is interesting your future colleagues, somewhat."

"Does it hurt?"

"Moderately." He smiled. "But I shall know more on Monday, when I go back for their report."

I was silent. I did not like the sound of this at all.

"So they might keep you to have it out?"

"We shall know next week. Possibly I might go later on to our base at Stonyhurst. At any rate, I wanted to say goodbye and wish you well in your university career. I have no doubts about you, because you have got it here," he touched his brow, "and here." He closed his fist and thumped himself hard on the chest. "I can't say," he went on, "that I have the same confidence in the future of your friend. Fitzgerald is like the curate's egg, good, very good, in parts, but the rest of it . . ." he shrugged and shook his head. "But, really, Alec, you must get to the dance or they'll think you're funking it. I'll see you downstairs, I am going to the church for a while."

He came to the door of the school, stood, and put out his hand, which clasped mine firmly while he looked straight into my eyes.

"Goodbye, Alec."

"Goodbye, sir."

He turned and moved towards the church, while slowly, very slowly and sadly, I made my way across the street and uphill to the Convent. I had read tragedy in Jaeger's brave eyes. And with reason.

He had a cancer of the tongue, already with secondaries in the larynx and elsewhere. Six months later, after three operations, and untold agony, he was dead. His one little indulgence in a life of stark austerity had killed him.

Some premonition of this must have been in my mind as I was admitted to the Convent. The dance was already in progress, couples moving sedately round under the watchful eyes of a group of senior nuns seated on the platform, Desmonde doing his best with a few capers to enliven the party.

Dancing had not been in my curriculum, but I took up one of the wallflowers, gathered in a distressful group, and made the circuit with her several times while she breathed heavily into my right ear as we trod on each other's feet. I then turned her over to an unsuspecting boy and sat down beside a nice, quiet, grey-eyed girl.

"Thank goodness, you're not dancing."

"No," she said. "I'm entering my novitiate tomorrow."

"For the Convent here?"

She inclined her head. Then: "Is that boy, carrying on there, Fitzgerald, the one who's going to be a priest?"

"Yes, he goes off to the Seminary on Monday."

"You're not serious. In two days' time?"

"Why not?"

"I couldn't believe anyone could go on clowning like that, practically on the eve of giving himself to Our Lord."

I said nothing, having no wish to be drawn into a discussion on pre-novitiate behaviour.

"You must be the Shannon boy. The good footballer who just won the bursary."

"How on earth do you know?"

She smiled. "We talk about you boys over here."

"Yet you're going to be a nun?"

"Yes, I am, I can't help it."

This delightful answer made me smile, and we began to talk very agreeably to one another, until suddenly she checked herself. "I think I must go now."

"So soon, just as we are beginning to like each other."

She blushed, most attractively. "That's why I must go . . . I'm beginning to like you too much."

She stood up and held out her hand.

"Good night, Alec."

"Good night, dear little sister."

I watched her to the door across the room. I hoped she would look round. She did, for a long, long moment, then lowered her eyes and was gone.

I decided to go too, but at that moment all the nuns on the platform stood up as a very old and venerable nun appeared, escorted by a young sister and walking slowly with a stick. Instantly a chair was produced, placed in the centre of the stage. She sat down.

The dancers had immediately become still, for this was the Convent's Mother Superior. After gazing down benevolently she said quite distinctly:

"Would the Fitzgerald boy come forward?"

Immediately, nimbly, Desmonde mounted the platform, bowed and stood before her to attention, then gracefully sank to one knee.

"You are the Irish boy who sings?"

"Yes, Reverend Mother."

"Father Beauchamp has spoken to me of you. First, dear Desmonde, for your peace of mind, I would wish to assure you that I did not receive my education at the Borstal Reformatory, which you seem to know of, in the vicinity of Eton."

Desmonde blushed as the surrounding nuns dissolved in giggles. The famous letter had apparently become a Convent joke.

"Do forgive me, Reverend Mother. It was stupid fun."

"You are already forgiven, Desmonde, but you must do penance." She paused. "I am an old Irish woman, who still pines for her homeland to which now she will never return. Would you oblige me, therefore, by singing one, just one, Irish song, or ballad, that might ease my longing?"

"I will indeed, Reverend Mother. With the greatest pleasure in the world."

"Do you know 'Tara'? Or 'The Minstrel Boy'?"

"I know both."

"Then sing." She closed her eyes and turned an expectant ear as Desmonde took a long breath and began to sing, first

one, then the other, of these old ballads. And never did I hear
him sing better.

> 'The harp that once through Tara's halls,
> The soul of music shed,
> Now hangs as mute on Tara's walls
> As if that soul were fled . . .'

> 'The minstrel boy to the war is gone,
> In the ranks of death you'll find him.
> His father's sword he has girded on,
> And his wild harp slung behind him . . .
> The minstrel fell, but the foeman's chain
> Could not bring his proud soul under.
> The harp he loved ne'er spoke again,
> For he tore its chords asunder.
> And said, 'No chains shall sully thee,
> Thou soul of love and bravery.
> Thy songs were made for the brave and free,
> They shall never sound in slavery.'

And what a tableau! Against a frieze of nuns, the old, the
very old Mother Superior, eyes closed, half reclining in her
chair, and at her side, this angelic fair-headed, blue-eyed youth
pouring his heart out in song.

When it was over, no one moved, until the Rev. Mother
spoke, through streaming tears.

"Thank you, dear Minstrel Boy. May our Lord bless and keep
you for giving an old woman a taste of heaven, before she may
get there."

She rose, helped to her feet, and smiled to us below.

"Now let the dance resume."

When she had left the stage, the fun did indeed begin, led by
Desmonde, elated by his triumph, and ready for action.
He had induced the jolly stubby little number, now identified
as captain of the hockey team, to join him in a combined
version of the Irish Jig and the Highland Fling.

I would have wished to go over to him for just one last
goodbye. But we had really said this after the game, and to the
lively strains of 'The Campbells Are Coming', thumped out on
the piano, I went out into the cool night air.

My mother was waiting on me when I got home. As I kicked off my shoes in the hall she called out:

"I hope you're hungry, dear. I have a lovely Welsh rarebit for you."

I was hungry. I stepped into the kitchen. She was there, arms outstretched, the brooch gleaming on her bosom.

TWO

DESMONDE ENTERED THE Seminary of St. Simeon in the village of Torrijos, some ten kilometres from Toledo. His letters to me thereafter were frequent but irregular. Following the initial letter, which gave an interesting account of the seminary and its whereabouts, they became rather dull and repetitious, since they had little to offer beyond the minutiae and monotony of monastic life. However, towards the end of Desmonde's preparation for the priesthood two letters reached me which had a definite interest and, indeed, a direct bearing on Desmonde's subsequent career. I shall therefore reproduce the first and the two terminal letters in detail.

As for myself, since I shall eventually come into Desmonde's life again, it may be briefly noted that my career at the university was proceeding rigorously in circumstances little different from those that had attended my school days. The same half-empty little flat, the same plain food and porridge, the same loving devotion of my mother. Ambition alone sustained us. We did not complain, since we were not alone. Other poor students were there, vying with each other, desperate for success. In that era, now remote, large sustenance grants were not lavishly and indiscriminately bestowed. Clever, ambitious boys would come from poor farms in the north carrying a sack of meal to sustain them till the next Meal Monday, a free day by university statute to enable them to return to the parental farm for fresh supplies.

Yet however harassed by hard work and recurrent examinations, I often thought of Desmonde and, refreshed by his letters, I had an odd conviction that when he was ordained I should again see, and be near, him.

My dear Alec,

Behold your beloved friend, your *fidus Achates*, in Spain, within sight of the noble walled city of Toledo, embraced by the benign sun of the Midi, but miserable, forlorn, desolated at the parting from my mother, and in dread of the long joyless future stretching endlessly before me.

But first I must serve the sweets before offering you the bitters.

Two days after our last meeting, I set out for Rome with my dear mother who, although far from well, insisted on accompanying me. Our journey was pleasant and uneventful and, on arrival, we proceeded to our hotel, the Excelsior in the Via Veneto, where we were shown to our rooms, both large, cool, and away from traffic noise.

The purpose of our stop in the Eternal City was not only to rest, although this was almost a necessity for my mother, but to renew certain contacts made by my father during his frequent visits, when he had come to purchase old manuscripts or books, and to review and catalogue the libraries of great houses. It was pleasing to find that he was not forgotten. And soon, indeed, our telephone began to ring, and cards were left for us at the concierge's office. Old Monseigneur Broglio called, a frightful old bore, with a large appetite, who did however get us the *entrée* to the Vatican. There were others. Most delightful and hospitable of all, the Marchesa di Varese had us several times to her absurdly large and beautiful old house on the Via della Croce. My father had spent many weeks as her guest arranging and cataloguing her enormous, and enormously valuable, library. I feel sure she was half in love with my dear dad, for she was particularly nice to me, promising to help me in any way if I had need of her.

She it was who supplemented the old Monseigneur in arranging our audience with His Holiness. And how memorable, how touching was that meeting—not a private audience, of course—this is accorded only to royalty or to the famous—but a meeting in the great hall, fifteen minutes in advance of the general audience.

We were there in time, I assure you, I in my black suit, my mother also in the required black, the fine dress and lace mantilla provided by the Marchesa. We waited in a little ante room, then were conducted to the near end of the audience chamber, a part sealed off by a velvet rope. There again, we waited for perhaps two minutes. When the Pope entered, accompanied by the papal secretary, I experienced a tremor almost ecstatic. Such dignity, serenity, such an abiding sense of goodness that it radiated towards us as, briefed by the secretary, he greeted us by our names, spoke, in perfect English, of my father—whom he had known when Cardinal Pacelli—and of 'all that he had done for the Church'. He talked first to my mother, then to me, extolling the great good that active young priests could accomplish in the world of today and, with a look in his eye that may have previsaged Toledo, discoursed on the virtues of self-sacrifice and penance. This might well have continued beyond the specified fifteen minutes, for I could see His Holiness was not bored with us, but suddenly behind us, at the far end of the hall, the great doors swung open and a horde swept in of . . . guess what, Alec? . . . American Navy sailors, who came forward en masse with unsuppressed excited cries: "There he is, fellers! There's His Holiness. Quiet now, don't shout!"

When silence was restored and they were all grouped in their own section, the secretary indicated that we should kneel.

I did so, but His Holiness made a restraining touch upon my mother's shoulder and whispered: "Do not kneel, dear lady."

He then blessed us, before these silent attentive witnesses.

Do you remember, Alec, that moment in your empty room when I asked you to bless me? This was the same unreal, unworldly, inexplicably presanctified feeling, magnified, of course, but in essence indentical. In future, therefore, I shall with difficulty refrain from addressing you as Your Holiness.

We were conducted out by the private staircase, and that evening dined in state with the Marchesa. Next day we were in the *rapide* for Madrid.

Since my mother had looked forward to this Spanish visit and had saved a substantial amount from her annual stipend to pay for it, I decided not to go direct to the seminary but to spend two more days in the Spanish capital. On our arrival I took a taxi direct to the Ritz Hotel, where, with dispatch and supreme courtesy, we were installed in a suite overlooking the gardens.

What a superb hotel, Alec—I unhesitatingly award it two extra stars beyond the four it already possesses. My mother had a real rest, relaxing under the orange trees, while I took a good look at the Prada, disappointing rather, too many huge portraits of Spanish kings, but with, of course, that wonderful, unsurpassable Velazquez: Las Meninas. Mother did worry a little over the lateness of dinner, but when we sat down all was forgiven. A mouth-watering cuisine.

On the morning of our third day I made all arrangements

for a courier to see my mother safely, that evening, into the compartment I had booked for her on the Madrid, Paris, Calais express. We set off in a large Hispano Suiza limousine for Toledo and the seminary.

At the forbidding gates of that institution, as my dear mother embraced me in a last goodbye, I had a sudden frightful premonition that this was indeed a final parting, that I should never see her again. I waited, watching the car until it was out of sight and also, let me admit, until I had wiped my eyes after a good weep, then I passed through the huge gates of the seminary and asked the gateman, in Spanish, to take me to the Father Superior's office. He seemed surprised that I spoke his language, and very willingly picked up my suitcase and escorted me across a wide courtyard towards the central part of the college, a delightful old Andalusian abbey on which, however, two horrible tall modern concrete wings have been added. Inside, we went up a fine old black olive wood staircase, then outside a forbidding door, of the same dark wood, he put down my bag. I gave him a couple of pesetas. Again, he seemed surprised and pleased.

"It is useful the Señor has Spanish. All the servants are Spanish."

"All men?"

"But assuredly, Señor. Father Superior Hackett would have no others."

I knocked at the door, received no answer, but went in, unutterably startled and surprised to see a tall dark priest kneeling in prayer at a prie-Dieu before a crucifix fixed on the wall. Beneath the crucifix in an enclosed glass receptacle lay, believe it or not, Alec, a severed human hand. Before I could recover, the kneeling figure spoke.

"Go outside and wait."

I removed myself, still carrying the bag, and stood outside for at least ten minutes before the voice again materialized.

"You may enter."

I entered, put down the bag, and as a chair seemed to be placed for me in front of the desk, sat down.

"Get to your feet."

I obeyed, surveying my future Superior with considerable misgiving as he sat there, studying a folder that, with deeper misgiving, I knew to be my dossier. Have you ever seen the

Phiz drawing of David Copperfield's stepfather? This was it—
the same stature and general repulsive appearance, the same
dark, brooding, sadistic eyes. I did not at all like him, in fact, he
made me feel exactly like little David before they sent him to the
factory to wash bottles.

"You know, dear Desmonde with the final 'e', that you are a
full three days late in coming to me." The sarcasm in his voice
was bitter, not amused.

"I am sorry, Father, my mother accompanied me, and as
she seemed tired, we spent two days in Rome, before coming on
to the Ritz in Madrid where, again, I felt it prudent to stay
overnight."

"A truly filial devotion. And what did you do in Rome, my
child?"

"We had a private audience with His Holiness, the Pope."

I thought that would sink him. It did not. He continued to
smile and I assure you, Alec, I did not like that smile.

"And what did His Holiness say to you?"

Misguidedly I spoke the truth.

"He extolled the virtues of penance and self-sacrifice."

Immediately, he raised his big fist and suddenly thumped the
desk so hard it made everything on it jump. Alas, I jumped
too.

"These are the very words I should have spoken to you. And
I speak them to you now, for they are the motto of this college
and they are particularly applicable to you, an effete, completely spoiled mother's boy! If I did not already see it written
on your face, it is here, written in your record." He glanced at
the folder on his desk. "Tell me, do you know *anything* of
mortification?"

Again, misguidedly, since, though still fearful, I was becoming
rattled, I said:

"Yes, I do. My greatest friend takes an ice-cold bath every
morning and runs two miles before he even has his porridge."

His eyes glistened hungrily. "That's my man. Could we ever
get him here?"

"He's already on his way to becoming a doctor."

"Pity! What a missionary I would have made of him. We
specialize in missionaries here, Desmonde with an 'e'. I have
in the past twelve years already sent out seven, of whom three
have shed their blood in Darkest Africa."

This blood-thirsty fellow was now alarming me, Alec. He was worse than Jack the Ripper.

"To come to the point. I am obliged to punish you for your flagrant disobedience of my order. You are gated for two weeks. And the room I shall give you will possibly not remind you of the Ritz."

He banged the bell on his desk. Immediately a servant appeared. The Ripper instructed him. The man looked surprised, but picked up my valise and we departed, moving out of the lovely abbey and across to a remote part of the concrete erection. Here, he led the way down the basement steps to a small dark cellar-like cubicle with a minute window that afforded a horrid vista of some outdoor lavatories. The cell itself was foully dirty and in frightful disorder.

I gazed at the dirty sagging bed, then turned to the fellow who was still holding my bag.

"Who occupied this room?"

"A student expelled only yesterday."

"What for?"

"I believe for smoking the cigarette, señor." Then he added in a low confidential voice: "This is the punishment cell, señor."

I brooded for a moment. I would not, simply would not have it.

"Do not go! Wait here with my baggage. I will return."

He seemed almost to expect this. He smiled and put down the bag.

I went up the beastly steps, straight back to the Ripper's office, and went in.

He looked up from his desk. I was convinced he expected me.

"Yes?"

"I will not accept that stinking dungeon. I am at least entitled to cleanliness and decency."

"And if I don't obey your demands?"

"I shall walk straight out of here to Toledo, charter a taxi to Madrid, take train to Rome and report the matter to the Holy Father."

"Very well," he said mildly. "Goodbye, Desmonde with an 'e'."

I stood there, blazing, while he resumed his work at the desk.

Then, I turned, went out, and slowly made my way back to the cell. Now I no longer felt like little David, but like one of the bottles he had half washed out. I could not, of course I could not do it, and the Ripper knew it. How should I look, returning to my mother at the Ritz . . . No, never, never, I must make the best of it. There was still some spirit left in me. The servant was still standing by me. He knew I'd be back.

"The little room would look better, much better, señor, it if were cleaned."

I met and read his eyes. Thanking God for my fluent Spanish, a fact unknown to that sadistic bastard in his study, I said:

"What's your name?"

"Martes, señor."

I took out from my pocket book a beautiful new, crisp fifty peseta note and held it towards him. I knew it was a fortune to him. He knew it, too.

"Martes! Bring a friend, with soap and water, everything for cleaning. Get fresh bedlinen, fresh curtains, find a carpet from another room. Make everything lovely, and fresh, and the money is yours."

He put down the valise and was off like a flash. I waited just long enough to see him return with another of the college servants, whom he introduced as José. Between them they were loaded with a variety of brushes, cloths, and buckets of water. As I went up the steps I heard them getting madly down to the job.

For about an hour or more I wandered round the grounds, inspecting some dilapidated tennis courts, into which cows from the neighbouring fields had obviously strayed to leave cards, a yard with several high Pelota walls, an old football field. I looked into the church, old Spanish and, I admitted to myself, most devotional, unspoiled, quite lovely. Classes were apparently in being, I met no one.

Finally, I returned to my quarters. Both servants were awaiting me outside and, indeed, followed me inside. In a word, I was staggered by what they had accomplished. The little room had been scrubbed and polished until it shone. A new linen curtain adorned the clean little window and a natty little Spanish rug lay on the tiled floor. Another gift from some empty room upstairs was a padded wicker arm chair. The chest of drawers, still exuding a healthy aroma of beeswax, was now revealed as a veritable Andalusian antique. And finally, the wreck of a bed had been put together and serviced with well bleached fresh white linen.

I looked gratefully at my two benefactors, both smiling and expectant.

"Nice room now, señor. Quiet. Lovely cool in summer."

I took out my pocket book and extracted another brand new fifty, fresh from the cashier at the Ritz. When I handed one fifty to each, their joy was a pleasure to behold.

"We come often, when everything is quiet, to keep it nice, nice, señor."

"Do that, Martes and José, for now you are my friends."

When they had gone, looking back with more smiles, I unpacked, put my things away in the newly papered drawers. Then stood my two little pictures on the chest, pushed the empty suitcase under the bed, and with a last look round, went out.

And there, in the yard, coming towards me, was my enemy.

"Been busy, Fitzgerald?"

"Not more than usual, father."

"Let's have a look."

He went down the steps. I did not follow. Presently, when he had obviously examined everything, opened my drawers and fingered my underwear, he emerged, smiling. And how I distrusted that smile.

"Congratulations, Fitzgerald. You've done a wonderful job. I didn't know you had it in you." And he put a genial hand upon my shoulder.

Retreating from this false embrace, I looked him in the eye.

"You know I did not do it. So don't try to make me out a liar. Whatever you think of me I have never been that, and you'll never trick me into being one."

He was silent, then in his normal voice, he said:

"Not bad, Fitzgerald. I may make a missionary of you yet. Now it's time for our delicious merienda. Come, and I'll show you the refectory."

This was a large hall in the far new building with a platform at one end and below perhaps twenty long tables at which my future comrades were getting ready to stuff themselves. Hackett showed me to the end of one of the tables while he took the centre chair at the platform table where, on either side, he

was flanked by two priests. Grace was then said and, as a youth
began to read at a lectern from what apparently was the *Book of
Martyrs*, the lunch was served, which suggested I might receive
some tasty bits.

Alas, the dish was a tasteless *olla podrida* of rice and peas,
semi-liquid, and floating with snippets of tough beef, which
must have been severed with a hatchet. I nerved myself to eat
my portion, knowing that if I did not learn to get down this
fodder, I would undoubtedly starve to death. Some sour goat
cheese followed with a hunk of bread, which actually was not
bad, this followed by a bowl of black liquid masquerading as
coffee. I managed this bitter brew in gulps. At least it was
hot.

Meanwhile, I had been surveying the other inmates whom,
for the most part, I detested on sight. In particular, a big ugly
brute of a youth who sat at the head of the middle table and was
addressed as Duff.

In regard to the clergy, one, and only one, seemed aware of
my existence, a little waif of a man, red cheeked and grey
haired, who kept moping and mowing in my direction. When I
inquired of my neighbour as to his identity, he muttered, since
silence was imposed:

"Father Petitt, music master."

Dear God, I thought, this is the last straw, and when we got
up and gave thanks, and he seemed to be making signs to me, I
hurriedly rose, mingled with the crowd and made tracks
for my little cell. This was the free hour in which I began to
compose and write this letter, now completed late, by candle
light, on the following day.

As I cannot risk subjecting it to the censoring of bloody
Hackett, I shall entrust it to my little Spanish friend, who will
mail it in the village. Do forgive this long laboured screed, dear
Alec. I wanted you to know exactly how I am situated and
what, if I survive, is in store for me over the next four years.

Do remember me to your dear mother.

Most affectionately yours,
Desmonde

P.S.   The neat little severed hand is now revealed as the relic
of one of the boys, a young priest, killed and mutilated in the
Congo, his body recovered by Belgian troops who preserved and

sent the hand. This gives Hackett one good mark in my book, that he should preserve and reverence it.

II

WHAT WAS ONE to make of that long and rambling, so typical letter? I allowed my mother to read it, since she was fond of Desmonde and interested in his priestly progress. She shook her head. "Poor boy. He will never do it."

But a long succession of letters, arriving periodically, seemed to contradict this foreboding. Moody, complaining, lit by occasional humour or bursts of fury against Hackett, they were so repetitious and, indeed, so unworthy of Desmonde, that I have suppressed them. Weighed against the events that were to follow, this was a dull period in Desmonde's life. In the early stages of his novitiate, his only friend amongst a rough lot was a boy as sensitive and intelligent as himself, nicknamed 'Looney', with whom he forgathered at recreation hour to play dreary games of tennis with antique racquets and worn out balls on a court well marked by sun-baked bovine excrement. At other times they would pace the cloister of the old abbey in silence, absorbing the beauty and peace of this much neglected part of the college. On wet days they forgathered in the library to read, although not from the volumes of the martyrs, with which the shelves were loaded, but other and less saintly books. They also got together to compose rude limericks, mostly dedicated to Hackett. These, written in disguised hand, were discreetly dropped in the lavatories and other more public places.

With the one exception of Fr. Petitt, Desmonde received little comfort from his priestly instructors, whom he often offended by revealing that he knew more than they were attempting to teach. But Petitt, the elderly, pink cheeked, rather timid little priest, already described as 'moping and mowing in an introductory manner', was from the first extremely well disposed towards Desmonde, whose school report had been of paramount interest to a choir master lost in a musical wilderness. Petitt could not really lay claim to this attribution. He played the church organ, taught the piano or violin on

demand, and mustered enough voices decently to control the
hymns, litanies and plainsong, which would otherwise have
been bawled beyond recognition. How he had come to the
seminary was a matter for conjecture since Petitt was not only
reticent but so painfully shy that a direct question would make
him flush. He had undoubtedly been musical from an early age,
and while still in his teens had played with one of the Midlands
orchestras, his instrument, appropriately enough, the flute.
How, or why, he had suddenly decided to study for the priesthood he would never reveal. So, also, was he silent on the many
changes, the shuttling from one parish to another, to which he
had been subjected after his ordination. He was not made to
be a success, even in the service of the Lord, but his knowledge
of music remained, and he felt it a blessing to find himself
finally at St. Simeon's. Here he was beloved by all and particularly by Father Superior, who favoured 'the little fellow' in
many ways.

Soon after Desmonde's first meeting with Fr. Petitt, he was
gently lured to the music room, a long, low, raftered chamber,
high above the cloisters of the old abbey, remote from concrete
and from all other distracting sights and sounds.

"Sit, Desmonde, and permit me to talk to you."

As they sat together on a frayed old sofa near the upright
piano, Desmonde saw that the little fellow was nervous, and
breathing quickly, as he began:

"My dear Desmonde, your report from St. Ignatius made
special mention, amongst your other attributes, of your
exceptional voice. When I read of it, I trembled, with ill
suppressed anticipation. Now, do not be alarmed." He laid a
hand on Desmonde's arm. "I would not for worlds throw you
to the wolves by requesting you to sing with that howling mob
in church, who yell their way through the hymns and the easy
pieces of Bach and Haydn I have drummed into them. No,
my dear Desmonde, I have a long treasured hope." His voice
trembled. "A possibility, a dream, a project that I have nursed
through many fruitless years." He paused. "Before I go on,
would you oblige me by singing to me?"

Desmonde had now been captivated by 'the little fellow'.

"What would you like me to sing, Father?"

"Do you know Schubert's 'Ave Maria'?"

"Of course, Father."

"It is difficult." He indicated the piano. "Shall I accompany you?"

"It's not necessary, thank you, Father."

Desmonde loved this beautiful hymn, and he sang it now with real enjoyment.

When it ended he looked down at Fr. Petitt. The little man was sitting with his eyes closed, his lips moving in silent prayer. At last he opened rather watery eyes and, inviting Desmonde again to sit beside him, he said:

"My dear Desmonde, I was thanking our Blessed Lord for answering a prayer I have made to Him for more than three years. Will you listen while I explain? And by the way, may I continue to call you Desmonde?"

"I wish you would, Father."

It was the first time Desmonde had been so addressed since he entered the seminary. And he listened intently while, for almost ten minutes, Fr. Petitt poured out his heart to him. A long silence followed this emotional outburst. Then:

"Will you try, Desmonde?"

"If you think I should."

"I believe it a God-given opportunity you should not throw away."

"Then I will."

They shook hands. The little man smiled.

"My idea is that you come up here during your free period in the afternoon, twice a week, say Tuesdays and Fridays, from three till five. We'll chat together and work, yes, work hard. For your relaxation I'll play you Beethoven, or whatever you prefer. And at the end I'll arrange for some refreshment to be brought up. I didn't do so today since I was not sure you would accept."

Desmonde went down to the stark austerity of seminary life with a new interest, the prospect of relaxation he had always enjoyed, and an objective impossible almost to achieve, but which stirred his blood when, occasionally, he permitted himself to visualize a possible victory, murmuring, savouring the words, 'The Golden Chalice'.

The Tuesday and Friday sessions began and were regularly continued. In all his singing Desmonde had never had a tutor, he sang naturally and had acquired many technical faults. Little Fr. Petitt set him many difficult pieces and did not fail to criticize.

"Desmonde, don't dwell on that last note as if you loved it and were afraid to let it go. That's a vulgar, sentimental trick. Try that passage again, you had just a trace of vibrato there. Avoid vibrato like sin. It's the damnation of many a good tenor. Don't blow up your high notes for effect, dying away like an expiring frog." Fr. Petitt resumed: "And now, Desmonde, what will be your 'choice' song at the contest? This is important, for much of the judging is based upon it."

Desmonde reflected for only a moment.

"I would wish to sing the Prize Song from *The Master-singer*." He added: "Wagner is not a favourite of mine, but this song is magnificent. Not only inspiring, but aspiring, reaching out for success, which makes it suitable for us."

Petitt nodded.

"Yes, a superb song. But long, very long, and difficult. Well, soon we will see what you can do with it."

On certain days Desmonde was not permitted to sing; he rested on the sofa while 'the little father' sat, with a cushion, at the piano and played, played selections from Brahms, Liszt, Schubert and Mozart, many of them Desmonde's favourites.

Regularly at a quarter to five, Martes would come up with something from the kitchen, normally reserved for the priests' table. Often he would come earlier and stand outside the door, listening. From some remote cupboard Fr. Petitt produced a kettle and spirit lamp on which he brewed tea.

This undreamed-of relaxation from the rigorous seminary routine, so in accord with Desmonde's tastes and natural disposition, undoubtedly saved him from abandoning his vocation, or perhaps from a breakdown. He referred to it continually in his letters, relating how gradually, subtly, he came to take possession of the attic room until he could come to it whenever he was free from the routine of the day. He wrote all his letters in this blessed seclusion and, stretched on the old couch, rested for half-an-hour, fighting down the inedible lunch, before starting work for the afternoon. He had uncovered a great pile of German music from the cabinet in the piano stool. He played through this and sang from it too, until his sight reading became perfect. Some of the lighter pieces he learned by heart. Two of Schubert's songs, 'Der Lindenbaum' and 'Frühlingstraum', he particularly liked, and that sweet love song of Schumann, 'Wenn ich in deiner Augen seh'.

Serious songs there were, also: Brahms' 'Der Tod das ist die
kühle Nacht', and surprisingly, in English, some excerpts from
Handel's *Messiah*, best of all the touching, 'I know that my
Redeemer liveth'.

One afternoon, when he was singing his heart out on a
favourite piece from Handel, 'The people that walked in
darkness', he did not hear the door open behind him. And
when he turned, there was the great, the ominous figure of
Hackett. He had been listening in the doorway.

Desmonde almost fell off the stool. He trembled, thinking,
this is the end, as Hackett slowly came towards him. But what
was this? A huge, approving hand laid on his shoulder, and the
words, not hurled at him, but mildly spoken:

"That was truly beautiful, Fitzgerald. I'm no professor,
but I know the best when I hear it. Keep on, keep at it, and
win, for the honour, and for the college, the Chalice."

He paused. "By the way, would you like to change your
bedroom to one of the bigger rooms upstairs?"

"Thank you, father, but no. I like my little cell."

"Good for you, Fitzgerald. I'll make a martyr out o' ye yet."

He smiled, actually smiled, turned and was gone.

Desmonde went down the old abbey staircase as noisily as
possible, singing a Hosannah at the pitch of his lungs. No need
to creep now. He was sanctioned, even sanctified; the little
attic study was his own.

Desmonde's dislike of Fr. Hackett had been modified by the
unexpected kindness his Superior had shown him. Yet he could
not quite accept the persistent and insistent missionary complex
that seemed the dominant factor in the teaching of the seminary
and the substance, more often than not, of Fr. Hackett's short
but powerful sermons.

One Sunday the morning discourse made a particular
impression upon Desmonde. Fr. Hackett began quietly
extolling the virtue and necessity of missionary endeavours, in
obedience to the command of Christ: " 'Go therefore and make
disciples of all nations'—Matthew 28.19. And St. Paul
had voiced the same command: 'Woe to me if I do not
preach the Gospel'—Corinthians 9.16. Christ had repeatedly
stressed the Church's evangelical mission, the need to preach
the Gospel and to educate its members to the greater knowledge
and consciousness of God.

"The core of the Catholic Church is missionary in nature," Hackett insisted. "An obedience to the command of Christ to exert a moral influence for social justice, to build schools, hospitals, dispensaries for the poor, the ignorant, the oppressed."

He then moved on to the great names in the missionary history of the Church, a subject dear to his heart, beginning with St. Paul, who had carried Christianity to the Gentiles, the Apostle James the Greater in Spain, and the Apostle Thomas in his conversion of the Malabar Indians. And, thereafter, St. Martin of Tours in France, St. Patrick and St. Columban in Ireland, St. Augustine, the first Archbishop of Canterbury in the year 597.

Fr. Hackett then went on to speak of the great Jesuit missionaries, citing the case of the Jesuit Matteo Ricci who early in the sixteenth century made the great breakthrough in China by an intensive study of the Chinese language and culture. His gifts of a clock and a spinet won the favour of the Emperor Wan-li and subsequent freedom to preach and teach. And in India the Jesuit Robert de Nobili, adopting the dress and manner of life of the Brahmins, outdid them in austerity and made thousands of converts among the upper classes.

"Do not imagine for one moment," Hackett resumed, "that all this sublime work was accomplished without sacrifice, the supreme sacrifice. In one year in the Congo alone, one hundred and six priests, twenty-four brothers and thirty-seven sisters were cruelly murdered in the performance of their holy work."

Fr. Hackett paused and with a break in his voice declared:

"Here, from this seminary, one of the many young missionaries we have sent forth over the years to all parts of the world, that noble and distinguished youth, Father Stephen Ridgeway, was brutally murdered and his body hacked to pieces while bearing the word of God into the wild and unexplored jungles of the Upper Congo.

"You are aware of the sacred relic recovered by Belgian soldiers and sent to us by the Belgian fathers at Kinder, the hand of this brave and noble youth, severed from his arm by a slash of the savage panga and miraculously, I repeat, miraculously preserved, fresh and undefiled, as though it still were a living part of Stephen's living body.

"You have viewed this relic, exposed to you for veneration at the Mass we celebrate on the anniversary of Stephen's glorious martyrdom. It is my most precious possession and will be shown in all its miraculous freshness when I apply for the canonization of this saintly youth, the pride of this seminary and a model, an inspiration and incentive to all of you here.

"What joy in Heaven, and to me, humble advocate of the missionary life, if, beyond these brave good souls who have already chosen this *via dolorosa*, others amongst you would come and say to me: 'I too, accept the message, nay, the command of Christ to "Go forth and preach the Gospel." ' "

Again a pause, then: "Stand up, and let us all sing that splendid hymn, the battle cry of all who lead the fight for Jesus, 'Onward, Christian Soldiers'."

Clearly, Father Hackett was now better disposed to the novice he had formerly so harshly treated. Yet Desmonde could not altogether respond to the advances made by his Superior. An unpleasant thought kept nagging him, and on the afternoon following the Father Superior's impassioned sermon, this found expression in the music room when he suddenly exclaimed to his tutor:

"Doesn't Father Hackett's missionary complex strike you as being rather cheap? If he feels so strongly on that subject, instead of urging us out to martyrdom, why won't he take a turn out there himself?"

Little Petitt dropped the sheet of music he was holding and looked at Desmonde sternly.

"That is a most uncharitable and uncalled for remark."

"But isn't it true?"

Again he studied him with a kind of angry surprise.

"Don't you know that Father Superior spent twelve years of his life as a missionary? Immediately after ordination he went to India to work among the Untouchables—the lowest and most despised of all humans. With his own hands he built a little dispensary, then started a little school, began to clothe and teach ragged, starved children whose days and nights were spent in the gutters of Madras. He literally pestered his friends at home for money to clothe and feed these little unwanted children, taught them the catechism, led them into Christianity while all the time living in the humblest, poorest quarter of the city where cholera is almost endemic.

"Of course, through his unsparing tending of the sick, he

went down with cholera, recovered, and was invalided home.

"In his absence a young American priest had carried on his good work and joined up with Father Hackett when Hackett returned. Together they achieved miracles until an epidemic of yellow fever struck the up-country province of Lingunda. Leaving his fellow priest in charge of the Madras mission, Hackett left for the plague centre. Six weeks later, after heroic devotion to the sick and the dying, he was himself stricken, nearly died, and was invalided home so wrecked, so devastated by that frightful disease, he was refused permission to return. Since it was now imperative for him to live in a warm climate, he was given this relatively easy appointment in Spain."

A long silence followed this brief exposition by Father Petitt, during which Desmonde remained perfectly still, a strange expression on his face. Suddenly he sprang to his feet.

"Please excuse me, father. I must leave you." And he rushed from the room.

Perhaps little Petitt had an inkling of the meaning of Desmonde's sudden departure, a premonition that he would soon return. He went to the piano and began softly to play his favourite 'Ave Maria'.

He was still playing, and continued to play, when Desmonde did come back, at the same time turning to inspect his pupil and to murmur slyly:

"You look happy. Good confession?"

"And forgiveness from a saintly priest," Desmonde said humbly.

III

DESMONDE WAS NOW settled down at the seminary, almost comfortably, rescued from earlier miseries by his God-given voice. His fastidious palate had even come to tolerate the unsavoury messes of the regime, since these were now mercifully ameliorated by fruit, notably peaches, from the surrounding orchards. He was even on surprisingly good terms with the Father Superior, who had begun to suspect possibilities hitherto unforeseen in this strange novice.

Desmonde's letters were now infrequent, altogether less

anguished, indeed, full of hope and tinged with a sense of dedication, an ardour that seemed to grow as time went on. One might say enthusiasm but for the fact that the discipline of the college had tempered his natural ebullience.

During this phase, benign and prolonged, Desmonde passed through the various stages of his novitiate, becoming in turn sub-deacon and deacon. And how pleasing this was to his mother, who longed to see her son a priest.

At least once every two or three weeks we went on Sunday to lunch with Mrs. Fitzgerald. The conversation always was centred on Desmonde. Now almost an invalid, she was living for the great event, yet I doubted if she would survive to see her son ordained. I was now within sight of my final examinations, and her symptoms of cardiac involvement, pallor, shortness of breath and marked oedema of the ankles, were only too apparent to me, a diagnosis confirmed when she showed me the medicine prescribed for her: little pillules of Nativelle's digitalin. I was now 'houseman' to Sir James MacKenzie, living in, with full board and lodging, at the Western Infirmary, and so ameliorating the burden my mother had heroically borne for so many years. Soon I hoped to be able to recompense her fully by sending her resignation to the Winton Corporation, terminating the work that had kept us both alive for so many hard years.

This satisfactory, almost benign state of being, for Desmonde and myself, continued for some further months until suddenly, out of the blue, a letter arrived, stamped with the familiar Spanish postmark. A letter so bulky and hurriedly written that I suspected disaster even as I unfolded it.

My dear Alec,

I have been in despair, cast down, humiliated, abused, ground into the dust, almost expelled, my priestly vocation in jeopardy, and all, all, I repeat, in my honest and unprejudiced opinion, through no fault of my own. Only now am I able to raise my bowed and bloody head, to give you the full circumstances of the case and to invoke your sympathy.

I believe I already mentioned, in a previous letter, that one of the few ameliorations in our strict regime is the weekly walk we are permitted to take to the town every Thursday afternoon. We go in a group, unchaperoned, with permission to buy fruit, or other legitimate refreshment, from the various vendors who are always about, in anticipation of our visit. Our absence from the seminary is never permitted to exceed one hour.

I need not tell you how eagerly we anticipate, not only this brief escape from our hard routine, not alone our momentary contact with the normal outside world, but also the many delicious fruits which we may purchase for a few pesetas. What else is there in this typical little Spanish village to excite us: the single dusty, winding street, lined with little houses, all blinding white in the perennial sun, with groups of old black clad women seated in front, stitching and gossiping. Dark little passages lead into the dark little shops which, solely because of the nearness of the seminary, sell extraneous articles: soap, toothpaste and brushes, simple medicines, postcards and even sweets. In season, too, mainly to seduce the students, they are piled with grapes, Malaga oranges, and peaches.

I am especially fond of peaches, as indeed are many of the other novices, and we are always met at the entrance to the town by a young woman, a girl, to be exact, who takes advantage of the other vendors by coming towards us with a big, flat pannier, slung from her shoulder and heaped with ripe, delicious fruit. In the interest of her business she has established a friendly relationship with us, and it has become more or less customary for us to stand and chat with her for a few moments, practising our Spanish, before we continue into the town.

On this particular Thursday of ill omen, I had been held up by Fr. Petitt, my admirable music master, who was rather excited by receiving long looked-for news from Rome of the proposed Song Festival. I was, in consequence, late in passing through the gates and when, by hurrying, I made up on my companions, I saw to my chagrin that all the peaches had been cleared.

"Oh dear, Caterina, you have kept nothing for me."

She shook her head, smiled, showing her nice white teeth.

"You are too late, nice little priest, and you must never be late for a rendezvous with a lady."

My colleagues, in particular Duff, the raw-boned Aberdonian, who detests me, had begun to enjoy my predicament as I said:

"I am sad. I thought I was your favourite customer."

"So you are sad, truly sad."

"Yes. Truly sad."

"Then smile now, your beautiful smile." And, to my surprise and delight, she produced from behind her back two of the biggest and most luscious peaches I had ever seen.

The chuckles and guffaws around me had subsided, as slinging the pannier to one side she came up to me holding a peach in each hand.

"Did you think for one second that I would forget you? Take them."

I felt in my pocket to pay her and, to my dismay, discovered that I had no money. In my haste I had forgotten my purse. My distress must have been obvious, not only to the onlookers but to her, as I stammered:

"I am so sorry. I cannot pay you."

She came quite close to me, still smiling. "So you have no money? I am pleased. For then you must pay me with a kiss."

She placed a peach in each of my hands and, as I stood there helpless, threw her arms around me and pressed her lips against mine in an embrace that was unquestionably passionate, at the same time murmuring in my ear: "Come any evening after six, my darling little priestling, to 17 Calle de los Pinas. *For you it is free.*"

When finally she disengaged herself, looking up at me with her dark sparkling eyes, that same entrancing smile, the ominous silence was broken by a shout from the Aberdonian.

"Enough, fellows. On to the town."

I followed in a state of dazed euphoria. That close and luscious embrace, tinged with the fragrance of peaches, had quite unmanned me. More or less isolated at the tail of the procession, I did eventually and to some degree revive myself by consuming both of the delectable fruits.

Even on our return journey to the seminary, no one spoke to me. Temporarily, at least, and through no fault of mine, I had become a pariah.

Next morning it did seem as though a thaw had set in, but at eleven o'clock I received a summons to appear before the Father Superior in his study. Somewhat re-chilled, I complied, my anxiety deepening when, on entering the room, I observed the tall, cadaverous figure of Duff standing by the window.

"Fitzgerald, a most serious charge has been laid against

you." Father Superior, seated at his desk, made the accusation immediately. As I remained silent he continued: "That of embracing the girl Caterina and, furthermore, of having immoral relations with her."

I was stupefied and, suddenly, enraged. I looked at the Avenging Angel by the window. He avoided my gaze.

"Who makes these charges? Plum Duff?"

"The name is Duff, Fitzgerald. He was present when you embraced the girl, Caterina. Do you deny this?"

"Absolutely and completely. It was she who embraced me."

"You did not resist her?"

"It was impossible. I had a large ripe peach in each hand."

"She had given you these peaches. Without payment. Does not that suggest intimacy?"

"She is a jolly friendly girl. We were all her customers and, in a sense, intimate with her. We all laughed and joked with her."

"No' me." A sepulchral voice came from the window. "Ah saw frae the furst she was a hoor."

"Silence, Pl . . . Duff. Of all the others you were her especial intimate, her choice, in fact. So that she arranged an assignation for that evening, to which you replied O.K."

I was now livid with rage.

"I have never in my life uttered such a corrupt and vulgar term. Who accuses me of using it?"

"Duff has keen ears."

"They are big enough."

Father Superior ignored this and resumed the attack.

"I have made inquiries. This Caterina Menotti, if not precisely a prostitute, is regarded officially as a *fille de joie*."

"Didna' ah tell ye, yer Reverence? She even gi'en him her address."

"Quiet, you Scottish oaf." Father Superior's evident annoyance with Plum slightly cheered me. But he went on: "Do you deny that you have ever visited her at this address?"

"If I had visited her, why should she give me her address? I would certainly have known it."

Father Superior looked inquiringly at Duff, who blurted out:

"She must of telt him to remind him in case he had forgot it."

A chilly silence followed this assumption, then Father Superior made a gesture towards the door.

"You may depart, Duff."

"I'm sure your Reverence kens I only brought this to your notice from the highest possible personal motives of virtue and the good name o' the college and forbye because there's nae doubt in my mind but what Fitzgerald . . ."

"Depart, Duff, instantly, or I shall be compelled to punish you with marked severity."

When Duff had departed, shaking his head, the Rector was silent, studying me reflectively. Finally he spoke.

"I don't believe for a moment, Fitzgerald, that you visited that house, or that you had carnal knowledge of that girl. If I did, you would leave the college this very afternoon. But you behaved in a manner that laid you open to a suspicion of grave misconduct, and one which disgraced and dishonoured the college. I shall have to consult with my colleagues as to what your sentence must be. Meanwhile, whether you must go, or whether you stay, I give you this advice.

"You are obviously inordinately attractive to the other sex. Be on your guard, therefore, against advances that may be made to you. Remain always in control of yourself and your emotions. Be discreet, calm, ready to withdraw at the slightest sign of danger. Do this, and you will spare yourself much pain, grief, and subsequent disaster. Now you may leave me. You will know your fate by tomorrow afternoon. Go to the church and pray that I may not be compelled to send you away."

I bowed and went out, straight to the church, where, I assure you, I made my entreaties with fervour. I knew how severe Hackett could be—only a few months before he had dismissed one of the younger novices for smoking a little end of cigar. Warned once before, this fellow had disobeyed the order. It was enough.

On the following day I continued to suffer until five o'clock, when our good choir master Fr. Petitt came towards me, and put his arm on my shoulders.

"I am deputed to tell you, Desmonde, that you are to remain. You are gated until the end of the term but, thank God, you are saved, not only for your vocation but," he smiled, "for our foray in Rome next month."

I had begun to thank him when he added: "Yes, you may be grateful to me. I think I swung the decision in your favour. I don't have a voice like yours, not once in a hundred years."

So there, dear Alec, is a verbatim report on the latest and

most serious trial and tribulation of your most affectionate
friend. I long for news of you. Do write to me immediately you
have the results of your final examinations. You don't know
how often I picture you, studying hard, in your bare little room.
In return I will brief you on the proposed visit to Rome, with
all the details, everything I have hitherto withheld.

   Ever yours most devotedly,
    Desmonde.

IV

I HAD NOW passed my final examinations for the M.B.Ch.B.
and (while his partner was away) had taken a four weeks'
locum tenens with Dr. Kinloch, an old and widely respected
general practitioner in Winton. This was not my ultimate
objective, nor the simple M.B.Ch.B. the last degree I meant to
achieve, but it would keep me near my mother for at least a
month, and with an honorarium of £40 would enable me, at
last, to remove her from her work in the slums and to relieve the
hardships she had bravely borne for so many years.

When I called to see Mrs. Fitzgerald it was now in a professional capacity. I was seriously worried by her deteriorating
condition and, when she permitted me to examine her, the
diagnosis was never in doubt. Acute mitral stenosis with partial
occlusion of the coronary artery. I persuaded her to allow me to
bring Dr. Kinloch in consultation. He confirmed the diagnosis
and, while cheering the patient and prescribing for her, gave
an even more grave prognosis: she must rest in bed pending an
improvement in her general oedema. Indeed, as we drove back
in his little cabriolet, he said:

"With that heart she might go at any minute."

The dream of her life had been to see her beloved son
ordained a priest of God. Now it was necessary to tell her that,
in her present condition, she would never reach Rome. I
could not bring myself to deliver this crushing blow, and my
mother, now free to visit her friend every other day, and wiser
than I, begged me to refrain for at least one more month.

So it befell that Desmonde's mother, falling asleep one night
in a bright vision of her son's future, did not awaken to reality,

disappointment and despair. She had died peacefully and without pain.

Desmonde, summoned immediately by telegram, arrived the day before the funeral, his manner sad yet restrained, without the abject manifestations of grief that might have been expected of him. I saw at once that he had changed, that his five years in the seminary had left their mark upon him, leaving him more restrained, rather more in control of himself. My mother epitomised it: "Desmonde has grown up."

Even at the graveside he bore up well, although tears, and bitter ones, were shed. Immediately after the funeral, since he had been granted only three days' leave, he talked with the lawyer. His mother's annuity died with her, but she had saved for him an amount exceeding three thousand pounds. He would also receive monies accrued from the sale of the lease of the house. Many of her nice clothes, including her fur coat and a brand new costume, no doubt intended for the ordination, she left to my mother, together with some of her best furniture, eminently acceptable gifts that moved the recipient to tears. For myself, who expected nothing, there was a gift outright of one hundred pounds.

Desmonde's train did not leave till midnight and that night, after my evening surgery, I sat late with him in the silent house and drew close to him again, as if we had never been apart.

Inevitably he spoke of his mother, concluding with a truism:

"Isn't it amazing, the good a good woman can do to a man?"

"And the bad, a bad one can do. There's plenty of them around."

"Always the realist, Alec." He smiled. "What are your plans now you have your degree?"

I told him this was merely the first step, that I meant to write a thesis for my M.D., and then to try for the M.R.C.P., adding:

"That's a hard nut to crack. Terribly difficult."

"You'll do it, Alec."

"How do you see your future?"

"Less clearly than yours. I shall be ordained in a matter of weeks, and as I haven't always pleased the powers that be, I've a sad foreboding that I shall be sent to do penance in some rough parish, probably Irish, since I am an Irish citizen."

"You won't like that."

"No, Alec, but it may be good for me. My views have changed

rather, under the tender solicitude of the good Father Hackett."

I looked at him inquiringly as he went on:

"This Hackett is a strange fellow, Alec. I began by hating his guts. And he gave every manifestation of loathing me. I thought him a bully and a sadist. He's not really, simply a zealot. He's imbued, saturated with missionary zeal. He would like all his students to go forth into the wilderness to preach the word of God. I thought him a maniac. I don't now. He's a throwback to one of the Apostles, probably Paul. I have come to like and respect him, in fact he has rather got me."

"Do you see yourself as a second St. Patrick?"

He flushed. "Don't laugh, Alec. How do we know what's ahead of us? You might suddenly chuck medicine and become an author. I might one day lay my bones in some tropical jungle."

Impossible not to laugh, loud and long. And in a moment he joined me.

"Anyway, I understand and respect Hackett now, and I'd like to repay him. There's a competition in Rome. Promoted by the Società Musicale di Roma with lots of backing from the Vatican, open to young priests newly ordained or to novices on the eve of ordination. The basic idea is to encourage the use of the voice, in the sung Mass, the litanies, and so forth. Quite a noble idea, and nobly named the Golden Chalice. Father Hackett would like me to try for it." He paused. "We're a small college at Torrijos, with an inferiority complex, far less well-known than our counterpart at Valladolid. What a lift it would give us, and what publicity, if we could put the trophy—it's a golden chalice—in our front window."

"When is the happy event?"

"Next June. So you can picture me following scores of others —Italy is bristling with young tenors—on to a platform decorated with a blasted panel of experts, lay and clerical, and singing my heart out before an audience, normally in the hundreds."

"You'll win, hands down, Desmonde. Want to bet?"

He smiled. "With my ordination so near, Alec, I am barred from donating coins of the realm to a very dear, canny Scot." He looked at his watch. "I'm afraid we'll have to go now. Let's walk down to the Central."

When he had taken a last look round the house he took his

C

bag and, pausing sadly on the threshold, shut and locked the front door. "It's a Chubb lock. The agent has the key."

As we set out for the station, he took my arm with his free hand.

"Too bad keeping you up so late, Alec."

"I'm often up late, or in the middle of the night. Let me take your bag."

He shook his head. "I carry my own these days. Listen, Alec. May I ask you a medical question?"

"Of course." I wondered what was coming, but never expected what followed.

"It's rather an odd question, but do answer me seriously. If a human hand was severed at the wrist, would it eventually decay?"

"Absolutely! After a week it would stink to high heaven, putrefy, then liquify and finally rot, leaving only the bones which would in time separate into the carpals and metacarpals—little knobs of disintegrating calcium."

"Thank you, Alec. Thank you very much."

No more was said, and soon we were in the Central Station. I saw him to his third class compartment.

"Don't wait, dear Alec. These prolonged farewells are hell. Besides, I know, absolutely know, that one day our lives will be together again."

We shook hands, then I turned away and walked quickly from the station. I hoped he was right, that we should one day meet again. I also hoped the last tram for Western Road had not gone.

Six weeks later Desmonde was ordained and, fulfilling his forebodings, officially notified to proceed to the Church of St. Teresa in the country parish of Kilbarrack in Southern Ireland. But much was to happen before then, as Desmonde will now relate.

V

ON THE MORNING of our departure, Father Superior came himself to my little cell to awaken me one hour earlier than usual. When I had dressed, he stood while I threw some things in my suitcase, then we went together to the church where little Petitt was awaiting us. Both he and Fr. Hackett had already said their Mass, but both remained in the front seat while I said mine, and I assure you I did not omit a petition for heavenly aid in the endeavour now before me.

When I had finished, Fr. Hackett took me by the arm and conducted me to his study, where Martes was standing by with good hot coffee, not the habitual refectory sludge, and fresh hot rolls. My Superior watched me in silence while I made a good meal, but refused, quite nicely, when I asked if he would take a cup.

When Martes had cleared away he said:

"I have arranged for you to have a car to Madrid."

"Oh, thank you, Father. That local is a beastly train."

"It is not a beastly train. It is a most useful train for our peasants and farmers taking their produce to the Madrid markets. It is, however, rather slow and uncertain in its arrival. Hence the car, not a Hispano Suiza, nevertheless a car."

"You are right, Father," I said at once. "I am always putting my foot in it with you."

"Not so much as usual, Father Desmonde. Not nearly so much. In fact, while you are far from perfect, you are a much improved young man. I have taken great pains with you, and in return," he paused, fixing me with a steady eye, "I want you to bring the Golden Chalice to the college. It is, in itself, a bauble, a sorry trophy, but it would bring great prestige, not only to you, which is unimportant, but to the college."

He stood up, as did I, and moved to the prie-Dieu. I followed.

"I am going to accord you a great favour. Kneel, take this blessed relic and say a prayer for your success and mine."

I knelt and, I assure you, with great reverence took the little hand, so smooth, the skin so pliable it had the feeling of a living hand. Gently I pressed it and it seemed as though the fingers responded, enfolding mine with a touch both intimate and tender, as though unwilling to release, unwilling to relinquish this contact with a life once experienced and remembered now in tranquillity and joy. In this manner I made a truly fervent petition, not only for immediate success, but for a good life and a happy death.

"Well?" said Fr. Hackett, when I stood up.

"It is miraculous. There is the touch of heaven in these fingers."

"You must tell that to your doctor friend who demands putrid flesh and rotting bones. Now come, it is time for you to go."

The car, a solid little Berlier, was already in the yard and beside it, with my suitcase and his own carpet bag, Fr. Petitt. When we were in the car, the luggage safely in the boot, as we set off I saw Fr. Hackett make a big sign of the cross, blessing us. In the beginning I had hated this dedicated priest. Now, though he deliberately repelled all affection, I truly revered him.

In about an hour we were in Madrid and in the *rapide* for Rome, Fr. Petitt, exercising an almost maternal solicitude upon me, imposing silence, forbidding the window to be widely opened, suspecting draughts from all points of the compass, as though I were a chicken just out of the egg. At Rome station, however, his confidence evaporated, and he was glad to have me summon a porter to transfer our bags to a taxi which I duly directed to the Hotel Religioso, where rooms had been reserved for us by our Superior.

Alas, the Religioso was a sad blow. Piety might be practised here, but all temporal virtues were totally in abeyance. As I surveyed the bare, linoleumed, liftless hall, the precipitous, uncarpeted stairs, and finally our two monastic little rooms overlooking the railway shunting yards, from which, amidst a grinding, snorting, puffing consortium of engines and their appendages, clouds of steam and smoke billowed towards us, my heart sank. With four full days remaining before the song festival, what a preparation for our ordeal! And I had hoped for such leisured, pleasant ease in this reunion with my favourite city.

I glanced at little Petitt. He did not mind, not a bit, but I was bitterly cast down, and at the midday meal, a polenta mélange served on a wax-clothed table with flies embracing the sauce stains, my melancholy deepened and continued until the shades of night began to fall.

And then, Alec, heaven responded to my unspoken prayers. As we sat staring at each other in what I might call the commercial room, a frightened youth in an outsize porter's uniform approached us at the double.

"A lady at the door, sir, in a car, asking for you."

I made for the door, also at the double, and there, yes, yes, Alec, there in a big new Hispano Suiza was my friend the Marchesa. She had read of our arrival in the evening paper, *Paese Sera di Roma*, and had instantly gone into action.

"Come, come, at once, Desmonde. You must not remain here an instant longer. I am afraid even to enter. Come to me."

"I have a little friend, a priest, Madame. He wouldn't take up much room."

"Bring him, bring the little priest at once. Come, both of you."

Needless to say, we did not refuse, and in no time at all we were in the big car with our belongings, I in the back seat with Madame, Fr. Petitt, still dazed, in front with the chauffeur, gliding towards distinguished affluence, leaving the youthful porter gaping in our wake, stunned by the tip I had recklessly thrust upon him.

It was after ten o'clock when we reached the Villa Penserosa, past the hour of dinner, and although refreshments were pressed upon us, I declined.

"Dear Madame, we have been stuffed with so much polenta since we became inmates of the Religioso that all we now long for is a good restful sleep."

"You shall have it." She spoke aside to the maid who stood waiting for instructions. "And as you are obviously tired, I shall say *buona notte* until tomorrow."

Our adjoining rooms, with a luxurious bathroom between, were, to the last detail, perfection. A suit of silk pyjamas had even been laid out on my bed. Fr. Petitt had not the habit of a nightly bath, so I luxuriated for half-an-hour in deep hot soapy water, rubbed myself down with a turkish towel, donned the gift pyjamas, in which I felt more unreal than ever, and fell into bed. Instantly sleep overwhelmed me.

Next morning, agreeably late, we were awakened by breakfast: a large pot of steaming freshly roasted coffee, with a little napkin-covered basket holding a tier of warmed Roman rolls, that special and richer variety of the French croissant. When I had dressed I went downstairs to find my hostess awaiting me in her little boudoir sewing room, where all her charitable stitching was accomplished.

"Good morning, my dear Reverend Desmonde. I see from

your fresh and shining air that you have slept well. Your little friend is safely ensconced in the library with a book. So now you belong entirely to me."

She stood there smiling, facing the hard morning light without a qualm. Inevitably, she looked older, her hair now a silvery white, but her fine eyes were as lively and her mind as wittily alert as ever. How unutterably irresistible she must have been as a young woman. Even now she was a darling.

"However," she added, "all fresh and dewy you may be, but where, oh, where did you get these trousers?"

"Madame, these trousers, now only three years old, are the finest work of the finest sartorial artist in the village of Torrijos."

"They are certainly unique. And the jacket?"

"This jacket, Madame, although venerable, is virtually a religious object, cut down, and suitably adjusted by the aforementioned tailor, from a discarded jacket previously in the possession of the very reverend Father Hackett."

"It is undoubtedly a relic. Come, Desmonde, and view yourself."

She pulled open the door of a cupboard on which a large pier mirror had been inset.

I had never seen so much of myself for a long, long time, and while the face remained passable, the rest of me might have been found on the trunk and legs of an aged and decrepit tramp.

"Yes," I reflected thoughtfully, "a little sponging and pressing would make me as good as new, Madame."

She laughed outright. "Desmonde, you are incorrigible. Listen, you must be quiet and rest until Saturday, but this morning you are coming with me, to visit my friend Caraccini."

"A priest?"

"No, merely the best tailor in all Italy. Don't worry about your friend, he is very happy in the library."

We set out in the beautiful big landaulette, not the Hispano as I had imagined, but a brand new Isotta Franchisi, drove down the Via Veneto to the Excelsior, turned left, and drew up at a window displaying no goods, adorned simply with the word, Caraccini.

We entered, Madame greeted with immense deference by a dapper little man in an immaculate dark grey suit. My needs, my situation, were fully discussed, bales of cloth were inspected, felt and selected. I was shown into a commodious cubicle where an underling in shirt sleeves taped and measured all over me.

"You understand, Caraccini, everything must be finished and delivered by the evening of Friday."

"Madame la Marchesa, it is impossible. But for you," Caraccini bowed, "it will be accomplished."

All was not over, since Madame still wanted more fun, for thus she regarded and named her charity to me, and I was led into a nearby haberdasher's of obvious and unimpeachable distinction. Here my dear friend went a little wild and, in the end, a variety of elegant and expensive garments had been chosen and set aside for immediate delivery. Finally, we dropped into the custom shoemaker's in the same street. Here my extremities were sedulously measured and two leathers selected, one light and the other somewhat heavier, both pairs commandeered for the following Friday. How, one might ask, could such skilled work be accomplished in so short a time? The answer is in the fact that Rome is a city of craftsmen, and of women too, tucked away in little rooms and alleys throughout the city, receiving the work for speedy delivery and labouring, often through the night, to complete it. One would hope that such expertise would be amply rewarded. Alas, this is not so.

"Just a light little lunch," Madame said, when we emerged from the shoemaker's. "Then home, to rest, rest, rest until Saturday."

She led the way into the Excelsior, where, seated at the bar, she proposed a sherry and a Parma sandwich. The car was still parked outside the hotel. Soon we were on our way back to the Villa Penserosa. When I tried to thank her she would not hear a word of it.

"Quiet, dear Desmonde. You know I loved your mother and was so sorry when you wrote me of her death." She added: "You know also that I love you too, my dear boy."

As we approached the house she murmured:

"I wonder what your little friend has been doing in your absence."

Immediately we were inside she took my arm and led the way to the library.

There, indeed, was the Reverend Fr. Petitt, seated in the same chair, with the same book, open at the same page, upon his knees, a beatific smile upon his face and a gentle rhythmic sibilation coming from between his lips.

"He has not moved one millimetre," Madame gasped.

"Oh yes, Madame," said the maid who had admitted us. "He ate a very good large lunch with a bottle of the good Frascati."

"He looks sweet when he is sleeping," Madame said. "Like a child."

"He has taught me a great deal," I said. "And if we should have any luck at all on Saturday I shall owe it all to him."

"What a nice thing to say, dear Reverend Desmonde. And now you must go to your room and rest. From now until Saturday it is rest, rest, rest, with little talking. Do you know that Enrico did not speak a word between his performances?"

"I am not Caruso, Madame."

"We shall see on Saturday." She smiled. "And now I must rest also, for I am tired. You see, I am an old woman now."

"Please don't say such evil words, Madame. You are as gracious, as charming, as darling as ever. And you have been an angel to me today."

She shook her head, still smiling, as she preceded me upstairs, then turned and went into her room while I entered mine.

VI

SATURDAY DAWNED FINE, and Desmonde, who had slept restlessly, rose early and drew up the Venetian blinds to let the sun into his room. He then lay on his bed for ten minutes considering the prospects of the day. Admittedly he was nervous, he wanted to win the Chalice, not entirely for personal success, but to please, and indeed repay, Fr. Hackett, the Marchesa and, especially, little Petitt. And, as he told me afterwards, his thoughts kept going back to the final of the Schools' Shield which I had longed to win and which, alas, had been lost.

A knock on his door cut short his foreboding. The little fellow, dressed, and having already said his Mass, came into the room.

"Good night?"

"Quite good. And you?"

"Perfect!" This with an emphasis that gave perfection the lie.

"Beautiful day for us."

"Perfect."

"I left everything for you down below, when you're ready."

Down below was the little sanctuary in the basement where, every day since their arrival, they had both said Mass.

"I'll be down straight away."

"Good!"

Desmonde did not shave but quickly got into his old suit and went downstairs to rejoin Fr. Petitt in the sanctuary, a little rough stone grotto equipped with a simple altar, a crucifix, a statue of the Virgin, and two prie-Dieux, a retreat for prayer and emergency services often found in large Italian houses. Fr. Petitt, with customary foresight, had brought everything necessary from the seminary.

Desmonde said his Mass, with Fr. Petitt acting as server, and it may be assumed that their prayers, those of the young priest and the old, were leavened by the same intention. Afterwards, when Desmonde had made his thanksgiving, they went upstairs to a substantial breakfast, English style, of bacon and egg, marmalade and toast.

As they were served the elderly tablemaid whispered to Desmonde:

"Madame la Marchesa begs you to make a large breakfast for it must be a very small lunch."

"We will obey," Desmonde said, smiling. "Madame la Marchesa will not herself be down?"

"Rarely she comes before ten o'clock."

The reply gave Desmonde a sudden understanding that his patroness, so lively and so charming, so active on his behalf, was, in years at least, an ageing woman. Now he knew that he must do his utmost to succeed, if only to reward her for her kindness.

After they had breakfasted, Desmonde with a good appetite, Fr. Petitt less so, they went together to the library.

"This is the beastly bit," Desmonde said. "Hanging on. By a thin rope over a cliff. I suppose I can't go out."

"Absolutely not. And you should talk little."

"God bless Caruso. If only I could sing like him."

"You will, if you remember all I told you. Be quiet, don't

move around. Half of these young Italians will be flinging themselves about the stage with hands on their hearts. Now listen, while you were shopping with the Marchesa I made inquiries. For your own choice song, which follows the set pieces, you will sing what?"

"As we decided. The Prize Song from *Meistersinger*, in the Italian translation."

"No, no. Listen to me. The Cardinal from the Curia on the committee of judges, a very, a most important man, is the German Cardinal. So you must, must sing your Wagner piece in the original German."

"I prefer it that way. Is the hall large?"

"Very large, with a wide high balcony. And it will be filled, every seat. The acoustics are excellent. On the stage will sit the judges, all important and informed people, teachers and professors of music, members of the Curia, including the Cardinal, and of the Society. I asked if our Marchesa might sit with them but the answer was 'no'. It would be deemed favouritism and would prejudice the judges against you."

"I can believe that. Where will the Marchesa sit?"

"All competitors—the number has been screened down to twenty—will sit in the front row. And in the row behind, railed off from the auditorium, will sit special guests, including our good hostess."

"Good! Steps up to the stage, I suppose?"

"Exactly. Each candidate goes up in turn, sings two set pieces, is judged, and given his marks. After all have been marked, and the marks are counted, ten are eliminated."

"And can go home, poor fellows."

"Certainly, they are dismissed. Again, for those who remain, one very difficult set piece, marked and the marks counted. The low six are eliminated. And again, for the remaining four, the other very difficult set piece, after which two are eliminated and two remain. These two must choose each one song, sacred or not, on which they are judged, one sent down and the survivor awarded the prize."

"A fairly cold blooded procedure."

"It is eminently fair, dear Desmonde. And for one to succeed all others must fail. Besides, it gives a whole afternoon of excitement and good singing to the aficionados. And there are many, many of these, I assure you, ready to cheer."

"Or to howl you down." Desmonde looked at his watch. "Only ten o'clock. Another two hours of waiting misery."

He got up and began to wander around the room, looking over the shelves so nobly stocked. Suddenly, on a bottom shelf, given over to smaller and more personal books, his eye was caught by a little green book entitled *Heraldry of Ireland*. Oddly it seemed familiar. He took it up from the shelf and opened it, turning the pages until he came to the fly leaf, and there, beneath his father's familiar bookmark, he read the words, written in ink, now faded:

'For my very dearest Marguerita with my deep affection and profound regard.   Dermot Fitzgerald.'

Desmonde remained motionless, holding the book, while a wave of emotion, of revelation and understanding swept over him. He knew now the reason for the kindness so warmly bestowed upon him in this house. He saw, too, that the book had been held and fondled many times. Quietly he replaced it, leaving it perhaps a fraction of an inch out of line with the other books, then he moved away.

"Going up to change now?" Petitt asked.

"Yes, it's about time."

He went slowly upstairs. As he was about to go into his room, he saw the Marchesa coming towards him, looking fresh and rested, beautifully turned out in a suit of dark Italian silk.

"Good day, Desmonde dear."

He did not answer, but took her hand and, looking deep into her eyes, he kissed her fingers one by one. Always Desmonde was full of these silly little tricks and always the recipients seemed to like them. She smiled.

"I would blush, Desmonde, if I did not have my rouge on. What have you been doing with yourself all morning?"

"I have been reading, Madame. A most interesting book on heraldry. I was pleased to find that we Fitzgeralds were mentioned therein."

Did she understand? Later that morning he saw the book had been lifted and replaced. But now, too quickly perhaps, though still smiling, she said:

"Now go and get ready for the fray."

Desmonde retreated to his room, washed and shaved more carefully than usual, brushed his hair, then put on his new clothes. How white and fine was the shirt, how light and well-fitting the suit. The shoes too, of pliable soft leather, had nothing of the rigid feeling of new shoes, but clung to his feet like gloves. The best is always the best, thought Desmonde, and what a pity it is always so expensive.

He could not view himself completely in the little bedroom mirror, but went downstairs smartly, hoping that all was well. The Marchesa was in the hall with Fr. Petitt, walking up and down, obviously awaiting him. Both stopped dead when he appeared, as, indeed, did he.

"I can't believe it's you, Desmonde," Fr. Petitt gasped.

Madame had not spoken but was circling him critically.

"Do clothes make such a difference?"

She smiled. "Dear Father Desmonde, how should I look in a washerwoman's old skirt and shawl? Never mind, I am pleased, very, very pleased with you. I knew Caraccini would not fail us. Perfection, there is no other word. Now come to lunch, such as it is."

"You both had a good breakfast?" Madame asked, as they sat down at the sparsely plenished dining room table.

"Wonderful." Little Petitt chuckled.

"The finest since I was a boy back on the farm!"

"You were never on a farm, Desmonde!"

"Of course not, Madame, but I must, at all costs, dramatize the breakfast."

"Well now, for every reason, you will get little. And all is for the voice."

A cup of strong bouillon was served with a raw egg, floating rather repulsively upon the top, and afterwards, thin slices of fresh pineapple floating in the juice of the fruit.

"This clears the throat," Madame asserted, looking at the clock. "And now we have time only for coffee. It is a bore, but they are so fussy and official at the Philharmonic, we must be early."

Coffee, strong black coffee, was swallowed, then they were in the closed car, driving through sunny streets to the big auditorium off the Via di Pietra, where already crowds were moving towards the long row of clicking turnstiles.

"We go to the offices. Everything is very stuffy and old-fashioned here," Madame said, briskly, leading the way to a narrow door beyond.

Here also a crowd was milling around, but the Marchesa, armed with Desmonde's letter, immediately commanded attention. They were shown into an inner office, thence to the auditorium proper, where Desmonde and Petitt found places in the front row, specially reserved for competitors. Madame la Marchesa was seated in a special reserved enclosure not far behind.

Already the auditorium was more than half filled, and crowds were flowing in. On the stage, too, where the trophy, the Golden Chalice, was enthroned on a velvet podium, activities were increasing, while from time to time young priests of various sizes and condition materialized and nervously seated themselves on the candidates' bench.

Little Petitt moved restlessly. "Such waiting. These preparations are very trying for you, are they not?"

"Yes," said Desmonde. "I'm going to close my eyes. Nudge me when they're ready."

For perhaps twenty minutes Desmonde kept his eyes resolutely closed, ignoring the noise and the sense of movement around him, until his vision was restored by a tap on the shoulder. He then saw that the other candidates were lined up beside him and that the committee of judges had assembled on tiered seats to the left, while at the rear of the stage a vocal quartette with string orchestra were about to open the proceedings with *Veni Creator Spiritus*. Everyone joined in this beautiful hymn, candidates, pianist, audience and committee alike, so that a great volume of sweet sound swelled and filled the hall.

The secretary of the Society now stepped forward and in a brief speech outlined the object of the contest: to sustain and increase public interest throughout all Europe in the sung Mass, to maintain and keep alive that most historic, most beautiful offering to God, which now, alas, was threatened by the rush and hurry of this modern age, sacrificed to the demand for shorter and still shorter services. He then thanked the members of the Curia, and in particular His Eminence Cardinal Gratz, for attending on the committee so that the judging and allocation of marks would be absolutely just and impartial. He looked meaningly towards the crowded balcony and begged the many partisans who had come to support their candidates to realize that justice would be done and to refrain from demonstrations of all kinds. He then decided that the contest should begin.

Immediately ten candidates on the far side of Desmonde got up and mounted the steps to the stage where they were seated on a long bench in one of the wings. The first test piece was announced, and the candidates, named one by one, came forward to sing it.

Desmonde, as may be imagined, listened intently. All were good choir voices, somewhat lost in the big hall, but two of the younger candidates were so manifestly nervous they obviously did not give their best, while a third almost provoked laughter by a variety of enticing gestures, hand on the heart, first one then both arms outflung, all implying dramatic and emotional fervour.

Now came the turn of the second ten. Of these Desmonde was the last to come forward, somewhat disturbed, not only by the fact that the candidate immediately before him, a novice from the Abruzzi, had sung superbly, ending to a great ovation from a crowd of supporters in the gallery, but also by the fact that his appearance, so quietly distinguished, had evoked catcalls and laughter from the same gallery.

Desmonde, however, remained quite still before the great sea of faces stretching beneath him, waiting in apparent calm until he achieved complete silence. Only then did he signal the pianist to launch into the lovely Brahms. Now there was no jeering from the gallery, but a great burst of applause swelling up from the main body of the auditorium.

Presently the marks were announced and the ten losing candidates removed from the stage, and the process of elimination was resumed.

The next set piece for the remaining ten was the *Ave Maria* of Gounod, a particular favourite of Desmonde's. His appearance, no longer greeted by derision from the gallery, was warmly applauded from all other parts of the hall. He was at ease now, and sang even better than before. As he went back to his place to prolonged applause he caught the eye of the Cardinal fixed benignly upon him.

Again the marks were read aloud, to the usual mixed reception, and the disconsolate six removed from the stage. Now, no more than four candidates were alive to face the final set piece, and of these it had now become apparent that

Desmonde and the novice from the Abruzzi would survive to meet in the grand finale.

An intermission now occurred during which the string orchestra played the first part of Vivaldi's 'Four Seasons'.

Meanwhile, Desmonde and the Abruzzian were called before the committee and given the respective totals of their marks, which indicated that Desmonde was leading by nine points. They were then asked to name their 'choice' piece. The selection of the little novice was 'O Sole Mio', a great favourite, in fact a crowd pleaser to an Italian audience, though less so to these informed committee critics, who now looked expectantly at Desmonde. Obviously, since he was already ahead, he must choose a simple piece to avoid all possibility of technical error. However, to the astonishment of the committee, he said: "I choose the Prize Song from *Die Meistersinger*."

A silence, then:

"You will sing in Italian?"

"Not at all." Desmonde permitted his glance to rest for an instant on the Cardinal. "I will sing in the original German."

Another silence, then the President said:

"That will be a great treat for all of us . . . but of course you know, the difficulties . . . the risk . . ."

At this point the Cardinal intervened.

"If this brilliant young priest wishes to sing this superb song, then you must let him sing it. He is not afraid, nor am I."

Thus, when the Vivaldi came to an end amid some polite applause, the President of the Society stepped forward and announced the choices of the two finalists. The novice from the Abruzzi must sing first.

And some moments later the lovely melody of 'O Sole Mio' fell upon enraptured Italian ears, long familiar with a song popularized, sung by countless mediocre tenors, throughout the country. The gallery went wild, even joining in the song. Alas, worse was to come, for the little Abruzzian, scenting triumph in this mass success, actually raised his right arm and conducted the yelling choir. More, more applause when he had finished. He returned to his seat flushed and smiling.

Now Desmonde must sing, to a restless, excited, seething gallery. He advanced, handed his music to the pianist, and

waited patiently at the front of the stage, calmly observing the
Marchesa and Fr. Petitt watching him with straining intensity.
Then at last there was total silence. He began to sing.

As the superb opening bars of that magnificent song swelled
upwards, the test song of the Meistersinger, purposely difficult,
a strange, trance-like stillness seemed to embrace, to elevate and
ennoble the listeners. Desmonde himself seemed to lose himself
in the Wagnerian meaning and intention of this noble song, the
straining aspiration it bestowed upon the singer. He became
Walther seeking the recognition of his splendid voice and
admittance to membership of the élite, the immortals. All, all
he gave, knowing, and rejoicing in, the supreme effort.

When it was over and he stood, his eyes uplifted, exhausted
and unknowing of his surroundings, a dead silence fell upon his
listeners. Then came a roar that lifted the roof, sweeping
upwards from all parts of the great auditorium, from the standing, cheering crowd.

A standing ovation, unsurpassed in the history of the
Society, which went on and on until the President came forward and, his face wreathed in smiles, took both of Desmonde's
hands and shook them repeatedly.

"My dear Father Desmonde, words fail me. Believe me, we
shall know more of you in Rome, and soon, since I personally
will see to it. You are too precious to be lost in the wilds of
Ireland." Then he raised a hand to still the audience.

"Members of the Society, ladies and gentlemen. Your
overwhelming response has confirmed our careful markings
that Father Desmonde Fitzgerald is the winner of the Golden
Chalice. And as Honorary President of the Society I have
great pleasure in presenting the Chalice to him now, together
with a little replica that he may retain as a constant reminder of
his triumph here today."

Amidst further cheers, he held up the Chalice, to which was
attached a small jeweller's box, and presented it to Desmonde.

People were now leaving the hall, indeed, the Abruzzi party
with other disappointed groups had already sadly departed.
The Marchesa and Fr. Petitt had come forward to the foot of
the platform steps, to catch the attention of the Cardinal.

"Your Excellency, may I present my hostess and my tutor?"

"Present! Good Heavens! Come here at once, Marguerita,
you naughty girl." He kissed her hand. "I see you are at your

old games, entertaining distinguished Irishmen, always handsome ones, too."

"Father Desmonde has just lost his dear mother. So I have
adopted him."

"Then we must get him back to Rome, soon, for you."

"And you, little Father . . ." He had turned to Fr. Petitt.
"It is you who have taught your pupil some useful tricks."

"Oh, your Excellency!" Between past tension and present
excited delight, Petitt scarcely knew what he was saying.
"Desmonde is himself bursting with all sorts of tricks."

The Cardinal smiled. "Let them give you the case for that
lovely thing, otherwise it may be coveted and stolen. You have
your car, Marguerita? Good! Then I shall bid you all a very
happy *auf wiedersehen*."

When he had gone, the Marchesa took Desmonde's arm and
pressed it to her side.

"You see, darling Desmonde, my heart is still beating like
mad. Oh, I am so excited, so deliriously happy. I can't tell you
how wonderful you were, standing before all that crowd, like
a young god, and singing, singing like an angel. But we must
get home. Father Petitt has his case, and I have got you. Now
come."

They left by the stage door. The car stood outside and they
were off, exhausted but triumphant, to the Via della Croce.

Together in the rear seat, while little Petitt sat in front
clutching his trophy to his breast, the Marchesa drew
Desmonde's head upon her shoulder.

"Tonight we shall rest and tomorrow also, for you must be
worn out with strain, and I, an old woman, am quite exhausted, supporting you with all my strength when you were
singing. But on Monday and all of next week we shall have fun,
with lots of parties, the opera too, here in Rome, and also a
quick trip to La Scala, where I have an *abonnement*."

"But, dear Madame, I should be in Ireland next week."

"The Irish won't mind, they are an easygoing people. And,
also, you have earned and deserve a holiday. Finally, as my
adopted son, you must obey me. I want you to be happy."

"Father Petitt will stay, also?"

"We could not detain him if we wished. Once he has the
Chalice engraved with your name and college he will be off
like a rocket to give Father Hackett the joyful news."

When they reached the peace and comfort of the Villa Penserosa Desmonde went immediately to his room and wrote a few words on one of his cards. He then took the card and his little gold replica, summoned the maid and asked her to place both on Madame's dressing table. He then took a hot, relaxing bath and, wrapped in a big towel, lay down on his bed. How pleasant to think of his success and of the coming festivities. Kilbarrack seemed a long way off, a different world, in which he would return to the crudities of peasant life, to a dilapidated church filled with artistic horrors, stations of the Cross so lurid as to hurt the eye, little faceless, factory-made statues of the Virgin in blue and white, a pervading smell of candle grease, stale incense, and odours normally associated with the stable. Well, he must endure it. In the meantime, let there be joy, music, refinement and all the pleasures he had so richly earned.

THREE

I

THE ARRIVAL OF Desmonde at Kilbarrack was not auspicious, nor did it raise the dampened spirits of the new curate. The day had been wet from morning and the railway journey from Dublin to Wexford a painful reminder of the native indolence of Irish trains. One hour late at the junction, he had to wait another hour for the local that dawdled to his destination. Here, disgorged with his suitcase on to the rain-swept single platform, he looked in vain for a cab. Ten minutes went by before one appeared, drawn by a nag that in all probability had never won the Irish Derby.

"Hey! Hey! Can you give me a lift?"

From beneath a mantle of sodden potato sacks came the answer.

"Sure and I can. Step up, your reverence."

Desmonde stepped up, hoisting his valise to the rear of the cab and taking his seat beside the driver.

"So you expected me?"

"I did." The driver laid the whip gently on the horse's dripping rump. "I met the noon train for ye on the Canon's instructions. I'm Michael."

"Sorry you had the double journey, Michael."

"Ah, 'tis no trouble, your reverence, no trouble at all. I do all kinds of a job for the Canon, besides bein' sidesman at the church. I'll take you by the Cattle Market and up the High Street, 'twill give ye a look at the town."

Kilbarrack, no different from a hundred other unflourishing country towns, was no surprise to Desmonde. He had known them as a boy. But as they jogged past the litter-strewn yard, the corner pubs, the licensed grocer, the butcher, baker, the ironmonger's spread of farm implements across the pavement, and again more pubs, all viewed through a curtain of mist and rain, he felt himself a long, long way from the Via Veneto and the delightful mansion of the Marchesa in Via della Croce.

Did the jarvey read his thoughts?

"Bit of a change for you, your reverence. And for us an' all. The whole town is buzzin' with the luck we have getting our new young father fresh and straight from none other than the Holy City."

"I hope I'll do well for you, Michael. I'll try."

"You will an' all. When I saw ye standin' there on the platform sae young and handsome, for a' the rain, I fair took to ye." As they had turned uphill away from the main street, he bent down to Desmonde, lowering his voice. "You'll forgive me, your reverence, if I give ye a bit of a word to the wise. The Canon's a fine man, a grand man, he's done wonders for us here, but 'tis not a bad notion to go sweet and gentle with him for a start. Once ye know him and he knows you . . . he'd fight the Devil himself for ye, if you grasp my meaning. Well, there's the church for ye, with the school to the side, across the yard, and the presbytery behind."

The church, built of a good grey stone, twin-spired, and surprisingly large, impressed Desmonde with its size and quality. It dominated the town and, with the adjacent school and presbytery, all of the same fine cut stone, was offset by a grove of trees that merged up into the woods beyond.

"It's wonderfully fine stonework, Michael, both the church and the school."

"It is, sir, an' all. And 'twould have to be, to please Madame Donovan."

But now they had drawn up before the neat porticoed stone house and the driver was lifting out the valise. Desmonde jumped down.

"What do I owe you, Michael?"

"Nothing whatsoever, your reverence. It's all a little matter between the Canon and myself."

"Take this, Michael, from me."

"May I live to be a hundred," Michael touched his hat and whipped up, "before I let your reverence pay me."

Desmonde watched him go with a sense of warmth behind his damp, chilled ribs. Then he turned, took up his bag and pressed the bell.

Almost at once the door was opened by a short, neat, full-fleshed little woman in a well-laundered, well-ironed white overall, who greeted him with a smile that revealed her own even teeth, creditably white, for her age, which could have been fifty.

"So it's yourself at last, Father. Come right in. We were

afraid you had missed the noon train. You must be drenched. Let me take your case."

"No, no, thank you."

"Then let me have your coat, it's fair soaked." He removed the coat and gave it to her. "Now, I'll show you to your room. The Canon is out to a meeting of the school board, but he'll be home by six."

As they went into the tiled hall, which afforded Desmonde a fleeting impression of a massive hat and umbrella stand, a statue in a niche and a huge brass gong, she continued, after neatly arranging his coat on a hanger: "I am Mrs. O'Brien, the housekeeper, and have so been, by the grace of God, for the past twenty odd years."

"I'm very happy to know you, Mrs. O'Brien." Desmonde held out his free hand. She took it with a pleasant smile that made her dark eyes sparkle. Almost black they were, against her smooth pale skin.

"But how cold and damp you are," she half turned as she led the way up the waxed oak staircase, "and half starved no doubt. Did you miss your dinner?"

"I had breakfast on the boat."

"So here you are all the way from Rome to Kilbarrack with nothing but rolls and coffee in your stomach." She turned towards him in the upstairs corridor and pushed open a door. "This is your room, Father, and I trust you'll find it in order. The bathroom is the end of the passage. I'll be with you again in no time at all."

The room was small and simple. A white enamelled single bedstead well made up with spotless linen, a crucifix above; a plain deal chest of drawers against one wall; a little fold-down mahogany bureau against the other; behind the door a prie-Dieu of the same polished wood; a square yard of carpet beside the bed on the glistening linoleum floor; and over all, the polished sheen of cleanliness and care. A room such as Desmonde had hoped for—not quite a monastic cell, of course, but suggestive of the ascetic life without loss of essential comfort. He put his suitcase on the chest, opened it and began to unpack his things, slipping them into the drawers below. The photograph of his mother he placed on top of the bureau, and beside it his little framed replica of the Bartolommeo 'Annunciation'.

He then became aware that his feet were uncomfortably

wet, and, kicking off his shoes, he had begun to peel off his
sodden socks when there came a knock on the half open door.
Mrs. O'Brien stood there with a tray.

"I'm relieved, Father," she smiled, "you've had the good
sense to change your feet—they were fair squelching. Now just
leave your wet things and I'll take them down for a proper
drying." With one hand she lowered the flap of the bureau and
put down the tray. "Now here's your tea, with something to
keep you going till supper at seven o'clock."

"Thank you, immensely, Mrs. O'Brien. You are terribly
kind."

"Have you plenty dry socks?"

"I believe I have another pair."

"One other! That will never do, young Father—not in
Kilbarrack with our roads, not to mention our weather.
We'll have to start the needles clicking." She had been
glancing at his pictures. "I see you have your treasures set out."

"One is of my mother, who died last year. The other Lady, I
believe, needs no introduction to you."

"Indeed not, and how nicely you put it. And what would
befit you more, Father Desmonde, than to come to us in such
company? Now take up your tea while it's good and hot."

She gave him a smile of real warmth, picked up his wet socks
and shoes, and went out, quietly closing the door.

The tea, indeed, was hot, strong, immensely elevating.
Equally delectable were two hot, buttered, home-baked soda
scones and a thick slice of Madeira cake that still bore the
fragrance of the oven.

Desmonde's view of Kilbarrack, pre-formed with deep
foreboding, but softened already by his reception, now mellowed
further, melted one might say, under the succulent impact of
that heavenly cake. Restored, fortified, he thought: I will take a
look at the church. He found the socks, pulled on his slippers
and went downstairs.

Approaching with the inimitable Michael he had noticed a
glass-covered passage leading across the courtyard. Con-
spicuously, it opened off the far end of the hall. A moment later
he was on his way to the church.

On his last day in Rome Desmonde had made a final
sentimental pilgrimage to St. Peter's. The image of that noble
creation was fresh in his mind, as he entered the parish church

of that dirty, impoverished Irish country town. He expected, and braced himself for, a shock, a chapel of conventional design with a lurid altar and daubed horrors of the Stations of the Cross deforming the walls.

He did, indeed, receive a shock, which caused him abruptly to sit down. He could not believe his eyes. The church was exquisitely and supremely beautiful, pure Gothic, the stonework of the finest quality and workmanship. The nave was lofty with aisles on either side. The Gothic pillars, supporting arches of delicate tracery, led the eye upwards to the lofty roof. The Stations of the Cross were also cut from the stone, simple in design but executed with grace and delicacy. The main altar, richly gilt, with a magnificent fretted reredos, lit up the Sanctuary and compelled the eye.

Instinctively Desmonde dropped to his knees, to give thanks for this heavenly, unexpected blessing, a noble church in which he felt he could strengthen and expand his sacred calling, increase his love and devotion to his Saviour. He was still in prayer when, suddenly, an organ pealed, and a choir of boys' voices began to sing the hymn 'Crown Him with many Crowns'.

Immediately, Desmonde rose and hurried to the rear of the church, then up a winding staircase to the organ loft. A choir of boys, conducted by a young man, were practising the hymn and, at Desmonde's sudden materialization, they broke off.

"Oh, please don't stop. I'm sorry to interrupt you." He went forward to the young man and held out his hand. "I am Father Desmonde Fitzgerald."

"I'm the schoolmaster, John Lavin, Father. We're having our usual practice."

"Forgive me," Desmonde said. "I'm literally stunned to hear such fine singing . . . and that unusual lovely hymn too, down here in the wilds of Wexford."

"It's all due to Madame Donovan, Father. She loves the boys' voices, in really fine part singing, so of course she had to have them."

"You've trained them splendidly. And you know your timing well."

"Thank you, Father." He paused. "If you're on your rounds, and free, one day perhaps you'd call in on my wife and me, and our new baby." He smiled shyly. "We're very proud of him."

"I will, I will." Desmonde lapsed into the Irish idiom, then shook hands, smiled to the boys and went out of the church, still barely recovered from what he had seen and heard therein.

At the presbytery Mrs. O'Brien met him in the hall.

"The Canon is back, Father Desmonde. And he'll see you at supper. Which I'm serving right away. Would you care to go into the dining room, the door's open and there's a nice fire for ye."

Desmonde washed his hands and went into the big dining room, where a glowing peat fire lit up the fine old mahogany furniture: table, chairs, sideboard, all of that solid, serviceable wood. At the double windows he had a striking prospect of the distant sea, some fine fields and woodland, and, the roof visible amongst the trees, a large country house.

"Do you like our view, Father Desmonde?"

Canon Daly had asked the question. A short thickset man with the chest and arms of a coalheaver, a round cannon ball of a head, dusted with grey, topped by a red biretta and without benefit of neck, sunk deep into the massive shoulders. His face was brick red, with deep-set honest blue eyes, his expression candid, open, but with the capacity to be formidable.

"I do like your view, Canon. And I love, am completely bowled over, by your magnificent, most tasteful and artistic church."

"Ay, there's none to beat it. I was pleased your first thought was to go down to it."

Mrs. O'Brien had now brought in supper. A noble joint of beef, side dishes of potatoes and green vegetable.

"Sit in," said the Canon. He took his place at the head of the table and picked up the carvers, which he proceeded to use with such vigour and dexterity that Desmonde quickly had before him a plateful of well sliced beef, floury potatoes and fresh spring cabbage.

"We are not fancy here, but we get enough to eat."

"It's delicious, Canon," Desmonde responded after the first few mouthfuls. He had eaten little during the journey, and now joined the Canon in attacking the good food with enthusiasm.

Watching him covertly, the Canon seemed pleased.

"I'm glad you're no' one o' they fancy finnickers as I feared

ye might be. In fact ye're a hale lot better than the Roman dude
I was led to expect."

"I'm no Italian, Canon, just an Irishman who has lived a
long time in Scotland."

"Do ye say so? Well, well, ye're like myself. I was near
eighteen years in Winton with my parents before they came
back to their homeland. And you can tell it frae the way I
talk."

"Your accent makes me feel at home, Canon, and it suits
your rugged strength."

When full justice had been done to the main course, Mrs.
O'Brien cleared and brought in a deep dish apple tart, then
quietly went out.

"You've got the right side o' Mrs. O'B. already, lad. She was
a' excited when I came in, singin' your praises." He handed out
a generous section of apple pie with lots of juice, and helped
himself in similar fashion. "And I think the world o' her
opinion. She's been with me over twenty years and never has
she failed me."

"The church, Canon. Your superb church. How under high
heaven did you get it? I know Ireland and the Irish. You
never got it from the pennies of Kilbarrack."

"You are dead right, lad. A' the pennies in a' the collection
boxes in a' the country, for ten years, would never have built
it." He had finished his dessert and, rising, he went to the
sideboard, took up the bottle that stood, openly, thereon, and
measured into his tumbler exactly two fingers of amber liquid.

"I got it from this, lad, and from the most lovely pious,
charitable, munificent lady in all Ireland."

Burning with curiosity, Desmonde watched the Canon sit
down and hold the glass up for his inspection.

"I don't allow liquor in the house, lad. But I'm an old man,
and this is different. It is the one drink I have in the day, two
fingers, and not a drop more, of Mountain Dew."

Desmonde was now wildly interested, but he dare not press
the Canon, who took a little sip of Mountain Dew, inhaled
slowly, then set it down tenderly, saying:

"The finest, purest, maist exquisite and devilish expensive
malt whisky in a' the world. Made with the finest peat water and
bottled in a special Donegal distillery, matured at least six
years in bond, then sold by the Dublin office all over the world,

to them that likes the best. And owned, lock, stock and barrel, by the lovely lady who planned, built, decorated and paid for our darlin' church."

After this peroration the Canon took another little sip, and gazed benignly at Desmonde, who murmured:

"What a wonderful thing to do. She must be a most charitable old lady."

At this, the Canon burst suddenly into a wild fit of laughter in which he was joined by Mrs. O'Brien who had come in to remove the dessert.

"Aye, she is charitable," the Canon resumed, when quiet was restored. "I'd be feared to tell ye what it a' cost. There was just one thing left out, worse luck, by sheer oversight. Did ye notice the altar rails?"

"Actually, I did, Canon. Very old, and wooden. Rather out of place."

"Ye see, ye noticed it right away. But never mind, lad, I'll have them changed one of these days for a set worthy of the church. It's the main object of my life now. I'm hintin' at it to Madame Donovan a' the time."

"Madame Donovan!" Desmonde echoed.

"You know the name?"

"Never heard it in my life until I came here."

"Well, ye'll hear it plenty now. That's her house ye were lookin' at through the window. And forbye she has another beautiful residence in Switzerland."

"Why on earth Switzerland?"

The Canon's left eye, viewed over the glass, took a slow, significant droop and he murmured a single word:

"Taxes."

Allowing this to penetrate, he added: "Madame is not only a lovely, accomplished, talented woman, but as clever and tough a business woman as you'd meet in the City of London. If you knew her history you'd know I am speakin' the truth."

A silence followed while the Canon enjoyed and finished his Mountain Dew. Then, in a different manner:

"I was prepared for a hard case before ye came, lad. And to deal with you hard. However, from what I see of you, the trouble simply is, ye've had far too much social life, gaddin' about Rome and gaein' to parties wi' rich," here he looked at Mrs. O'Brien, "old ladies. In fact ye've been a bit o' a playboy.

So my order is this: and if ye look at my ugly auld face ye'll see I'm a man to be obeyed: no invitations to be accepted here without my permission."

"Yes, Canon."

"Ye understand."

"The schoolmaster, Canon, whom I met in the church, asked me to look at his first-born baby."

"Babies is different. Ye may go, but don't stay, just look, say somethin' nice, then out."

"Yes, Canon."

"Good! Now, we're early bedders here, and as I'm sure ye're tired after the journey ye may turn in now if ye wish. I'll take the ten o'clock and you'll do the eight. Michael's always in the vestry, he'll show ye a'. Mrs. O'Brien will wake ye in the mornin'. Now, a good night to ye, lad. And it may please ye that what I have seen o' ye is highly satisfactory."

In Desmonde's room, all his damp things had been dried, ironed and neatly laid out, the bed was turned down and a hotwater bottle placed between the immaculate sheets. When he had knelt to say his usual prayer, and glanced at the two familiar photographs on the bureau, he got into bed and, with a profound feeling of gratitude, closed his eyes.

His first day at Kilbarrack had been a most surprising success.

II

AT HALF PAST seven Desmonde, refreshed by a sound sleep, was in the church where Michael, in the vestry, had laid out the vestments for the day.

"Usually we have only a scattering at the early Mass, your reverence. But there's quite a crowd this morning."

"Piety, Michael? Or curiosity?"

"Maybe a touch of both, your reverence."

Now Desmonde, in fact, was himself in a state of high curiosity in regard to the donor of the superb church.

"Does Madame Donovan, by any chance, frequent the eight o'clock Mass?"

"She does indeed, sir, every weekday and the ten o'clock on

Sundays. That's her own private little pew at the end of the front seat."

"Indeed, Michael."

"But she's not here this mornin', being in Dublin on business at her office. They do say, however, that she'll be back Saturday."

Desmonde knew always when he had said a good Mass rather than one impaired by personal worries and distractions. He was satisfied with himself when he had left the altar, made his thanksgiving, and returned to the presbytery.

After an excellent breakfast he set out for his initial tour of Kilbarrack. How pleasant to be saluted and greeted as he made his way down to the Cross Square. Not all, however, were so friendly. Outside Mulvaney's tavern on Front Street the crowd of youths and men idling on the corner were silent, barely allowing him passage room, and when he had gone, following him with laughter and rude remarks. Desmonde was not perturbed, for the Canon had warned him that this was the pest spot of the town.

Recollecting the invitation of the schoolmaster, he inquired the way to Curran Street where, closely regarded by the neighbours, he knocked several times on the door of No. 29. He had decided to avoid an afternoon call lest he be pressed to stay for tea and so contravene the Canon's injunction.

Now, however, there was no response except for sounds of an infant's wailing coming from inside the little house, so, as the door stood ajar, Desmonde pushed it open and went in. And there, in the corner of a neat living room, a sweet little baby was howling its little head off in its cot. Embarrassing, no doubt, but not for Desmonde.

He immediately went forward, picked up the child, burped it, and cradling it warmly against his breast, began to pace up and down the room, singing Schubert's 'Frühlingslied', which he conceived to be the nearest thing to a lullaby. The result was magical. The little thing snuggled against him and immediately went to sleep.

Elated by his success, Desmonde dared not spoil it by putting the baby down and so continued singing and walking up and down the room. The front door, meanwhile, had blown open and, in no time at all, a gathering of the neighbouring women, mostly in their morning *déshabillé*, had clustered round on the pavement like bees round a honey pot, and were even pressing into the house.

"Oh, God, Janie, take a peek at his reverence."

"Did ye ever in your life? 'Tis the new swate young Father from Rome."

"He may be young, begor, but he can handle the wean."

"Oh, God, 'tis a lovely sight, and the lilt o' the voice of him, the doat."

Then one, bolder than the rest, exclaimed:

"Excuse me, Father. Mrs. Lavin has just slipped out a minute to the baker's up the street."

The room was slowly filling up, causing Desmonde some anxiety, not for himself but for the child. He decided to go outside to meet the mother.

"Gangway, please! Gangway for his majesty the baby."

Once he was outside in the cool air he felt more comfortable. But he had reckoned not of his audience. As he padded slowly up the street, still crooning, to keep the child asleep, his followers, swollen by more and more spectators dashing out from their homes, had become a legion.

Worse was to follow. Janie Magonigle at the outset had shouted to her own little nipper:

"Tommy, dear, sprint down to the *Shamrock* office and beg Mick Riley to slip up quick with his camera."

Scenting a sensation Mick had obliged, and before Desmonde reached the baker's, he responded to a call from behind, turned, and was startled by two sharp clicks.

"Thanks, your reverence. We'll have ye in the *Shamrock* Saturday."

At this precise moment, fortified by a long chat with the baker's wife, Mrs. Lavin came out of the shop, a loaf under each arm.

"Oh, dear Lord, what in all the world . . . ! "

Even as she ran forward, Desmonde soothed her, then briefly explained all.

"Will you take him now?"

"I can't with the bread, father. He's sleeping so good and peaceful with you, please, please take him back with me to the house."

It was a procession to arrest and enchant the eye. The young priest with the baby, the young wife with the loaves, followed by a horde of ecstatic admirers. Mick Riley had finished his film by the time they reached No. 29 Curran Street.

"Come in, do come in, Father," the mother breathed, in a visible tremor, as she flung the loaves on to the hall table.

"Another time," Desmonde answered hurriedly. "I'm due back at the presbytery. But let me tell you this, you've got the best and sweetest baby I've ever held in my arms."

The infant was handed over, still angelically fast asleep, and Desmonde set off hard for the upper town. But not before three hearty cheers were called for him, and with these still ringing in his ears he dashed into the presbytery, hoping that subsequent days in Kilbarrack would be less memorable than his first.

At supper that evening the Canon remarked casually:

"Old lady Donovan will be back from Dublin on Saturday, Desmonde. No doubt you'll see her on Sunday."

"Did she telephone you, Canon?"

"No, indeed. And it may interest you to know how news travels in Kilbarrack. This morning Madame telephoned Patrick, her butler. Patrick naturally gave the news to Bridget, his wife. Bridget told the girl in the kitchen, who told the milkman when he called, the milkman then told Mrs. O'Brien and Mrs. O'Brien told me."

Desmonde smiled. "You know the event before it happens!"

"Yes, lad." The Canon leaned forward and patted Desmonde's hand reassuringly. "And that's why I know you'll be front page news, with photographs, next Saturday morning. Now don't upset yourself, I understand it was all done with the best intentions, and 'twill do ye a power of good in the parish."

III

SUNDAY DAWNED WARM and fine, hopeful harbinger of a good summer, a season of the year that Desmonde loved, particularly since he had known the benign, perennial sunshine of Spain. The Canon had announced that his curate would take the ten o'clock Mass, while he, though preaching at the ten, would take the eight o'clock. This unusual arrangement puzzled Desmonde, until his superior, sitting across at breakfast, remarked, with a side glance at Mrs. O'Brien who had just come in with a rack of fresh toast:

"I want to display you in style to the old woman. It would suit my purpose fine if she sort of took to ye." The Canon added: "What the purpose might be ye'll learn in the Lord's good time."

This pre-arrangement annoyed Desmonde. He had no wish to be made a puppet in the Canon's schemes and made up his mind to ignore the private pew, whether occupied or empty, at the end of the front seat.

When the ten o'clock bells had ceased and he was fully robed and approved by Michael, he followed the four little altar boys dressed as friars to the altar with his eyes determinedly lowered. Yet as the Mass proceeded in this fashion he was absurdly and annoyingly conscious of a scrutiny, penetrating and prolonged, on himself and all his actions.

After the gospel, the Canon ascended the pulpit to preach; Desmonde, two little boys on either side, was seated on the right side of the altar. Only then did he direct a cold and impassive glance towards the private pew. He started, started so visibly and with such surprise that his little acolytes looked at him in wonder.

A young woman was in the pew, stylishly, elegantly dressed in a grey tussore silk suit, a flat-brimmed straw hat tilted rakishly on her nut brown hair and, with a calm, self-possessed expression, she was deliberately studying him. As her cold grey eyes met his and did not fall or falter, he immediately averted his gaze. This was not Madame Donovan, perhaps her daughter, or some rich relation, and her open, rude curiosity in regard to himself he found both objectionable and offensive.

The Canon had now concluded his sermon, notably shorter than usual, and during the succeeding hymn the collection baskets were being passed. Out of the corner of one eye Desmonde noted that this modish interloper, in her expensive clothes, contributed nothing, not even a silver sixpence.

The hymn over, Desmonde returned to the altar and proceeded with the service. At the Communion he did not expect the woman to receive the Sacrament. He was wrong, she knelt, last of all, at the altar rails, and as he placed the Eucharist upon her tongue he saw with relief that her eyes were closed.

Soon the Mass was over. A final hymn, and Desmonde

D

returned to the vestry. His thanksgiving completed, he hurried to the presbytery, eager for his breakfast-lunch and for enlightenment on the mystery of the woman.

The Sunday midday meal of roast beef was not quite *au point*, but Mrs. O'Brien had coffee and a toasted scone on the dining room table for Desmonde to break his fast.

"Canon," exclaimed Desmonde, when he had swallowed his coffee, "who is that excessively rude young woman in Madame's pew?"

The Canon exchanged a look with Mrs. O'Brien who had come in with fresh coffee.

"You mean that good lookin' one in the good claes and the swanky wee hat?"

"Exactly! Was it Madame's daughter?"

"Could it be the granddaughter?"

"Possibly! She looked young enough!"

"Desmonde!" The Canon glanced at Mrs. O'Brien repressively. "We're not makin' fun o' ye. And our bit of a joke has gone far enough. You fancied Madame an old woman, and we had a little fun over it. That was Madame Donovan herself in the pew this morning!"

Desmonde sat up. "You can't mean it. She was no more than twenty-four or five."

"Add another ten to that, lad, and ye'll just about hit Madame's age. She is a fine woman in body and spirit. And young in heart. Forbye, she takes care of herself, she *does* look young."

"So, she is actually the head, the owner of . . . everything . . ."

"When you know Madame's story, if ever she tells it tae ye—and I cannot, for I'm her confessor—you'll fully understand the way she's capable to run her business, control it, and a' her other affairs, with a will of iron."

"I can believe that! The way she stared at me."

"Now, don't be hasty, lad. I've an idea she has taken tae ye. When we chatted after Mass she invited you to tea, Tuesday, at Mount Vernon."

"It shows her manners when she invites me second-hand."

"Again, don't be hasty, lad. I'll warrant you a written invite comes by Patrick—that's her butler—when he's up for Benediction. Now wait and see if I'm right or wrong."

The Canon's prediction was fully justified. At half past six that evening, Desmonde opened a sealed envelope, unfolded a sheet of finest quality hand-made note paper, embossed in block letters with the address: Mount Vernon, Kilbarrack.

Dear Fr. Fitzgerald,

If your clerical duties permit, would you come to me for tea at four o'clock next Tuesday?

Sincerely,

Geraldine Donovan

"What cheek," Desmonde muttered. "What bloody awful cheek. *Would you come.* I'll show her I'm not her lackey!"

IV

THE FINE WEATHER continued and Tuesday was sunny with a refreshing breeze that sent fleecy clouds chasing each other across the sun. Desmonde had been fully occupied during the morning and after lunch he decided to take a siesta. He lay down on his bed in his underwear with an eye on the clock, not to ensure punctuality but because of his determination to be late for his command appointment at Mount Vernon.

He had a nap, rested for a further half hour, then got up, shaved, washed and brushed his hair. He then put on his fine light Caraccini suit, with a clean shirt and collar. The result was satisfactory, indeed, pleasing, and as the clock now showed four o'clock, he set out in leisurely fashion for his destination.

When he passed through the wide gateway of Mount Vernon and advanced up the broad drive it was in fact almost half-past four. He did not hurry. The house was now in view, a fine Georgian house, with a pillared portico such as may be seen in many an Irish estate. But this house differed, in that its immaculate appearance indicated a care and maintenance rarely, if ever, seen in the run-down dilapidated quasi-historic mansions of the Emerald Isle. The long double row of windows gleamed, the frames freshly painted, as was the door on which the heavy brasses shone, the sloping roof immaculate and in front a cut stone terrace with balustrade, obviously an addition, which completed a picture worthy of the front page of *Country Life*.

Desmonde mounted the steps and rang the bell. The door

was opened by an elderly manservant, not in tails, but in a livery waistcoat, who showed the visitor into a large hall, the marble squares superbly covered by a Kirman Lavar flower carpet which Desmonde, as his feet sank into it, correctly deemed to be of the seventeenth century. A fine Lavery portrait of an elderly man hung on the near wall above a silver-laden Chippendale side table, while on the opposite wall there was a portrait of a woman in fancy dress by the same hand. At the rear of the hall a lovely broad staircase swept gracefully up, with a statue, probably Greek, on the landing, while below, two wide passages led away from the hall to the right and to the left.

Following his mentor to the right Desmonde did not fail to observe through an open door the comfortable library, appropriately lined with volumes.

At the end of the corridor he was shown into a large domed apartment which had once been the great conservatory of the mansion but which, with skill and taste, had now been converted to a variety of drawing room known in Ireland as the saloon. Again, Persian, or perhaps Chinese, rugs, faded with antiquity, littered the parquet floor. A grand piano, open, at one end, silk covered settees and armchairs on either side, flowers everywhere in careless abundance, suffused, too, by the warmth and radiance of the April sun, it was a rococo setting sufficiently overpowering to the uninitiated visitor.

At the far end a slender, elegant woman was seated at a small buhl table, reading. Her complexion was pale, carefully tended, her features fine and regular, her expression, even while she read, firm and composed, her beautiful chestnut hair in a bobbed shingle which intensified her youthful appearance. She was perhaps rather more than thirty, simply yet beautifully gowned in dark grey silk, entirely without ornament but quite strikingly adorned by an oriental scarf of grey and scarlet silk.

Desmonde, by no means overpowered, had given his hat to the servant who admitted him and was now standing quite erect, hands by his side. Indeed for some moments he stood thus, silent and still, delightfully aware that, as he had intended, his lateness had annoyed her.

At last, having failed to force him into some rustic gaffe, she looked up, but did not rise. After studying him for a further moment, with critical unfriendly eyes, not neglecting to note, however, the smart Roman cut of his clerical suit in which, she was obliged to admit, he looked stunningly handsome, she said coldly:

"So you are our new curate."

"I believe so, Madame." He did not move.

"I hear that, for a playboy, you are good with babies."

"If you hear nothing worse of me, Madame, I shall be grateful."

She half smiled, yet suppressed it.

"Since you are apparently known in the town, affectionately, as Father Desmonde, shall I so address you?"

"I could not so presume at our first meeting, Madame, but later I might be worthy of your affection."

Feeling that she was getting the worse of these exchanges, she said:

"Sit down."

He did so, quietly, easily, without affectation. She continued to study him, with her clear steel-grey eyes.

"At least you are a change from our late curate. I had him to tea. Only once. It was enough. He sat on one corner of his chair, lips clamped together, his cup clanking in his hand, speechless with fright."

"At least he was not a playboy, Madame."

"No, he was not. A good, hard-working priest, dull as ditchwater. I rejoice that he has been given his own little parish. Would you like tea?"

Desmonde smiled: his beautiful smile.

"I came here in the expectation of your justly famous tea. I am glad you won't disappoint me."

She pulled the wall cord beside her chair and put down her book, a superbly bound copy of the *Imitation*, saying:

"My Kempis came from your father. I knew him and liked him greatly."

"I thank you, Madame. For my father, and from myself."

Almost at once tea was brought in by the manservant. He carefully put down the heavy silver tray with its service of antique Spode and a three-tiered cake stand.

"Thank you, Patrick."

He bowed and went out, shutting the doors silently behind him. Beginning to pour the tea, she remarked:

"Irish servants are the best in the world, Father, if you

train them. If you don't, if you spoil them, they are the worst. Remember that, in your dealings with the presbytery staff."

"Our good Mrs. O'Brien is more likely to spoil us than to be spoiled."

She seemed to regard this as a mild rebuke, but said:

"I have no wish to be spoiled. Or to be surrounded by flunkeys. The good Patrick is my butler and chauffeur, his wife, Bridget, my excellent cook, aided in the kitchen by Maureen, a local girl. For my simple garden the son of one of my farmers comes to attend to it three times a week."

He received this information in complete silence, as though he considered it redundant or even in rather bad taste.

She was obliged, therefore, to turn her attention to the tray. "Cream? Sugar?"

He made a quiet gesture of negation.

The cup she handed to him, pure and undefiled, was hot, fragrant, delicious. She watched him sip it like a connoisseur as she sipped her own, then raised her eyebrows questioningly.

"Irish tea is always good, Madame. But this, like manna, must come from heaven."

"No, from a special plantation in Ceylon, shipped direct to us here. What would you like to eat?"

He took two of the wafer thin watercress sandwiches. They were delicious. Then put down his plate.

"What! No cake? Bridget won't sleep tonight if you don't take a slice. I thought all curates liked cake." Obediently, he took a slice of the rich home-made cake, saying:

"Not only curates. The clergy, in general." He went on to relate, quite amusingly, the episode of Fr. Beauchamp and the chocolate cake. But, reminding herself that she had meant to be severe with this young priestling, she barely smiled.

"I don't care to hear a good priest ridiculed. I once heard your Father Beauchamp preach a sermon that was truly memorable."

"In Winton, Madame?"

"Yes. I was briefly in that city."

Desmonde was silent, swept by the strange and indeed incomprehensible conviction that once before, briefly, he had seen this remarkable woman, who was now offering him his second cup of tea.

"I am still waiting for your horrendous impression of Kilbarrack. It must be a shock to you after Rome."

"It is not a shock, Madame, for I am as Irish as your dear good self. What is a shock, a great undreamed-of joy, is the truly beautiful, the superb, church in which I am permitted to serve our Blessed Lord. Nor can I forbear to add, the unexpected pleasure of this invitation, to take tea at her house, with the blessed donor of the church."

"What a lot of words, Father Desmonde!"

"Yes, I'm a fool when I'm deeply moved, I spoil it all with a tirade. Simply, I love and adore the church and bless the giver of it."

"I love my church too, Father Desmonde. That is what keeps me in this remote part of Ireland, that and my house which I also love. For ever since my husband's death I am a woman of many affairs, with fully staffed headquarters in Dublin. I must go there often. Yet, with a direct private wire I make many of my decisions here, and go as seldom as possible." She paused. "But why am I speaking of myself?"

"Because I am listening with the greatest interest and attention. Madame, you may have heard weird and untrue stories of me from Rome. I was merely polite. And bored. But now, to be in my own country, in the society of an Irish lady, so charming and fastidious, so noble and . . . oh, heavens, dear Madame Donovan, you must stop me . . . I came determined to be as rude to you as you were to me in church on Sunday. I have just so loved being with you this afternoon, that I have run away with myself again." He stood up. "And it's time now for me to leave . . . I have Benediction tonight and the good Canon insists on punctuality."

"Then you must come earlier next time." She smiled, warmly, and stood up. "I'll walk with you to the door."

She stood with him for a moment on the paved portico. The first distant stars were already showing through the still warm air.

"Is it not heavenly?" she breathed. "A heavenly evening. If you are late Patrick will drive you."

"Thank you, no, Madame. I shall enjoy the walk."

"We have a short cut through the upper wood to the church. One day I will show you. Good night, Desmonde." She gave him her soft warm hand.

"Good night, dear Madame."

She watched him go smartly down the drive, hoping suddenly, strangely, that he would turn back to look.

He turned and looked back.

When he had vanished between the high pillars of the gate, she went to her room and looked at herself, all warm and glowing, in the mirror. It was a pleasing sight, she half smiled, then moving away sharply, she said, out loud:

"Don't be a fool, Gerry. Please don't!"

V

DESMONDE, NOT A notable walker, was a full six minutes late for Benediction. But after the service, when he appeared at the Presbytery, the worthy Canon, usually a stickler in the manner of punctuality, chose to ignore the peccadillo. And later, as they sat down to dinner, he unfurled his napkin with a flourish, tucked it securely around his neck, and smiled.

"You had a nice time with her ladyship, lad?"

"Delightful, Canon. I'm afraid I overstayed my leave."

"Ah, what of it! Did she . . . sort of, as ye might say, take to ye?"

"After her preliminary attempt to take me down a few pegs, she was most kind. In fact we got on famously."

"I kenned ye would, I kenned ye would." The Canon chuckled, as he took up the carvers and slashed through the crackling of a promising leg of lamb. "All in a good cause, Desmonde, lad."

During the next few days there was no word from Mount Vernon. On Sunday the main ten o'clock Mass was normally reserved by the Canon for himself since the later hour gave him time to prepare his thunderbolts and a much larger congregation on which to discharge them. The earlier sparsely attended eight o'clock service was therefore taken by Desmonde.

On the following Sunday as he came to the altar he could not fail to observe that the sacrosanct reserved pew at the end of the front seat was occupied by Madame Donovan, who normally came at eleven o'clock. She was wearing a short black cashmere coat cut in a military style with a wide collar and flap pockets, pleated skirt, silk stockings and stitched shoes, and on her head, a chic black cloche hat, worn low on the forehead. She looked a full ten years younger than her age, and to say that she was smart would be a vulgar understatement. In any of the fashionable Paris churches she would have drawn admiring glances.

During the Mass Desmonde did not once look towards her, but at Holy Communion when she came forward and knelt at the little wooden altar rails, looking up as he placed the sacred wafer between her parted lips, her eyes remained open and met his in a spiritual exchange that was touching and sweet.

In the vestry, as he disrobed, he saw that the Mount Vernon closed landaulette stood outside, and when he emerged she was waiting on him, brisk and slightly impatient.

"I am driving to Dublin today. Important business that I must see to. Will you let the Canon know? I shall be at the Shelbourne, as usual, for ten days or thereabouts." Suddenly she smiled, showing her small, white, even teeth. "By the way, my spies inform me that you got a thorough drenching on your rounds the other morning. Haven't you a raincoat?"

"It's not a garment much worn in Rome." Desmonde laughed, and his teeth were quite as attractive. "I have the parochial umbrella, a tremendous canopy which blows inside out with delightful facility."

"You must have a raincoat," she said, laughing. "If not in Rome, it's a garment much worn in Kilbarrack. Now, au revoir." She held out her hand.

After the Sacrament he could not do more than gently press her fingers. But when she had gone he knelt and, before beginning his office, said a prayer that she might journey safely on the crowded Sunday roads. And return soon.

Life moved on normally for the next few days, during which Desmonde became more and more conscious of the absence of his new friend. But on the Thursday, evidence that she had not forgotten him came by express delivery in the form of a superb new raincoat. A Burberry, quietly grey in colour, and, when he tried it on before the expectant Canon, a perfect fit.

"It's the very thing for ye, lad. Downright handsome, and that clerical grey is just right." He smoothed the fine proofed gabardine, well pleased by this sign of interest from Madame Donovan. "She's taken to you, Desmonde, and later on, if you watch your step, she might listen if ye bring up the matter of the altar rails."

Desmonde was silent. He had already made up his mind to treat this oppressive and delicate matter with great reserve.

Six days later, evidence of Madame Donovan's return reached the presbytery: a telephone call asking both Desmonde and the Canon to lunch on the following Sunday.

The Canon was pleased but sent his regrets, accepting only for his curate.

"It's yourself Madame wants to see, Desmonde. And you know how I enjoy my nap after the Sunday dinner."

So Desmonde set off alone for Mount Vernon, bare-headed and wearing, as a gesture of gratitude, his fine new raincoat. As he came up the wide drive Madame was strolling on the terrace, very informal, in a pink blouse and grey linen skirt, a straw garden hat strapped under her chin. She held out both hands with a smile.

"Good heavens! Is it raining?"

"Madame, the weather is irrelevant. I am modelling your delightful gift so that you may admire it."

"I do admire it. And you! You look most unclerical, like a young fawn disguised as an advertisement for Burberrys. Now, take it off at once."

He did so, thanking her, simply. She took the coat, folded it over one arm, and offered him the other. "Now we must saunter for at least ten minutes or Bridget will be serving everything half raw."

They began to walk up and down on the terrace.

"You were absent longer than I had hoped," Desmonde said.

"There was an annoyance that I had to squash." As he looked at her inquiringly she went on: "Some enterprising little Japs in Tokyo, already making bogus Scotch whisky and selling it under faked Scottish names, like 'Highland Fling' and 'The Sporran', have now turned their attention to Irish whisky. In bottles similar to ours, practically the same labels, they have titled their rot-gut stuff 'Mountain Cream'. " She paused. "Of course it does not bear comparison with our superb matured malt whisky, but the confusion is damaging."

"You sued them?"

"In Tokyo! Good heavens, no. And I've had enough of

law suits. No, I simply sent out an S.O.S. to all our agents, dealers, and wholesalers that if they stocked and sold the Japanese imitation they would cease to act for us." She paused. "Before I left Dublin we had been flooded with obedient, consenting cables, telegrams and express letters." Abruptly she dismissed the subject. "Are you hungry, after your walk?"

"Ravenous!"

"Of course, I must warn you that you will not get anything half as satisfying as Mrs. O'Brien's Sunday dinner. What is it to be today?"

"Boiled pork, I believe, with whole onion sauce."

"How the good Canon will snore after that! I admire and esteem the Canon, Desmonde, but sometimes he is too possessive. My beautiful church was not given to him but"— she lowered her voice—"to Almighty God, for His most blessed help and support during a period of suffering and trial."

Desmonde was silent for a moment, then he said quietly: "I would wish you to understand, my dear, most dear Madame Donovan, that I would never, but never, accept your most kind and welcome invitations, to use and debase them, by seeking some advantage, spiritual or temporal, from you."

She pressed his arm, turned, and looked at him.

"I knew that, Desmonde, from the moment I saw you."

The melodious notes of a gong broke into the silence of this touching intimacy.

"My punctual Patrick is calling." They went into the house. "There is the wash room. And at the end of the passage, the dining room. I'll be with you in a moment."

The dining room was all Chippendale, polished and gleaming, the long formal table unset but, by the window where the sun came in, a small oval side table laid very elegantly for two.

"Isn't this cosier?" she said, coming in. "I always feed here by choice."

They sat down. She was still wearing her fetching little straw hat.

"Madame," Desmonde was compelled to say, "I must still use the word with discretion, in a personal sense, but may I tell you that I love your darling little hat. It's a Boulter's Lock Sunday hat. I want to take you on the river."

"Could you punt? In your Burberry?"

"No, but I could look at you, lying languidly on cushions in the stern, an unopened parasol by your side, one lovely hand trailing in the cool, limpid water, as we glide under drooping willows."

She smiled, looking happily into his eyes. Then she collected herself and looked away.

"I warn you, Desmonde, you will get nothing but fish here today. And it was all in the sea not later than six o'clock this morning."

Patrick was now serving the soup, in two-handled thin Dresden bowls, and whispering in Desmonde's ear, "Good day to your reverence. 'Tis the *bisk domard.*"

The thick lobster soup was delicious, floating with little ends of claw and served with cheese straws and a blob of cream on top.

"Again?" asked Madame Donovan. "If you will, I will. There's not much to follow."

"Oh, please. It's delicious."

After the second serving of soup there was a pause while the butler carefully uncorked a mildewed bottle.

"Don't decant it, Patrick."

"Will Madame try it?"

She made a gesture of negation.

"It ought to be all right. It's been waiting long enough."

The clear, amber wine was poured. Desmonde sipped and looked at his hostess across the little table, with silent reverence. It was a venerable Chablis, mellowed to a honeyed fragrance.

"Yes," she smiled. "It's awfully good. And so rare, we must finish the bottle."

Now the next course was being served. Grilled fillets of sole, garnished with anchovies, and ringed on the platter by honest Irish mashed potatoes.

"Eat lots," Madame said. "There's only fruit salad to follow."

The delicious fish, grilled to a turn and impeccably fresh, was irresistible. Desmonde did not reject the platter when it came round again. Nor, indeed, did Madame.

And afterwards, how cooling and refreshing was the compote of fresh fruits, well chilled and served in antique silver communion cups.

"Coffee in the sun room."

They seated themselves on the big settee facing the window to drink the strong, black mocha. Desmonde, suffused by a euphoria almost beatific, felt his eyes drawn compulsively towards her.

"Well . . . what next?" she asked, smiling. "Do you wish to emulate the worthy Canon?"

"That is an insult, Madame . . . as if I could leave you."

"We could rest on separate ends of the sofa. It is most comfortable, perfectly pure, and known, I understand, as toe to toe."

"Are you sleepy, Madame?"

"Decidedly not."

"Then I must speak to you, Madame, if you permit, of a matter which has been on my mind, insistently, from the moment I saw you."

"Yes?" she murmured, doubtfully. Surely, helped by the Chablis, he was not about to make some premature declaration that would spoil everything. No, he was not. Taking her hand, he said, very seriously:

"Dear Madame, ever since our first meeting at Mount Vernon, I have had the conviction that I had seen and heard you before. And now, after two delightful hours spent intimately in your presence, I must tell you how insistently you remind me of Geraldine Moore who in Winton some years ago brought me to my feet, cheering like mad, by her sublime performance as Lucia, in Donizetti's *Lucia di Lammermoor*." He paused. "And then your lovely portrait in the hall . . . as Lucia."

She seemed slightly put out, then she smiled.

"Ah, Donizetti, how he could wind himself round your heartstrings. But, my dear Desmonde, I thought all of Ireland, including your dear self, knew that I was Geraldine Moore before my marriage and that for four years I had sung with D'Oyly Carte and the Carl Rosa. And I recollect that I did sing Lucia during that visit. And also, I believe, Tosca."

"We heard you, Madame, in *Tosca*, my friend and I. We left the theatre in tears."

She half smiled: "You can blame Puccini for that, not me."

"Then, why, dear Madame . . .?"

She stood up. "One day, Desmonde, when we know each other better, I will bore you with the story of my life. Now, what we both need is a good brisk walk. Give me a moment to change my shoes and I will show you the short cut from Mount Vernon to the church."

They set off uphill through the grounds, crossing trim lawns that surrounded the rose garden and the little pillared pseudo Greek summer house, which stood beside a well-tended en-tout-cas tennis court.

"I keep this in good order, since some of my office staff like to play, when they come down. My school-girl niece likes to play, too."

Now they were in the big orchard.

"All apples, and a few plums," she said. "We can't grow much else here."

And finally they reached the pine wood. Desmonde saw that a path had been cleared through the trees.

"It's all good walking," she said. "I have it trimmed regularly. And look, over the tops of the trees, you can just see the roof of the church."

"It is lovely," he said. "What a view!"

"Yes . . . I come up here every day to look." She held out both her hands. "Now, go and wake the Canon. And come again soon . . . soon."

She turned and was gone.

VI

THE BLIGHT OF Lent had now fallen upon St. Teresa's, and the worthy Canon, who loved his joint of prime beef, his leg and saddle of lamb, his fat boiled pork, and perhaps best of all, his daily dram of Mountain Dew, yes, the worthy Canon who disciplined others, was even more severe upon himself. He abstained and fasted rigidly. In a word, he suffered. It was in this season and in this mood that he composed and discharged his famous thunderbolts.

During the month, as a further penance, the Canon took the eight o'clock Mass, Desmonde the ten o'clock, and after the Gospel of this Mass, while Desmonde and his servers sat beside the altar, the Canon mounted the pulpit to preach.

Today, the second Sunday in Lent, the church was packed to the doors, a tense and quivering congregation, aware from experience of what to expect, as the Canon, a long lace surplice over his scarlet soutane, the red biretta firmly anchored on his skull, slowly mounted the rostrum and, with a brooding

brow, turned, faced his audience and paused. The pause
lengthened until, in a rising crescendo, with a voice of Stentor,
there came forth, thrice repeated, to a final shout:

"Hell! Hell! *Hell!*"

When the shock wave beneath him had passed, the Canon
began.

"Do I utter that dreadful word as an oath, as a foul and
ribald curse to be tossed about by, and between, the ungodly
on the street corners or in the pubs? Go to hell! The bloody hell
with you! A hell of a good time! Damn it to hell! I'll see you in
hell before I stand you another.

"No! I speak of hell as the bottomless fiery pit into which, to
their everlasting doom, Satan and his rebel angels were hurled
from heaven. Hell, the tortured, hopeless home of the damned
throughout the ages. Hell, the inevitable ending of the wicked,
the fearful bourne to which come all who spit in the face of God,
of those, even in this congregation, now before me, who per-
sistently refuse Grace and die, God help them, in mortal sin,
and are plunged into Gehenna to join the infernal legions of the
damned, writhing, entangled in their agony. Did you never
pause to contemplate the fearful unending agony of the
damned? Did you ever burn your finger, holding the match
short, when you lit your pipe? Would you ever want to try and
hold a finger for one minute only in the flame of a simple
tallow candle? Never! No one but an idiot would so harm
himself. Reflect, then, on such a pain, multiplied a million
times, and suffered all over your body. Not for one minute, not
for a million years, but for all eternity.

"Immersed in a boiling lava, flames ablaze around and upon
ye, suffocated by the smoke, steam and all the foul stinks and
spume of the inferno, pronged and tortured by a' the little
devils with red hot forks and pincers, the groans, the shrieks
and the curses of a' the other lost souls about ye, a seething,
writhing, intermingled mass of hellish agony, and through it all,
the wan continuous torturing, eternal thought that ye have
only yerselves to blame, that ye had yer chance and threw it
back, with a curse, in the face of the Almighty, that if only ye had
listened to yer poor auld Canon on a certain Sunday, ye wad be
above, in Heaven, in the company and companionship of the
Elect where, clearly seen, mind ye, where reigns light, sweetness
and eternal joy in the Divine Presence of the risen Lord."

Silence, complete, deathly, followed this peroration. And the Canon was quick to seize the advantage.

"I speak to all here in this beautiful church, this veritable Cathedral, gift of the munificent, saintly lady, our Madame Donovan. Many of you, thank God, are good true practising Catholics. But there are others," the Canon's voice rose, "you at the back there, jammed in the back seat, slinkin' in to stand by the door, you that never take your coat off for an honest day's work, but only for a fight. You that get corns on your behinds, wearin' out the arses of your trousers, sittin' on the pavement with your backs to the wall of the corner pub. And you bedizened Jezebels, hidin' yourselves with pretended modesty behind the pillars, you what gets yoursels aal done up pretty with the powder and paint, puts on a fancy shawl, and strolls out of an evening by the front, seeking whom you may devour . . . and God pity the poor fool when he wakes up of a mornin'. To you I say, and to all in this church, steeped in the filth of Mortal Sin, I say again, the eye of the Avenging Angel is upon you. And if you deny that, and toss it off with a curse, then I tell ye: *Mine is!*"

Seated on the narrow bench, weighted down by his heavy vestments and deafened by the Canon's thunder, Desmonde felt himself begin to wilt. His meagre breakfast, scrupulously apportioned, did nothing to sustain him—he was not built to live on Lenten fare, and to ask a dispensation would be sheer futility. Wistfully he thought of his dear friend, absent so many days now from Mount Vernon, wondering what could delay her return, pervaded by a sense of longing to be with her again.

He had been out, on his daily rounds, when she telephoned ten days ago, and the Canon had taken the message that she must leave immediately for Switzerland. Could this be for fiscal reasons? Impossible! Her three consecutive months in summer, spent at her residence near Vevey, must surely maintain her necessary Swiss domicile, already well established by law.

Puzzled and confused, he had a sudden longing that Madame might return soon. But at that moment, a long sigh of repletion, followed by the scraping of chairs and boots, warned him that the sermon was over. He stood up while the Canon stalked by, genuflecting in passing to the tabernacle.

Immediately Desmonde returned to the altar and, with

increasing fatigue, succeeded in completing the Mass. Within twenty minutes he was upstairs in the presbytery.

He went immediately to his room and lay down on his bed, already made and spread with a clean coverlet by Mrs. O'Brien. After a few moments of complete inertia his thoughts returned to Madame and, once again, to wonder if she had returned. The nature of her absence remained an enigma. And why, why must his thoughts turn so insistently to this woman, herself, in a sense, an enigma? Was he in love with her? He stirred restlessly. Pure love was permitted between man and woman, and she was, admittedly, ten years older than himself. But how sweet she was, how lovely, fragrant and charming, witty too, and with a keen and lively intelligence . . .

The faint sound of the gong, always tactfully muted by Mrs. O'Brien in the Lenten season, forced him to his feet. In the dining room the Canon was already seated, mournfully regarding the small plate of macaroni cheese which, with its counterpart at Desmonde's place, constituted the sole decoration of the table.

As Desmonde sat down he felt the Canon raise his eyes, a glance that was considerate, almost tender.

"You're pale, lad. 'Twas a long Mass. I'm going to break the rules and give you a glass of sherry."

"Only if you take one also, Canon."

The Canon, who had half risen, sank back, reached out across the table and took Desmonde's hand. He pressed it, warmly.

"That is a sign of true affection and regard. I shall treasure it. And so we'll suffer together."

"At any rate, you gave us a smashing sermon."

"Smashing, may be." The Canon carefully conveyed a string of macaroni to his jaws. "But I'll tell you straight. The maist o' the bloody lot o' them will have forgotten it a' before they're half way down the hill to Murphy's shebeen. Do you think there's enough cheese in this sludge? It's tarnation tasteless. And why don't they grow the macaroni thicker?'

No answer was expected. The Canon resumed.

"Mind ye, lad, I don't go a' the way wi' the med-evil conception o' devils wi' toasting forks, I only use it to try and frighten them. But there is a hell and the punishment is the worst of a', sadness and desolation, the loss for ever of the sight and presence of our Divine Lord. And I tell ye, lad, I'm down-right depressed, not alone by the state of the parish, but by the immoral condition of the whole bloody world, at large."

Another string gone, sucked off the fork.

"There's na difference now, at all, at all, between what's right and what's wrong. Everything goes. Cheating in business, infidelity in marriage, in the beastly irregularities of sex at all ages. Go down by the pier of an evening. What do ye see, washed out by the tide, a shoal of filthy condoms, like diseased fish, floatin' out to God's ocean, as evidence of man's immorality."

The Canon skilfully forked and engulfed the last of the macaroni.

"I tell you straight, Desmonde lad, in no uncertain terms—the world of today is fucking its way to hell!"

Having delivered this powerful aphorism the Canon picked up his plate and, with a circular motion of his large tongue, licked it clean of sauce.

"There now—clean as a whistle. No need to wash it at all, at all."

He rose and patted Desmonde on the shoulder.

"Now out you go for a breath of air. 'Twill dae ye good. Stroll down to the Mount and see if Madame is back yet."

VII

DESMONDE LEFT THE presbytery by the side door, cheered by the kindness of the Canon, a man of iron rarely given to expressions of approval or affection. The lane leading to the wood was steep. Desmonde took it slowly, pausing when he reached the great belt of trees above, then, resisting the temptation to rest on the grassy dell that marked the end of the lane, he entered the private cutting that reached down to Mount Vernon.

The resinous scent of the firs was reviving, full of promise of the estate beneath. Desmonde felt his spirits liven and his heart quicken. How fond he had become of the lovely old house which, within and without, fitted so exactly his sense of beauty and good taste. Perhaps, too, though he doubted this, the lady of the manor would have returned, Madame Donovan, his friend, his dear friend whom he loved, in the best and purest expression of that noble feeling.

Alas, when he broke from the wood and Mount Vernon lay exposed beneath, the house was shuttered, the garden deserted. Nevertheless, he went down, pausing to study the little Greek atrium which served as a tennis pavilion, then on to the terrace of the great house. Here he began to walk up and down, enjoying an amusing, vicarious sense of ownership.

Suddenly the front door swung open and there, in her best Sunday clothes, was Bridget.

"Oh, your Reverence, do please come in. To see you walkin' outside, like a born stranger!"

"But you are all closed up, Bridget."

"Not at all, sir. I'll have the blinds of the sun saloon up in a second. Madame would never forgive me if I left you out there, all by your lone. And an' all, there's a letter for ye."

The prospect of the letter was decisive. Desmonde followed Bridget into the house and, true to her word, she quickly rattled up the Venetian blinds of the sun room then, before he could stay her, she put a match to the kindling beneath the logs arranged in the fireplace at the far end of the room.

"Now, sir, may I give you a good cup of tea and a nice bit of cake? Patrick is off for the day and the gurl is down to her mother's, but 'twill be a pleasure to serve you."

"If you're sure it's no trouble, Bridget. I would love a cup of tea . . . but no cake."

"Ah, 'tis that blessed Lenten starvation on ye. I'll have a real good cup to you once the kettle boils. And your letter."

When she had gone Desmonde sat down by the fire. The good, well-seasoned logs had already begun to blaze and crackle. How good it was to be here again. He let the warmth of the fire and the ambience of the room sink into him, longing to read his letter, yet protracting the pleasure of anticipation until he had had his tea.

This came quickly, a large steaming cup. Never had he tasted anything so good, so fortifying, so delicious in flavour. Indeed, when Bridget came again to the door to ask if he would have a second cup he exclaimed:

"That's the best cup of tea ever, Bridget. Was it something special?"

"To tell the truth, your Reverence," Bridget smiled, "seeing you so tired like, I put a good drop of the 'Dew' in it."

"No seconds, then," Desmonde laughed. "But I'll tell Madame how wonderfully you revived me. Bridget, may I sit by the fire and rest for half an hour, since you've had the kindness to light it?"

"It's not you may, sir, but you must. Madame told me the freedom o' the entire house was yours should ye come down."

When she had gone, silently closing the door, Desmonde took a deep breath and opened the letter.

My dear, my most dear Desmonde,

I hope you will have honoured me by visiting Mt. Vernon in my absence and that you will then receive and read this letter.

When I telephoned the presbytery to speak to you, the Canon answered, since you were out on a sick call. I therefore said no more than that I was leaving urgently for Switzerland. You will now learn the reason of my sudden departure.

Claire, my niece, daughter of my poor sister who died, tragically, some four years ago, after a horribly disastrous marriage, has been in my care ever since. Undoubtedly she had an unhappy childhood which may account for a certain irresponsibility, one might even say wildness, in her character. For the past two years I have had her at Chateau-le-Roc, undoubtedly one of the finest finishing schools in Switzerland. The school, beautifully situated high above La Tour de Peilz, is most conveniently near my house at Burier, where she spends her holidays with me during the summer.

All has seemed to be reasonably well with Claire, although her reports have indeed referred to some indiscipline and breaches of rules, mainly attributed to high spirits. However, last evening I received a telegram from the headmaster, Major Coulter: Claire had been expelled and I must come to remove her.

Naturally I telephoned at once. It appears that Claire, accompanied by another of the girls, after going to the dormitory as usual at 9.30 p.m., climbed out by one of the windows, after dark, jumped to the ground, removed their cycles from the bicycle shed and free-wheeled down to Montreux. Here, wearing their school uniforms, they went to a dance hall where they readily found partners in a jamboree that went on till after midnight. Fortunately their uniforms had given them away and the doorman of the hall telephoned the headmaster, who tore down in his car, arriving in the nick of time, just as the two girls were preparing to take off with a very doubtful looking young man, in his sports car.

*I need not tell you, Desmonde, how upset I am or how I begged Major
Coulter not to do anything decisive until I arrive. I hope to be able to
persuade him to keep Claire for another year, after which she would
surely be less irresponsible and more adaptable to our quiet way of life.
At present I fear she would be rather unmanageable here, if Major
Coulter insists on an immediate expulsion.*

*I shall leave immediately for Dublin by car, and hope to get there in
time for the afternoon boat.*

*While I am away, do walk down to the Mount occasionally and go
into the house—you will be expected, and Bridget will give you the
freedom of the larder. Sit in the sun room and think a little of me. I
assure you my thoughts will be of you.*

Most affectionately yours,
Geraldine

Desmonde read the letter twice, and not because he failed to
understand it. His heart lifted at the intimacy, even the
tenderness, of the hurried phrases. And while he regretted the
necessity of her sudden trip to Switzerland, this absence had
given proof of the feeling that bound them, respect, devotion,
love in the purest sense of that misused word. Convinced that
she would quickly induce the headmaster to keep her trouble-
some niece, he could now look forward to her almost immediate
return.

Desmonde folded the letter, thrust it in his inside pocket and
jumped to his feet. Elation, induced by Madame, and perhaps
by Madame's Mountain Dew, demanded action, an immediate
response. His eyes fell upon the piano. Impulsively he sat down,
opened the keyboard and ran his fingers over the keys. A
soft-toned Blüthner, exactly to his taste. For some months now
he had not sung, but now, irresistibly compelled, he filled his
lungs and broke into that loveliest of all hymns: 'O salutaris
hostia'.

How well his voice sounded in the big room. Rest, perhaps,
was the reason; he knew that he was singing better than ever
before. In the same mood his next choice was Pergolesi's
'Salve Regina', then light-heartedly, for a complete change, he
sang Edward Purcell's 'Passing By'.

He now began to play and sing snatches of his favourite
operas, improving as he went along and thoroughly enjoying
himself. Finally he let himself go over Paco's last aria in an
opera he loved: *La Vida Breve*. Suddenly he glanced at the

clock above the mantelpiece. Good Heavens, it was ten minutes past four, his First Communion children would already be gathering for him at the side altar. He had less than fifteen minutes to be there.

Bridget was in the hall, seated, as he came out of the sun room. She rose at once.

"Father Desmonde, I've been listening to your wireless, fair entranced. Never did I hear Dublin so loud and clear. It's them records they play: John McCormack, Caruso, all them great ones."

"I'm glad you enjoyed it, anyway, Bridget. And thank you for all your kindness and hospitality. Especially the lovely tea."

"Come again, father." She opened the door. "And soon. Madame would want it."

Desmonde took the hill at a good pace, recovered his breath going down the lane and was in the church at exactly half-past four.

The little children, a round dozen, all five or six years old and all from poor families, stood up as he drew near. Desmonde's mood was radiant. Rather than address them from the altar he sat down and gathered them around him in a little group.

This was only the second lesson and he picked up the thread of the first by describing how Jesus, entering Jerusalem with his disciples, knew that He was going to His death. As He was soon to die He wanted to leave something by which He would be remembered. And what better if that symbol of remembrance were Himself. So Desmonde resumed, simplifying the Mystery in words which the children might understand and, as he went on, feeling that he had captured the attention even of the little ones.

At the end he invited questions, careful to encourage rather than belittle, and, when possible, to praise. He then fixed the hour and the day of the next session, handing to each of his pupils a sweet from the supply he kept in the cupboard behind the altar, and dismissed the class.

As he walked towards the vestry a little girl, one of the smallest, followed and took his hand.

"When Jesus comes to me, will I love Him as much as I love you, Father?"

Desmonde felt the tears spring to his eyes.

"Better, my darling. You'll love Him much, much better."

And lifting her up he kissed her on the cheek, put an extra sweet in the pocket of her pinafore and carried her back to the others.

VIII

DESMONDE'S POPULARITY WAS not confined to the children of the town, who would run to him and take his hand whenever he appeared on the streets. The adults of the community, at first regarding him with curiosity and suspicious awe, were now almost entirely his friends, won over by his ready smile, constant good nature and the interest he displayed in listening to those who chose to inflict woes upon him. After all, he was an Irishman just like themselves, although fancied up a trifle by the Pope in Rome.

He was generous too, scarcely a week would pass without Mrs. O'Brien coming to him with an apologetic smile, after the shades of evening had cast a friendly obscurity upon the back door of the presbytery.

"You're wanted again, Father Desmonde."

"Who is it this time? Old Mrs. Ryan, or Maggie Cronin?"

"No, it's Mickey Turley . . . just out the nick."

"Tell him I'll be down in a couple of minutes."

"You're too good to all these dead-beats, father." Half smiling, Mrs. O'Brien shook her head. "They take advantage of ye."

Desmonde put his hand on her shoulder and gently, affectionately shook her.

"What's a shilling or two in the sacred cause of charity? Here am I, warmly housed and wonderfully fed by the best housekeeper in Ireland, who washes and irons my linen to perfection, brushes my suits, keeps my room spotless and, no matter how hard she's been working, greets me always with a charming smile, who am I to turn away some poor soul with nothing but the few rags that cover him?"

"The maist o' them will drink it."

"At least a good Guinness will warm them and send them on their way. Now lend me half-a-crown from that purse you always carry on ye and I'll pay ye back tomorrow."

Still laughing, but still shaking her head, Mrs. O'Brien handed over the coin. She was still there, waiting on him, when he came up from the back door.

"I'm not trying to buy popularity, Mrs. O'B. There's a tough crowd in this town that will never, but never, have anything to do with me."

But not long after he had made this remark, the Thursday before Easter to be exact, an event occurred that caused him to modify his views.

It was the monthly market day, an event of some importance in the little country town, when the farmers of the neighbourhood came in to sell and buy their livestock. The streets were crowded with carts, wagons, trucks and a constant slow moving procession of farm animals being driven in and out of the town. All was bustle, excitement and confusion.

Desmonde enjoyed these market days, and on this Easter Thursday he walked briskly down from the presbytery to enjoy the spectacle. He was half-way down the hill when, at the main cross roads below, an old farm truck, descending too fast, collided violently with a heavy wagon cutting across from the side street. No one seemed hurt but the shock of the impact broke the tailboard of the truck and instantly a stream of little pink piglets gushed out, leaping and frisking, their silky ears flapping, their tails curled with delight, their little trotters scampering towards freedom. Instantly a crowd formed, yells and curses rent the air, blows were struck and everywhere hands reached and grabbed after the elusive little porkers.

Out of the mêlée two little piglets sneaked away unseen and took off up the main street at full speed, still unobserved, making direct for Desmonde. He saw he must stop them, lest they come to an untimely end, and raised both his arms arrestingly. But the two truants, instead of halting, turned left and bolted into an insalubrious narrow alley, known as the Vennel. This was worse than before since here, unquestionably, they would be stolen for the stew pot. So Desmonde gave chase, running hard, following all their jinks and capers, and finally running them to earth in a blind close with no exit.

Quite as exhausted as he, they gazed at him fearfully but seemed reassured when he picked them up, one at a time, and held them in his armpits under his raincoat where, indeed, they snuggled warmly against him. Desmonde then waited until he had recovered his breath and set off for the scene of the disaster.

Here, indeed, the crowd had multiplied, all hell had broken loose and a police officer, Sergeant Duggan, whom Desmonde recognized as one of his parishioners, was trying, but failing to control it.

"Sergeant!" shouted Desmonde. "Make way for the Church."

This unusual demand did actually cause a passage to open, and Desmonde found himself in the centre of the ring facing the two combatants.

"Michael Daly! You know me and I know you. Your farm's along the road from Madame Donovan's estate." A dead silence had now fallen upon the mob as Desmonde went on:

"You have lost two of your pigs."

" 'Deed an' I have, two of the best, sows they were, for rearin' and breedin'."

"Farmer Daly, if you could have them back would you shake hands with this fellow here that ran into you?"

" 'Deed an' I would."

The silence was now petrifying as Desmonde slipped open his coat and, with a gesture that would have done credit to Maskelyne and Devant, produced and, one in each hand, held up on high the two little porkers.

For a full minute that dead silence continued, broken only by a feeble female voice, recognizable as that of old Maggie Cronin:

"Oh, God! 'Tis a bloody miracle."

Then pandemonium broke loose, yells of surprise, laughter, stark bewilderment. The Deity and the Devil were equally invoked. Then, as Desmonde handed over his trophies to their owner and brought the two men together to shake hands, there was a roar of applause.

"You got me out of a nasty situation, Father." The sergeant spoke into Desmonde's ear. "I'm going to see you get what you deserve." He held up his hand. "Listen all of ye. The trouble has been settled to perfection. Instead of fighting and a bloody riot, blessed peace has been restored. And all through the efforts of the cleverness of wan man—his reverence here, known affectionately as Father Desmonde. Come on now, all of ye, three hearty cheers for his reverence."

The cheers could, indeed, be heard at the presbytery, to

which Desmonde returned, between laughter and, absurdly enough, a warm satisfaction and sense of accomplishment.

As he passed by the side door of the church he noticed that a small girl, who stood there alone, had raised her right hand, making a timid signal in his direction. He immediately moved towards her, recognizing her as one of the brightest of his Communion class. He saw also that she had been crying. He put his arm round her thin little shoulders.

"Why, Peggy, what's the matter?"

She burst into tears again. "I can't come for my Communion, father. I don't have a proper frock."

He remembered saying that it would please our Lord if the girls could come dressed in white.

"It's not really important, Peggy. You can come as you are now."

"Like this, Father? The other girls would laugh at me."

He saw now how poorly she was dressed.

"Did you ask your mother?"

"Yes. She was angry." The tears flowed again. "She said if I wanted a new dress I could go to Jesus for it."

Desmonde was silent. He had made a mistake. In the face of such poverty one should not command. But this child must not be hurt. He smiled at her and pressed her thin shoulder blades.

"Tonight, Peggy, before you go to bed, I want you to kneel down and, just as your mother said, ask Jesus for your new dress." She looked up at him in wonder. "Don't tell anyone, just say your prayer. You promise?"

"Yes, Father." The answer came in a tearful whisper.

"Now, off you go, and we'll both see what happens."

Briskly Desmonde entered the presbytery and immediately was met by Mrs. O'Brien.

"Oh, 'tis glad I am to see you safe back, Father. There's been such a fearfu' commotion down the street. What in all the world was the matter?"

"Just a little bit of trouble for your friend Sergeant Duggan. He'll tell you about it, no doubt. Now, never mind. Here's that half crown I borrowed off you. And in return . . ."

"In return? Isn't it my own half crown?"

"In return," he smiled winningly, "I want you to do something for me . . ."

He spoke to her earnestly for just four minutes, then before she could protest, he was off, bounding upstairs to the study.

That evening, as they sat down to supper, the Canon leaned forward, with narrowed eyes and a quivering of the lips that betokened some fearful joke.

"They tell me y'are a great success in the lost property business."

IX

EASTER SUNDAY DAWNED fine, in splendid colours of gold and pink. Desmonde's prayer for a good day had been answered, or perhaps the Irish weather man was for once in a good mood. So too was the Canon, rejoicing in the feast of the Risen Christ and the blessed ending of his Lenten martyrdom. He greeted his curate with the traditional cheek to cheek embrace.

"You will celebrate High Mass, Desmonde. And I shall assist you."

Desmonde flushed at this unexpected honour.

"Ye deserve it, lad, the way ye have bothered wi' the children. And besides, I've gotten sorta' fond of ye."

A vast quantity of spring flowers had been sent up from Mount Vernon. The high altar, superbly decorated with narcissi and Easter lilies, was a sight of splendour and fragrant beauty. Michael, the sidesman, himself with a flowery buttonhole, reported to the vestry that the church was overflowing, packed to the door.

"Never saw the like, they're standin' in the aisles."

"Ye're not nervous?" the Canon whispered. Desmonde shook his head. "I tell ye because Madame's home, and will be watchin' all." He added: "I hope she notices our poor ould altar rails!"

The organ pealed, the voices of the choir rose in the opening Anthem and the procession moved into the church, Desmonde, superbly robed in festal vestments of gold and white satin, preceded by eight little altar boys dressed as friars, and followed by the Canon in stately humility.

Desmonde's first glance was towards his communicants, seated in the front seat: all as he had wished, the boys with white and gold armlets, the girls all in white, some merely in white starched pinafores, others in white summer frocks and one, in particular, neatly, beautifully dressed, in a white voile tunic, that could be serviceable thereafter. Desmonde looked no further but mounted the altar steps, genuflected, and the Mass began.

Slowly, with perfection of movement and colour, the ceremony continued, a tapestry woven in gold and scarlet, slowly unrolled. Only when the Canon turned to read the Epistle did Desmonde look towards that end front pew, realizing with a start that Madame's eyes were steadily fixed upon him. She looked happy, a good augury for the news she would give him from Switzerland, and in her neat suit of fine blue Donegal tweed, as fascinating as ever.

The service resumed, the bell rang for the Consecration and again, presently, for the moment of Holy Communion. The children stood, came in perfect order, knelt at the altar rails and Desmonde, alone, came slowly to place the Eucharist, for the first time, upon the childish tongues. Then came the parents of the children, followed by great numbers of the congregation, the Canon descending now to assist Desmonde. And finally, the last of all, came Madame, kneeling, looking upwards to receive, and meeting, in that same glance of spiritual love, the eyes of Father Desmonde.

Soon, now, the Mass was over, the organ played, the choir sang the final hymn 'Christ the Lord is risen today'. Back in the vestry, as they disrobed, the Canon whispered:

"Perfection, lad. You never put a foot wrong."

Back in the school hall the children were seated at a long table for their Communion breakfast, a substantial meal of cereal, bacon and eggs, toast, tea, and fruit cake, served under the supervision of the schoolmaster. Madame was already there with a little prayer book, *The Key of Heaven*, for each child, and soon Desmonde and the Canon came in.

"Don't rise!" called the Canon, stifling an incipient movement. "Go on with your breakfasts. And God bless you all."

He turned to Madame Donovan and bowed. "Happy to see you home again, Madame. Didn't you think, thanks to you, that the church looked beautiful?"

"The Mass was beautiful." She turned to Desmonde. "It was perfection. I was deeply touched. And these sweet children, so well prepared . . ."

"Ah, yes, Madame," cut in the Canon. " 'Twas a lovely sight. If only the rails at which the poor little things knelt had been more in keeping . . ."

"Be quiet, Canon," Madame laughed. "You may get your rails sooner than you expect. In the meantime, how do you stand with your Dew?"

"I have not lipped it during Lent, Madame. And even out of Lent I sip, once a day, no more than two fingers full, as Desmonde will testify, yet, an' all, I have a feeling I may be getting low."

"You'll have a fresh case from Dublin immediately."

The Canon bowed low. "I thank a most generous lady."

"And what of you, Desmonde? Would an invitation to drink tea be acceptable?"

"Eminently, Madame."

"Good heavens," Madame smiled at him. "We're behaving like characters in one of Cavalli's horrible operas—*Ormindo* for choice. You may come at four."

When she had gone Desmonde walked round the long table, before following the Canon to the door. As he passed the girl in the voile dress, he met her radiant glance and whispered: "That was a good prayer, Peggy dear."

Upstairs in the presbytery, Mrs. O'Brien, looking flurried for once, was in the dining room.

"I'm sorry, Canon, and Father Desmonde, I've been so busy with the children's breakfasts, as ye see, I have only a ham sandwich for you. But I've a lovely saddle of lamb for this evening."

"Don't worry, Mrs. O'Brien. You never fail us. And I'll take my daily drop of the Dew with the sandwich."

"Wasn't it a tremendous congregation?" said Mrs. O'Brien, putting the bottle on the table. "Never, never in my life did I see the church so full . . . and with some of the tough characters from Donegan's Corner."

"Are you acquainted, Mrs. O'Brien," said the Canon, measuring an exact two inches into the glass, "with that old song that begins: 'As I came out one morning from Tipperary town . . .'?"

"No, Canon."

"Well it ends like this, or nearly so." And the Canon boomed forth: "'Twas the little pigs that done it, och the dear little pigs."

"Desmonde," resumed the Canon, when Mrs. O'Brien had departed, shaking her head, "I see a case of the Dew on the horizon and also, God willing, a set of altar rails in pure Carrara marble. Go down for your tea to dear Madame and be very, very sweet to her."

X

IN THE EARLY afternoon Desmonde set out to walk to Mount Vernon. He was happy, supremely happy: that admixture of spiritual joy and physical well-being that matched the brightness of this lovely day. How well everything had gone this morning: his splendid Mass, the sweetness of the children's First Communion. He prayed every day to the Holy Spirit for success in his vocation. That prayer had indeed been answered.

As usual he was early at the Mount: Madame had gone out on a round of visits to her tenants, but Bridget, emerging from the servants' hall, where she appeared to be entertaining friends, assured him that he was expected for four o'clock tea. And indeed, Desmonde had barely begun to walk up and down the terrace when the big landaulette swished up the drive and Madame stepped out, briskly, before Patrick could get to the door.

"Take all these things to Bridget." She spoke sharply. "The scones, soda bread and vegetables."

"May we have some of the scones, Madame?" Patrick spoke with unusual humility. "You did say, Madame, with your kind permission, that we might have a few friends in to have a bit of a Easter party."

"Take them all!" She turned on her heel, came up the steps and to Desmonde, who had bent forward to kiss her hand, "Not now, please."

Only when Patrick had removed the car did she smile, faintly, a rather forced smile, barely showing her beautiful teeth, pressed firmly together.

"You must forgive me. I'm in a teasing mood. The more you give, the more people demand from you. New water pipes, more tiles on the barns, a new floor in the kitchen and, if you please, two new bathrooms with hot and cold showers."

Desmonde smiled. "What a pity, Madame, that today's Irish peasant won't walk in his bare feet to the yard pump to wash himself."

"No wit, please. And last evening a worrying, most ungrateful letter from Claire. But enough. Go into the sun room and I'll be there presently."

Madame was indeed in a bad mood, and not alone for the reasons she had stated. Always she had been regarded as the luminary, the leading figure, the cynosure of all eyes at her own beautiful church, St. Teresa's. But now, this handsome little curate, emerging from nowhere, or at least from Italy, had stolen her thunder. This morning she had felt herself slighted, almost ignored and, though she repressed the feeling, had even wished that he might make some slip, a human *faux pas*, in the perfection of his performance.

She had decided, while making the upsetting round of her tenants, that Desmonde must be taken down. He was altogether too complete. There must be a flaw in his perfection and it had become her duty to expose it.

She was smiling when she entered the sun room, took both his hands, and made him sit beside her on the sofa.

"Desmonde, dear, Bridget has given me the weird story of the song recital on the wireless that afternoon when I was out. Come, now, you really were regaling yourself with a few student ditties."

Desmonde smiled. "The piano was open, so inviting. I trust I was not taking a liberty, Madame."

"Good Heavens! Of course not. And as it's still some little time until we are served tea—they're having quite a party in back—I would love you to sing to me now."

He glanced at her oddly.

"I have hitherto refrained, Madame . . . since you don't sing yourself."

"Tut, tut! You'll hear about that one day, and perhaps soon . . . I adore to hear good singing and now I wish to be entertained."

He paused: "What shall I sing to you? A hymn, an old Irish song, something operatic?" She was looking at him inquiringly. "When I was in Italy I had the advantage of hearing many of the best operas . . . in Rome, but mainly at La Scala in Milan."

She forced a laugh. "Did you make the pilgrimage to Milan on foot?"

"No, Madame. I had the extreme good fortune to be taken by Madame la Marchesa di Varese, in her magnificent Isotta limousine. As you may know, she is an elderly lady, with her own box at La Scala, passionately devoted to music."

"And to you?" As he ignored the question, which was almost a sneer, she continued: "So what is your taste now, in operas?"

"I tired of the little tear-jerkers." He smiled as he used the phrase. "Of dear Donizetti, and Bizet, and Puccini: *La Bohème*, for example, is such nonsense. My taste turned to the grand operas. Verdi and Mozart. *Don Giovanni* is a great opera. I also love the Spaniard de Falla."

"Surely you forget Wagner."

"I am always carried away by Wagner's thunder, against my will. But he has written some extremely fine pieces."

She looked up at him endearingly. "Do you know the Prize Song in *Die Meistersinger*?"

"That is probably one of the most beautiful songs ever written . . . Yes, Madame, I know it . . . moderately well."

"Could you, would you sing it for me? It is frightfully difficult . . .?"

"For you, Madame, I will try . . ."

She seemed almost to relent. "Don't worry if you break down, dear Desmonde. We'll choose something simpler."

"Thank you, Madame," Desmonde said simply. He was now perfectly aware that she had chosen this song, deliberately, to embarrass him, a feeling that became a conviction as she explained:

"You won't mind if I call the servants and their friends into the passage? They are all dying to listen to you."

Desmonde suppressed a smile. She could not know that this was his winning Prize Song or that he had sung it in the salon of the Marchesa, to an audience of over a hundred of the best of Roman society.

"It will make me more nervous, Madame, but if you wish, please do call them."

He waited until she had called and settled them in chairs outside, leaving the door half open, until she had seated herself, almost purring like a dear little cat about to sip cream.

"You forgive me in advance, if I disappoint you, Madame?"

"Of course, dearest Desmonde, now do begin, we are all waiting."

He did wait, another moment, then quickly he played the introduction and, lifting back his head, began to sing, in the original German.

Firmly determined to sing well, he knew after the opening that he was at his best and would never sing better.

Indeed, he sang it to listeners enchanted, and when at last he finished, the silence persisted for a full minute before a perfect crescendo of applause broke forth in the passage.

Desmonde did not leave the piano, but when quiet came, called out: "As this is Easter Sunday, when we praise with joy the Risen Christ, I can't leave you without one hymn in His honour." He began, without delay, to sing his favourite hymn, the lovely 'Panus Angelicus'.

No applause when he finished, but a reverential silence, immeasurably more impressive. He glanced towards the sofa. Madame Donovan was in tears. Blindly, she made a sign that he should close the door. He did so, then again she signed, that he should join her on the sofa. Here, half reclining, she took his head in both hands, and pressed it towards her, so that he felt the warmth of her tear-stained cheek.

"Desmonde," she whispered, "you have overwhelmed me. Your beauty, your charm, your perfect manners, your inviolable purity, and now . . . that lovely, lovely voice. What must I do? I wish you were my confessor—but that would hurt the good and worthy Canon. I wish you were my son . . ."

"Madame," Desmonde interposed reasonably, "that is a physical impossibility . . . you are no more than nine or ten years older than I."

"I wish, then, that you could offer some solution in my extremity. I am Heloise, and you are Abelard."

"No, dear Madame, I am not Abelard who was a rather dirty, unpleasant fellow. I am a priest truly in love with a charming, distinguished woman who, I believe, has an equal fondness for me. There is no solution other than to love purely, in the sight of God, and to be content with that love."

She sighed, disengaged herself, and sat up.

"Desmonde, we must first have our tea. If only in the cause of propriety. Then I will try to explain why I feel so bewildered and so lost. Do ring for Patrick while I try to repair my face."

E

Desmonde pulled the bell cord, then wisely stood looking out of the window, with his back to the room. He foresaw eulogies from Patrick, who was indeed on the point of erupting, stilled only when Desmonde half turned and raised one finger to his lips.

Presently, Madame returned, looking fresh and apparently composed. She poured the tea and they drank it in silence. Some fine slices of buttered soda bread were on the tray. He took several, remarking that it had been some time since he had tasted this home-baked Irish bread.

She said: "I imagine Mrs. O'Brien is too busy to bake it."

This was the limit of their conversation, until Patrick had re-entered to remove the tray.

Only then did Madame turn to Desmonde, and in a firm voice, she began:

"I had been singing two years with the Carl Rosa when, during the Dublin season, it became evident that an elderly gentleman had become interested in me. Always the same stage box, and only when I was singing. He was Dermot Donovan, owner of the Donovan Distillery Company, a rich and prominent Dublin personality. I was flattered, and when, one evening, a note came round asking if I would take supper with him, I accepted. We went to Jamme's, where, treated almost with reverence by Jamme himself, he commanded a delicious supper. It was delightful to be entertained by such a man, tall, solidly well-built, and with trimmed grey hair and grey moustache. He drank only a thimbleful of his own Mountain Dew. I had a half bottle of Perrier Jouet.

"When we had eaten, in the seclusion of our private room, he took my hand and said, very seriously: 'Gerry! I am in love with you and wish to marry you. I am seventy years of age, comfortably rich, and able, I believe, to give you a full and happy life. I don't ask you to decide at once. Come down to Mount Vernon, my place in Wexford, and see for yourself.'"

She paused. "In a few words, I came here. I married Dermot Donovan. There were, of course, the usual screams in the newspapers: 'Spring weds December.' 'Little Song Bird in a Golden Cage.' But I never, no, never, regretted my marriage." She paused. "Strange though it may be.

"Dermot was a man of high principle. He was one of those Irishmen, and they are not uncommon in Ireland, taught in the

Jesuit schools and colleges that sex is a dirty and offensive thing, to be avoided at all costs. He had lived his life as a lay priest, and now at seventy he had no desire to possess me sexually. All this was explained to me beforehand. He had his own bedroom, I had mine, an arrangement acceptable and agreeable to me, since my love for him had nothing of sex in it. I was his dear companion, he loved me to sing to him of an evening, and as time went on I learned shorthand and typing and became his personal secretary. We travelled, usually to the spas of Europe, in winter we took a cruise, to the West Indies, to Jamaica, to Tahiti.

"We spent five happy years together, then, quite suddenly, in Vichy, after complaining for only a few days of a pain in his chest, he died. He was buried in France.

"Back in Dublin his will was read. The dear, dear man had left everything to me—his personal estate and the business. Naturally, I was grateful, and happy too. But before the will was probated an objection was raised by two men in the Dublin office: the manager and the cashier. They demanded a post mortem, on the grounds that the sudden death of my husband was suspicious."

Madame paused, moistened and compressed her lips and went on.

"So the body of my poor man was dug up, brought to the Dublin mortuary for examination The certain cause of death: rupture of an aortic aneurism. Was that enough for those two devils in the office? It was not. They brought a plea that the marriage was invalid since it had never been consummated. I was forced by law to be medically examined." Again Madame paused, and her eyes were hard as steel. "You may understand the misery and humiliation this caused me. The finding: I was *virgo intacta*.

"The case came before old Judge Murphy, a wise and, thank God, an honest man. He tore these two scoundrels apart. 'Because this good woman was faithful to her old husband, because she did not allow herself to be seduced by some younger man, you would deny her the rights and rewards of her fidelity. Case dismissed without possibility of appeal.' "

Madame took a long sighing breath, but her eyes were steely.

"You may imagine that I was now a nervous wreck, but I was not quite out of it. For it was my turn now. I put the best

London firm of chartered accountants into the office. They went through the books with a fine toothed comb. As I had already suspected, the two would-be beneficiaries had been quietly helping themselves to the till for months. And they had stolen even more: the foreign receipts were short by nearly one hundred thousand pounds. They are still in Mountjoy Prison."

"Madame, how brave you were!"

"That's about all, dearest Desmonde." She took his hand. "Except to say that I had a breakdown to end all breakdowns. I was dead out for two months, and when I came to, my voice was gone, they told me I would never sing again. But what of it?" She smiled. "I'm a fighter, Desmonde. I've taken charge of the business, built it up to treble what it was before, established Swiss residence, cutting taxation in half, and here I am, as good as new."

XI

WHEN DESMONDE RETURNED to the presbytery, he found the Canon upstairs in the study, drinking coffee before a fine, glowing peat fire. No one could manage this intractable fuel better than the Reverend Daniel Daly.

"They drove you back, lad. I heard the car." He added, inquiringly: "A good ten minutes ago."

"I went into the Church. To thank the good Lord for a wonderful Easter Sunday. To say a prayer for my little Communicants, not forgetting your kindness, and Madame's also."

"Well done! Will you join me in a coffee? Ye observe I keep my vow—I had my Dew middleday." He handed Desmonde his cup. "Go in the kitchen, fill me up again and take a cup to yourself. Mrs. O'B. is out, but the pot's on the stove."

When Desmonde returned, a cup in each hand, the Canon had drawn forward a chair for him at the other side of the fire.

"Thank ye, Desmonde. Not bad stuff this, though it gets one up, the middle o' the night. Did you have a good dinner down by?"

"Quite simple, Canon. The kitchen was rather on holiday."

"We had a grand saddle o' lamb here. The best I ever put

my teeth into. Mrs. O'Brien was real upset you missed it. She kept a bit for you for tomorrow. And mind you, cold saddle of lamb with a baked potato is even better than the hot." He paused, to sip coffee. "By the way, I heard ye had a bit of a sing-song down by."

Desmonde smiled. "Canon, you get the news in Kilbarrack even before it happens."

"Not at all, lad. 'Twas Patrick when he rang up to say you'd not be here for dinner. He near burst the wire. You know, lad, the more I hear of your accomplishments the more I get depressed. For it means that I shall lose you soon. The Archbishop has been speakin' of you, your talents, your manner, your personality. He wants you in Dublin for his own entourage, or for the Cardinal. And what shall we do then? Myself, and Madame. You know she loves you, Desmonde. And so do I." He paused. "By the way, how did Madame seem to be, today?"

"Much as usual. But she did seem upset early on."

"And well she might be." The Canon finished his coffee and put his cup down on the fender. "She rang me late last night, told me not to say a word to you, not to spoil your Easter Sunday." He shook his head. "On Saturday evening she had an express letter from that headmaster in Switzerland. After all the trouble she took to smooth things over, the niece has been expelled." The Canon drew a long distasteful breath. "There appears to be an Italian gentleman, if I may use the word, from Milan, where he seems to have a substantial business of an unknown nature, and is rich, aged, say twenty-eight, with one of the choicest and most expensive Italian cars, staying, presumably for tax purposes, at the most exclusive hotel on the Lake and who, like a gentleman of the type I've implied, has three times persuaded the niece, Claire, to break bounds at night, for purposes unknown, returning to her dormitory just before dawn." After this sardonic peroration the Canon paused, then, in his natural voice, added: "Third time out, the little bitch was bloody well caught, and deservedly."

"I'm terribly sorry for Madame," Desmonde said. "Is she all bad, the girl?"

"It seems she's like her mother. Wilful, attractive and fond of the men. Anyway, at eighteen it's high time she was finished with school and under stricter supervision. And that is just what Madame has asked me to give her."

"Shouldn't Madame take charge of her, now that she's going to her Swiss house?"

"And let this Italian bastard keep after her? No. No, Desmonde, she must be removed from his illicit attentions. I promise you I'll knock some sense into her, and you must help me. I'm meeting her in Dublin the day after tomorrow. Patrick will drive me up."

"It's a long journey for a young girl to take alone."

"Tuts! 'Twill all be arranged, lad. She'll be put in the train at Geneva. At Paris a representative of the school will meet her, put her on the Calais express. At Calais it's a step to the boat, and in London a man from Madame's London office will put her on the train for Holyhead. And I'm on the quay waiting for her in Dun Laoghaire."

"Anyway, she must have made the trip several times before." Desmonde added: "Does Madame leave soon?"

The Canon nodded. "To add to her present woes, the boys of the Inland Revenue are asking if she intends to give up her Swiss Residence. She must get there presto, once she has settled the girl down at the Mount."

"Such changes!" Desmonde said. "I don't like them. Canon, if you're not thinking of bed yet I'd like to ask you about a letter I had this morning."

"I saw the envelope, with the heading on it, in your mail. Don't have anything to do with them, Desmonde. Or their Movement."

"You know about it, Canon?"

"Small though it is, I do. They're puttin' out circulars to all the young members o' the clergy: protest against the continuance of priestly celibacy! Pah! They're just a bunch o' bastards wantin' weeman."

"You're all for celibacy, Canon?"

"My views on celibacy can be expressed in five words: 'Lump it and like it.' We priests are men, Desmonde, which makes it hard at times. But we are followers, disciples of our Lord Jesus, also a man, who was celibate. And from the practical point of view, what use would a wife be in a presbytery? Before long she'd be wearing the vestments and hearing confessions. Don't you know, too, from your experience in the confessional, how many marriages are failures, bringing misery in their train—the nagging, the quarrels, the fighting, the

infidelities, the get to hell out of here you bloody bitch. Less
than a tenth of the marriages of today are happy and successful.
And the children? Do you want half a dozen o' them yelling,
squabbling, playing hide and seek in and out o' the con-
fessionals?"

"The High Anglican Church, very near to us, seems to
sanction marriage with some success."

"They're situated differently from us, lad. We priests live
beside, or on top of our churches. The Anglican vicarage is
often a mile or more away, private and secluded. Married life
to them is a thing apart. No, Desmonde, the rosy dream of
matrimony of any young priest is not based on reality. 'Tis
just a projection of his own two balls."

A silence fell, broken by the sound of the side door being shut
and bolted, followed by the footsteps of Mrs. O'Brien moving to
her room below, then quietly closing her door.

"There's the answer to your question, Desmonde. Who could
look after us better than that good, pure, I repeat, pure
woman?"

He stood up and stretched. "I'm weary, I'll take the bathroom first tonight, if that's all right with you."

Desmonde laughed. "Then I can soak a bit longer. Shall I
put the light out here?"

The Canon nodded. "Good night, my dear, very dear lad."

"Good night, Canon, with my deep affection and dutiful
respect."

Thus ended Easter Sunday in Kilbarrack. The happiest,
and the last, that Desmonde Fitzgerald would ever spend there.

XII

ALL ARRANGEMENTS HAD been made, as pre-viewed by the
Canon, and at eight-thirty on Thursday, after he had said the
seven o'clock Mass to a mere handful of the faithful, and break-
fasted substantially thereafter, that worthy dignitary departed
for Dublin in the landaulette, driven by Patrick. He was
wearing his best Sunday suit and was wrapped tightly in a
thick black ulster which would undoubtedly protect him from
the elements should he be obliged to wait, exposed, on the

Dublin quays. His expression was firm and composed although, indeed, for a cleric who rarely quitted his own diocese, the expedition was both an excitement and an ordeal.

"All being well," he remarked to Desmonde, who saw him off, "we'll be back around four o'clock. Though, mind ye, I can't guarantee the mail boat."

"Don't omit your lunch, Canon," said Desmonde, with solicitude.

"If I have the time, I'll drop in at the Hibernian—they know me there," added the Canon, with the air of a man of the world. "But if I'm pushed," he made an inconsequential gesture to the left, "Mrs. O'Brien has put up a bit of a sandwich for me."

Glancing left, Desmonde was relieved by an outsize package on the seat, carefully wrapped in oiled paper, and bulging with assorted food. Assuredly the Canon would not starve.

"Take care of yourself while I'm away, lad," cried the Canon, as the big car began to move.

What a good, simple, honest man was this old parish priest, yet strong, too, formidable in the cause of virtue. So thought Desmonde as he went towards the church. When he had said Mass he made his way over to the school. He had not visited there for some time, and after a chat with the master he went round the classes, saying a few words to the children in each, pleased by the morning freshness of the children and the greeting they all gave him.

Desmonde was still smiling as he went to the presbytery. Here Mrs. O'Brien was waiting on him.

"There's a message for you, Father, from the Mount. 'Twas Madame Donovan herself, she's expecting you to lunch today. You're to come when you're free. A light luncheon, she said." Mrs. O'Brien shook her head. "And what a pity. Here am I with two of the nicest sweetbreads ye ever saw, ready to cook for you special."

"I *am* sorry. But keep them, Mrs. O'Brien. The Canon and I could share them for dinner."

"I will, I will. But sure, one of them is but a couple of swallows for the Canon. I'll have to put in some chops as well. And now, there's a sick call for you, as well. Old Mrs. Conroy at the Point. She's bedridden, you know, and would like you to take the Sacrament. I'll give you something else for her too, she's a poor old soul, though a terrible talker."

The Point was on the far side of the town, so Desmonde decided to take the car. After he had washed, he went back to the church, removed a host from the tabernacle and placed it in the little purse reserved for that purpose. He then drove off in the old Ford. Mrs. O'Brien had already placed a parcel on the back seat.

Mrs. Conroy, one of those old ladies who like to make the most of a visit from the clergy, was sitting up in bed, wrapped in her best shawl, with a lace cap upon her head. Neat and tidy, adorning the poverty of the little cottage, she welcomed Desmonde with effusion.

After he had administered the Sacrament she pointed to the chair, which at her direction the neighbour who looked after her had placed beside the bed.

"Now, Father dear, 'tis a great honour. I'm sure ye understand, the fella that was here afore ye, I disremember his name, never had it, nor deserved it, but then he was a dull sort of a clod, and never came but three or four times to see me aal the time he was here. Ye are the chip of a different tree, it's clear to see, even with my poor ould eyes, lookin' at your dear handsome smilin' face, and they tell me it's wondrous things ye have accomplished, the two pigs that was killed stone dead by a truck in the market and ye put your fair blessed hands upon them and lifted them back to life, I tell ye, the neebours tell me the cheerin' could be heared down here. What's that you're callin', Lizzie, a parcel from Mrs. O'Brien? God bless her, there's a kind wumman for ye. And what would be in it? Scones, butter, the half of a boiled fowl and a hale can o' tay! Ah, now, the saints be praised, and Mrs. O'Brien too, just when we're near outa the tay, 'tis mate and drink to me. Let Lizzie give ye a cup, Father."

Rather than disappoint the old chatterbox Desmonde accepted and drank the tea, which he duly praised. Thereafter he sat and listened until he felt he might leave without giving offence.

After his escape, Desmonde drove the long way round to the Mount with both car windows down, deeming it wise to aerate himself from the odours of Mrs. Conroy's bedroom, before presenting himself to Madame. Thus, it was precisely noon when he arrived.

"You are barely in time," Madame said chillingly. "Bridget

has just sent word that the soufflé is *au point*. Once it falls in it is of course uneatable."

"I have been on an errand of mercy," Desmonde excused himself, as he followed his hostess into the house. "To Mrs. Conroy."

"That old gossip! Not half so ill as she pretends. Is she still complaining?"

"Yes, Madame, that you don't send her enough of your delicious hothouse tomatoes."

"You'll soon see if they are delicious. With Patrick away, I warned you it would be a light lunch. Salad and cheese soufflé, followed by," she smiled, "coffee."

They seated themselves and almost at once Bridget's girl brought in the soufflé, golden brown, beautifully risen, puffy as an old man's breath.

"Tell Bridget it is a success," Madame said, already slicing into the glorious bubble.

Each place had already been set with oval plates heaped with a fresh vegetable salad.

"It is unbelievably delicious, Madame." Desmonde sighed after a few forkfuls. "Like an angel's kiss."

"Do they kiss up there? Don't the wings get in the way?"

A silence followed while they devoted themselves to the food. A single glass of the same Chablis had already been poured, ice cold.

"We were enlivened this morning," Madame said, looking up, "by the strains of martial music. A fife and drum band to be exact."

"I believe the Hibernians were on the war path."

"A route march."

"Possibly."

Madame shook her head, smiling. "Desmonde, my dear Desmonde, Bridget's girl, who was at the ten o'clock, brought back a very different story. You are now numbered amongst the elect, surpassing even the Canon." She paused to spear a reluctant slice of cucumber. "Did he get off safely this morning?"

"He did, Madame, exactly to the second, fully accoutred and stocked with rations, against all hazards and contingencies."

"What a dear old man he is—simple, faithful, strong and true. A saint, in fact. I love him." She added: "Even when he annoys me."

"Have you a grain of affection left over? For his curate?"

"Don't tease me today, dearest Desmonde. You know you have become half of my life. And I shall miss you dreadfully for three whole months. How I wish you could come to my place in Burier. It is quite lovely, and large, a real country house. I hate to be confined. Lots of parkland and a heavenly view of Leman. A convent near, at La Tour de Peilz, very convenient in Protestant Switzerland, where I hear Mass in the little chapel. Beauty, peace, complete isolation. But no Desmonde. And, besides, I shall worry all the time about Claire." She paused. "I dread meeting her today. We are always at odds. She is exactly like my poor sister, intractable, irresponsible, unpredictable. I have begged the Canon to try and put some sense in her. And you must try, too, Desmonde. Can you stay with me till they arrive?"

"I am free all afternoon, Madame."

"Splendid! Then we'll have coffee in the sun room, and afterwards you must sing for me."

"Won't you . . . try to sing with me?"

She smiled, sadly. "I am not Trilby, and you, Desmonde, are not Svengali, if such people ever existed. No, my phrenic nerve is irreparably gone. Yet my speech, thank God, is not impaired."

She rose, gracefully, as usual. "I'm afraid that's all. No good offering you cheese after the soufflé."

The afternoon had passed, ecstatically as planned, and now, some three hours later, having taken tea, they were seated on the long settee in the sun room.

"Desmonde," she murmured. "This, I believe, has been the sweetest afternoon of my life."

"You speak for me, too, Madame."

"Tinged, intensified, by the agony of separation, Desmonde." She paused. "I must leave within the next few days, first to Dublin, where I shall spend a week at the office, reviewing everything, then to Geneva. So this may be the only time I shall be with you alone." She took both of his hands. "I therefore wish you to know, that once I have persuaded my friends at the Inland Revenue that I am back in Switzerland, I shall take the express that goes direct, through the Simplon, to Milan, and there I shall proceed to the firm of Moreno and Calvi, expert in all arts and skills appertaining to ecclesiastical marble.

Desmonde, because of you, I intend, at last, to embellish my church with altar rails of the finest Carrara marble. There I will kneel when I receive the Eucharist from you."

"I am overwhelmed, Madame. And the Canon will be in the seventh heaven."

"You may have the pleasure of bringing him the good news. So that is settled." She stood up, still holding his hands. "Desmonde, just this once, it may be a sin, I do not care. I embrace you as a woman who loves a man."

Opening her arms, she took him to her, offering all her body, withholding nothing. Their lips met in a long, exquisite, prolonged kiss.

Where this might have ended must remain in doubt, since the crunch of the big car on the gravel caused reason to intervene. They drew apart, and almost at once the Canon burst in, buttoned to the throat and followed by a tall, thin girl with a white, dirty face, the front of her dress stained with vomit, her big dark, weary eyes drawn fearfully towards Madame.

"So you are back, Canon," pale and breathing rapidly, Madame managed to remark.

"As ye see, Madame, safe and sound. And with your young lady, who's a bit the worse o' the wear. 'Tis a deadly crossin' from Holyhead when the wind's high. Waitin' there on the quay I was glad of my ulster."

"You did famously, Canon, and I am grateful."

"'Tis a pleasure to serve you, Madame, and as I happened to be in Dublin I took the liberty of calling at the warehouse for the case ye so kindly promised me."

"That was wisely done." Madame inclined her head. "Claire, you may go to your usual room. I am quite sure you need nothing to eat. Take a bath first."

"Thank you, Auntie. And thank you, Canon." Claire turned and went out.

A brief silence followed.

"I took the further liberty, Madame, of asking Patrick to wait. I thought you might kindly permit him to finish the day by drivin' us home."

"Naturally, he will do so. I am sure you are weary yourself, so I will not detain you."

She escorted them to the front door. Here, the Canon bowed

and went down the steps. Madame gave Desmonde one swift, burning glance.

"Three months is not forever. Remember that I love you."

Back at the presbytery, welcomed by Mrs. O'Brien, the case of Dew safely in the hall, the Canon was himself again, and in an answer to his housekeeper on the question of supper, thoughtfully replied: "I had a chop or two at the Hib, sampled some of your sandwiches on the Quay and finished the remainder off with Patrick on the way home. However . . . ?"

"Something light, maybe, Canon. A sweetbread?"

"The very thing, with a bit of cheese and a biscuit to follow."

Mrs. O'B. smiled at Desmonde. "I believe you would like that, yourself, Father."

During supper the Canon, in the manner of Marco Polo, reverted to the rigours and hazards of the expedition. As regards the niece, he merely said:

"She seemed a poor bit of a thing, half dead wi' that awfu' journey. And starved as weel. Onything she had to eat went ower the rail into the Irish Sea."

"She seemed terrified of her aunt."

"And with good reason. Onybody that does wrong to Madame knows what to expect." He paused to sip his Dew, perhaps a slightly larger portion than usual, because of the fresh stock on hand. "How did you get on yerself today, with Madame?"

"Wonderfully." It was the appropriate moment. Desmonde rose from the table. "Canon, I am deputed by Madame Donovan to inform you that before the end of the year you will have altar rails of the finest Carrara marble."

As though electrified, the Canon sat, motionless, then he sprang to his feet.

"Oh, thank God! And thank you, Desmonde. I kenned ye would do it, that Madame would do onything for ye." He put his arms on Desmonde's shoulders and embraced him. "Oh, glory be to God, and to Madame, we'll have the finest church, all complete, in the whole of Ireland. Wait till I tell Canon Mooney in Cork. He's aye been sneerin' at our auld rails, the Carrara will kill him. Oh, I must get on the phone instantly to Madame, to thank her . . ."

"No, Canon, wait. She's not in the mood now with the niece just back on her. Compose one of your beautiful letters overnight and send Michael down with it in the morning."

"Oh, you're right, lad, right as usual. I'm in no fit state. But I'll phone Mooney, 'twill give him a bad night. And I'll give Mrs. O'B. the great news straight away. Och, lad, I'll never forget you for this, never, never. Sit down by the fire, I'll be back in two ticks, then we'll talk it all over from beginning to end."

And the Canon, his Dew forgotten, dashed through the door, and downstairs to the kitchen.

XIII

MADAME HAD GONE and the days seemed less bright. No longer did her charming, attractive figure adorn the church. Instead, the little end pew held only a solemn faced Patrick and a subdued, sulky Claire. Sadly missed, too, was the generous hospitality of the Mount.

"It's no' quite the same without her," the Canon commented more than once, adding: "I hope she hasn't forgotten her promise."

Madame had not forgotten. Towards the end of the second week two architects arrived and, without delay, began their operations in the church, measuring, calculating, discussing, and with a silence more cutting than speech, ignoring the Canon's suggestions and proposals, which would undoubtedly have ruined the entire project. They conversed only with Desmonde, in rapid Italian, that had the warmth of expatriates discovering their own language, spoken perfectly, in a foreign town. And from these exchanges Desmonde was able to assure his Superior that all would be perfect, both in quality and design.

Indeed, after three days, before the two strangers departed, they presented the Canon with a skilfully tinted design, a picture, in fact, of the finished work. The Canon gazed, and was immediately in ecstasy.

"'Tis beautiful, 'tis superb, oh, dear Lord, it is heavenly!"

Looking over his shoulder, Desmonde was equally enchanted. A superb curve of veined white marble, supported, in groups of three, by delicate yellow pilasters, saved from over elaboration by a median gate of beaten bronze.

"You were right, Desmonde, lad, to leave them to it—

they're experts, artists, ah! what a joy 'twill be when it's here. Did they mention when the work would start?"

"Almost at once, Canon. They asked me where their men could stay—the Station Hotel, I thought . . ."

"Ay, they'll get dacent rooms there. I'll see to it. I'll speak to Dolan myself."

Hugging the drawing, the worthy old man went immediately to the church porch and hung it there for all to admire.

Every week now, on Tuesdays and Fridays, the Canon, accompanied by his curate, made the pilgrimage to the deserted Mount to see that Madame's instructions were being strictly observed.

On the Tuesday following the departure of the Italians, the Canon and his curate took their leisurely walk to the Mount, the Canon remarking as they approached the house: "'Tis like a body without a soul."

Patrick, as usual, anticipating their visit, met them at the front entrance.

"Well, how is your charge today, Patrick?"

"As usual, I'm afraid, your reverence. Miserable all the time, nothing to do, naebody to talk to, barring ourselves, she wanders around like a knotless thread."

"No letters written or received?"

"None whatsoever, your reverence. Not a scrape of a pen. I check the post carefully myself."

"Does she not take up a book?"

"She's not a reader, Canon." Patrick hesitated. "Don't you think, your reverence, that Madame is just a bit over severe with her? With all respect, that's the opinion of ourselves in the kitchen. She's a slip of a thing who's been a bit wayward maybe but there's many o' us makes mistakes when we're young. Why, Madame has even forbidden the glass of light wine to her lunch that she's used to at her school. She's no appetite without it. Don't you think t'would be a kindness to let her have just one glass o' the Barsac we have on occasions ourselves, mild stuff, from Findlater's in Dublin?"

The Canon pondered, glanced at Desmonde.

"I say no." The response came firmly. "Madame must be obeyed."

"Weel," said the Canon slowly, "I say yes. Justice must be tempered with mercy."

"Thank you, Canon," Patrick said. "She'll maybe eat a bit now. She's up by the tennis court if ye wish to see her."

He led the way through the house and out across the rose garden to the pavilion. On the court, dressed in her ordinary blouse and skirt, Claire was making the best of her solitary state, serving six balls from the far end of the court, walking slowly to the near side, collecting the balls, then carelessly, absently, banging them back again.

"That's no sort of a game!" growled the Canon, and after a further listless volley, he touched Desmonde on the shoulder. "For pete's sake, lad, take your coat off, get a bat and knock the balls back to her."

"I have no racquet."

"There's plenty in the pavilion." Patrick disappeared, and was back in a moment with a brand new racquet. "'Tis a good one, a Spalding."

Desmonde stripped off his jacket and stepped on to the court, where he was greeted by a surprised, welcoming smile.

"I'm not much good," he said. "But I'll try and give you a game."

They started off with a knock up. She began by moderating the speed of her serves, and he in turn served with an underhand stroke. Desmonde had a good eye and soon they had some creditable rallies that provoked applause from the spectators. Finally they played a set which Desmonde, still serving underhand, lost, though only by six games to four.

The change in Claire was remarkable, she looked a different girl as she followed her opponent from the court. Flushed and smiling, she thanked, in turn, the Canon, Desmonde, and finally Patrick.

"It's just what I've been longing for," she added.

"Father Desmonde looks the better o' it, too," commented Patrick. "Maybe you'll let him play again, Canon, when he comes down."

"I sanction it." The Canon nodded amiably. "But look at the way he's sweatin'. He'll need tennis claes."

"There's plenty o' them. Madame had white shirts and shoes and pants in the lockers—for the office fellas when they visit us. I'll have Bridget wash and iron a set o' them."

Claire's eyes had brightened. She's nothin' like as bad as Madame makes out, thought the Canon. Madame can be

gey hard, ay, hard as steel, when she's crossed. And, aloud:
"I perceive it's been dull andmiserable for ye, missie.
We'll ease up a bit on ye now. If Father Desmonde is free, he'll
give you a game Thursday. Away now, and get yourself
shifted, you're all sweatin'!"

They watched her run down to the back door of the house
where she turned to wave to them.

"I'm in the same condition." Desmonde laughed. "Wringing
wet. Perhaps Patrick would drive us home."

"'Twould suit me," said the Canon, who was not looking
forward to the uphill walk back to the presbytery.

"I'll see that the water is turned on in the pavilion," Patrick
murmured to Desmonde, as he led the way to the garage.
"You'll get a dacent shower after your game Thursday."

The two visitors were driven off, suffused by a comfortable
feeling of a kindly act, well done. Watching from the window
of her little bedroom, Claire felt happy, for the first time in many
weeks.

XIV

THE FOLLOWING THURSDAY was wet and the official visit
to Mount Vernon was postponed. In the forenoon Desmonde
worked with the Canon over the quarterly accounts, writing
off the expenses of the presbytery against the income from the
church collections. The balance was small indeed, so small that
the Canon shook his head.

"We'd never manage to keep things going, Desmonde, if
'twasn't for Madame. Think of all that she gives us, or pays for.
The fine wax candles, lovely vestments, and flowers, the heating
and lighting, even the incense. And now, them wonderful
rails." He paused. "I wonder how she is now, over there?"

As if in answer to the Canon's query, the noon mail delivery
brought a letter from Switzerland, addressed to Desmonde, who
immediately read it aloud to his Superior.

My dear Desmonde,

*I have been frantically busy since my arrival here, but now I seize a
moment to unburden my troubled lonely heart and also to inform you that
all arrangements for the new altar rails have been completed. You must*

tell the good Canon that I have sanctioned the proposed design, it is quite lovely. I have also chosen the various marbles, also superbly beautiful, and now Signor Moreno, head of the Moreno Company, has just telephoned to say that all these precious goods have been crated, and will be shipped by freighter direct to Cork one week from today. Accompanying them will be four of his best workmen who will see to the delivery of the crates, unpack and instal the marbles. This should take a week or ten days, so perhaps the good Canon will accordingly reserve rooms for the men. I suggest the Station Hotel. Tell Dolan to give them rice and macaroni dishes—that's their usual diet.

Amongst all my longings, I cannot wait to see my lovely gift actually in being, in my lovely church, and to kneel there, to receive the Sacrament from your dear hands, dearest Desmonde, what joy, spiritual and, yes, temporal—but of the purest ray serene.

Desmonde flushed and paused, looking across at the Canon, who nodded understandingly, saying: "I know, lad, I know. If it hadna' been for you I might have waited long enough . . ."

Desmonde resumed. *Nor must we forget our worthy Canon, who will soon be in a position to exult over his friendly enemy in Cork.*

The Canon chuckled. "She kens aal . . . What a woman!"

The letter continued. *On other matters of less importance, I have had a most unpleasant time, interviewing Major Coulter, Claire's late headmaster, who, in addition to lecturing me, as if I were to blame, on the adverse publicity suffered by his school through Claire's escapades, presented me with a sheaf of bills sent to the school after her departure, debts unofficially incurred by my darling niece, for showy dresses, a bead necklace and white gloves, all quite unnecessary. To put it as charitably as possible, she seems to have no sense whatsoever, not only of the standards of common decency, but of the value of money, particularly when it is not her own. I do trust that, with the Canon, you are supervising her behaviour and ensuring that she doesn't communicate with her former confederates, or get into mischief here.*

Again the Canon intervened. "Isn't that just what we're doin', and seein' to, forbye, that she stays in good health?"

Desmonde concluded. *And now dear friends, with all good wishes, I must say au revoir. Let me know at once when the shipment arrives.*

Most sincerely yours,

Geraldine Donovan

Desmonde hesitated, then folded the letter and returned it to its envelope. A postscript had caught his eye which he thought wiser not to disclose.

Desmonde, I cannot sleep. I, who always slept peacefully, soundly as a child, lie awake at night, often for hours, une nuit blanche, *thinking, thinking . . . of whom? Write to me soon, my darling.*

Gerry

Leaving the Canon to his final additions, Desmonde rose and went to the church to kneel before the tabernacle, always his solace and comforter, his refuge in every difficulty. He prayed that Madame's insomnia might yield to refreshing sleep, but beyond all, he prayed that their mutual love might be restrained, to remain within the bounds prescribed by Holy Church. For himself, he had no fear, but as for his dear, dear friend, his patroness, the postscript of her letter troubled him. He promised himself, and Heaven too, that his reply to the letter, while no less affectionate than before, would be tempered by a cautionary prudence.

The children were now beginning to assemble for his Confirmation class, amongst them the little ones he had brought on for Holy Communion. The Bishop's visit was not due until late September, a week or ten days after Madame's return, but Desmonde, who wanted his pupils to shine before his Lordship, had started early. Assuring himself that the glass jar, in the cupboard behind the side altar, was still amply stocked, Desmonde began his instruction, which went on until noon.

The sun continued to shine and at lunch the Canon remarked:

"You better do Vernon this afternoon, lad. 'Twill take us over the weekend." Then as Desmonde looked at him inquiringly: "I have a four o'clock C.C. meeting on my hands. And to tell the truth, I don't care for that stiff uphill walk on the way back, instead of my usual nap. So you might as well run down yourself in future, see that all goes well, and have your bit of a game forbye."

Desmonde, accordingly, made his way alone to the Mount, arriving soon after two o'clock.

Claire, already on the court in short white ballet skirt and singlet, greeted him joyously.

"I'm so glad you've come, Father Desmonde. I was desolate yesterday. Patrick has put your togs all ready in the pavilion, and he's most decently given us new balls. So do hurry and change."

Desmonde went into the pavilion. As promised, everything

was there, beautifully washed and pressed: white flannels and singlet, white sweater and blancoed shoes. An inviting sight. In four minutes flat, Desmonde emerged, transformed.

"I say, you do look spiffing!" Claire's dark eyes had widened. "Absolute Wimbledon."

"All but my game, Claire."

"We'll see to that! Now, come on, the first thing is to teach you the overhand serve. No more popping the ball over, underhand, as Auntie might do if she tried it."

The lesson began. Desmonde was an apt pupil, he felt so free and easy in his light clothing, and soon Claire decided that the set might begin. Her serves came crashing in, unsparingly, until at last Desmonde learned to time and return them. His own serve began to take shape, affording him the delicious sensation of a brand new ball, hit hard and true with the centre of a first class racquet.

Claire took the first set six games to one, and the second six to two. Half way through the third, Patrick appeared with a jug of iced lemonade and glasses on a tray, which he placed on a table in the veranda of the pavilion.

"You *are* kind, Patrick," Desmonde said, coming to the net. "Please thank Bridget for doing my things so nicely. And thank you for the new balls."

"It's a pleasure to see your reverence lookin' so well, ye know, you were quite pale and peaky for a while, just before Madame left. As for the niece, the good exercise has made her a different cratur."

He waited, watching the game resumed, then joined Bridget, who had a vantage point by the pantry window.

"They're a beautiful pair out there," Bridget commented. "But . . . do you think it's quite in order, quite safe, so to speak, to let them be thegither . . . alone?"

"Ah, they're just playin' like a couple of children."

"Madame wouldn't like it, Pat."

"What Madame doesn't see won't grieve her. It's my opinion she's been far too hard on the girl. Ever since we've been kind to her she's blossomed like the rose."

"Cut the poetry, Shakespeare! Ye never ca'ed me a rose. Ah, well . . . ah, well. Just look at that Father Desmonde, there. Anybody but a blind man would see she has fallen for him. He would turn the head and the heart of any wumman, young or old." Moving off, she added a parting shot. "As Madame could well tell ye."

When the third set was over, the players retired to a bench on the veranda and poured the lemonade.

"I did enjoy that," Desmonde said. "And I've always rather stupidly despised ball games."

"There's one or two of them warrant investigation." Claire put both feet on the railing, leaning slightly back to allow the breeze to exert its full cooling effect which was, indeed, assisted by a slight billowing of her short skirt. Hurriedly, Desmonde averted his eyes from the delectable vision thus revealed.

"Shall we play again?"

"I don't want you to overdo it, Desmonde. You'll feel stiff tomorrow from that overhead serve. But do come again on Monday. I'll be seeing you, Sunday, in church. Take your shower now before you cool off. I'll bring my dressing gown over tomorrow, so I can take one too. It's more companionable by far."

She got to her feet and, before skipping down the steps, planted a light kiss on his cheek.

On her way to the house she turned twice to wave her racquet and to blow another kiss.

XV

GREAT EXCITEMENT NOW animated Kilbarrack as the cry went round 'the Eyetalians are here'. Accompanied by numerous crates, large and small, four quiet, debonair little men had been welcomed by the Canon and shown in state to their hotel. Almost immediately the work on the altar rails began. And how skilfully, how expertly did it proceed. And so silently, since the Canon, after some misguided attempts to interfere, was obliged to watch, which he did almost continuously, without words. And with what envy did he regard Desmonde, chatting away to them, making them smile, and chatter back.

"What was that a' about?" snarled the good Canon.

"They are happy to be here, and with the accommodation so kindly provided. But as they are all highly skilled and experienced technicians they wish not to be disturbed. Also they have brought with them all their own delicious food and wine and wish no food from the hotel."

"Ma Goad!" groaned the Canon. "What will Dolan do with a' them lashin's o' macaroni I made him buy?"

Not alone was the Canon in his silent vigil. Piety suddenly became the rage in Kilbarrack, crowds flocking to the church to cross themselves, kneel, stare, and wonder.

"Have ye been up the day, yet, Mick?"

"I have indade, but I'll go up with ye again. 'Tis as good as the theayatre. The way them little fellers slide around in their sandals, knowin' where everything goes and slidin' it in like clockwork. And a lovely job 'twill be when it's done, an all."

Parochial duties were necessarily reduced to a minimum, and Desmonde, with time on his hands, was drawn even more frequently to Vernon, to the tennis court. He had become fond of the game, and with his keen eye and swift reactions had surprised Claire on his latest visit by winning in three straight sets. Far from annoying Claire this had delighted her. Always gay, full of fun and in her own phrase 'ready for anything', she had proved herself an amusing, uninhibited, and carefree companion. Now they shared the pavilion together as a living-room in which towels, clothes, slippers, bath robes and the rest were scattered and littered around.

"Isn't this fun?" Claire would exclaim, coming out of the shower, loosely robed. "I'm glad I got kicked out of Chateau-le-Roc. First of all because I hated the bloody place, and secondly because now I've got you."

And she began to sing: "Falling in love is wonderful . . ."

"Enough, little birdie, you're off-key. This is how it goes."

And he sang it through for her.

This was the good summer which occasionally, though rarely, steeps the south-west of Ireland in benign and constant sunshine. Desmonde was now deeply tanned and he had put on muscle, so that the Canon, scanning him approvingly, had exclaimed:

"You're lookin' great, Desmonde, and more of a man."

This afternoon, striding down towards the pavilion, to change before Claire should appear, Desmonde did indeed feel unusually fit, carefree and cheerful, a euphoria that owed much to the prospects of this lovely afternoon, and the pleasure of being with his carefree opponent who was, in fact, on the spot when he leaped up the steps of the veranda.

"Out, birdie, out," he cried. "I'm going to strip."

"And what difference does that make? I'm putting a new lace in my shoe. And aren't we the best of intimate pals?"

"Turn your back, then."

"What for? Are ye like Nora Macarty on her weddin' night?" And without moving she began to sing.

'Little Nora Macarty the knot was goin' to tie,
She washed all her trousseau and hung it up to dry,
Then up came a goat and he saw the bits of white,
He chewed up all her fal-de-rals, and on her weddin'
    night,
Oh, turn out the light quick, poor Nora cried to Pat,
For though I am your bride, sure, I'm not worth
    lookin' at,
I had two of everything I told you when I wrote,
But now I've one o' nothing, all through Paddy
    McGinty's goat.'

Claire burst out laughing: "That's a great song, Des, you should hear the two Bobs at it. So let's see you with one of nothing."

Desmonde shook his head and began, with as much discretion as possible, to change.

"And don't call me Des, Claire. The name is Desmonde, with the final 'e'."

"Ah, what's the odds, I'll soon be calling ye' darlin'. Here I go again, just once more." And she sang: " 'Let me call you sweetheart, darlin', I'm in love with you . . .' "

Out on the court, Desmonde said: "I'm going to knock the stuffing out of you, for that."

They played, without rest, two hard sets, and, after a short adjournment to the pavilion, a final two, leaving the honours even. As they came off the court shortly after four o'clock, Patrick was waiting on them.

"Bridget thought you must be tired of that ould lemonade and wonders if ye wouldn't like to come in the house for your tea."

Desmonde glanced at Claire, who exclaimed: "I think we'd love it, don't you, Desmonde?"

They went into the pavilion to change, Claire, according to custom, taking the shower first while Desmonde went into the men's changing-room. He had barely stripped off his singlet when a wild shriek from Claire brought him out again.

"Oh, Des, quick, quick, look at my eye."

Standing stark naked, bedewed by the shower, like Aphrodite risen from the foam, she now ran towards him, put her hands on his shoulders and upturned her face.

"Something in my right eye, a fly perhaps, hurting, hurting. Please look."

Desmonde inspected the eye, pressing back the lid, but could see no insect of any kind. He did, however, see Claire, her slim beautiful body, tight little pink-tipped breasts and the delicate little tuft guarding the ultimate mystery from which, perhaps, came the strange fragrance that made his head swim. He felt his own body react, violently, hotly, as he stammered: "I see nothing . . . perhaps the spray . . ."

"Oh, it was so sharp, and sudden . . ." She let her face rest against his. "I was frightened. Don't move, dear, this is helping me." Now she was almost in his arms. "This is what I was longing for, hoping that you would hold me close, wanting you. You know I'm crazy about you, darling. Hold me this way, often, often . . ."

When at last Desmonde disengaged himself, his heart was beating fast. He took one last look at her, standing there with arms outstretched, then stumbled into his changing cabinet.

Fifteen minutes later, they were both in the sun-room, oddly silent, relieved, almost, when Patrick, who had just brought in a well-stocked tray, seemed to hesitate before leaving the room.

"Might I take no more nor a minute, sir, to ask you a favour?"

"Certainly, Patrick."

'Well, 'tis like this, your reverence. The A.O.H. will be givin' their annual concert next month, for charity, ye understand, and bein' one of the officials they've asked me to ask you a great favour . . . if you would consent to appear on the programme, just to sing no more nor a couple of songs, not classical, ye understand, just two o' the good old Irish ballads."

"Go on, Des, say yes," Claire urged, as Desmonde hesitated. "I've promised to do a turn myself."

"She has indeed, sir."

"Well, I will, then," Desmonde said.

"Oh, thank ye, sir, thank ye, indeed, the boys will be delighted. Ye've made yerself so well liked, so popular, goin' amongst the people, bein' one of us, despite your position and education, 'twill fill the house to hear you."

When Patrick had bowed himself out, Desmonde turned to Claire.

"Give me my tea, you hidden persuader, and some of that cake before you finish it."

When the tea and cake had been given and absorbed, Desmonde said, seriously:

"Claire, dear, we must be careful in future. No more of these sudden sorties from the shower. They are dangerous."

She did not answer, but smiled, her tight-lipped enigmatic smile, which barely uncovered her little white teeth. When they had finished tea, and thanked Bridget in the kitchen, she said:

"I'll walk up the hill with you."

She took his arm and, in silence, they set off. At the summit of the woodland cutting, in the little grassy glade, he held up his hand.

"No trespassers, please. This is private property, where I come to meditate."

"Will you think of me?"

"Unfortunately, yes."

"What a nasty thing to say. You must atone by kissing me."

He kissed her.

She watched him as, without looking back, he walked down the hill.

XVI

DESMONDE WAS NOW in better physical condition than ever before, or indeed, than ever he would be again. Unhappily there was a fly in the ointment, possibly of the species that flew out of Claire's eye. No matter how hard he worked in the parish, winning commendation from the Canon for completing tasks that had long awaited attention, he seemed unable to tire himself out, and often at night he would lie for hours inviting the sleep that did not come.

Mentioning his trouble at supper one evening, the Canon nodded understandingly.

"I had the same thing myself, when I was a young priest. It's in the nature of man—repression taking its revenge. You don't play so much tennis these days?"

"I was overdoing it, Canon. A priest has no place on the tennis court, every day of the week."

"Maybe . . . maybe," the Canon said thoughtfully. "Why don't you take a good hard walk at night before ye turn in? Or a little drop o' the Dew might send you over."

"Thank you, Canon." Desmonde smiled constrainedly. "I think I'll try the walk."

He wondered if his worthy Superior had an intuition of the struggle going on in his mind, of the fight he was waging to keep away from Vernon and from Claire. He did, nevertheless, set out about an hour after supper, striding up the hill and half running down. This, followed by a hot bath, gave him some relief, an exhausted sleep of two or three hours' duration, before the restless tossing set in again.

Often he thought of the casual manner in which he had treated Madame's mention of her insomnia. The mild remedy he had suggested, aspirin before retiring, proved useless to him. Were they suffering, she as a woman, he as a man, from the same malady? He did, however, continue with the palliative of the hard nightly walk, setting off with his torch when the darkness was oppressive, meeting the Canon's anxiously approving glance when he returned. That wise old man knew precisely the cause of Desmonde's disorder; as a young celibate he had suffered it himself.

One night of unusual humidity, the air warm and still, Desmonde breasted the hill and flung himself down on the grass to rest. He had closed his eyes, instinctively wondering if sleep might come to him. He did not hear the sound of quiet approaching footsteps rustling the fallen leaves. Only when his whispered name, and the sound of hurried breathing, caused him to turn on his side, did he sense that Claire lay beside him. Was it reality or was it a dream? Her arms enfolding him, her voice, breathless from hurry, whispering again: "Darling, darling, why didn't you come to me? I've waited, waited, hungry for you. And when I saw your torch tonight I couldn't wait another sleepless night. Come, darling, come to me, love me."

He was in her arms now, lost in the blessed relief, the joy of her embrace, their lips together, hands touching, fondling, seeking and finding, finding, with her skilful guidance, the entrance to appeasement and the delirium of undreamed delight.

A long sigh broke from her, she was still, remaining locked in his embrace. Then she whispered:

"Darling, wonderful darling, that was the best ever—" She checked herself. "I felt that it was love, true love, I came to you, did you not feel it, how I quivered? I had been longing for you so long." Then, after a silence: "I must go now, dearest, or they will miss me at the house."

Another kiss and she had risen, was gone.

Desmonde lay for a moment, as though dazed, his eyes still closed, his being pervaded by a calm satisfaction, as though every nerve in his body were at peace. At last he got to his feet and began to walk downhill.

Alas, the nearer he came to the presbytery, the more a realization of his predicament dawned upon him. His glow faded, supplanted by a slow fear and chilling remorse, that drove him directly to the church. He entered by the side door and, without turning on the switches, flung himself down upon his knees before the altar.

The side door banged open and, flashing his torch, the Canon came barging into the church. He did not at first discern Desmonde, but finally a beam of light caught up and illuminated the still, kneeling figure of his Curate.

"So this is where ye've been hidin' yerself. And me lookin' for ye all over. There was a sick call for ye. The old Duggan man, way down at Ardbeg. I had to do it fer ye. And ye know how I hate drivin' at night."

Desmonde remained silent.

"What's the matter with ye?" The Canon angrily drew near. "Are ye deaf or dumb."

Still no answer. The torch flashed into Desmonde's face. A brief silence. Then:

"Good God! What's the matter? Are ye ill? This bloody night walkin' has exhausted ye."

A tremor passed over the kneeling figure. A hand was raised

shielding the death-pale face against the light. The Canon's voice altered.

"Here, lad, enough of these midnight vigils. Let me give you my arm. And come away up to my room." He helped Desmonde to his feet. "Mrs. O'Brien is long gone. But I'll make ye a good strong cup o'coffee. I'm needin' one for my own self onyway."

So presently Desmonde was in the Canon's warm room, seated in the Canon's deep arm chair, eyes down, gulping his coffee with a shaking hand.

"And now, lad, what's the matter?"

"Father, I must confess to you."

"Ah?" The Canon raised a restraining arm as Desmonde attempted to kneel. "Sit where ye are, lad. I'm listening."

"Father . . . I am in love . . ."

"Ah! A wumman?"

"Yes."

"Well, there's naething so wrong with that, so long as ye've come out with it to me. Wha is't? That little bitch, Claire?"

"Yes, father."

"I'd sworn it. There's nae good in that little bitch. She would make love to a lamp post."

"No, father. No . . . no . . . no. She is a sweet, innocent little thing."

"Indeed, now. Well, lad, you'll put that same sweet and innocent little thing right out of your sweet innocent stupid head."

A silence. In a voice that trembled:

"I cannot, father. We . . . we have already consummated our love."

"Consummated . . . your love. What in the name of God do you mean?"

"Tonight, as you are aware, I went walking . . . in Kiloan Wood . . . couldn't sleep . . . deeply troubled . . . by chance we met . . ."

"You met."

"We tried to resist, Father. It was impossible. We . . . we loved each other."

A shocked look came over the Canon's ruddy face. Slowly he said:

"You mean you had her?" Then, peering into Desmonde's half lowered eyes, ear cupped for the faint answer.

"We loved."

"A physical union? Oh, God Almighty. Holy Mary and all the Saints. What a bloody to-do! You went fucking in the dark in Kiloan Woods, come back half dead and call it love." The Canon's voice rose to a shout. "I see it all now. And ye come back to be petted and gi'en coffee. Go to your room, you dirty little brute, but first take a bath. Ye'll get no absolution from me yet. But what's to do in the parish . . ." He threw up his hands. "If this gets abroad 'twill mak' all the devils in hell dance the fandango!"

XVII

PHYSICALLY AND EMOTIONALLY exhausted, Desmonde slept as one dead until the persistent whirr of his alarm clock, set for six o'clock, awakened him to the realization of his position. For some moments he lay motionless, then raised himself on one elbow. He had the seven a.m. morning weekday Mass. He must get up. But before he could stir, there came a knock at his door which opened to reveal the Canon, fully dressed.

"Good morning, lad. How do you feel?"

The sympathy, the humanity in the Canon's voice startled Desmonde, who stammered an answer.

"Well, well, now, that's good news. Though you do still look a bit white about the gills. So there's no need to hurry. I'll take the seven o'clock for ye. I've asked Mrs. O'Brien to give ye a right good breakfast, since you missed your dinner last night. Over that sick call." The emphasis on these last two words was stony. "And if you'll step down to the church around eight, I'll be in the sacristy."

A nod, what might have passed as a smile, and the door closed quietly.

Desmonde got out of bed, knelt, according to his custom, to pray, then shaved, washed and dressed. His appearance in the small square mirror above his washstand was disheartening, but he went fairly steadily along the passage to the dining room where, beyond the hatch that opened to the kitchen, Mrs. O'Brien greeted him.

"Good morning to you, Father. You must be starved. And

out so late too, at poor old Mr. Duggan. I'll have your breakfast through to you in a minute."

Indeed, with her customary efficiency, she was as good as
her word. This cheerful, bustling, dark-eyed little woman of
fifty who must, in her youth, have been pretty, and who now,
with no more help than one village girl in the kitchen, managed
the Presbytery in all its ramifications.

The breakfast was exceptional, even in a house noted for its
table. Fried soles that had come fresh from Wexford before
dawn. New baked rolls and dairy butter. Honey and cream
cheese. Strong steaming coffee with clotted cream.

Desmonde, faint from lack of food, did justice to this noble
spread and, though he divined it some part of the Canon's
design, when he rose from the table much of his anguish and
apathy had gone.

He knocked on the hatch and lifted it to thank Mrs. O'Brien,
whom he knew to be favourable towards him, and this surely
was a moment when he needed all possible good will.

"Did you enjoy it, Father Desmonde?"

"Immensely."

Her dark eyes sparkled and she smiled, showing her nice
white teeth. She loved to be praised, especially from this nice
young priest, such a handsome boy.

When Desmonde entered the church Mass was over and
the Canon, having finished his thanksgiving, was in the vestry.

He smiled, a conciliatory smile, as Desmonde appeared and,
surprisingly, held out his hand.

"Did ye have a good breakfast, lad? I told Mrs. O'Brien to
make it special."

"A wonderful breakfast, thank you, Canon."

"Good, good. And I'll warrant you slept well."

Desmonde reddened, murmured almost inaudibly: "Yes."

"Then come and sit by me, lad, we'll have a bit of a chat, and
forgetting all the hard words of last night, try and straighten
things out for you and all of us.

"Now don't be thinkin' that the sky has fallen in on you
because you've made a bit of a false step. You're not the only
one, by a long chop, that's done so. It's hard for human nature
to be celibate. It would surprise ye to know how many a dacent
priest has made a slip, once in a while, and has had to pick
himself up quick and tell the Lord he was sorry."

The Canon paused reflectively, and looking at him, Desmonde became suddenly the victim of a strange optical illusion. He saw, not the Canon's ruddy honest features but, just for one second, the sweet, docile, dark eyed face of Mrs. O'Brien.

"Well now," the Canon sighed. "One thing is certain, you cannot have anything more to do with the girl. To do so would be fatal. Do you see that yourself?"

"Yes, Canon. It's hard . . ."

"Of course it's hard, and if it were harder 'twould still have to be obeyed. You want to continue as a priest, where already you have made a great success and where the future is so bright and shinin'. You want to continue to serve the Lord God Almighty as his blessed and anointed servant."

"I do, I must."

"Well, then, leave everything to me. I will see to it that Claire does not come near you again. I have the power and the influence in that quarter, and believe me, I will use it. Just you put her out of your mind. If you don't, 'twould be stark ravin' madness, the disaster that all Hell is awaitin'." He stood up. "Now, take the car, and away down to see how poor old Duggan is this morning. I think it's maybe pneumonia, and if it is he'll have to be lifted to the infirmary."

As he was bid, Desmonde drove out to make the sick call. He found the old man better, which he thought a good omen, and attended by the district nurse, who assured him it was only a chill.

On the way home he saw that they were putting up posters for the Hibernian concert, and was able to distract his mind by thinking of the songs he would sing—all truly Irish, he decided, tender, sentimental, patriotic. He parked his car at the Cross, scene of his adventure with the piglets, and went on foot to visit another of his invalids, greeted all the way by touched caps and cheerful, friendly, respectful salutations. How good to be on such pleasant terms with his parishioners, to be revered, yes, even loved, in this old country town. He began gradually to realize how foolish, how dangerous, had been his conduct.

It was lunch time when he got back to the presbytery, and after that light meal the Canon had more work for him, which kept him busy well into the evening. And how comforting, at dinner, to find the Canon as well disposed to him as ever.

The days that followed were filled, by the Canon's design, with a plenitude of parochial duties, comings and goings that kept Desmonde busy and on the move. There was no sign of Claire, not a word was heard from her, and Desmonde, true to his given word, tried to banish her from his mind.

The day of the concert finally came round and Desmonde, his spirits restored, decided to give of his best, the more so since the Canon had honoured him by promising to attend.

The night was dry and fine, crowds began early to flock to the town hall and when the Canon and Desmonde arrived and took their places, reserved on the front seat, the hall was filled to capacity, overflowing even into the streets.

Desmonde had been given the final place of honour on the programme. He had feared, greatly feared, that as she had promised Claire might appear. But as the evening wore on, mildly entertaining, there was no sign of her. And now it was his turn. He mounted the stage by the wooden side steps and, amidst applause, sat down at the piano, immediately behind the footlights.

Dead silence as his fingers moved over the keys, then he began to sing.

> 'The minstrel boy to the war is gone,
> In the ranks of death you'll find him;
> His father's sword he has girded on,
> And his wild harp slung behind him . . .'

He could not have chosen a better opening. Cheers echoed to the roof, stilled only when he raised his hand. He had decided to give of his best, to honour Ireland and his Irish birth.

He sang next 'Killarney', then, in turn, 'The Star of County Down', 'Terence's Farewell to Kathleen', that lovely song composed by Lady Dufferin, 'The Meeting of the Waters', then, as a touch of comedy, he suddenly launched into 'I met her in the garden where the praties grow'. His heart swelled as he filled the hall with the dear old Irish melodies. Finally he sang 'Off to Philadelphia in the morning!'

It was sensational, a triumph beyond triumphs. Deafened by the thunder of the applause, amongst the great mass of cheering faces, he could see the Canon clapping like mad and behind him Mrs. O'Brien, waving her tear-damp handkerchief wildly.

They would not let him go. He had to sing more. It was of course his favourite end-piece, his favourite hymn.

Dead silence when he began. Dead silence when he finished, then the riot broke loose. They were up on the stage, crowding round, shaking his hand, patting him on the back, he had to be rescued and rushed back stage through the wings and down to the dressing rooms below.

He was sitting here, exhausted, when the Canon came in, accompanied by Sergeant Duggan.

Coming directly to Desmonde, the Canon took both his hands.

"Never, never, in my long life, did I have such a heavenly treat. And Mrs. O'Brien too. You could see it in her face, she was just in the seventh heaven."

"Count me in too, Father Desmonde," said the Sergeant. "I'm not a Roman. Before I come here I was an Orange Lodge member up North. But I tell you straight, when ye sung that last hymn, I could have dropped on me knees. And now to be practical, I can't let you out the front doors, it's too dangerous, there's hundreds outside waitin' for ye." He looked at the Canon. "But I'm sure you know the back way up, sir, by the Vennel. I could let you out the side door . . ."

"That would be fine, Sergeant. Father Desmonde looks tired, I'd like to get him home."

Out in the cool night air, the Canon took Desmonde's arm, leading him through a network of narrow passages.

"You have Kilbarrack in the hollow of your hand, lad, the people love ye. Wait till ye see the church on Sunday, packed to the doors. Your little slip is over and forgotten. You're on top of the world."

As they drew near the presbytery, the Canon continued. "I know ye, lad. Ye'll want to go in by for your little prayer of thanksgiving. I'll go in the house and see what's doin' in the way o' supper."

Desmonde entered the church by the side door. Although tired, he was in a state of suppressed elation, of thankfulness and joy.

Except for the sanctuary lamp, the church was, as usual, in darkness. No, perhaps not completely dark, since in the further aisle a single amber light had been switched on, above his own confessional. He drew near and there, in that faint glow, standing, waiting, was a woman, a girl, Claire.

F

The shock was severe but Desmonde stumbled across the darkened church, came close to her. He was the first to speak.

"Claire. Dear Claire, we have been forbidden to meet. You should not be here."

"You think, darling, that because your bloody Canon lashed and lambasted me with his tongue, you think I could keep away from you?" Her voice was perfectly calm and contained as she continued: "You know that I love you, and I know that you love me. We could never be separated."

"No, Claire dear, but . . ."

"There are no buts, Desmonde." The voice was hard now. "We are tied together unalterably."

"Yet, darling Claire . . ."

"Unalterably, Desmonde, for you will be the father of our child. I am pregnant, Father Desmonde, by you, and in a few short months there'll be a little one really calling you father."

"But Claire dear," Desmonde stammered. "How can you be . . . I mean, only three weeks since we were together."

"I thought you'd say that, and that your bloody Canon would throw it at me too. Now listen to the God's truth, and like it.

"When I came to you that night in the wood my period was just due, that's why I came, I was burnin' hot. You served me and I was caught. No period, instead sick in the mornin', and the feeling a woman gets all over and especially down there. I knew I was pregnant."

"Darling, how could you be sure?"

"Ah, it's out, as I expected, not from you, but from the Canon. After three weeks with no period, I took the train to Cork, to Dr. Dudley Martin, the best known woman's doctor in Ireland. He examined me, outside and in, and gave me this signed certificate."

Dazedly, Desmonde took the paper, a prescription form written over in black ink.

"I can't read it here, darling, I'll have to take it upstairs. Do you want to wait or will you come back tomorrow?"

"I'll be at the presbytery. Eleven o'clock sharp, and see that you're all there ready for me, as I'll be ready for you."

Her voice altered, softened to entreaty.

"Now hold me, darling, only a minute, and kiss me just the

once. You know I love you with all my body, heart and soul, just as you love me. And I'll never let you go."

She threw herself into Desmonde's arms, passionately gave him her lips, then spun round and a moment later was gone. Desmonde turned slowly and stumbled out of the dim church. Alas, the Canon must be told immediately, and joy turned into sorrow.

XVIII

IMPLACABLY, THE NEXT day dawned. The Canon, who normally slept like a felled ox, had passed a restless night. Desmonde had not slept at all. Even the good Mrs. O'Brien admitted that she had not closed an eye till three in the morning. Gloom lay heavy on the presbytery as breakfast was eaten, the Canon insisting that strength must be maintained for the coming ordeal, the two Masses had been said, a telephone call to Dr. Martin in Cork had, alas, proved the authenticity of Claire's certificate, and now, as the eleventh hour drew near, Mrs. O'Brien had polished the dining room table while the Canon, after arranging four chairs squarely in position, placed an enormous Douai Bible in the centre of this formidable set piece.

"We have to frighten her," he muttered. "Then I'll lay into her. And let us be all ready, seated, like a court of law before she comes in."

Accordingly they seated themselves, the Canon at the head of the table, Desmonde opposite, Mrs. O'Brien on his left.

"Ye're not really wantin' me, Canon," Mrs. O'Brien quavered, uncertainly.

" 'Tis more dacent to have a woman, a good woman on the board. Besides, 'twill confuse her. So sit where ye are, Mrs. O'B."

The silence of expectancy fell upon the group, broken by the little clock on the mantel, which chimed eleven cheerful strokes.

" 'Tis fast," murmured the Canon.

"No, Canon dear, 'tis four minutes slow. I forgot to put it on this mornin'."

Again silence. The slow little clock now showed six minutes past the hour.

"She's feared," exclaimed the Canon with a note of triumph. "All may be well, Desmonde."

At that precise moment the door bell rang, firm, rapid steps were heard on the stairs, and Claire, beautifully turned out, swept into the room. Wearing a smart light navy Swiss dress, Madame's cloche hat and short black cashmere coat, both appropriated, sheer silk stockings and patent leather shoes, she looked stunning, as though she had stepped out of the Place Vendôme into the Ritz Bar.

"I'm so sorry to be late." She apologized, sitting down and tossing her gloves on to the Bible. "I simply had to have my hair done." She then leaned over and kissed Desmonde lightly on the cheek. "How are you, my darling, darling? I've brought you a little present. A lovely soft shirt with soft collar attached. You'll need it when you drop the dog collar." And she placed a neatly wrapped flat parcel before him.

For a full two minutes, stunned silence held the court speechless, then the Canon cleared his throat.

"You know, young wumman, what a serious, a deadly serious situation you have placed us in?"

"I, Canon? Was there no partner in the crime?"

"Yes, our Father Desmonde here was inveigled into it. A brilliant young priest with a great, a grand future in the Church, made that single slip. Do you want him to lose everything, to suffer all his life for it?"

"Leave out the suffering, Canon. So far Desmonde and I have had a lot of pleasure together and we want it to continue, don't we, Des?"

Desmonde flushed. Claire's smart, charming appearance, her style and composure, had restirred his vital organs. He did not reject the hand she held out to him.

The Canon leaned forward and his voice rose.

"Let's cut the fancy talk. What will ye take to let Desmonde off the hook?"

"Do you mean take a pill, Canon, maybe from your lady here, to have an abortion and kill my baby?"

"You'll excuse me, Canon," Mrs. O'Brien faltered. "I have to go."

She got up, slowly, and no one made the effort to detain her as she left the room.

"I am talkin' of money, that's what I mean!" the Canon

shouted. "How much will ye take down, and to go with the money in your hand to a nice quiet maternity home where all will be done for you?"

"And come home with me bastard in the mornin'," Claire sang. Then, in a hard voice: "How much down?"

"Two . . . three . . ." Watching her face, the Canon went on slowly: "four . . ." Then explosively: "five hundred golden sovereigns."

Claire laughed, a low, amused, bitter laugh.

"Admittedly, Canon, 'tis more than the thirty pieces of silver that sold Our Lord, but it won't buy me, Canon. I'm no little dirty farm servant, knocked up by the plough boy, that can be paid off in cash. I love Desmonde, and I know, Canon, know that he loves me. We'll give our beautiful little baby our name, together."

Silence, then the Canon, now thoroughly enraged, played his last, his trump card.

"Then there's only one thing for it. We'll disown you, totally and absolutely. Desmonde will continue here with his priestly duties, and you'll be left with your misbegotten bastard."

Claire laughed outright, throwing back her head and showing all her little white teeth. Then her teeth came together and her lips firmed in a hard narrow line.

"'Tis just what I expected of you, Canon. So go ahead. And I will go ahead!" Her voice hardened, and her eyes narrowed. "I'll take the first train to Dublin, to the office of the *Irish Citizen*, a popular paper, ye may know, with Protestant tendencies and noted for its anticlerical attitude. I'll give them the whole story. It will be a front page feature, with photographs an' all, they'll be down after you with cameras and reporters. You'll be the talk of Ireland, laughed at, cursed, spat on, prayed for, despised."

A long silence, then in a low voice: "You would not do such a thing, Claire."

Claire leaned forward, staring straight into the Canon's eyes.

"Don't you know me yet, your bloody, stupid reverence?" Again, a long, long silence. Then the Canon sighed, stood up, and threw out his hands.

"I've done my best. But 'tis no use, Desmonde. I couldn't stand the shame, the dishonour on my beautiful church, the new altar rails and all, and Madame returnin' the end of the month and the Bishop due for Confirmation. You'll have to clear out with her. And the sooner the better."

But suddenly, as though inspired, he raised his eyes and his arms to heaven and, in a grief-stricken voice, while Mrs. O'Brien, standing by the door with tears in her eyes, gazed in awe, he cried out:

"Oh Lord God Almighty in Heaven, there's something wrang wi' your Holy Roman Catholic Church, when a sweet young priest, the flower o' the flock, just because he makes a single mistake, then corrects it by honestly marryin' the girl and givin' his baby a name, must be kicked out o' the Church like a mangy hound dog.

"It's a' the fault o' these auld bastards at the Vatican, wrapped in cobwebs, and sae bluidy holy they think it's a sin tae haud their article when they go and make their watter. 'Tis no' only unjust, 'tis bloody unreasonable and agin nature. 'Twill have to be changed, oh, 'twill have to be changed, dear Lord, that is my humble prayer before Yer heavenly throne."

The Canon then confronted Desmonde sternly.

"One thing I must do, and will do, even though I may break the rule of the Church, though God knows not the spirit. I'm not having you go out of here and live and sleep in sin with that girl. And I'm not having your child born in sin, a bastard. Regard this as a marriage *in extremis*, but a marriage it will be. So fetch up the girl here within the hour. I'll be at the side altar with Mrs. O'Brien as witness. Don't fail me, Desmonde, or ye'll never have a moment's peace thereafter."

And so, within the hour, Desmonde stood with a very frightened Claire while, in the presence of Mrs. O'Brien, the Canon solemnly read the service and made them man and wife. He then blessed them and abruptly turned away. Only Mrs. O'Brien remained, and with tears in her eyes kissed first Claire then Desmonde.

"Kneel down both of the two of you and pray for God to bless you in your marriage, as I will pray for you myself."

The poor old Canon, indeed, was at the end of his tether. He offered no resistance when the following day, Saturday, was hurriedly fixed for Desmonde's departure. Claire made her preparations and took the tickets, while Mrs. O'Brien packed Desmonde's things, weeping at the memory of the happy day of his arrival. Desmonde forced himself to make, as he then thought, a final visit to Mount Vernon, to say goodbye to Patrick and Bridget.

Everything was accomplished quietly and well, since Desmonde wished, above all, to make his exit in peace. Alas, on the morrow, when the farewells were over and he was in the cab with Claire, driving to the station, the sound of the fife and drum band burst suddenly upon his ears, the cab was surrounded by marching men, the horse loosed from the traces, and replaced by men on either side of the shafts. Then, as the bank struck up 'Wearing o' the Green', with redoubled vigour, the cab slowly rolled off.

"Oh, God, Des!" Claire cried in high glee. "They're pulling us to the station, giving us the royal send off. What an honour. What fun! And look at the banners!"

Now that the horse was gone, the processional Hibernian banners held aloft were clearly visible, each covered with a white sheet on which, in black paint, slogans had been splashed.

GOOD LUCK TO OUR DES
WE LOVE YOU DES. HAPPY WEDDING
FAREWELL DEAR MINSTREL BOY
CHANGE THE LAW
LET OUR PRIESTS WED

Claire was beside herself with pride and delight. When, finally, they were out of the cab and in the train, she lowered the window of the compartment, waved and blew kisses to the sea of faces below, then taking Desmonde's hand she drew him beside her.

How the cheers rang out! Three for Desmonde. Three for Claire. Then a voice shouted: "Three for the baby."

This set the crowd into a turbulence of laughter and cheers. Then, as the train started slowly to move, all else was stilled and the band struck up fortissimo: 'Will ye no' come back again?' In this manner did Fr. Desmonde Fitzgerald take leave of his parish in Kilbarrack.

FOUR

BEFORE LEAVING KILBARRACK Desmonde had wisely written to his father's old housekeeper, Mrs. Mullen, now indeed a very aged though still active woman, asking her to find him a decent three room and kitchen apartment well situated on the Quays. Desmonde knew the Quays since boyhood and felt that he might find there a simple and quiet retreat until he knew more clearly what lay ahead for his wife and himself. By the same post he had also written to the former headmaster of his preparatory school, St. Brendan's.

When the happy couple arrived at the station Desmonde took a taxi direct to the Quays, Claire viewing the busy streets en route with delighted anticipation.

"Dear old Dublin! Here we come!"

At Mrs. Mullen's the bridal pair were welcomed with less enthusiasm, the old woman's face expressed concern and bewilderment, but she had found a modest furnished house almost next door, which she thought might suit, and towards which, after she had draped a shawl about her, she conducted them.

Desmonde, who had expected the worst, was relieved and pleased as he viewed the three rooms, not ill-furnished, and the bathroom with hot and cold taps. As the rent was reasonable he immediately took it for a preliminary six months and had the luggage brought in from the waiting cab. Mrs. Mullen, dismissed with the present of a pound, promised to tell the landlord to send the lease.

"Well, darling," Desmonde exclaimed cheerfully, "how do you like our new home?"

"It's not what I'm used to, Des. It's *low*."

"I think we're lucky to get it, so soon."

"You're used to this low class district, Des. You were born here. But I was brought up in more lady-like surroundings."

Ignoring this, Desmonde said:

"Well, how about stocking up with some grub? As I remember, there's not a bad little grocer's on the next corner."

"Then you go, Des. I want to unpack and rest. Do remember my condition, dear."

Desmonde went out to Kelly's little corner shop, where, fortunately, he was not recognized, and bought tea, coffee extract, milk and sugar, bread, tomatoes, plain biscuits, a pot of Robertson's marmalade, cheese, butter, some slices of cold ham, bacon and a dozen eggs. Pleased with this substantial cash order, the aproned proprietor, no longer John Kelly, agreed to send the boy round with them at once.

If Desmonde expected congratulations for this neat show of efficiency he was disappointed.

"Look, Des, look, will ye." Exposing a dress somewhat creased, Claire continued: "That bitch of a Bridget that I told to pack my things has made a rag of my lovely new muslin."

"Won't the creases iron out, dear?"

"Where's the iron? Will ye oblige me by telling me? No, 'twill have to go to the cleaners."

At this point came a knock at the door. It was the boy 'with the messages'.

"Well, let's have some grub, darling, we'll both feel better after that. Would you like to knock up something while I unpack?"

Claire stared with hostility at the packages on the table.

"I must tell you at the beginning, Des, I'm not the cook and washerwoman type. I've been well brought up and I'm not used to it. Why don't we just nip up to the Hibernian for supper?"

"And come back to find the bed not made up, all the sheets and blankets still in the hall out there, and my clothes still unpacked!"

"Ah, Des, you're lovely when you get a bit red and excited." She stretched out her arms. "Come and kiss me, love. Wasn't it darling in the train, all the little bumps helping us up and down and in and out. And ye're right, we must get the bed sorted. I'll do it, if you make the supper."

Desmonde had set two eggs to boil on the little scullery gas stove and was beginning to lay the table when loud lamentations drew him, running, to the front room.

"It's the bed, darling. It's been taken down, the bits are all over, and so heavy I can't shift them."

It was one of those old Irish beds, solid oak and large enough to hold a family.

Desmonde approached the backboard.

"Let's try this first, and get it against the wall."

Together, straining hard, they lifted the bed which seemed to weigh a ton, until Claire, with a gasp, let go her end. With a thunderous crash the backboard resumed its situation, flat on the floor.

"We'll need help, Des. It's too much for us."

"We must do it, Claire. It's a challenge. We can't sleep on the floor."

As Desmonde bent over the backboard once again, the doorbell rang.

"Who the hell can that be?"

Without answering this pertinent question Desmonde went to the front door and opened it.

A young man stood there, bareheaded and smiling.

"I'm Joe Mullen, Father, sir, old Mrs. Mullen's grandson. She thought you might need a bit of a hand, getting in. With the bed, especial."

Desmonde held out his hand.

"Come in, Joe. I'm very glad to see you. It's the bed, of course."

He led the way to the front room where Joe looked at the bed and nodded.

"It's one of the old brigade, sir. I think I know its tricks."

He took off his jacket, revealing splendid arms, and took the backboard in both hands. One straining heave and it was up, tilted against the wall.

"If you'd just put your hand on that, sir, so it doesn't slip, I'll have the end piece up in no time at all."

As good as his word, Joe soon had the end piece up and arranged in position. Then, holding it up with one hand, he took the two side beams and slotted them into position back and front. The centre piece followed. And there the framework of the bed stood, awaiting the mattress, a huge affair that Joe expertly slung into position.

"There you are, sir. I think I'll leave the blankets and sheets to madam."

"Thank you, Joe, a million times. Now you must tell me what I owe you."

"Not a brass farthing, sir. The name of Fitzgerald is still honoured on the Quays. Besides, I'm not so ill off myself."

"What do you do, Joe?" asked Claire.

"I'm a professional footballer, Madam. Centre forward for the Dublin Harp. I get good money for that, then, since I'm free, afternoon and evening, except on Saturday, Mr. Besson has made me wine waiter in the lounge of the Hibernian."

"Mr. Besson?"

"He's the Swiss gentleman that bought the old Hib, and with his good Irish wife has made a wonderful place out of it, you wouldn't know it from the old Hib. Come in and see me there, both of you. There'll always be a glass of sherry for you on the house."

"Thank you, Joe," said Claire. "We will."

"Well now, I'll be off, wishing you both a good night's rest in that fine old Irish bed."

When Desmonde came back from showing Joe out, he looked at the bed, then at Claire.

"What a fine young man that is, so strong, so well built, and so polite."

"He certainly is, dear. And mighty handsome too."

In the kitchen, the eggs were hard boiled but, sliced with tomatoes and eaten with toast and coffee, they made a satisfactory meal.

"And now for bed, darling. I'm dead beat. We'll leave the dishes till tomorrow."

As they undressed and rolled into the cosy big bed, Claire breathed:

"Isn't this lovely, darling, the big bed, after dark woods and fusty railway coaches, so warm and cosy? Come to me, darling, please, please."

He came to her, knowing that twice in one day was a bad, sad practice, but unable to resist, and afterwards, hand in hand, they fell deeply into sleep.

Never, over many, many years, had this old Irish bed, that had witnessed so many lyings-in and so many layings out, never had it harboured such a strange and ill-assorted couple as this young man and woman who now lay upon its broad expanse fast asleep, still holding hands.

II

IT WAS EIGHT o'clock when Desmonde awoke from a good
night's sleep. After a moment he got up and rolled up the
blinds, letting a flood of sunlight into the room. Claire, one
eye open, lying there like an indolent cat, murmured sleepily:
"Come back, Des. It's so lovely, with all that sun."

"I would, Claire, but I have my appointment with Dr.
O'Hare this morning."

"Ah, yes. Well, get yourself a cup of coffee, love, and some
toast." As he pulled on his dressing gown and prepared to go,
she added: "While you're at it, dear, you might make it a
double order—'tis just as simple as one."

Five minutes later, he was back with a small tray on which
two cups of coffee steamed invitingly beside two slices of hot
buttered toast. Removing his own share of the breakfast to the
little dressing table, he handed in the tray to Claire, now
propped up on both pillows.

"Des, what a darling you are, I picked the right one when I
picked you. We really ought to make this a regular feature
every morning."

Sipping luxuriously in bed, she was silent, then after a
substantial bite at the toast she shook her head sadly: "Des,
darling, I have a confession to make to you and I had better
get it over with now, and have your absolution, rather than go
on worrying myself to death. Des, dear, I am no use whatsoever
in the kitchen. I can't cook, never have done, and as I have been
brought up as a lady . . ." He looked up quickly to see if she
was joking, but she was not, and went on with a kind of proud
sadness: "I have never put a finger in dish water or scrubbed a
dirty pot, in my entire life." Allowing this to sink in she continued: "So maybe your old Mrs. Mullen would give us a hand
or find us a scullery girl."

"We'll see what can be done, dear, when we're settled
in."

"If we want to eat, there's lots of good cheap little restaurants
just round the corner in O'Connell Street, that's to say if the
Hibernian is too expensive for you, dear Des."

"We'll see about that, too, dear. In the meantime I must be off."

"I do hope you get the job, Des. It's awful to have you hanging around here just doing nothing."

"And what do you propose to do this morning?"

"Oh, I'll just take a stroll up Grafton Street to look at the shops. By the way, love, have you just a little something for pocket money to see me around and so forth?"

"Certainly, darling, I'll just see to the dishes and get dressed first."

Desmonde took the breakfast dishes back to the kitchen and washed them with the left-over supper dishes. Mercifully there was hot water. The good Joe must have switched on the heater last night before he left. When he had dried the clean dishes Desmonde put them back in their places on the dresser shelf. He then shaved quickly before the miniature mirror hung over the sink and went back to the bedroom, where he dressed, then, unlocking his suitcase in the cupboard, he took ten pounds from his store of ready cash, not failing to look at his passbook, which showed a disquieting balance of eight hundred and sixty-two pounds. He now realized how much he had spent or given to charity of the three thousand inherited from his mother.

"I'm off, then, Claire dear. Will this serve you for the time being?"

She came out from cover of the sheet where she had been watching his every movement.

"What, oh, Des, 'tis you. Oh, yes, dear." Taking the money: "This will see me around for a bit. Now good luck to you, darling. I'll say a little prayer for you."

When he had gone she counted the notes, then snuggled down for another nap.

Desmonde walked to the end of the Quays, turned right and made his way up to Grafton Street, pleased to find himself again in the famous street, justifiably the pride of Dublin, and continued until he reached the corner affording a view of College Green. He had intended walking to Ballsbridge, but now a sudden exacerbation of the tiredness he had felt all morning made him decide to take a tram. He knew very well the reason of his fatigue, and decided that he must take the matter up, nicely and reasonably, with Claire.

A tram soon came round the bend and stopped at his signal.
Once seated inside Desmonde was again swept by nostalgia,
hurtful memories of his early boyhood, as the tram clanged its
way along this very route he had so often followed on his way to
school, feelings intensified as he descended from the tram at the
Ballsbridge terminus and walked through the public gardens to
St. Brendan's School.

Some late scholars, in the familiar green and black blazers,
were hurrying across the playground as he slowly followed
them to the entrance doorway. No need to ask for directions.
He well knew his way past the classrooms and along a private
corridor leading to an end door, on which he knocked discreetly. Voices within indicated that Dr. O'Hare was engaged,
so Desmonde seated himself on the bench outside. As a sup-
pliant he was well prepared to wait. In perhaps a quarter of an
hour the door was opened and a well dressed, officious looking
woman was shown out by the headmaster and escorted
courteously to the end of the corridor. Returning, Dr. O'Hare
saw Desmonde and silently beckoned him inside. Ensconced at
his desk, he indicated a chair and when Desmonde was seated
studied his visitor for a long, long time. Desmonde, too,
respectfully returned that look, shocked, almost, by the signs of
age on the headmaster's lined and sagging face.

"Well, Desmonde, I had your letter and perused it with deep
surprise and sadness. What, I wonder, would your dear father,
so honoured, so distinguished, have thought of it? In his old age
it would probably have killed him. Were you unhappy as a
young priest?"

"Far from it. I loved my work at Kilbarrack, but it was a
choice between behaving like an honourable man or leaving
a young woman of good family to suffer shame and dishonour
alone."

"So the girl was pregnant."

Desmonde inclined his head in silence.

"Well, now I see you in a better light, Desmonde. So now
you are married, a cast-off from the church, in straitened
circumstances and badly in need of work."

"As always, sir, you put the case with lucidity and a sense
of justice."

"Don't flatter me, Desmonde, or I shall have nothing to do
with you. Now listen, what can you offer me as a teacher?"

"I could teach Latin, French, Italian and even Spanish. I am fluent in these languages. And I believe I am reasonably good with the younger boys. I was quite successful with my First Communion and Confirmation classes at Kilbarrack."

"Just so," Dr. O'Hare reflected. "Well, Desmonde, I could take you on to teach Latin and French to the two lower forms. For the rest, you could help me in the office, correcting papers, helping me with my correspondence, filing, and so forth. The normal salary would be £20 a month, but because of our past pleasant association and because you are obviously in need, I would make it £25 a month."

"Oh, sir, I am so . . ." The headmaster held up his hand.

"All this, Desmonde, is on one condition. That I am now, and will so remain, completely ignorant of the circumstances of your life. You are simply an old, esteemed pupil who had come to me seeking employment."

"I . . . I think I understand, sir, and of course I agree."

"Yes, Desmonde, if it came to the ears of any of the parents that I had knowingly engaged a man with your reputation to teach their young children, I should be in a very difficult position—unless I could instantly disown you."

"I understand, sir. And I agree. There hasn't been a word here in Dublin, about . . . about Kilbarrack."

"Then you are engaged, Desmonde. As from tomorrow at nine o'clock. I repeat the terms. The normal salary would be £20 a month. Because I am truly grieved for you, I shall make it £25."

"Oh, thank you, sir. From my heart. You will see how I will serve you."

"Good, Desmonde. Now leave me. I have the sixth form in five minutes."

Desmonde left the school walking on air. He was saved. A regular position, one he would love, and a salary that would keep Claire and himself beyond all want.

He no longer felt tired, and stepped it out all the way to Dublin. Here he felt he must celebrate, and he stopped off at Bewley's for a large cup of coffee and two wheaten scones, each with a pat of fresh butter. He knew Bewley's coffee of old, quite unbeatable, so fragrant and strong, with a little pot of thick fresh cream to enrich it. It was heaven, although he did rather fancy one of the good looking pork pies his neighbour was biting into, but that was an expense and must come later. Afterwards he strolled to St. Stephen's Green and sat there on a bench in the sun amongst the students who usually passed the midday hour in that pleasant square of greenery in Dublin's busy heart.

He got back to the little house on the Quays, now known as 'home', at three o'clock. Claire had not yet returned, but almost at once the door bell rang. A smart van stood outside, and on the doorstep the driver, in a natty green uniform.

"Does Mrs. Donovan Fitzgerald reside here?"

Quite taken aback, Desmonde nevertheless answered in the affirmative.

"From Switzer's," said the man, placing two large, beautiful, beribboned boxes in Desmonde's arms. He then leaped into the van and was off.

Desmonde re-entered the house slowly, placed the two luxurious looking boxes on the living room table and studied them with mixed emotions, murmuring to himself with a questioning wonder: "Mrs. *Donovan* Fitzgerald."

He was not long in doubt. At four o'clock Claire dashed in, beautifully smart in her best clothes, and bursting with exhilaration and excitement as she flung her arms round him and exclaimed:

"Oh, darling, I've had such a wonderful time. Let's sit down and I'll tell you. Well, I went, naturally, to Switzer's in Grafton Street and spent a marvellous hour there. You've no idea what wonderful things they have there, regular Paris style, and better. Well, besides looking, I did a bit of shopping . . ."

"Is this it here?" he interrupted.

"Yes, darling, some of it. Two heavenly dresses, latest models, I just couldn't resist them. Of course I can't wear them now, darling, I'm really beginning to show, but after, you'll love me in them."

"But, Claire, these must have cost the earth. How did you manage to . . . ?"

"Very simple, darling, I told them I was Madame Donovan's niece and wanted to open an account. You've no idea, Madame's name is a password in Dublin. You should have seen them all round me bowing and scraping."

"But these things will have to be paid for."

"Ah, they don't send their bills for six months at Switzer's. especially to anyone with the name Donovan."

"I see you have adopted it."

She laughed. "Ah, what's the odds, darling, I'm entitled to it."

"Did that conclude your adventures?" he asked, after a pause.

"Not at all, not at all, by no means." She giggled. "Remembering Joe's invitation to the Hib I dropped over to the lounge and had the promised glass of sherry. Joe is a darling. He must have mentioned me to Mr. Maley, the manager, the nicest fellow you could hope to meet.

" 'Joe tells me you are niece to one of our most distinguished clients.'

" 'Yes,' I said. 'I am Mrs. Donovan Fitzgerald.'

"We shook hands.

" 'Are you lunching with us?'

" 'I had intended to,' says I, bold as brass. 'Unfortunately I find I have rushed out without my purse.'

" 'Oh, Madam, don't let that trouble you. I'll reserve your table now. And you may lunch *à la carte* as a guest of the hotel.'

"Well, Des, to cut a long story short, I had the best lunch ever, the lunch of a lifetime, *pâté de foie gras*, grilled salmon, strawberry mousse, and Irish coffee. Then, bowed out with smiles. So here I am, darling, back home and dying for a pee-wee, I must rush. Will you get us a cup of tea, Des, while I'm occupied in the bathroom?"

When she had gone to execute this laudable performance, Desmonde went slowly in to the kitchen to make the tea. She had not once asked him if he had succeeded in his interview with Dr. O'Hare. Now, for the first time, he realized the folly of his marriage and was struck, as by a blow, with the premonition of disaster.

III

APART FROM THE monthly salary, itself a life saving asset, Desmonde was happy in his new position, and as the weeks and months passed he became accepted and, always good with young children, liked at the school. He did not see much of his colleagues, since when out of the class room Dr. O'Hare kept him busy in the office, often after school hours, and, observing the new master's efforts to please, had come to take an interest in Desmonde, suggesting that later on he might study for his Ph.D.

Claire, too, in her own fashion, welcomed and approved Desmonde's bread-winning effort.

"It'll be a blessing, Des, not to have you hanging around the house, like a sick dog, when I'm out and about in the town."

Claire, however, was less out and about the town than before, since she was now most perceptibly pregnant and approaching the date of her delivery. Desmonde's wish that her confinement should take place in the Mater Misericordia Hospital had been brusquely negatived.

"I want none of that Convent Miserarium."

"But the Mater has a worldwide reputation, Claire. My friend Alec took his obstetric training there."

"It may be all right for the students, Des. But for the patients—stand outside and hear the screams. I want no nuns hanging around, flinging Holy Water at me. I've had a good long talk with old Mrs. Mullen. She's brought many a child into the world and she'll bring ours."

Desmonde, naturally, was constrained to acquiesce, doubtfully, yet impressed by Claire's hardihood. He had a talk later on with his father's old housekeeper which did partly reassure him. And indeed, when the event did take place, everything passed off with the greatest ease and facility. Desmonde, who had spent no more than an hour pacing anxiously outside, was called in by Mrs. Mullen, truly official in a large starched white overall, to be presented with a lovely baby daughter, all warm and cosy from the soapsuds, her dark eyes, as she lay in his arms, bent upon him in tender wonderment. Claire, surveying this touching scene from her position of leisured indolence in bed, exclaimed:

"Did I do well for you, Des?"

"Wonderfully, thank you, dear, dear Claire. A lovely child, with your lovely dark eyes."

"Thank you, Des, dear. I'll remember these kind words when we have our next set-to."

"I hope it was not too hard for you, dear."

Here the old lady professionally intervened.

"I tell ye, sir, in all truth and honesty, I never had such a patient in all my life. She bore down hard without a scream, and when the baby came out, that's the worst bit, sir, she no more than uttered a little whimper. And I tell ye this, for I'm sure it's of interest to ye, there's not a cut, not so much as a scratch on her dear little you-know-what. 'Tis as fresh and good as ever 'twas."

The old woman was in her best form, and when she had done everything to her satisfaction, she smiled at Desmonde.

"That's the lot, sir. Mother tidied up, baby washed and asleep, the little crib set up there by your bed, all ready for her, the mother comfortable in bed and half asleep, so I'll be off, till first thing tomorrow morning."

"Good night, and thank you, Mrs. Mullen," said Claire. "You're a darling."

Desmonde followed the old woman into the passage, put his arms round her, and kissed her withered cheek.

"Dear, dear Mrs. Mullen, you're an angel, and have made us all so happy with your goodness and skill. Money can never repay you, but please tell me your fee."

"A couple of pounds is the usual, sir. But from you I'll take one."

Desmonde felt the ready tear spring to his eye. He took from his pocket the two five pounds he had removed from his store in the cupboard and silently handed them to her.

"Oh, I couldn't, sir, indeed I couldn't . . ."

"You must, I insist, after all you've done, borrowing the crib for us, and everything."

"Well, sir . . . I'll take one, and thank ye kindly, but no more." And she tucked one of the notes into Desmonde's breast pocket. "And now, good night. I'll be round first thing in the morning." On the doorstep she turned. "'Twould have been a happy moment for your dear honoured father if he could see his lovely granddaughter, just her alone, and no more."

Desmonde went into the bathroom and got ready for bed. As he climbed in beside Claire he whispered:

"Are you asleep, darling? If not, I want to tell you how happy you have made me. I feel that baby will draw us closer together, close the little gap that seems to have sprung up between us."

"And who made that little gap? And what would any wife think of a husband that walks in one night and tells her straight he doesn't want her six nights in the week?"

"It was stupid and tactless of me, Claire. I love to love you. But I'm like a bit of chewed string if I get too much of it."

"There's some men can't get enough of it. But there's still a lot of the priest in you, Des. Well, now that I'm in milk and *safe*, I'll maybe see more of you." She kissed him, adding: "If baby wakes in the night, get up and bring her in to me."

Almost immediately she was asleep, and soon Desmonde followed her, clinging to her soft warm body.

IV

AND NOW, ON Saturdays and Sundays, when the weather was fine, the little family might be seen taking the air, along the Quays across the bridge, even as far as Phoenix Park, Claire beautifully turned out in one of the new Switzer dresses, the baby in the handsome pram her father had bought for her, and, of course, Desmonde, enjoying the admiring glances directed towards his equipage. Claire had taken advantage of this happy interim to present Desmonde with the bill for the dresses, some sixty odd pounds, sent again with a threatening letter. He could not protest, particularly when she, alone, had attended to the difficult matter of the child's christening.

"You wouldn't want to do it, Des?"

He hesitated. "But it must be done."

"Give me the marriage lines the Canon gave you and I'll see to it Sunday at the Carmelite. There's always a crowd lined up there after the eleven o'clock. You're still agreed on the name Geraldine?"

Claire had insisted on this, as a propitiation to her aunt whom she still hoped to win round, with the help of the lovely child.

So Claire had set off while Desmonde waited in an agony of pained suspense, dispelled when Claire reappeared, smiling broadly.

"All over, lad. The little one's a Christian now, God bless her."

It was then she presented him with the Switzer bill. Yes, Desmonde was happy, at least happy as one might be in his invidious position. His teaching at St. Brendan's had saved him from at least the worst of his remorse, and when this did at times torment him, when he was alone, he would cry: 'You threw me out like a rotten apple. Why should I come back to You?'

His better relations with Claire were enhanced by the help he gave her with baby Geraldine. Every evening when he returned from school he would bathe, dry and powder the little one and make her comfortable with a fresh napkin for the night. On Saturdays and Sundays he was exclusively the baby's nurse, rewarded now with a smile of loving recognition that warmed his heart.

One day when he was so occupied, while Claire sat reading the morning paper, she remarked idly:

"What's a note of hand, Des?"

"A bit of paper, some sort of agreement that you sign with your own hand."

"Is that all there is to it?" She laughed, and laid aside the paper to watch him powder and re-diaper the babe. "You've a real way with her, Des, you handle her a treat. And she loves you now, you can see it in her eyes."

Desmonde smiled. "Are you about ready for our promenade now?"

"I'll just go and change my dress. It's a pity we can't all go out for lunch somewhere, we would be the admiration of the Hib!"

"She's a bit young for that yet, darling."

"Ah, yes, of course. But speaking of lunch at the Hib, Des, didn't you promise to take me for a slap-up celebration when I had stopped being a milk bar!"

"I did indeed, Claire dear, and I'll not fail to keep my word. How about next Saturday? We'll get Mrs. Mullen to look after Gerry."

"It's a date, Des. And I'll want it with all the trimmings. Saturday's the best day at the Hib. All the gang's there."

For the next few days, the prospect of the coming luncheon was never far from Claire's mind. Never failing to remind

Desmonde of his promise, and preparing herself, in her own ways, for the celebration, she departed on unknown missions several times during the week, returning with sundry parcels that caused Desmonde to wonder how much money had been expended on these apparent luxuries, and what might be the source of such unsuspected wealth. However, he refrained from pressing the matter, anxious to preserve the benign harmony that now lay like a sweet melody upon the house.

Now that Claire was lactating and self-declared to be 'safe', Desmonde was induced, more or less by Royal Command, to perform his marital duties more frequently than before.

"You really are a great lover," Claire complimented him after one strenuous performance. "I don't want to swell your head, darling, but you leave a woman satisfied and fulfilled. There's some, God knows, that leave you up in the air, waiting for what you haven't got. But you're the goods. I knew that the first time I had you in Kilbarrack Wood."

"That was a short and," he added quickly, "sweet event."

"I've no time for them that drags it out, darlin', like layin' down a cigar and goin' back to it. Besides, 'tis a sinful perversion in the eyes of the Church. No, no, I'll take your way, lad, you've got *poon tang*."

"I'm always afraid of hurting your breasts," Desmonde murmured, in an effort, perhaps, to get off the hook. "They must be full and tender, darling."

"They are, darling, and it's sweet of you to think of it. So next time why don't you just go in from behind? There's them that tell me it's even better."

Accordingly, two nights later, suitably exhorted, Desmonde, although trying to postpone the event, did as he was bid, but all the time haunted by a horrid recollection of two mongrels he had once disgustedly observed performing in identical fashion in the main street of Kilbarrack.

At last Saturday dawned, faintly grey, yet full of the promise of sunshine. While Desmonde made coffee and attended to Gerry's needs, a task in which he was now skilful, Claire rested in bed, rising at eleven to prepare herself for the pleasures of the day. Meanwhile, Desmonde had dressed himself and visited Mrs. Mullen, who promised to look after the baby that afternoon.

At twenty minutes after noon Claire strolled into the living room and struck an attitude, inviting Desmonde's admiration. She was wearing a smart green dress he had not seen before, new green gloves and a large flashy green hat, also new.

"How, Des?"

"Stunning," he murmured sadly. "You look like a very expensive French tart out for the kill."

She laughed. "I like that, Des. I just came into a little money unexpectedly and thought I'd go the limit. Today, especial, I want to attract attention. There's some of the fellows up there at the Hib think I don't have a husband. Did you order a cab?"

"It's such a lovely day I thought we'd just walk up."

"All right, penny pincher. At least we'll give the neighbours a treat."

They set off, arm in arm, when Mrs. Mullen appeared, followed by the old lady's shocked and sorrowful gaze. At one o'clock precisely they strolled into the hotel and through the lounge to the dining room. Here, the head waiter obsequiously bore down upon Claire.

"Have you a nice table for us, Jules?"

"The best, madam. Your usual, by the window." And he conducted them thereto and seated them, whispering: "May I tell madam how ravishing she is looking today?"

"None of your blarney, Jules dear. What have you got to eat for us? And we'll want a bottle of Perrier Jouet. This is a delayed wedding celebration. Meet my husband, Desmonde."

"Oh, I am pleased to know you, sir. Will you choose?" He produced two large elaborately ornate menu cards, offering one to Claire, the other to Desmonde. "Now, if you'll excuse me, I'll go and instruct the wine waiter as to your champagne."

Eventually a choice meal was ordered, the champagne opened, sampled and served. Meanwhile Claire surveyed the long room, commenting upon the various personalities she recognized. Her own attire and affected mannerisms were certainly attracting attention, looks, whispers, suppressed laughter, that seemed equally inspired by Desmonde. A quietly dressed man in a dark business suit, lunching alone at the adjoining table, had several times encountered Claire's smiling glances and now, inclining towards her politely, he said:

"Forgive me, dear lady, but from the proximity of our tables I have gathered, without seeking to do so, that I am in the presence of a happy wedding celebration."

"It is indeed, sir," replied Claire, delighted at last to have someone to talk to. "And long delayed through the remarkable circumstances of our love and marriage. Would you take a drop of champagne to celebrate with us?"

"I must not drink at luncheon, since Saturday is a very busy day, but, dear madam, if you would allow me one little sip from your own glass . . ."

Willingly, Claire proffered her glass to which the stranger barely applied his lips.

"You were speaking, dear madam, of difficult circumstances."

"I was indeed, sir. Would you believe it, looking at him now, so gay and happy, that my darling husband was once . . . ?"

Desmonde pressed her arm and tried to turn her towards him, but she shook him off.

". . . once a young and much beloved priest at Kilbarrack?"

"Don't tell me, dear madam, that he is the famous Kilbarrack curate everybody has been looking for over the best part of two years, and that you, dear lady, must therefore be the niece of our own Madame Donovan?"

"For God's sake shut up, Claire," Desmonde groaned.

But Claire was now fully wound up.

"You hit the nail on the head both times, sir. But that's not all the story by a long chop. Desmonde darling, keep your feet out of the way, you're hitting me with them all over. I could tell you, sir, of the difficulties of our courtship, both of us madly in love. I thought I would never get him, until one lovely starry night I made after him in the lovely woods of Kilbarrack."

"Waiter, the bill!" Desmonde called wildly. But the waiter, with arms folded, his back turned, and listening hard, would not have missed this for a five pound note.

"Yes sir, the lovely woods of Kilbarrack, where he used to stroll of an evening. And there indeed we consummated our love with such unrestrained passion that, while I caught Desmonde, I was caught too."

"Oh, God! Shut up, you drunken fool," Desmonde hissed into her ear.

"Pregnant, dear lady?" This from the benign stranger.

"You have it in a word, sir. And at the first go, showing the depth and strength of our love."

"Oh dear, oh dear," sighed the kindly gentleman. "And that's where your troubles began."

"You've said it, sir. But I had picked the right one. This handsome, brilliant young priest, fresh and famous from Rome, walked out of the Church and made me his dear wife."

"True nobility, dear lady. And how did your aunt, dear Madame Donovan, take the news?"

"Like one of the furies of hell, sir. For just to whisper in your ear, she was madly in love with Des herself. Des, for God's sake stop kickin' me. And what's Joe doin' there making faces at us like a madman?"

"Just one little point more, dear lady. How did you adjust yourself to the non-sacerdotal life?"

"Just to perfection, sir. We have the loveliest little baby in all the world, called Geraldine after my aunt, a comfortable house on the Quays near where Desmonde's very famous dad used to live, while my brave bold husband has got himself a splendid position . . ."

"Be quiet, Claire, you damned idiot," Desmonde hissed in her ear. "Stop it at once."

". . . splendid position," Claire continued blandly, "teaching languages at St. Brendan's School."

"Madam, I am overcome with admiration."

Desmonde leaned across his wife and interposed furiously.

"Sir, I'm afraid my wife and I are somewhat exalted. Perhaps on another occasion."

"In point of fact, sir," he looked at his watch, "the pleasure of listening to you has kept me late, very late, for my office. But you must permit me. A little belated wedding gift, and a small honorarium in acknowledgement of the wonderful information you have freely given."

He signalled to the waiter and asked for both bills, his own and that of the adjoining table. Both were brought and quickly signed by the generous gentleman. He then stood up.

"Again, thank you madam, for a truly remarkable and most fortunate experience. No need to wish you well. I foresee for you a sensational career. As you for, sir," he offered Desmonde his hand, "you have my sincere and profound sympathy." Turning away, he added: "I have added the tip to the bill."

He swung round and made his way quickly to the door. Immediately, Joe approached their table. He was in his waiter's uniform and had obviously just come on duty.

"Hello, hello, Joe." Claire chuckled. "Come and drink our healths in champagne."

"I never touch the stuff, madam, and if I may say so in the presence of your husband, you've had a damn sight too much of it today." He turned to Desmonde. "Didn't you see me give you the warning to shut her up?"

"He must have, Joe dear. He near kicked the shoes off me."

"Well, I'll tell you straight now, madam. That gentleman that was pumping you is the head editor of the *Sunday Chronicle*. And every word you told him, multiplied by ten, will be in the paper tomorrow."

"Good God, Joe!"

"You may well say it, sir. You'll find yourself bang on the front page tomorrow."

Claire gave way to fits of delighted laughter.

"I've made you famous at last, Des darling. Am I not a darling wife?"

In the effort to refill her glass she upset the bottle, flooding the table with the last of the champagne.

"Don't you think, sir, if I gave you a hand with her and got her into a cab? She'll begin to sing in a minute."

With Joe's help Desmonde got his darling wife on her feet, and taking one arm firmly, while Joe took the other, made an erratic progress towards the door, during which Claire bestowed her proudly smiling glances all around. But all was not yet over.

As they came to the entrance steps two photographers were waiting upon them, with flash bulbs and clicking cameras. But at last they got her into a taxi. On the way home she did indeed begin to sing, maudlin rubbish, clasping him to her the while in voluptuous embrace. And he had a horrid feeling that another taxi was following them.

At last they were in the seclusion of their little house where the good Mrs. Mullen sat awaiting them.

"For God's sake get her to bed," Desmonde cried, releasing

her so that she fell, in all her absurd finery, spreadeagled on the sofa. "I've had enough! And I'll stand no more of it from her, the drunken bitch."

He turned and walked out of the house, turning inevitably to his usual retreat, to the quiet and solitude of Phoenix Park. He knew that he must free himself from her. And that without delay.

V

DESMONDE DID NOT leave the park until evening, almost closing time. As he walked slowly back to his house it seemed that more than the usual weekend promenaders were on the Quays. And Mrs. Mullen in her best shawl was pacing up and down on the pavement as though awaiting him.

"I'm glad you're back, sir. There's been a regular commotion around here. Have ye seen the papers? An early special edition of the *Chronicle*."

"No, I haven't."

"Well, ye may do so now. A fellow from the *Chronicle* office just opened your door and flung in a copy."

"Bad news?"

"The worst, sir. Oh, God, I'm heart sick and sorry for ye. Me that lived to serve your honoured father. And held you in my arms as a child."

"Oh, well! I'll go in and look. Have you seen to baby?"

"I have indeed, sir. She's had her bottle and is all bathed, tidied up, and asleep in her cot." She paused. "Madam's in the bed too, snoring her head off."

"Thank you, Mrs. Mullen, from my heart. What in all the world would I do without you?"

He went into the house, locked the door and picked up the paper lying on the rug. In the living room he switched on the light and opened the paper, shocked instantly, appalled and horrified by the banner headlines screaming from the front page.

'RUNAWAY PRIEST FINALLY HUNTED DOWN

'The handsome young ex-cleric all Ireland has been seeking, found at last luxuriating with his would-be fashionable over-dressed lady wife, lunching in state . . . Salmon and champagne . . . postponed wedding celebration . . . As the champagne flowed in Madam's direction, we had the story in full from her sweet painted lips . . . "I wanted him from the first moment I set eyes on him," she burbled, ". . . a sweet schoolgirl from my exclusive Swiss finishing school . . . My dear Aunt, famous Madame Donovan, had for some time been after him also . . . Indeed, on my unexpected return from school I caught her with arms around him in a passionate embrace." '

Desmonde closed his eyes in agony. But he forced himself to read on, shrinking from the block headlines of every para-graph.

'Tennis *à deux* . . . walks in the lovely woods . . . already he was mine . . . saw it in his eyes. The first kiss . . . But alas his sacred office . . . Adored by all the parish . . . Certain advancement promised by the Archbishop. Would he be promoted from the parish? I shivered at the thought. It was now or never . . . knew he went walking at night . . . fighting down his passionate love . . . Caught him in those same lovely woods! And there on the green sward under the stars, I made him mine!'

Desmonde could not continue. He felt physically sick, but even as he put the rag away from him his anguished eye caught two more headlines:

'Pregnancy shyly confessed to him in the Confessional . . . He stood by me. Love conquered all.'

And the photographs, emphasizing her drunken stagger as they left the hotel. And worse was to follow:

'Now living at No. 29 the Quays, masquerading as lan-guage master at the select St. Brendan's School, this son of a famous Irish father, striving desperately to regain his self-respect, has succeeded in passing himself off as a clean young bachelor . . .'

It was the final blow. Desmonde lay back on the couch, overcome by shame, disgust and blind rage.

His marriage had, from the first, been a tragic mistake into which his own folly had forced him. He had used every effort in adjustment and propitiation to make a success of it. And he had failed. He could not continue, indeed, it was now only too apparent that Claire was tired of him, that while he had certainly not been the first man to possess her, he would be, sooner or later, superseded by another, richer or more attractive than himself.

These were his thoughts as the sounds of slow movements in the bedroom, followed by dragging footsteps and the opening of the inner door, caused him to look round. Claire stood there, a loose dressing gown flung over her nightdress, slippers on her bare feet. She scuffed to the sofa and sat down.

"Get me a cup of tea."

He had resolved, above all else, to keep his temper. He handed her the paper.

"Wouldn't you like to read this first?"

She glanced at the news-sheet with befogged vision until the headlines caught her eye. Then she began to read, mouthing the words to herself.

Meanwhile he went into the kitchen and made her a cup of tea. Continuing to read, she slobbered this down, still half asleep, still not quite free of the alcohol in her blood.

"Well," she said at last, "I've put you on the front page, Des."

"By making a drunken exhibition of yourself, and of me. I shall most certainly be kicked out of the school on Monday, and I'll never, never get another decent job in Dublin. I'll be out on the streets without a penny to support you and our child." He paused, continuing in a controlled voice. "Don't you think, Claire, that it's time we called a halt in our marriage? Take Gerry to your aunt and stay there for a while until we see how things are with us."

"So you're sick of me. Well, Des, I'm just as sick of you. You're a dull fellow to live with and, to speak the truth, you're no longer much good in bed. There's others could lick you at that job. You never take me to the movies, but keep nagging me to go walking in Phoenix Park. And I'm sick to death of the kind of life you've brought me down to, this little slum flat, me that's used to living like a lady with servants and all. Not to speak of an empty purse when I go shopping, so I have to get everything on tick. For weeks now I've had the idea to go back to my aunt with Gerry. We'll be welcome there."

Desmonde took her hand.

"I'm truly sorry to have been such a failure, Claire. Yet I'm relieved in a way, it makes my suggestion that we separate for a while more reasonable."

"Oh, shut up your talking, Des. You're full of words. I'm just as ready for a change as you, and I'm glad we can do it without a fight. Now go in the kitchen and cook me a bit of supper. Lunch is long gone and I'm half starved. Can you do me some rashers and a couple of eggs?"

"I believe that's about all that's left," he said, getting up.

He hesitated. An hour ago he would have refused to serve her, but now, with the prospect of an amicable parting in sight, he thought it better to obey.

"Fry some bread with them, I'll stretch for a bit, I'm still a bit woosey."

The larder was indeed bare, only the bacon, a couple of eggs and a stale loaf remained, but he fulfilled the order, reserving two strips of bacon to make a sandwich for himself. He had eaten nothing since his morning coffee and toast.

"I've made a good cook out of you, Des," she commented, using a crust to polish the plate. "Before I had to do with you, you could scarce boil an egg. Ah, I feel better now. But would you mind giving baby her bottle tonight? Everything's there in the cupboard. I'll have so much to do to-morrow I'll just toddle back to bed."

When she had gone Desmonde set about preparing the child's feed, an operation to which he was now accustomed. Later, with the little one on his knees, gurgling at her bottle yet watching him always with her dark, wide open, loving eyes, he felt an immense sadness sweep over him. He loved the child and would miss her dreadfully. Yet it was better she should go to Madame Donovan, who, whatever her feelings towards him, would ensure that she was properly

G

cared for. Yet this must be no more than a temporary expedient. When he had picked himself up and restored his position in life, he would claim her again.

The feed over, he changed her napkin and tucked her in her cot. Mamma was already giving tongue in measured snores that indicated she was again asleep.

Desmonde returned to the living room, arranged a make-shift bed for himself on the couch and, having removed his suit, lay down in his underclothes. The prospect of facing Dr. O'Hare bore heavily upon him, but at last he fell asleep.

VI

ON MONDAY MORNING Desmonde awoke feeling rested and refreshed, but excessively hungry. He had eaten almost nothing over the weekend. He got up, made tea and break-fasted on a jagged slice of the remaining loaf, supported by two strong cups of tea. He then went through to the bathroom, washed and shaved with extreme care and returned quietly to the living room, where he brushed his suit and dressed. Nothing was stirring in the bedroom as he let himself out of the house and set out on the long walk to the school.

He walked slowly, since he was early, trying to avert his thoughts from the interview with Dr. O'Hare that must surely lie ahead. And once again he was swept by an over-whelming impulse to pray, to implore help from Heaven, for some Divine act of intervention that might save him. Once again he resisted it.

And now he was at the school, some little boys from his class, lifting their caps, waving and smiling to him as they walked on ahead to the class room. Some moments later he was about to follow them, when at the doorway one of the head boys of the school, a sixth-former, held up his hand.

"You are not to go in, sir. Dr. O'Hare's orders. He wishes to see you in his study immediately."

Desmonde's heart sank. He stood there, looking at the boy, who averted his eyes, then, without a word, turned abjectly away and walked slowly to the headmaster's room. He knocked and was immediately bidden to enter. He obeyed.

Dr. O'Hare was seated at his desk facing two women, both overdressed in their Sunday clothes, both armed with rolled umbrellas and an expression of outraged propriety.

"Mr. Fitzgerald," Dr. O'Hare began, without delay, "these two ladies, each mother of a boy in your class, have startled and shocked me with a horrifying story that apparently appeared yesterday in the *Sunday Chronicle*, a paper that I myself never read. Fitzgerald, answer me truthfully, were you at one time a priest in the parish of Kilbarrack? Did you seduce a young girl in your congregation, and when she was with child, marry her and leave the Church?"

"I did, sir."

"Then why in the name of heaven did you not reveal this when I engaged you?"

A pause, whispers between the women: "I was sure the good doctor didn't know nothing."

"Well, sir," Desmonde said, slowly, painfully, "I was afraid that if I told you, you might not take me on."

"We was sure, doctor, that you never had the least suspicion," said one of the women. "But now?"

"Yes, now, madam. Fitzgerald, I am obliged to tell you that your position in this school is now terminated. You will leave instantly without returning to your classroom. Here is your salary paid until the end of the month."

Desmond took the envelope held out towards him, stood for a moment in silent anguish, then said, in a muted voice:

"I'm truly sorry, sir, to have caused you this distress, and I thank you for all your kindness to me." He half turned. "As for you, ladies, may I congratulate you on your charitable efforts, which have effectively destroyed my one chance to redeem and regenerate myself. The children in my class had nothing but good from me, and I believe they loved me."

He then turned and went out, closing the door quietly, then, slowly and sadly, set out for the house on the Quays. No longer could he think of it as home, so sickeningly was it identified with his misery and ruin.

When he reached the Quays it was almost eleven o'clock, and the inevitable Mrs. Mullen, harbinger of good or, more frequently, of evil, was walking up and down in some distress outside the house.

"Oh, I'm glad to see you back, sir. The lady has gone out, all dolled up, and she's locked the door. Now I hear the baby crying pitiful and I can't get in."

"Thank you, Mrs. Mullen. I have the key. I'll go in and see to the child."

He opened the door and went in. When the child saw him it muted its cries to a little whimper. Quickly he set to and, since there was no milk in the cupboard, heated some of the prepared cereal that the baby seemed to prefer to the milk, and when it was ready he fed her with tiny spoonfuls until she was satisfied. Then he must change the napkin. He lifted her from her cot and carried her to the living room, where the better light from the large windows would enable him to see what he was doing in this complex operation.

He had barely removed the soiled diaper and begun to clean the little soiled bottom when the door bell rang. He thought, with relief, that Mrs. Mullen had come to his aid, and called:

"Come in!"

But it was not his friendly neighbour who entered. There, in the doorway, stood Mrs. O'Brien and the Canon.

"May we come in, Desmonde? Mrs. O'B. and I are in town buying some fine linens for the new altar rails. And we couldn't go back without giving you a call."

"Please come in," Desmonde said faintly. "As you see, I'm rather busy at the moment."

"Enjoying the pleasures of a father," said the Canon, as the baby, naked and unattended, began to howl in misery.

"Let me, please, Desmonde. Please, where is the bathroom? Through there?" Quickly Mrs. O'Brien stepped forward, lifted the child, whipped the obscene napkin from the table and disappeared. The Canon then came in and closed the door, sat down, and in silence viewed the stale end of loaf, the half empty pot of cheap jam and the dirty tea cup.

"Well, lad," he said at last, "I see you're not only in the headlines, all over Ireland, but at home, by the look of it, you're on the verge of starvation. You're pale, thin, hollow cheeked, a miserable shadow of what ye were when I had the pleasure of knowing ye. But then ye have the recompense and all the joys of a faithful loving wife. We spotted her at the Hib on our way out, in the lounge at an early drink, lookin' like the Queen o' Sheba, with three of the flashiest young toughs ye'd ever meet at the Baldoyle Races."

Desmonde remained silent.

"'Tis wonderful, of course, the true nobility of sacrifice for love. To abandon your religion, your vocation, your splendid standing and propriety in the church, in fact everything, all for the sake of some sexy little bitch that got round you in a weak moment in the dark. Are you still proud of it? Or, now, do you think it was folly?"

Desmonde did not raise his head.

"Not folly," he muttered. "Madness. And how savagely I have been punished."

"If only, when ye felt the need of a bit of lovin', why did ye not turn to Madame? She was completely gone on you, head over heels. Then, when the first flurry was over, ye could have settled down quietly, in loving friendship, and nobody a bit the wiser. After all, didn't some of our best Popes have their women, in the good old days? But no, you chose to play the gentleman, the hero, all for a worthless little bitch who has dragged you down to her own level, to the gutter, and will now, sure as God's in Heaven, give you the soldier's farewell." Desmonde remained silent. The Canon continued: "A true daughter of her mother, who left a decent husband to run off with a worthless scamp who had his will of her for a few months, all over Europe, then left her without a penny, in the middle of nowhere." He paused. "She threw herself under a train in Bregenz station."

A long silence followed, then the Canon exclaimed with a sigh so deep it was almost a groan:

"If only ye were back in Kilbarrack with me, lad. Just up from your own good Mass, or from teaching your little Communion class, and were sat down at the table and I was slashing the carver into a lovely leg o' lamb, all crisp with cracklin', cooked to a turn by Mrs. O'B., and you were due for a quiet afternoon stroll to Mount Vernon for tea and music with Madame, and the Archbishop had just sent me a letter full of your praises . . . making me as proud as if ye were my own son . . . Oh, God, it fair breaks my heart to think of it . . ."

He broke off. A long pained silence followed, broken only when Mrs. O'Brien came back into the room.

"Well now," she said cheerfully, "Baby's all cleaned up and washed and is cosy in her cot, almost asleep."

Abruptly the Canon stood up.

"Then we'll be off, Mrs. O'B. There's no more for us to do here. The mischief is done and canna' be undone. Goodbye, Desmonde dear, and God succour you." He made the sign of the Cross over the bowed figure at the table and turned to the door.

"Goodbye, dear Desmonde," murmured Mrs. O'Brien. "I pray for you every night and will never forget you."

When they had gone Desmonde made an effort to throw off the misery into which the Canon's melancholy soliloquy had plunged him. He got up and went into the bedroom, where the little one, freshly bathed and neatly tucked into her cot, was fast asleep. The room had been tidied and the bed properly made up, something of a novelty, since the sheets were usually flung back in a tangled bunch. The bathroom, too, had been cleaned, the towels straightened out, the soap and sponge retrieved from the bottom of the bath, and correctly placed in the wash basin. And there, on the little shelf above the basin, tucked in beneath a tube of toothpaste, was a brand new five pound note.

This was the last straw, the final touch of loving pity and compassion, that broke through Desmonde's self-imposed restraint. He returned to the living room, sat down at the table, put his head in his hands and wept, bitterly, bitterly, he wept.

At last he pulled himself together and forced himself to think of the future. The envelope from Dr. O'Hare contained twenty-five pounds. His reserve of fifty pounds, carefully preserved in his suitcase, and the five pounds from Mrs. O'Brien, made altogether a total of eighty pounds. The rent of the house was paid until the end of the year. At least he was not insolvent. He unlocked the suitcase, put the twenty-five pounds in the pocket of the lining with the original fifty, locked the case, and with the five pound note in his pocket went out, and along the street to pay the grocery bill.

"I was afraid ye had forgotten it, sir," remarked the shopkeeper, when the note was placed on the counter. "Let's see, now. You have seventeen and ninepence coming back to you. Shall I send the morning milk round to you again?"

"If you please. And some of these apples you have over there. I'm sorry for the delay."

"No harm done, sir. Whatever they may say of ye, the name o' Fitzgerald is good enough for me. Let me give you one of the apples, on the house. They're the first of the season's Cox's."

With the apple and seventeen and ninepence in his pocket Desmonde left the shop and went home, relieved, on his arrival, to find Mrs. Mullen in the house.

"I thought you might be needing a bit of a hand, sir. You've had lots of callers. Can I do anything?"

"If you would keep an eye on baby, Mrs. Mullen, I'd like to go out for a couple of hours. I'll give you the key of the house."

"Ay, sir, go and get some fresh air to yourself. For in God's truth ye're not lookin' at all well."

Desmonde handed over the key and went out, with a strange sense of escape, as he slowly set out for his inevitable resort where, as a boy, he had so often walked with his father.

The afternoon was fresh and fair, the park deserted and, though he felt he should walk, he soon was seated in his usual secluded corner, with trees around and the songs of the birds to soothe him. He ate the apple, skin and all, threw the core to some friendly sparrows, lay back and closed his eyes. Soon he was asleep.

VII

IT WAS NOT a lazy sleep but, so poor was Desmonde's physical state, a sleep of sheer exhaustion, a benign blackout that lasted a full three hours. Twilight was falling as he awoke and hurried to the park gates, lest he be shut in for the night. Then, at a more moderate pace, he started on the return journey to the Quays and reality. He felt better, and better able to face whatever lay in store for him.

As he approached his house he saw that Mrs. Mullen was again on patrol, now always a presage of evil. She half ran to meet him.

"Oh, God, sir, thank God you're back. I've been at my

wits' end. What's happened wouldn't bear repeating." She paused to catch her breath. "Just after ye'd gone your lady came back in a flash little car, driven by a flash lookin' man. Into the house she swept, and in no time at all she was out again with her luggage, then in again for a longer time, then out with more things, and baby, wrapped in a blanket. Into the car they crowded with everything in the boot o' the car, or packed in the seat behind them.

"'Where are ye off to, madam?' I ventured to call.

"'To Cobh Pier,' she called back, tipsy like. 'And to hell with you, and the rest of you, old bloody Mullen.'

"So off they went with a blare o' the horn." Again she paused. "I've had a look in the house, sir. It's like all the Furies of Hell were let loose in it."

Desmonde entered the house. The living-room looked a shambles—the table upset, chairs turned over, cutlery and china strewn on the floor. In the bedroom the crib was lying on its edge, blankets and sheets in a twisted knot upon the floor, and, on the chest of drawers, his two prized little pictures, the Bartolommeo Annunciation and the photograph of his mother, were totally destroyed, smashed, no doubt, on the hard edge of the chest, the glass broken, frames bent and twisted, the pictures pierced and torn beyond repair.

Desmonde sat down on the mattress and silently viewed the damage, such an expression of wanton rage and actual hatred that his heart sank within him, in bitterness and pain. Suddenly a thought struck him. He jumped up, ran into the living room and flung open the cupboard door.

His suitcase was still there, but the lock had been forced and hung limp and useless. He dropped to his knees and lifted the lid. His money was gone, gone to the last pound note. She had finished as she had begun, with unutterable selfishness and inherent unfaithfulness. She had cleaned him out.

He was still on his knees and motionless, a petrified figure, when Mrs. Mullen came into the room.

"Do get up, sir," she said soothingly. "I'll send Joe in to clear up the mess. He'll soon put things to right."

He permitted her to raise him, and to lead him to a chair, which she set back squarely on its four legs. There he sat, an acrid bitterness in his mouth and a chill sense of fear in his heart. No longer a priest, a schoolmaster sacked in disgrace, he had exactly seventeen shillings and ninepence between himself and starvation.

A voice roused him:

"Don't take on, sir. I'll have everything straight for you in no time."

Joe had come in and, in his shirt sleeves, had begun the work of restoring decency and order. Desmonde simply sat there in a state of dazed inertia. But when Joe had finished and both rooms had resumed their normal shape and form, he motioned Joe to sit near him.

"Thank you, Joe, from my heart. I can't understand why you and your grandmother are so kind to me. I'm not worth it."

"You are worth it, sir. And we're truly sorry for you. Besides, we remember that your father was very good to us. When my widowed mother died he bought our house for us so that Gran should always have a roof over her head."

Desmonde was silent. Always his father's virtue, distinction and nobility returned to confound him, and now more so than ever.

"I would love to give you something myself, Joe. But I am absolutely and completely broke."

"I thought she would skin you to the bone, sir. We waiters at the Hib see and hear more than you would ever guess. We summed her up as a right bad lot!" He paused. "Now that you're up against it, have you any idea as to what you'll do?"

Desmonde shook his head slowly. "I'm down and out. With no way to pick myself up."

"I think you're wrong there, sir," Joe exclaimed, then hesitated. "You forget about your gift in your voice—I read all about it in the *Chronicle*, and I believe I could get you a job."

Desmonde looked at him doubtfully.

"It's like this sir. Up at the Hib in the big lounge after dinner it's usually chock full, and Mr. Maley, the manager, very often has an artiste in, to sing or play to the customers. Last winter we had Albert Sammons the violinist. So if you'd permit me to talk to Mr. Maley, he might give you an engagement."

Desmonde was silent. To sing in a pub, had he fallen so

low? Better to sing in the streets. And why not? He had an
impulse to degrade himself still further. Yet the reality was
not quite so bad: the Hibernian was a first class hotel patronized by the best of Dublin society and by many distinguished
visitors. Above all, he urgently needed work, not only because
he was destitute, but as an escape from the brooding solitude
that now hung over him.

"Joe, you are a real friend," he said at last. "I'll come to
the hotel with you any time you say, and take my chance with
Mr. Maley."

"Right you are, sir. He's a fine man, is Mr. Maley, I've a
feeling he'll take to you in your distress." He paused. "Could
you manage to come up around four o'clock tomorrow afternoon? Tog yourself up nice and quiet, try and look your best."

Desmonde nodded and held out his hand. "I'll be there."

When Joe had gone Desmonde glanced at his watch. Almost
eight o'clock. Exhausted, mentally and physically, he wanted
only to rest. But first he forced himself to eat: a bowl of hot
oatmeal and milk, followed by one of the apples sent earlier
in the day, which Mrs. Mullen had stowed away in the cupboard. He then took a hot bath and lay down on the big
bed, conscious immediately of the peace, the blessed quiet
and roominess, the divine solitude of lying alone and un-
molested, in the slow search for sleep.

VIII

AT TEN MINUTES to four o'clock next day Desmonde set
out for the Royal Hibernian Hotel. He had shaved and
groomed himself with more care than he had lately come to
bestow on his appearance. He had brushed his sadly neglected
shoes until they shone, and put on his best Italian suit with
a soft collar and dark tie. Let it be admitted: although frightfully pale, he was as handsome as ever, and so young looking
he seemed little more than a stripling. He was in fact not yet
thirty years of age.

Outside the hotel the usual string of cars was lined up,
some small and ordinary, others larger and of a more distin-

guished lineage. He went in and passed through the entrance hall to the lounge, directed thereto by the chatter and hum of many voices. The place was indeed crowded, mainly with women, for this was the fashionable hour for tea in Dublin, and the Hibernian the fashionable resort. Desmonde remained standing outside. Threading in and out of the tables he could see Joe who, obviously expecting Desmonde, soon caught sight of him and presently came over.

"You're looking grand, sir. And there's a lovely crowd here today. I'll send a word to Mr. Maley that you're here."

Desmonde waited, still standing, and presently Mr. Maley came towards him. The hotel manager was a well set-up man of fifty or thereabouts, with a commanding presence and an expression firmly indicating that he would stand no nonsense. He looked Desmonde up and down, and said finally:

"You have had your troubles. Joe tells me you are practically down and out."

"Your information is correct," Desmonde said.

A pause. The reply had created a favourable impression.

"Well, there's your audience. Get in and show me what you can do with them. I'll sit here to watch and listen."

Desmonde inclined his head and without a word walked firmly to the platform, no more than a foot high, on which stood the grand piano. His appearance had caused an immediate cessation of the chatter, followed by the murmur of many whisperings. Desmonde waited until this too had ceased. Then he bowed and, in complete silence, sat down at the piano.

His first choice, with an eye towards Mr. Maley, was that lovely little song of Schumann's, 'Wenn ich in deiner Augen seh'. He sang it in the original German, softly and sweetly, as befitted the words, then, without pausing, passed immediately into the most tender of all songs, 'Jeannie with the light brown hair'. When this ended, in a silence of rapt attention, he was obliged to stop, so warm was the applause. Across all the upturned faces Desmonde could see that Maley was smiling and applauding vigorously.

Desmonde gave no sign whatsoever of gratification at his success but continued with his programme, wisely interpolating his Irish ballads with German lieder, 'Der Lindenbaum' and 'Frühlingstraum'. How often he was obliged to stop for spontaneous and prolonged applause need not be recorded. But when he ended with his favourite 'Tara' and immediately stepped from the platform, so demanding were the cries for an encore that he was obliged to return to sing the last verse again. Only then was he free to escape through the little side door at the rear of the platform that led into the waiters' mess hall. And here he found himself face to face with Mr. Maley, who pulled two chairs forward from one of the tables.

"Sit down, Desmonde. Are you tired?"

"Slightly, sir. And rather hungry."

"All that will be attended to, my boy. Now listen to me. I have the name of a fair and honest man and I will not, I say not, take advantage of your dire need. You gave a marvellous performance and I know what I'm talking about. I believe you could fill these rooms until people would be falling over themselves to get in!" He paused, looking Desmonde in the eye. "Now what I propose is this. If you would sing at tea time for one hour and no more, for I don't want to kill you, then rest in a room I will reserve for you and be served there with our full à la carte dinner and an appropriate wine, then, after another little rest, sing again for just one hour for the after-dinner crowd, I would be prepared to pay you thirty pounds a week, provided you stay with me the entire season, right through the Spring Show."

Desmonde had turned very pale. He murmured:

"You are noble, truly noble. You know my absolute need."

Maley smiled. "But yes, I could have swindled you. But that's not James Maley. Besides, I've a hunch you'll fill the hotel. Now," he stood up, "I'll send Joe in with a drop of tea. He'll show you to your room. And your dinner will come later."

He took Desmonde's limp hand in a firm clasp, turned, and was gone.

Alone, Desmonde felt torn between a rising tide of joyful relief and the nervous reaction of tears. The entry of Joe, smiling all over his face, saved him from giving way.

"I know how you feel, sir. You've made a smash hit and I'm delighted. Now drink up your tea, it's good and hot."

"Thank you, Joe. Thank you a thousand times." His voice broke. He could say no more.

Joe watched with a paternal air while Desmonde gratefully gulped the hot tea.

"There's a couple of ladies, Mrs. Boland and her sister from Ballsbridge, really nice people, ladies of quality, I know them well. They asked if you would favour them by coming to their table."

Desmonde shook his head.

"No, Joe. Please thank them, but let it be known that I have made a resolution never, never to accept such invitations."

"I understand, sir. And I respect you for it. Of course, these ladies, and others like them, who come to us, are quite first class—real good people. Now, if you're finished I'll take you to your room."

The room, conveniently near on the ground floor, was small with a wash basin and a neat single bed, a window that looked out on the yard, completely quiet at this hour. Desmonde threw himself down on the bed and closed his eyes.

"You've a good hour and more before dinner, sir," Joe said, as he closed the door.

Desmonde slept until seven o'clock, awakened by Joe bringing in his dinner.

"Mr. Maley chose it himself for you," Joe said, laying the well equipped tray on a small table near the window. "He thought something light might be in order for your first night." He added, on his way to the door: "You should see the evening papers, sir. They're a fair treat!"

Desmonde had no interest in what the papers might say of him. Hardened by the scurrilous treatment he had already received, his mind was passive, his state of being in a cloak of total indifference, of curious non-receptivity. Good or bad, everything was superficial, nothing important.

Yet he was perfectly able to enjoy his dinner: a cup of delicious beef bouillon, followed by a thick slice of turbot and string potatoes, suitably accompanied by two glasses of white wine. The dessert was chocolate soufflé with whipped cream.

Not for many, many months, not since his happy stay in Rome with the Marchesa, had he savoured such a meal, and one which by its very excellence so revived and fortified him. He smiled faintly as he thought of what he would give his audience tonight, and how he would play upon it with careless skill. He was still planning when the door swung open, admitting none other than Maley himself, a smiling, hand-rubbing Maley, a warm, solicitous Maley.

"Was everything all right, Desmonde, the dinner to your taste?" And then, reassured: "You should see the evening papers, they're ecstatic, they say you're even better than John McCormack. We are absolutely booked out in the dining room, and we've had to cram another thirty seats into the lounge. I hope the big crowd won't worry you."

"Not in the slightest. But if I should feel tired might I spend the night in this room?"

"Of course, of course, man. And tomorrow I'll find you a better one."

"Thank you, Mr. Maley, but I rather like it here. It reminds me of a little room I had in Spain during my novitiate."

"Well, well, just let me know. You know I want to please you." He paused. "You'll be all ready by eight o'clock?"

Desmonde merely smiled, a pleasant indifferent smile, symptomatic of his present mood. And at eight o'clock he was ready, brushed and freshened by a wash in cold water. He left the room, impassively, with no thought of a little prayer for renewed success, calm and untroubled by the hum of many voices that came to him, resolved to maintain that calm, never to smile, but to use without stint or reserve the wonderful gift that was within him, to use it as a bitter answer to those who had so viciously abused him.

IX

WHEN DESMONDE HAD been singing for three weeks at the Hibernian an event occurred that could be regarded as unusual. It was the Spring Show, the great Dublin festival that attracts many hundreds of visitors to the city. Maley was at his wits' end, not only to provide accommodation for his many wealthy patrons clamouring for the best rooms in the house, but, in a word, to cope with the unbelievable demand for Desmonde. He had extended the lounge by throwing in two extra rooms and, wisely, had placed a cover charge of two guineas on the seats. He was thereby, apart from preventing a riot, coining money hand over fist, and his attitude towards Desmonde had become more deferential than ever.

"Anything more I can do for you, Desmonde, just say the word. You know, of course, that I'll give you a bonus at the end of the Show."

"Very well, Mr. Maley. You know, of course, that I shall be leaving you then."

Maley started. "Good God, man! You can't do that! We're not near the peak yet!"

"Nevertheless, I shall go. You remember the terms of our agreement. You definitely said, till the end of the Spring Show."

"But you see, Desmonde . . ."

"I do not see, Mr. Maley. And as you are, in your own words, an honest man, I hold you to your word."

"I'll pay you the double—and more."

"The answer is no. You cannot expect a singer of my quality to continue without some respite. In addition," Desmonde lowered his voice, "I have a personal reason for leaving."

"Then you'll come back, Desmonde, lad, you must come back."

"We shall see, Mr. Maley. We shall see."

That evening, Desmonde was at his best, singing with a distant look, as though, oblivious of his audience, he envisaged a joy that was to come. At the end of the performance he found Joe in the waiters' room apparently snatching a moment from the tearing rush of his job.

"Listen, sir. There's a fat little woman, sitting at the very corner of the platform, has ordered me to ask you to see her." Anxiously he exhibited a five pound note. "I wish you would, sir, for my sake. She's far from beautiful, I assure you, and I could bet this fiver she's somebody important."

"I'll go, Joe. Just this once. For you."

When the crowd had thinned, Desmonde moved quickly across the platform and stepped down to the table Joe had indicated. The woman, rather as Joe had described her, was seated with a tumbler of whisky and soda, barely touched, before her. She was wearing a low necked Paris gown that emphasized her fat bosoms and suited her ill.

Desmonde stood, silent, with an expression of distaste, awaiting her request, he assumed, for an autograph. She, too, studied him in silence. At last, in a vivid southern American accent, she threw out:

"So you're the little Fitzgerald priest they kicked out for adultery."

His face hardened. "As you say, madam."

"Was the fornication pleasant?"

"Excessively." He bit out the word and spat it at her.

"And you're a little bit of a singer too, it seems."

"As you say, madam."

A pause.

"Don't you use your bottom for sitting on?"

"I prefer to enjoy your pleasantries standing, madam. And now that you have exercised your wit, may I leave you? But before so doing, may I tell you that you are the most foul, fat, obscene, vulgarly got-up and, in a word, repulsive creature I have ever encountered in my entire life."

Surprisingly, she burst out laughing and, although he had begun to move away, she shot out a fat arm and little podgy fingers, one adorned with a diamond the size of a hazel-nut, and gripped and swung him into the chair beside her.

"Don't run away, Desmonde. I think I like you, very much. I'm so used to people pandering to me, lying, licking my boots, trying desperately to win my favour, that it is refreshing, for once, to be told the truth." She paused. "You know, of course, who I am?"

"I have not the faintest notion, madam. And I have no wish to know."

"I am Bedelia Basset. Known all over the U.S.A. as Delia B. Now you know of me?"

Silently, Desmonde shook his head.

"My God! You are the original backwoods boy. Don't you know I am syndicated in sixty of America's best-selling newspapers, that top Hollywood directors tremble in my presence, that famous stars beg and beseech me for kind words that may make them more famous, or dread the words that may send them back on the streets selling candy bars?"

"Madam, I know, and care, nothing of this. My sole knowledge of your fabulous kingdom comes from my friend, my

dear friend, the only one I have in the entire world. He
is Alec Shannon, now a novelist, he has been to Hollywood
and indeed sold his first two novels to the pictures."

"Alec Shannon! I believe I know the name. But novelists
are two-a-penny in Hollywood. We regard them as keech!
You say your only friend?"

"Yes. Except for big Joe, the waiter. I am cast off by all
the others."

"What about your wife?"

"I hate her," said Desmonde simply. "Yes, as much as I
love my darling little babe. I am going to see her soon. She
is with my wife's aunt, Madame Donovan, whose whisky
you are now drinking."

"My God, Desmonde, I'm a hard case, yet you startle
me. Madame Donovan must be worth millions, she donates
cathedrals, yet here you are . . ."

"Singing in a pub for a few quid a week." He paused.
"It's my own choice, I don't care any more. And of course
I'm leaving Mr. Maley to visit my little one."

"He'll not let you go. You're manna from heaven to him.
Unless . . . you've signed nothing?"

Desmonde shook his head.

"Thank God. That would have been a bad start. Now
listen to me, Desmonde. I don't like often, but when I like
. . . I like all the way. And what I must tell you is this. You're
wasting your time and your talent here. Your magnificent
talent! I know you've been hurt and you want to hide. But
it's got to stop. I'm off tomorrow to the west country to look
at a little village I believe my forebears came from, but I'll
be back in about a week. Before I go will you do one little
thing for me?"

Desmonde inclined his head.

"I'll be at this same table tonight. Don't sing those lovely
little Irish songs. Sing something big, classical, out of the
operas. Do this, and I'll know you're with me! Now go and
get your dinner. I'll sit here awhile, send off some cables,
and finish your auntie's whisky."

Despite his habitual indifference, Desmonde was somewhat
taken by this unusual little woman. When he had finished his
dinner he felt compelled to write one of his periodic letters
to his friend.

'This afternoon I was accosted by a little fat weirdie of a woman, fearfully ornate and calling herself, with great éclat, Bedelia Basset. Believe it or not, she seems to have taken a fancy to me, or rather to my prospects. It's a joke, of course, but she does know you, although despising all authors and dismissing them with one unprintable nasty word. You know I am chucking my job at the pub here. The delicious and nourishing food, supplied gratis by the good Maley, has quite put me on my feet again, and I am going to Vevey to see my little darling. I am terribly fond of her, Alec, although no doubt you will regard this as further evidence of my weakness. What has happened to my wife I neither know nor care. We are irreparably parted, and I have no doubt she is finding her own kind of fun elsewhere. Are you by any chance in the mood to take a short vacation and to come with me to Vevey, just for two or three days? It's too long since we have met, and the Swiss mountain air would do you no end of good . . .'

When the letter was finished, sealed and stamped, Desmonde gave it to Joe to post. He had just come in to remove the dinner things, looking particularly jubilant.

"You know that queer little fat Yank, sir?"

"Intimately, Joe!"

"Well, sir, she just gave me a tip to keep that same little corner table for her. Guess what?"

"Sixpence, Joe."

"No, sir, this . . ." Joe exhibited another five pound note. "And she did ask me to remind you about them opera songs."

"She will be obeyed, Joe."

For perhaps the first time since his engagement at the Hibernian, Desmonde's mood was cheerful as he stepped on to the familiar platform at eight o'clock. He actually smiled as he faced his audience, which, as large as ever, was somewhat different in nature from those immediately preceding it. The Spring Show was over, most of the wilder elements had departed, and here, tonight, were members of the Irish gentry who had stayed on, either to hear him or for purposes of their own.

"I hope I won't disappoint you tonight," Desmonde began, very quietly. "As you may know, I sing a great many Irish songs and ballads. Tonight, however, at the request of a very distinguished and famous American visitor, I have consented to sing two numbers from operas. The first will

be from the beloved Puccini, from *Tosca*, the last heart-rending
song sung by Cavaradossi before his execution. The second
will be the Prize Song from *Die Meistersinger*, which, you
might care to know, I sang in Rome, when, as a young priest,
I won the competition for the Golden Chalice." He paused,
waiting for the hum that succeeded his announcement to
subside, then said: "I shall sing the first in the original Italian,
the second in German, exactly as Wagner wrote it."

He sat down at the piano, and from memory, partly im-
provising, played the haunting melody of *Tosca*, the motif
that runs through the last act of the opera, then began to
sing.

Tonight, perhaps because of his impending holiday, he
was in superlative form. Into that last passionate, loving,
despairing yet courageous cry from the condemned Cavaradossi, he put all the feeling that Puccini had therein ordained.

When he finished the applause, while orderly, was deafening,
led by a series of 'Bravos' from the corner table by the platform.
Desmonde bowed repeatedly, then sat down at the piano to
rest. He could not fail to see that the little American, her cigar
discarded, was writing like mad on a pad of cable forms.

Fully rested, he was ready to sing again. Dead silence.
He waited, just for a moment, then threw back his head and
began to give forth that sublime ascending volume of delicious
and arresting melody, the finest ever written by Wagner, in
whom the fatal Germanic mystique was so deeply rooted.

It is a long, an exhausting song, and Desmonde gave it
everything within him. When it ended, he felt spent, and
instead of immediately leaving the stage he sat with bent
head and let wave after wave of the applause roll over him.

Everyone was standing up. Vaguely he saw his little American friend fighting her way to the door and he thought, I'll
never see her again. At last he forced himself to his feet,
bowed and bowed again, throwing out both arms and repeating, again and again: "Thank you, thank you, thank
you." Then he turned, made his way to his room, and lay
down on his bed.

Joe was longer than usual in coming to him, but at last
he arrived, his hands crammed with cards and torn off pieces
of paper.

"You never saw such a commotion in your life, sir, at

least I never have, in all my days at the Hibernian. More
nor half the gentry o' Ireland, talking thegether about you,
sending in their cards with all sorts of messages, beggin' ye
to call on them, and to stay too. Shall I read them to you?"

"No, Joe, drop them in the wastepaper basket."

Joe seemed stunned.

"God bless my soul, sir, you're not serious. Here's one
from the Lord Lieutenant of Ireland and his lady. 'Do call
on us, Desmonde, we do wish to meet you.'"

"Drop that one in first, Joe."

"And here is one, sir," Joe dropped his voice to a reverential
whisper, "which is actually from no less than His Lordship,
Archbishop Murphy, that says: 'My son, now surely you have
expiated your sin. Come to me, Desmonde, and I will see
what might be done for you.'"

"Take that one, Joe," Desmonde said, bitterly, "tear it
in little pieces and flush it down the toilet."

"I will not, sir," Joe said, outraged. "That would be a
mortal sin on me. Whether you like it or not, I'll tuck it in
the pocket of your suitcase."

"Nothing from that nice, funny little Yank?"

"There is indeed, sir, scribbled on a Western Union cable
form. Will ye be wantin' me to put that one down the jakes
also?"

"Stop teasing me, Joe. Read, read, read!"

Provokingly Joe cleared his throat several times, then read:

"'Darling, darling Desmonde, you have given me the
scoop of the year. Tomorrow your name will be splashed in
the headlines of thirty newspapers all over the United States
announcing my discovery, young handsome ex-priest, Irish,
new, better than Caruso, singing for coppers in pub, a story that
would bring tears from a stone. Don't, don't, don't sign any
contracts till I see you again. Till then I remain with love
and kisses your most foul, fat, obscene, vulgarly got-up and,
in a word, repulsive creature you have ever encountered in
your entire life.'"

"That's a real person, Joe," Desmonde said.

"She is indeed, sir. Afore she dashed off she gave me another
fiver and told me to take care of you."

"And so you have done, Joe, all along. Drop that message
in the suitcase, at least it deserves keeping as a souvenir."

"And now, sir," Joe bent forward obsequiously, "what can I do for you in the way of dinner?"

"Cut it, Joe! Bring me something good. I'm hungry and tired. And if you can, pinch me a half-bottle of champagne."

"No need to pinch, sir, Mr. Maley will give you the pick of the cellar. I'll be along in half-an-hour."

Desmonde got up, took a hot bath and soaked in it, then a rub down, and into slippers, pyjamas and dressing gown. He did not know what to think, and therefore decided not to think at all.

FIVE

I

THE IRISH MAIL train was late, causing me to spend almost an hour in the dank beastliness of Euston Station. But at last it came in, the engine puffing and snorting as though it had climbed Snowdon en route. And there was Desmonde walking down the platform, carrying a limp hand bag. We both wanted to embrace, but refrained and shook hands.

"Is your luggage in the van?"

"No, I have it here."

"Splendid, then we can start from scratch."

"Give me your arm, Alec. I'm still rocked in the cradle of the deep."

"It was rough? As usual?"

"Tempestuous."

I had come to the station by bus, unwilling to throw my possessions in Desmonde's face. We quickly found a taxi and sat facing each other as we rattled off.

"You look terribly fit, Alec."

"You do too, Desmonde," I lied cheerfully. He was still entrancingly handsome as ever, but sad, and of course tired.

"And your dear mother?"

"Well and happy. She has a nice little flat on the seafront at Hove, just three minutes from the church. Of course, when my boys are home she is always with us."

"Where are you taking me?"

"Home. It's just a little house in Kensington, but nice, quiet, and within a few paces of the Gardens."

He wanted to know more, but, as always, was too well bred to ask. And presently we drew up at the little white house I loved so much, one of a quiet row, totally free of traffic noise. I got rid of the taxi and opened the front door with my key.

I took him upstairs to the guest room that opened on to the garden of the house.

"You can park here, your bathroom's just there. Now, how about some food?"

"Absolutely not, Alec. I'd love a good wash, then lots and lots of talk."

I smiled, put my hands on his shoulders and gave him a good shake to break down the constraint that lay upon us. After all, it was a very long time since we had last been together. Then I went down to the kitchen to see Mrs. Palmer, my especially good 'daily', who had consented to wait beyond her usual four o'clock departure.

"Everything ready for your dinner, sir . . . The chops on the grill, the spuds are peeled and ready, the salad made and in the fridge with the apple tart."

"Thank you, Mrs. Palmer. And it was kind of you to stay over."

"It's a pleasure sir, for the likes of you."

She picked up all her gear and went off, saying: "Your mail's on the hall table, sir."

Upstairs, I glanced at my letters, which seemed promising, then went into the drawing-room. Desmonde was already there, standing, looking about him.

"Oh, come, Desmonde, stop looking and sit here beside me."

"I can't, Alec, it's such a lovely room, everything, everything, and your pictures . . ."

I took his arm and drew him on to the settee beside me. But still he kept looking.

"That lovely Sisley, the early Utrillo, the Mary Cassatt, that lovely little violety conversation piece, is it a Vuillard?"

I nodded. "Madame Melo, the actress, and her daughter. But do stop, Desmonde, you're making me frightfully uncomfortable."

"I can't stop, Alec, I'm enjoying it so much and, my God! I believe that's a Gauguin over there! Pont Aven, just after he came back penniless from Tahiti."

"Good for you, Desmonde. Yes, he had not enough to buy a real canvas. That lovely thing is painted on burlap. Of course, I had it rebacked in New York, where I bought it. And it's housed in a genuine Louis XVI frame, stripped, of course. Now about you, Desmonde, what . . .?"

"Just one more, Alec, that lovely thing, of the Seine, I believe."

"I don't mind talking of that masterpiece, Desmonde, for it's my favourite. It's the Seine at Passy, the last scene painted by Christopher Wood. A letter from his mother is on the back."

"Just before . . . at Salisbury Station, wasn't it?"

"Yes . . . What a loss!"

Desmonde was silent, then said:

"You seem to be alone here, Alec."

"Yes, I am. My dear little wife and my two brats, both boys, are down in Sussex."

"At an hotel?" Desmonde asked, studying the photograph on an adjoining table.

"Of course not. I have an old shack down there. We use it a lot."

Idly, Desmonde asked: "That's a lovely old Georgian house with heavenly old brick stables made over into a loggia and with a view, it seems, of the Downs. Whose is that?"

"That's the Old Rectory, and of course it belongs to the Vicar. Very decent chap. And just up the road is Mellington Church. Genuine Norman, you can see the long and short brickwork. I can't tell you how lovely it is. One of these days I'll show you."

"Thank you, Alec. Perhaps the Vicar will let us stay at the Old Rectory." Then he said: "Alec, you are, as always, the best and dearest friend a man could ever hope to have. But for God's sake, because of the abysmal failure I've made of my life, don't try to minimize the success you've made of yours."

"Stop it, Desmonde! Your success is just ahead of you."

"I won't stop it. You put yourself through school and university on a shoestring. You've no money, so you have to find work as an assistant. It's hard work, often you're up at night, but you manage to pass your exams with flying colours, and in no time at all, you have a most successful practice. Before long you sell out, and now here you are, a best-selling novelist. You've really worked a miracle. And I . . . I am a kicked-out priest, deserted, thank God, by my bitch of a wife, with no more than thirty quid in my pocket."

"Please be quiet, Desmonde." I moved closer to him and put my arm round his shoulders. "I've been infernally lucky. And now we're going to work a miracle for you. Tell me, what did Bedelia B. say when she came back?"

"She said quite a lot, and once you get used to her, you rather like her. Well, here it is, straight. They are definitely committed to making a film based on the life of Enrico Caruso.

It won't be called that, of course, but some bloody tripe like
The Golden Voice, or *The Voice That Breathed o'er Eden*. Anyway,
they have an excellent script all ready, but the original idea
of using Caruso records has been ditched, all the old records
are terrible, besides, even if they were usable, the result would
be transparently mechanical and feeble. So they're urgently
looking for someone to act the part and sing, if possible, like
Caruso. Little Bedelia thinks it's made for me, and mind you,
she is no fool, and she knows Hollywood inside out. She seems
to like me, why God only knows, and is going to try to land
me the job."

I took both Desmonde's hands and wrung them.

"There's *your* miracle Desmonde. What a heavenly opportunity. It's God given. With a start like that nothing could
stop you. Now I promise you this, Desmonde, I'll do everything to help. Of course I'm coming with you. I've some
business of my own to do out there. We'll go shopping tomorrow. I'll take care of everything, tickets, reservations,
accommodation, everything."

"I must first go to see my little one. She's with Madame,
in Switzerland."

"We'll do that en route. Join the boat at Genoa."

I still held his hands. He raised mine and kissed them both.
I saw with distress that he was fighting tears.

"Alec, you are so eternally kind to a washed-up bloody
wreck of a fellow, and I love you for it as I always have."

"Enough, Desmonde. Come and help me get up the dinner."

We went downstairs to the kitchen where I switched on the
electric grill and lit the gas under the pot of potatoes.

"I thought you'd rather eat in than out, tonight. Are you
hungry?"

"Voracious, now I've ceased to rock and roll. I was in the
vomitorium half the voyage." He was sitting at the kitchen
table. I joined him.

"Wonderful ideas those old Romans had to regain their
appetite."

"But painfully, surely."

"Do you remember old Beauchamp and the cake? He had
such an appetite he must surely still be alive."

Desmonde smiled. "He did nourish himself assiduously. But
I'm afraid the dear old Mother Superior must be gone."

"Oh, yes. She's certainly in heaven. Desmonde, I'll never forget the scene when you sang to her. From that moment you were destined for the movies."

"I'll never forget the stumpy little hockey player. What a sport she was. And what buttocks!"

When the potatoes were ready I poured them and turned off the grill.

"Let's feed here, Alec. Such a fag carrying everything upstairs."

"Wouldn't dream of it. Go up to the dining room. You'll find the table already laid."

He looked at me indecisively for a moment, then obeyed. Quickly, I put the food into the little dumb waiter, sunk into the wall, and joined him upstairs.

"Where's the grub, Alec?"

I pressed the button on the wall, there came a faint whirring, immediately two panelled doors sprang open, and there was our dinner.

"What a topping idea."

"You won't get maids running up and down these Victorian stairs, nowadays. Our Mrs. Palmer is extremely good, but she would jib at that!"

We sat down to dinner, simple but good. Desmonde polished off two chops with commendable ease, and a good thick hunk of pie.

"I can't offer you wine, Desmonde. We don't go in for it here."

"This Perrier is awfully good."

"Another slice of pie?"

"Just a little bit. It's delicious."

When he had finished I said:

"Now the prescription is, hot bath and bed, so that you're all rested and fresh for tomorrow."

I put the dishes in the waiter and sent them down for Mrs. Palmer's attention in the morning. Then we went upstairs.

"Have you got everything you need? Pyjamas, tooth brush, razor, etcetera."

"Everything, thank you, Alec. And my room and bathroom are lovely."

"Good night then, Desmonde. Sleep well."

"Good night, my dear Alec."

II

Next morning I got up at my usual hour, seven o'clock, took my cold bath and my usual half walk, half run up Victoria Road and across the gardens to the Carmelite Church, just in time for the eight o'clock Mass.

On the way home I picked up the paper and fresh rolls. Mrs. Palmer, never failing, was already in and had my coffee ready, steaming hot.

"I think Mr. Fitzgerald would probably like his in his room. I'll take it up, Mrs. Palmer, in about ten minutes."

When I had glanced through the paper, hoping, without success, for some mention of my new novel, I took the tray Mrs. Palmer had prepared, added my second cup of coffee, and went up to Desmonde's room. He was awake, but still luxuriating. I placed the tray on the bedside table while he raised himself on an elbow.

"What a kind idea! I haven't had coffee in bed for at least a hundred years." He drank. "And such good coffee. Did I hear you go out?"

"My usual morning prowl. Up to the Carmelite for eight o'clock Mass."

He seemed to shrink slightly, but forced the words out. "And to Communion."

"Of course. That's routine too. And a jolly good start to the day."

He was silent, then said:

"I'm obliged to tell you, Alec, that I have broken completely with the Church. I never go. Never. I consider that the Almighty has given me a beastly rotten deal."

"Didn't you rather set it up for Him? Anyway, I'll bet you a new prayer book that you *will* go back one day. Now, it's a lovely morning and we're not going to waste it discussing theology. Get dressed and we'll get going on the town."

Within half-an-hour Desmonde came into my room, fully dressed. I had put on my dark suit, black shoes and bowler hat.

"I say, Alec, are you something in the City?"

I laughed. "On my first visit to Hollywood, a very important woman, she had just written and produced *The Big House*, took me quietly aside. I was all tweedy, with coloured shirt, flowing tie and suede shoes. 'Alec, don't for heaven's sake dress like an author, you'll get nowhere. Dress like a business man.' I've taken her advice."

We went downstairs and out. The morning was delicious, fresh, lovely and sunny. The prunus in the little front gardens of the quiet road were already in heavenly bloom.

We walked to the end of Victoria Road and took the No. 9 bus at the stop outside Kensington Gardens.

The gardens were green and lovely, some early nurse-maids already abroad with their prams. Green, too, and in fresh foliage, was the park, then past Marble Arch and into Piccadilly with its wonderful shops. What a lovely city London was in that era: uncluttered by traffic, the lively buses springing along, the pavements clean, uncrowded, the policeman on his beat, the milkman on his round, the whole enlivened by a sense of honest activity, beauty and order.

We got off at Burlington House and turned up left into Savile Row.

"Now your work really begins, Desmonde. All we're now going to do is frightful foppery, but all the people I know do it, so I've just fallen into line."

I did not take him to my usual tailor, but to Bluett's, a younger house I sometimes patronized.

'Ping' went the door as we entered, a delicious, reassuring, old-fashioned sound matching the rich smell, and sight, of good cloth, bales and bales, on the long heavy mahogany table, and the deferential gentleman with the inch-tape round his collar.

"I believe you know me as a customer?"

"Mr. Shannon, isn't it, sir?"

Impassive but inwardly delighted, I said:

"We would like two suits, if you could oblige us by making them within a week and sending them, without fail, to the offices of the Italian Line in Genoa."

He thought for a moment, then went through to the work room, emerging with a smile.

"As you are a customer, sir, I am sure we can oblige you,

without fail. I assume the suits are for the gentleman who
accompanies you."

Then the fun began, the long, careful choosing, the equally
protracted measuring, the plea for just one fitting, in two
days' time, then we were shown out with the utmost courtesy,
Desmonde the potential owner of a lovely herring-bone grey,
and a dark, softly bluey-black merino suitable for evening
wear.

Bond Street was near, always an interesting, though narrow,
thoroughfare, and here, in Turnbull's, we bought half-sleeve
sports shirts, six pairs of socks and half-a-dozen conservatively
hued Macclesfield silk neckties.

"I do badly need some ordinary shirts," Desmonde murmured.

"Not here, Desmonde. Hats first, then shirts."

Across the street we went to Hilhouse's where, very easily,
we found a dark checked tweed hat, that Desmonde kept on,
and a knockabout soft panama.

"Shall I send your friend's hat with the panama?" asked
Mr. Hilhouse, gingerly holding the battered relic by the brim.

"Oh, no," Desmonde said, hurriedly. "Please throw it
out."

"It's been a good hat in its day, sir. But now . . . I'll burn
it."

"Are you tired?" I asked Desmonde, as we stepped out
of the little shop. "There're two more measurings to be done.
So I think we'll now have lunch."

"Good idea! I spotted a good looking A.B.C. just up the
street."

"Silence, Fitzgerald. Do you think I'm going to spoil our
day by taking you for tea and buns?"

We recrossed the road and turned into Grosvenor Street.
As Claridges hove in sight, guarded by two uniformed giants,
Desmonde faltered.

"I'm not going in there, Alec. Not in these rags, I'd eternally
disgrace you."

"Come, child, take my hand, and stop howling."

We entered the magnificent portals and went downstairs.
Seated outside the restaurant, on one of the settees, and
obviously awaiting a guest, was that wonderful woman, Lady
Crayford.

"Well, Alec," she greeted us, "who is your handsome friend, in those atrocious clothes?"

"He is Desmonde Fitzgerald, and he's coming to Hollywood with me, next week. He's just come off the set and hasn't bothered to change."

"What are you making?"

"A modern version of *Hamlet*, madam," Desmonde supported me, launching his marvellous smile. "I am the third grave-digger."

"Weren't there only two?"

"It's a dreadfully deep grave, madam."

"Well, do wipe your boots before you go in. I see my guest coming. And do take care of yourself, Alec. Send me an autographed copy of your new book."

The head waiter had seen us chatting with Lady Crayford so we had a first-class table, when otherwise we might have been shunted to a corner of the long, lovely room. We studied our menus, gold printed on double pages of embossed tasselled board.

"Shall we be simple and have the table d'hôte? It's usually awfully good."

Desmonde agreed. "And no wine, Alec, please. Perrier, if you wish. Who is your nice friend?"

"Sybil Crayford. She's been terribly kind to my wife and me. Inviting us to her parties and to lunch. Even when we were new in London, and painfully green."

The lunch, as might be expected, was extremely good. We did not talk much since I had no wish to linger. More work lay ahead of us. Not long after two o'clock we had scoffed the finale, *mousse aux framboises à la crème*, drunk our coffee and, with the bill paid and the waiter tipped, we were on our way.

"Do let's take a taxi, Alec, and tip the head porter. I can't sneak out of this place in my broken down shoes."

I obeyed, saying, as we rolled away:

"Apropos of tipping, there's a story that a fabulously rich Eastern potentate, who often stayed at Claridges for months on end, never tipped the head porter, but repeatedly and affectionately promised him he would be remembered lavishly in his will. When Mahomet did take him to his bosom the will was read. Guess how much the head porter got?"

"Half-a-million."

H

"Absolutely nothing."

"What a sell," Desmonde murmured sympathetically. "But all rich people are not mean."

"I'm not rich, Desmonde," I laughed. "I enjoy spending money. And I can never, never forget how kind you were to me when *my* shoes were broken down."

We were now at the far end of the Burlington Arcade, the driver having kindly taken us the long way round by St. James's. But he duly received his tip—no Londoner ever has a row with his taxi driver, that fatal error is left to tourists.

At the Piccadilly end of the Arcade we entered a small shop which bore on its signboard the name Budd. Here we resumed our work: viewing, examining, feeling and finally selecting various materials: silk, poplin, cotton. And again Desmonde was subjected to various measurings.

"Now shoes, lad," I exclaimed, as we emerged, doubly reassured that everything would be dispatched on time.

"For heaven's sake, stop, Alec. It's all far, far too much. You make me feel as if I were going to boarding school."

"You're going to Hollywood, you dear idiot. Do you want to arrive in your bloody bare feet? I know from my own experience that those things you're wearing won't last much longer."

Quite near, a few doors below Lobb's, shoemaker by Royal Appointment, to whom I had not aspired, we went into the Churchill shop, less famous but equally good.

My position as a customer immediately rectified the shock conveyed by Desmonde's horrifying feet. He was seated, the remnants removed, and the usual careful measuring begun. I was glad to observe he had only one small hole in the toe of one of his socks. Finally, after the order had been given for two pairs of black, two of dark brown and one patent leather for evening wear, Churchill tactfully suggested:

"I am sure I have some shoes in stock, sir, that would serve the gentleman until his order arrives."

He went into the rear shop and came back with a brand new pair of black shoes.

"The old gentleman who bespoke these, sir, a very old and favoured customer, we've had his last for almost fifty years, died before delivery. Of course we did not press the matter."

The shoes fitted Desmonde very well indeed, although Churchill said, disparagingly:

"Not bad, sir. Rather slack across the base of the metacarpals, but they should do for the time being."

I thanked Churchill and said we'd take them and to put them on the bill.

"These you've got on, your good self, sir, they seem to be wearing remarkably well. Don't tell me you've had them re-soled."

"Good heavens, no, Churchill," I lied. "I wouldn't dream of it."

"Then it's my good leather, sir," Churchill said, adding sadly: "It lasts for ever."

When we got out of the shop I inquired:

"How do you feel standing in a dead man's shoes, Desmonde?"

"Totally rejuvenated. I can't tell you what a blessing it is to have something solid on one's feet."

The office of the Italian Line was our last port of call, and here we were fortunate. The flagship of the line, the *Cristoforo Colombo*, was due to sail from Genoa in ten days' time. I recognized the girl at the desk.

"Have you a double stateroom available, midships, on the port side?"

She examined the plan of the ship.

"You may have C 19, if you wish, sir. It is the accommodation you and your wife occupied last year."

"That would be splendid."

"Shall I reserve you a table in the restaurant, sir?"

"Oh, please don't trouble. I'll see Giuseppe on board— I'm sure he'll know me again."

With everything completed, I turned to Desmonde as we came out to the street.

"Now you're tired, so no more bussing, but home, James, and don't spare the petrol."

I hailed a taxi and presently we were back and thirsting for tea, which I asked Mrs. Palmer to bring up to the study, a cosy, book-lined little room, an addition to the house, that opened off the first landing.

"Any messages, Mrs. Palmer?" I asked, when she appeared with a well-stocked tray.

"Miss Radleigh called from Mellington, sir. Nothing important, she said, some contracts for you to sign, the little boys have gone back to Aylsford and Madam is well and hoping you'll be down soon."

"Thank you, Mrs. Palmer, and also for these very good-looking cakes."

"I hadn't that much to do, sir, so I just baked one. It's quite plain, the way you like them."

"Thank you again for your thoughtfulness."

She blushed and looked pleased.

We were silent, savouring the rapture of our first cup of tea. When I handed Desmonde his second cup he said:

"What a nice way you have with people, Alec. I've been noticing it all day. And how wonderfully fortunate and happy your life has become."

"Yes, I thank God for it on my knees every night."

Again I noticed that slight shrinking from the very mention of the Deity. But he persisted.

"You must really be very well off now, Alec."

"I am not. I have a good income and I spend every penny of it." I stood up and moved to the door.

"I must go and telephone my wife."

Downstairs in the hall I rang Mellington. It was Miss Radleigh who answered.

"Mum there, Nan?"

"She's just gone out, round the garden. Shall I fetch her?"

"No, Nan, this is just to say I'll be down tomorrow."

"Oh, good, I've some good news for you."

"Can't believe it. Tell Mum I may have a friend with me. It will just be for the day. How is the garden?"

"Coming on lovely. The strawberries are almost ripe!"

"Have you been pinching?"

"Maister! You're the one with that delightful habit. Besides, Dougal has netted them."

"Nan, I'm bringing down the big car and will leave it. I'll take the Morris. Will you mind coming with us to drive it back?"

"Of course not, Maister. But . . . I hope you're not going away again?"

"Just for three or four weeks, Nanno."

"Oh, dear. And it's so lovely down here in the early summer. I shall miss our walks on the Downs."

"I'll be back, Nanno. Do rest and take care of yourself. There'll be bag loads of work when I get home. Perhaps you'll tell Mum to have a nice light salady lunch for us tomorrow."

"I will, indeed, dear Maister."

I hung up, thinking, what a splendid girl, so good, trustworthy and hard working. What on earth would I do without her?

At the foot of the stairs I yelled up:

"Like to come with me to Mellington tomorrow?"

"Love it," he called back.

I went into my room, closed the door and lay down on the bed. I still had my letters to go through. But first I'd have a nap.

III

NEXT MORNING AFTER breakfast, coffee and fresh rolls for both, we set off for Mellington. The day was lovely and promised to continue so with a warm sun and bluey-grey skies. Happy to be going home, for Mellington was my home, the little London house no more than an outpost, I felt like singing, but was restrained by the presence of the maestro beside me. How good to see my dear little wife, and Nanno, and to have news of my two sons and to see, with Dougal, how my beloved garden grew. I could not resist the impulse.

"Sing, Desmonde. Something sweet, touching and home-coming."

Desmonde never resisted such an invitation. He loved to sing. And so we rolled through the Sussex lanes—I knew all the shortcuts—to the strains of 'The Bonnie Banks of Loch Lomond', leaving behind us a trail of bemused villagers, gazing fearfully through our dust, puzzled as to whether they had glimpsed a mirage or the advance guard of Barnum & Bailey's Circus.

But all was quietly expectant as we turned up Mellington lane and finally swung through the open white barred farm gateway, which I had insisted on preserving, and drew up before the old Rectory. Immediately there was an explosion from the house as Paddy, the Irish Setter, hurled himself upon me, almost knocking me down, then came my wife, on Nan's arm, followed by Annie, the strong, plump little country maid, all smiles, and inquiring if there was luggage. Behind, peering from the shadow of the portico, stood Sophie, our Austrian cook, while at the corner of the barn I caught sight of Dougal, dramatically attacking the wallflower bed.

I embraced and kissed my dear little wife, who looked remarkably well, gave a hand to Nan, and said:

"Darling, here at last is Desmonde Fitzgerald."

She smiled. "My husband has spoken of you so often and so nicely, I almost know you already."

"Madame." Desmonde bent and kissed her free hand. "Your husband has spoken of you so continually and so lovingly that I am enchanted to meet you."

"Enchanted? I am no witch, Desmonde. So do keep your fine words and manners for Hollywood. Do you know of our dear Nan?"

Rather deflated, and deservedly so, Desmonde murmured: "I have certainly heard of Miss Radleigh."

"Then let us go into the house. Would you like coffee? No? Then perhaps you'd rather go round the garden."

We went first to the old walled garden, my pride and joy, where, in the shelter by the lovely eighteenth-century rose-pink wall, Dougal had tended and brought to perfection all our early plantings. The herbaceous border was in bloom, the vegetable garden was nobly productive with lettuce, trenched celery, radish, endive, runner beans, delicious fresh peas, and Dougal's pride, the marrow bed, bulging with green balloons which, no doubt, would shortly be reduced to a single monstrosity for the village flower show. Then came the currant bushes, red, yellow and white dangling with variegated bunches, the gooseberries, rather ravaged for a reason I suspected, but still thriving, amber globes, next the raspberries, safely caged, loaded with ripe berries, the espalier peaches with alas, few immature fruits, many nipped off by the Sussex blight, and finally the strawberry bed, a glorious huge spread of ripening Royal Sovereigns.

I turned to Dougal, who had quietly followed us.

"Congratulations, Dougal. Everything looks wonderful, especially the strawberries."

"Ay, they've done fine, sir. I kent ye like them. But I've

had a bit of a struggle keepin' the wee laddies off them."
He smiled. "I even caught Miss Radleigh putting a dainty wee
finger through the net."

"She'll be suitably chastised, Dougal. The raspberries
are gorgeous too, Dougal."

"Ay, sir, they're splendid. Ever since ye gi'en me permission
to put the cage up."

I glanced at Nan, who was trying not to laugh.

"You were right, dead right there, Dougal, and I was wrong.
It's not at all unsightly."

He looked pleased, and I chose this moment to say coaxingly:

"Dougal, I ken how ye hate picking the fruit afore it's
ready, but could you manage to find just a few ripe strawberries for our lunch. My guest here is a very important man
from Hollywood."

"I jaloused he was important, sir, frae the terrible auld
claes he has on. Verra well, sir, I'll dae my best to let ye have
a nice wee punnet. And if ye've a moment, sir, I'd like to see
ye by yoursel' out by the barn doors."

"Certainly, Dougal. I'll come with you now."

Out by the corner of the barn I gazed with rising anger at
the ruin of my wallflower bed.

"Damn it to hell, man, who did this? Was it Paddy?"

"I thought, sir, ye'd be rightly angered, as was I. No, sir,
'twas not Paddy, he's a well trained animal. 'Twas these two
wee sons of yours, at their football. I begged them to stop,
but they just laughed and wouldna'."

I was indeed very angry, and I wisely exaggerated my
rage.

"My beautiful wallflowers! I'll let them have it, I warrant
you, Dougal. They'll play football in the far field and nowhere
else, I promise you. Can you do something with the bed?"

"Verra easy, sir. I'll pick up a couple o' dozen new shoots
at the nursery and have them charged to you." He smiled.
"Maybe ye'll let me order a dozen for masel'. Like you, I
love them wallflowers!"

"Certainly, Dougal," I said heartily. "Two dozen, if you
wish."

"Na, na, sir. The ane dozen will dae fine. And don't be too
sore on the laddies. Boys will be boys, ye ken. And thank ye
again."

I saw that he was not only appeased but pleased. I shook hands with him and saw him immediately depart for the strawberry bed. Dougal was a priceless gift from the neighbouring big estate that also supplied me with its pheasants. A trained and skilful man and a hard worker, he had come to me after a violent quarrel with the head gardener, to whom he was second in a staff of six. I valued him and made every effort to appease his rather craggy nature. He liked me because I was obviously Scottish, though masquerading under an Irish name. I felt sure now that he would stay with me. Half an hour later he handed to my wife a large punnet of delicious big ripe strawberries.

Meanwhile, I rejoined the others, who were emerging from the path that wound through our little wood.

"Why do you call it the Canon's Walk, Alec?"

"There's a story that a previous incumbent, Canon Herbert, walked here every day reading his breviary. My neighbour's pheasants are very fond of it. They usually find their way to our dinner table."

We paused in the orchard, the two ladies had gone on to the house.

"Tell me, Alec, why does Miss Radleigh address you as Maister?"

I laughed. "It's a silly story. When Dougal first came to us he wanted to put a cage over the raspberries. I said 'no'. There was an argument, rather hot, which I terminated by saying in broad Scots: 'Dinna' forget, Dougal, that I'm the Maister.' Nan, who was with us, thought this very funny and has adorned me with the name ever since. Naturally, next year Dougal talked me into the cage, a great success of course. He's a splendid fellow."

"And what a splendid girl is Miss Radleigh," said Desmonde wistfully.

Lunch was ready when we reached the house. Sunlight poured into the dining-room as we sat down to one of Sophie's Emperor omelettes and a huge bowl of gorgeous salad fresh from the garden. Afterwards came the strawberries served with fresh cream from the neighbouring farm. They were inexpressibly good. Then came coffee.

Oddly enough, conversation did not flow easily, and now it became apparent to me that neither my wife nor my secretary

was well disposed to Desmonde, a formality which he himself
seemed to feel, since he became increasingly anxious to please.

When we rose from the table he looked engagingly at
Nan.

"If you're in the mood for a walk, Miss Radleigh, would
you care to show me the Downs?"

She looked him straight in the eye.

"I am going to be very busy, Mr. Fitzgerald. But if you
walk out of our gateway, turn left, and follow your nose,
you will be on the Downs in exactly two minutes."

"Thank you," Desmonde said politely. "Can you spare
me for an hour, Alec?"

"Certainly, my dear fellow. Have a good walk, but be back
before three."

When he had gone off alone, I said:

"It's too bad. Everyone treats him as a pariah. Why must
you?"

"He is not good, darling," my wife said. "There's something
wrong with him inside."

I looked at Nan, who said, apologetically: "I feel like Mum.
And I can't stand his bowing and knee bending, and hand
kissing."

"That's because he's nervous. The poor devil has been
kicked into the mud, has had his nose ground into it, is absolutely down and out. I can never forget our friendship when
we were boys. I'm trying to help him make a come-back.
And I hope I succeed."

"You are always so kind, dear," my wife said.

"Nonsense! Go and lie down for an hour, then we'll run
over to Aylsford and see the boys, just for five minutes."

"Oh, do let's," she said.

I went upstairs with Nan to my little study that overlooked
the garden and the outbuildings. Dougal was hard at work
on the wallflowers. All the papers requiring attention were
on the desk. I looked through them quickly and signed where
necessary.

"Why do the Italians want four copies of every contract?
I see there are a couple of less than bad early notices here."

"It's too bad, Maister, that you're going off again. Mum
doesn't like it. We're very lonely here when you're away."

"I promise I'll be back within two weeks. Perhaps sooner, if

I sell the film rights. Then you'll have to put up with me for the next hundred years. I'm taking Mum for a quick run to Aylsford. Want to come?"

At half past two we set out for Aylsford, a run of not more than six miles. Desmonde had just come back, looking fresh, but rather bored with the Downs. He sat in front with me, Mum and Nan were in the back. In no time at all we were gliding to the large country house converted to a school, with playing fields around, and a swimming pool at one side. Our two sons spotted us at once and rushed over from the cricket pavilion. A scratch match was in progress and they were not fielding.

"Had a good innings?" I asked.

Robert answered: "Mine was short and completely un-eventful."

"In other words," James said, "he got a duck. I made twenty-seven."

"All flicked off the edge of the bat. Missed twice in the slips."

"Three jolly good boundaries and caught, at last, off a possible sixer."

"We can't stay, boys, but I did want to see you and to tell you, if you're out at the house before I come back, don't, don't, don't mutilate the wallflower bed. If you promise not to, Nan has something nice for you."

Both together: "We promise, Dad."

"Now first come and kiss Mum and tell her that you love her, then shake hands with my friend Mr. Fitzgerald who is taking me to Hollywood."

This was accomplished, and Nan was also kissed. She then produced the bag of gooseberries.

"I say, how lovely, Nan. James, I thought we'd cleared all the bushes."

"These must be new growth, ass."

"Don't eat them all over the car, boys. I'm sorry, but we must be off. You can sit under that tree and polish them off."

In no time at all we were back at Mellington. When I had put away the car I went immediately to Dougal and told him I'd made a special journey to the school to admonish the boys.

"Och, ye shouldna' have done that, sir." But he smiled.

"Ye may depend on me to look after the gairden weel while ye're away."

Then it was time to think of leaving if Nan were to drive back before dark. I brought the Morris Oxford to the front door and sought my wife, who was resting on the couch in her room. I knelt beside her.

"I'm sorry to be leaving so soon, darling. I'll be home again in about three weeks, then we'll have a lovely long time together. You are looking so much better, keep on taking care of yourself."

"Nan takes care of me. She's such a dear."

"You are a darling, darling. And I love you with all my heart."

I kissed her gently. Her lips were soft, passive, tender as a child's. Before I reached the door she had closed her eyes.

In five minutes we were off, Desmonde at ease in the back seat, Nan and I sitting up in front. I drove fast, very fast, not taking risks but cutting everything fine. I knew the road so well and it was practically free of traffic at this hour. None of us said anything, not a word. At four o'clock precisely we drew up outside my Kensington house.

"I hope I didn't scare you," I said to Desmonde, as we stretched, then went into the house.

"Nothing scares me now, Alec," he answered, with that same note of sadness. "Anyway, you're a magnificent driver. You do that well, as you do everything else."

"Come, come, now, Desmonde, that won't do. You're needing your tea."

As we went slowly upstairs I told Nan to ask Mrs. Palmer to bring tea for three in the study.

"I'll just have a quick cup with Mrs. Palmer in the kitchen. I want to be off and home before the traffic. Shall I take your mail for filing?"

"Yes, dear Nan, and answer as you think best."

We looked at one another. I knew then that I loved her and that she loved me. I had the overwhelming desire to take her in my arms.

"Goodbye, dear Maister, come back soon." She smiled faintly, she had seen love in my eyes.

"Goodbye, dear darling Nan." I touched her cheek lightly with my lips. Then I went upstairs to my room.

Only when I heard the sound of the departing car did I go upstairs to the study. Desmonde was already there, as was the tea tray. I poured his cup and gave it to him, then poured my own.

"Desmonde, I've a horrible feeling that my idea of giving you a breath of fresh air in the country has been a fiasco, a rush around in cars, simply a wasted day."

"Not at all, Alec. I've seen your beautiful estate and duly admired it."

"Good God, man, I did not take you for that beastly purpose."

"I've also seen your two fine boys and duly admired them."

"Oh, shut up, man. What's come over you?"

"I have also met your sweet wife who loves you, and the good Miss Radleigh who also loves and respects you. And I have come to the sad conclusion that in the society of good pure women I am nothing more than a cheap, posturing, broken down, unspeakable, lecherous, God-damned bastard."

I was about to remark that he would meet few pure, good women in Hollywood when I saw, with a start of pained surprise, that he had his hand across his eyes to hide the tears dropping into his cup. I immediately moved towards him and put my arm round his shoulders.

"Please, Desmonde, please don't, my dear old friend. You know all that's finished and done with. You're on the very threshold of a new and brilliant career. Just cut out all the bowing, genuflecting, hand kissing—stop and be yourself again. Damn it all, man, think how I've set you up for a big success, all that I've done for you, all the trouble I've taken. Are you going to quit when we're in sight of the promised land? Are you that kind of a lousy quitter?"

He slowly uncovered his eyes, and handed me his cup.

"More tea, quickly, you Scotch Irish American best-selling Roman Catholic, daily Communicant, and unutterable decent fellow. My hurts will heal, vanish, when I have Holly-wood at my feet."

"That's the spirit, Des, keep it up."

"Then I will thank you for all the wonderful things you have done for your old friend who loves you."

"That's enough, Des. You've just got yourself back in the groove. Here's your tea, and I'll have mine. When do you

want to go to Switzerland to see your wee lassie? We haven't
much time before we board the *Cristoforo Colombo*."

"Let's go now."

"Don't be an ass, my newly restored and fortified friend.
If you get up very early when I call you tomorrow morning
I'll have you in Geneva by tomorrow night."

"It's a deal, pal," he said, handing his cup for more tea.

IV

NEXT MORNING WE were up with the dawn and left immediately for Victoria Station. I had paid Mrs. Palmer the
night before and given her the keys of the house. She would
forward all mail to Mellington.

The daily boat train left on time, as did the cross-Channel
steamer when we pulled into Dover pier station to make the
transfer with five minutes to spare. The crossing was not
unduly rough, and at ten-thirty we were on Calais pier taking
the long walk to the Paris train. Some delay here owing to the
loading of baggage, but when we took off, to the accompani-
ment of shrill whistles, the train was non-stop all the way.
At the Gare du Nord it was of course necessary to change
stations, but a slow taxi took us to the Gare de Lyon where the
continental express, steaming at its platform, was ready and
waiting. At noon exactly we slid away in slow grandeur,
merging gradually into the speed, remarkable for that age, of
sixty-five miles an hour.

We had lunch in the restaurant car, a meal as different
from the British equivalent as the Ritz is from the Trocadero.
Desmonde apparently had little appetite, he kept looking
out of the window, occupied with his thoughts which were,
undoubtedly, directed towards his little daughter. He had
thanked me so often for my kindness in coming with him
that I no longer answered, merely shook my head and smiled.
After lunch we both nodded off into a nap that took us on to
four o'clock and a pot of rather indifferent tea. At five thirty-
four we drew up, in clouds of steam, at Lausanne station.
Nowadays, of course, air transport makes fun of our journey—
when the planes fly, are not delayed by strikes, crashed or

hijacked in transit. But, for the day and age, it was a good performance.

So Desmonde seemed to think when we stood on Lausanne platform. He smiled.

"Can't believe we're here. What next, Alec?"

"A taxi to Burier, just beyond Vevey. I believe there's a hotel near Burier, not large, but good."

"If it's small and good it'll be full up."

"Well, we'll see." I did not mention that my wire for reservations had been confirmed.

We found a man who would take us to Burier for the modest sum of thirty francs. It is a beautiful drive, the lake on one side, on the other hillsides draped with vines, great extents of famous vineyards, where the grapes were already large as currants. The sun, not yet setting, was low, drenching the still water with a glittering radiance. We passed through lovely little Vevey, always so peaceful, spread out along the lake, then on to La Tour de Peilz, where Courbet lived and died, still a village, dominated by its château, a gem in an antique setting. Here we turned off the main thoroughfare, moving uphill on a country road that took us past wide pastures to the little village of Burier, a handful of houses on a strip of high land, almost a cliff, overlooking the lake. On the other side was the little village station, embowered in rambler roses, vast stretches of pasture land beyond.

"What a lovely spot," Desmonde murmured, as we drew up at the hotel.

This, though named Reine du Lac, was not a large or pretentious establishment, but as we entered it gave manifest evidence of class. Our rooms, separated by a bathroom, overlooked the lake, with a superb view of the Dents du Midi, still snow-capped and now bathed in a rose-red, empurpled sunset.

"And all that lovely open country behind," Desmonde continued. "Trust Madame Donovan to find it."

We were both hungry and decided on an early dinner. We had an admirable table by one of the windows. Most of the other early diners were rich old ladies for whom this hotel was obviously a choice resort. One had a tiny toy Pekinese, supremely well behaved, on her lap, which she fed with minute snippets from her own plate.

The dinner was excellent, the fish unbelievably good, a grilled ferra, which the head waiter described as 'swimming in the lake only this afternoon'. Then, inevitably, chicken, but tender and nicely cooked. The sweet, a well-made crème caramel. Finally, as we drank our coffee, the moon came up in slow grandeur, over the distant Les Roches. Although slightly on the wane, visually the great white disc was as good as new.

"Let's spend the rest of our lives here," Desmonde said.

"That's what Madame Donovan seems to be doing. I gather she's in Ireland for no more than three months each year."

"Let's go out and see if we can spot her place."

Outside, in that lucent light, it was almost clear as day. We walked across the road to the little red tiled station which, on that single line, served perhaps three or four trains in the day. In the little garden the station master, so distinguished by his official cap, was taking the air. We approached him and Desmonde greeted him in French. I wish I might record the conversation in the idiom of that tongue, it was extremely amusing; but the translation must serve.

"Master of the Station, may I trouble you to answer a question?"

"You are not troubling me, sir. As you see, I am not occupied with my official duties, which have been fully and effectively completed for the day. I am regarding my artichokes, which, alas, do badly."

"I regret that your artichokes do badly, sir."

"I, too, sir. What is your question?"

"We are seeking a lady named Donovan."

"Ah, ha, the Irelander."

"Exactly! So you know her?"

"Who does not know Madame Donovan?"

"She is well known here?"

"Have I not said so, sir?"

"For what is she well known, Station Master?"

"For everything, sir."

"Everything?"

"Everything that is good, sir."

Desmonde looked at me and said aside: "Shall I go on?" I nodded.

"Station Master, what good exactly does Madame Donovan do?"

"Have I not said, sir, that she gives to all, to the village, the school, the home of old men there, at the end of the road, you observe it from here. Even in the smallest givings. There is a great oak tree where the old men used to gather to talk. Only this month she puts a good strong seat all round the tree where now they sit with comfort."

We could have gone on pleasantly in the delicious cool air, but now Desmonde put the final question.

"Where does the good Irish lady live?"

The station master removed his pipe and waved it widely, as he answered:

"Look over the other side of my little station, sir. Look to the right, very far, and to the left, as far as the village. Look then to the distance, the tall wood on the left, the home farm with cows still in the fields, on the right. Look then to the large house in the centre upon the little walled eminence. You will then have seen the domain of Madame Donovan."

Desmonde looked at me in silence.

"Thank you profoundly, Station Master."

"A pleasure, sir. Do you visit Madame?"

"Tomorrow, Station Master. Good evening."

"Good evening to you, sir."

"Some domain," I remarked, as we turned away.

"We must breach it, Alec."

Back in the hotel we took turn-about in the bathroom. The beds were excellent, the hand-washed linen sheets softly caressing. I fell asleep instantly.

V

AT SEVEN O'CLOCK next morning I was awakened by a knock at my door. A maid entered silently with coffee in a thermos and fresh rolls and put the tray on the table with a murmured, "*Service, monsieur.*" She seemed surprised, almost sad, when I said I would have my breakfast later. I felt sad too, for I knew the coffee was good and burning hot, while

the rolls, not the usual horrible *ballons*, were genuine crois-
sants, sure sign of a first class hotel.

When she had gone, I rolled out of bed, took a cold shower,
and quickly dressed. I then went downstairs and, following
directions received from the head waiter on the previous
evening, set off at a hard pace for La Tour de Peilz.

On the outskirts of that lovely village, I found the small
convent towards which I had been directed. Those of my
readers who still remain with me are, I fear, heartily sick of
my early morning devotions. However, this occasion of my
piety must not be omitted since, on entering the little chapel
in which the convent nuns, some twenty in all, were grouped
at the back, I observed that another member of the laity, in
addition to myself, had come for the eight o'clock Mass,
which now began.

She was a woman of perhaps forty years, possibly more,
quietly but most expensively dressed in black, a mink cape
about her shoulders, an English prayer book in her hands.
She was undoubtedly beautiful, yet her expression was so
withdrawn, intent and severe, one was impressed more by
her piety than by her beauty. As I had passed an antique
but magnificently maintained Rolls-Royce in the courtyard
with a uniformed chauffeur in the front seat, I guessed this
to be hers, and also that she was probably English.

We ignored each other during the service, although once
or twice I felt her glance upon me. But when all the nuns had
communicated and we rose simultaneously to receive the
Eucharist, she smiled faintly as I allowed her to precede me.

When Mass was over I left the chapel and set out at a good
pace for Burier. The lady had remained behind to talk with
the nuns. However, I had not gone far before the antique
Rolls purred alongside me.

"May I give you a lift, young man? Where are you going?"

"To the hotel at Burier."

She opened the door. "Oh, do step in, then."

I would much rather have walked, but the opportunity
was too good to miss. I stepped in.

"Are you English?" she asked.

"No, Madame. An Irish Scot."

"And what are you doing in this beautiful and still, mercifully, remote part of Switzerland?"

"I am on my way to Hollywood."

"Good heavens! Are you an actor?"

"No, Madame, merely an author. And I am sponsoring a friend who, in an admirable life, made one horrible mistake for which he has suffered atrociously. He now has a chance, quite literally, to pick himself out of the gutter."

"In Hollywood!"

"He is a singer, his one possession, his buried talent, a superb voice."

Now, I saw comprehension dawning in her eyes. I continued.

"He wants to see his child before he goes. I beg you to permit it. It is only for one day."

She drew back, with a sudden darkening of her face.

"He sent you specially to the chapel, in pretended piety, to get hold of me."

I looked at her steadily.

"If you think that, Madame, that I would so defile the Eucharist, I can only pity you."

Now she had turned pale. The car drew up at the hotel. I opened the door. As I stepped out she said, in a low voice:

"He may come."

My adventures, which I had certainly not anticipated, were not yet over. As the ancient Rolls drew away a voice hailed me from the far side of the hotel yard, where a man was cleaning the windscreen of his car. Now, as he beckoned, I went over.

He was a big fellow, in a flashy expensive brown suit, and his car was rather different from the vehicle I had just quitted. It was an Alfa Romeo, low, rakish, and incredibly fast, the finest product of Italy.

"Good morning!" He spoke excellent English. "I see you know Madame Donovan."

"Oh, slightly, she gave me a lift from La Tour."

"I know her niece, more than slightly." He flashed his big teeth at me. "My name is Munzio. I hope to marry her when she gets her divorce."

"Congratulations," I said, then quickly: "I am admiring your car. Very fast, I suppose."

"That is the finest car in the world. And fast? Let me tell you. After breakfast, which I often take at the hotel, since I garage my car here, I leave for my office in Milano, pass round the lake, a narrow twisting dangerous road, *over* the Gotthard, not by the tunnel, then across the frontier, again many bad roads, then to Milano, do my business, have lunch and am back *here in time for tea*."

It sounded impossible, yet I believed him.

"You must be a first-class driver."

"I am the best." Again he flashed the teeth. "I drive this car as I ride and master a good horse, a thoroughbred, between my knees."

"You go now?"

"Of course."

"Then I'll look out for you at tea."

Again he flashed the smile.

"I see you, then. I show you."

I went into the hotel, rather full of my recent experiences, which, after I'd had my coffee, I immediately related to Desmonde, who, breakfasted and dressed, was sitting on the balcony of his bedroom.

"I believe I saw that fellow," he said calmly. "He must be from northern Italy, he's so big and powerful." Then: "It takes someone like that to keep Claire in order." Then again: "How fortunate you met Madame Donovan. Now we won't be turned away at the gate. Although I'm sure she won't receive me."

And so it was when, at ten o'clock, we strolled down the village street, past the old men, seated round the oak tree, and presented ourselves at the heavy iron gates of the estate. These were immediately opened, but the lodge keeper said to Desmonde, in Italian:

"Madame does not receive today, sir. But you may proceed to the terrace."

We walked slowly towards the house, in bright sunshine, with rooks circling and cawing in the tall trees that bordered the entrance to the estate. The drive was freshly raked, the edges trimly clipped, the park stretching on either side, recently mown and in good heart. A large walled garden came into view on the left as we breasted the slight rise at the end of the drive. The house itself, of plain grey stone, was large and square, entirely unornamental, and surrounded by that invaluable protection against the Swiss winter, a covered terrace.

On the south side of this terrace, preparations had been made which caused Desmonde to hasten his pace. A rug had been spread on the clean tiles, and on this stood a substantial play-pen, beside which, seated erect on a hard chair, was an elderly, severe Schweizer Deutsch nurse, immaculately garbed in a fresh linen uniform, a small watch pinned to her breast and around her neck a high starched linen collar, of which the unendurable tightness and stiffness bespoke the wearer's implacable fortitude. And within the pen a little animated bit of life in petticoats was already cajoling with Desmonde, on his knees beside the pen.

"She knows me, the darling," Desmonde murmured, as I arrived, tears welling from his eyes, adding, equally mistakenly: "The moment she saw me, she smiled with recognition all over her darling face."

Yet who knows? He had bathed and bedded the little one so often, he might indeed have touched a slender chord of recognition. He had brought a present for his child, a little silver and ivory rattle, and wisely, oh, how wisely—for Desmonde knew women—he handed it to the nurse, who accepted it with a prim, gratified smile, looked it all over, wiped it carefully with a strip of clean linen, then gave it to the child. Immediately, rattles and delighted laughter filled the air. I thereupon left Desmonde to it, aware that he would presently win the approval, if not the sympathy, of the nurse, and be permitted guardedly to handle and to hold his own child. Already he had narrowed the breach by addressing her, with proper humility, in her own Schweizer Deutsch.

Back at the hotel I asked at the desk for a picnic lunch, went upstairs and changed into shorts, sweater and sneakers. When I came downstairs the neat packet was already at the bureau—what a good hotel was the Reine du Lac!

I went back into the estate, parked the lunch on a seat in the park under one of the big trees, and set off at the double. I had not had my exercise for some time and was sadly missing it.

Round the grounds I went at scout's pace, fifty yards running then fifty hard walking, an admirable method of progression in which you do not exhaust yourself and can keep it up indefinitely. In my circling I made out that Desmonde was progressing in his own particular way. First

he had a cushion for his knees, then a chair on which he
sat, actually with the child upon his lap. I also had a shrewd
suspicion that I was being watched from behind the long
curtains of one of the upper windows.

I was still going well when the noon bell tolled, not for the
angelus in this canton, but to summon the old men to their
dinner at the Home. I then felt it was time to have my own
lunch, the more so since Desmonde, nurse, and child had
disappeared from the terrace. I could have done with a
shower. Instead I rubbed myself down with the napkin that
enwrapped my lunch, put on my sweater, and sat down on the
bench.

What a good lunch! Avoiding the usual unwanted surplus,
one delicious ham sandwich, a slice of Emmenthaler between
two buttered digestive biscuits, then fruit: apple, orange, a
huge, heavenly Comice pear. How I enjoyed it all, after my
run! Then, having carefully tucked the fruit cores and other
fragments into the napkin, I stretched out on my back on
the tree-shaded bench. I would willingly have spent the entire
summer in this lovely place. Let me confess that at moments
such as this I felt rather tired of Desmonde. I had seen quite
a lot of him lately, and in his present embittered mood he was
not a stimulating companion. But I had given the poor devil
my word and, come what may, I would keep it.

I must have fallen asleep, for my watch showed half-past
two when I awoke. And now a charming little cavalcade was
in progress on the avenue that led to the walled garden.
The nurse, Desmonde wheeling the child in a little open
carriage, and two Kerry blue terriers following obediently
to heel.

I watched them for a few minutes, pleased that everything
had been accomplished without open rage or rancour. Then,
as I was no longer needed, I decided to take myself off. I
had crossed the park and reached the main avenue when I
saw a figure beckoning from the west terrace. Although I
had no wish to meet Madame Donovan again, I could not
well ignore that invitation.

"I could not let you go without apologizing for my atrocious
remark to you this morning."

"Please do not worry, Madame. I am used to hard knocks
in my profession."

She paused, leaning forward, as though in propitiation.

"Won't you let me give you tea? Here, on the terrace."

Again, I could not refuse.

"Thank you, Madame."

She smiled. "I'm sure you are thirsty after all your running. Do sit a moment while I tell Maria."

She returned a few minutes later followed by a stout Italian maid bearing a well-equipped tray. As I accepted my first cup I asked myself: how should one open the conversation?

"You have a very beautiful place here, Madame. And very large, too."

"Yes, when I came here, prices were not high, and I thought it a pity to break up the estate. I even took over the farm, and am very glad I did so." She paused. "I have Italian workers, and most excellent they are. You know, I suppose, that many Italians come to work in Switzerland, glad to find work and a decent wage."

"So you are really settled here, Madame?"

"I love Switzerland. Chiefly, of course, for its beauty. But in every way it is an admirable, contented country where the people work hard, the trains run on time, in fact, where everything is in order." She paused. "Naturally, I go home to Ireland for three or four months in the year."

"I am often tempted by Switzerland. But for a very base reason. Taxes."

"Yes, they are kind to us, and to their own people too," She smiled. "You would not settle in Hollywood?"

"Never, Madame. Authors are not persona grata there. They are regarded with contempt. Mere scullions!"

"And yet you go there tomorrow."

"I am going for two reasons. Mainly for Desmonde. But also to try to sell my new novel."

There was a silence, then she said:

"It is sad that Desmonde should not redeem himself more suitably, more nobly. I have been reading again today of a young priest who spent all his life in the remote, impoverished interior of China, giving himself, less to conversion, than to relieving suffering, sickness, and famine."

"Unfortunately, Madame, for Desmonde to attempt such a mission of redemption would be a complete negation of his character. He would get no further than Hong Kong,

returning by the first boat with a splendid assortment of Kang
Hsi china. No, Madame, he must sing his way to salvation!"

She barely smiled. "How do we know what lies ahead for
us, or for anyone? The future is unpredictable." She added:
"I can't understand why you are so good to him."

"We were great friends at school, and he was very decent
to me when I had nothing. I owe it to Desmonde that I sat
in the stalls of the Kings Theatre, enthralled by the wonderful
performance of Geraldine Moore in *Tosca*." Her expression
did not change. "Besides, he has had a very rough time since
he got mixed up with your attractive niece."

"It was of his own choosing. You know that Claire is seeking
a civil divorce. She is already living with Munzio."

"It makes no difference. We are leaving early tomorrow for
Genoa. He will never see her again."

There was a silence. I felt drawn to this woman and,
suddenly, immensely sorry for her. She was not made for a
virginal life, yet willed herself to it. What could one say?
I stood up.

"Now I must go, Madame. I expect Desmonde will stay
to see his infant in her bath. Thank you again for your
courtesy."

She smiled and said: "Don't fail to let me know if you settle
in Switzerland. And come to see me in Ireland when I am
there."

"And you, Madame. If you are in London, do visit us in
Sussex. My wife would love to know you. She does not get
about much, and would welcome you."

"I will come," she said. And in these three words was the
beginning of a long and precious friendship.

We shook hands, then I turned and went back to the
hotel. And there, sure enough, outside the hotel lockups,
thoroughly spattered, awaiting a wash, was the Alfa Romeo.
At the bureau I arranged for a car to take us to Genoa tomorrow, leaving at six-thirty. I also asked to have my bill
prepared at that hour tomorrow.

I then went upstairs to my room, feeling unaccountably
depressed, perhaps in the knowledge that I had spent a useless
week. I therefore sat down and cheered myself up by writing
a long letter home, inquiring tenderly, amongst other things,
on the well-being of the new wallflower bed. What a God's

blessing it was for a man to have a home and a wife and sons who loved him. Desmonde had none of this, so I must be tolerant of his unmanly rhapsodizing over his child.

He was late in coming to the hotel. I was half-way through dinner when he arrived. He seemed to have little appetite, and ate in absolute silence. Finally, he looked at me with misery in his eyes.

"I gather that my wife is about to divorce me and remarry. If she should claim the child, that would be the end."

What could one say in reply? Nothing. In view of our early start on the morrow we both turned in early.

VI

THE *Cristoforo Colombo* slid out of the wide harbour with flags flying, speeded away from her home port by the blare of sirens and the ringing of church bells. We had arrived in Genoa with two hours to spare, ample time to collect the packages awaiting us at the offices of the Italian Line. All that we had ordered was there, everything, neatly packaged and awaiting transit through the customs. What a triumph of London craftsmanship, skill, efficiency and integrity. Normal and expected features of that age, no doubt, but could they be duplicated in the present day? The mere question is absurd.

I had left Desmonde busily unwrapping in our stateroom while I went aft on deck, to watch the receding coast line and to renew my acquaintance with this lovely ship, in which I had voyaged once before. I was extremely fond of these Italian ships, not only because they followed the southern route, but for everything else—speed, comfort, and a typical Italian type of service, willing and friendly. Below, the head steward was already taking bookings for tables, and I reserved the side table on the portside where my wife and I had previously been seated. Then I looked in at the little chapel, a delightful feature of this line. Already an Italian padre was on his knees there, so I knew that we should have Mass every morning. One last trip to the sun deck, where I reserved two well-placed chairs. No covered promenade deck for me, on this perennially sunny voyage.

Back in the cabin I found Desmonde seated and steadily regarding his new clothes, all laid out on his bed. Ever since leaving Switzerland he had been in a queer, often morose, mood. I accordingly approached him with a guarded cheerfulness.

"Tried anything on yet, for fit, size, colour and cut?"

"No! I'm just thinking what a popinjay I shall look in them. Do you know that this is the second time in my beastly life that I have been outfitted by charity."

I laughed. "Keep on your old duds then, if you'll feel more comfortable."

"And waste all that you've done for me. It will be wasted anyway."

"Come now, Des! Pull yourself together. You haven't been at all yourself lately."

"Could you expect me to be!" Desmonde rarely used foul language, but now he did. "My child in charge of an old perpetual virgin who hates me. My wife in bed with a big Italian bastard, getting it hot and hard every night and loving it." He put his hand to his head. "Oh, God, I still love her, bitch though she was, still is, and ever will be. And here I am, bloody swine that I am, sponging, sponging on you, costing you the earth and all for nothing. That publicity freak won't get me to sing. And even if she does I'll fall flat on my face."

There was only one thing to do and I did it. I went out of the cabin and quietly closed the door. Naturally I was worried. If he broke down now, how should I feel, backing a horse that refused to go to the post? Nevertheless, I was hungry, and at half-past twelve I went down to lunch where my steward on the previous voyage greeted me with affection—I must therefore have tipped him handsomely.

"But are we alone, sir?" he inquired sadly, fitting me tenderly into my chair.

"Not at all. I have a friend . . ."

At that moment precisely Desmonde appeared, a new Desmonde, washed, shaved, brushed, attired in the smashing new grey suiting, the new soft-collared shirt and near Old Etonian tie, the new brown hand-made shoes, and silk hosiery. The steward, further overpowered by Desmonde's perfect Italian and his equally perfect knowledge of all Italian dishes on the menu, took our orders in an attitude of prayer, then retreated, backwards.

"I'm terribly sorry, Alec," Desmonde said, firmly unwrapping his napkin. "In fact, I'm damned sorry. But no more of it, I promise you."

He was as good as his word, never again did he lapse into that abysmal mood during the voyage, yet he was not the cheerful, lighthearted Desmonde I had once known. Moody and irritable, he seemed obsessed by an inward brooding.

The wind blew lightly, the sun shone, Desmonde did as he pleased, mainly on the flat of his back in his deck chair with his eyes closed, moodily avoiding all attempts at shipboard acquaintance. I followed my usual enjoyable routine: up fairly early for a run round the deck and some easy exercises in the gym, a plunge in the pool, then the short Mass and Communion in the chapel. I was then ready for a good breakfast and a lazy, lazy day in the sun. Unfortunately the nice little padre latched on to me. He came from a most laudable institution in Rome, to which I had been enticed on a visit to that city some years before, and which was run by young priests who taught useful handicrafts to the homeless boys taken off the streets. The purpose of his visit to the United States was, inevitably, to collect money from the various Italian communities in New York and other large cities. I should have had him at my side all the voyage had I not given him a fifty with the whispered confession that my doctors had prescribed silence and complete rest for me owing to an affliction of the liver. But before he left me I asked him about Desmonde, briefly explaining my friend's present situation. His answer was emphatic and immediate.

"He will never be at peace, never, never, never, until he returns to the Church. I have seen it before, many, many times. Once you quarrel with the Lord, you will never be happy till you make up and tell Him you are sorry."

Too soon we were across, the engines ceased their violent throbbing and we glided past the Statue of Liberty into New York harbour. How pleasant to disembark when one has little luggage. Carrying each a light suitcase we walked freely past crowds of passengers gathered in confusion around enormous piles of huge cabin trunks, baby carriages, golf bags, and other paraphernalia of travel *en famille*. Immigration had been passed on the ship; we simply took a taxi to Penn Station and the morning train to Chicago that connected with the Super Chief, on which I booked a double compartment.

Those who know only the utilitarian, strike-dislocated trains of today, or who simply travel by air, cannot conceive of the splendour and luxury of that magnificent trans-continental train. We changed stations at Chicago and there, awaiting us, was the Super Chief, shining with the potential of speed, a great greyhound waiting to be unleashed. The red carpet was already unrolled and, to the sound of music—preamble of Hollywood, ridiculous, yet agreeable—we boarded the monster. Our compartment was ready, indescribably immaculate, fresh antimacassars on the seat, the two bunks folded up against the partition, the bathroom spotless, and the car attendant, white teeth gleaming in a smile, asking if we wished breakfast. As we drank coffee the train pulled out silently on its flashing dash across America.

Twice before I had made this journey, but it was a novelty for Desmonde. Yet he was never interested or relaxed, gazing moodily through the window, and as we approached our destination he began to show signs of anxiety and tension only partly dispelled by a Western Union telegram handed to him at Albuquerque which said curtly:

GET OFF AT PASADENA WILL MEET YOU THERE

"At least she expects us," Desmonde muttered.

"Expects *you*," I corrected him. "I'll get the hoof!"

At Pasadena, where most of the Hollywood élite leave the train, we obeyed the telegram and got off. And there, on the platform, in full flesh, was the little Delia B. She reached up and embraced Desmonde, I heard the smack of the kiss.

"Glad to see you, darling. Everything's laid on. You're looking good." Then to me: "Why in hell are you here, Red?"

"I'm the valet."

"Then stay valet. I've only a single room booked for Desmonde at the Beverly Hills."

"In that case I'll make do with the four-roomed cottage I've reserved in the Beverly Hills garden."

She actually laughed. "You win, Red. You want to bunk in with him, Des?"

"Don't you think I'd better?" Desmonde said drily. "You see, I wouldn't be here but for Alec. He's paid cash for everything, even the clothes I'm wearing."

"Not bad, Red, not bad. You got anything of your own to do here?"

"Certainly, I'm here to sell my new book."

"I think I heard about that one. The Cuticle, ain't it?"

"That's the one, Delia B. The story of an Ingrowing Toenail."

We got into her car, not the opulence I had expected, but a knocked-about Ford which she drove with all the slap-dash abandon of her nature. She parked at the hotel, and when we had registered came through the garden to the cottage to make sure that I had not been lying.

"Not bad, not bad, Red. You got the doings. This will set you back plenty."

"My wife and I had it last year."

"Why didn't you let me know you was in town? Ah, well, this will suit nicely for you, Des. Just do nothing, rest up over the weekend. The big day is still uncertain but may come soon."

When she had gone, we unpacked and stretched out on long chairs in the sun. At that period before the increase in population, automobiles, and industries had darkened the light coastal mist into smog, Beverly Hills was one of the most enchanting resorts in Southern California, and the hotel at which we were staying one of the best.

We simply lay about that day, but after dinner in the hotel restaurant I rang my agent, Frank Hulton, at his home.

"How do you like your new job, Alec?"

"It's a lot easier than writing best-sellers."

"Well, if you can stop pressing pants tomorrow morning, will you come out here for breakfast?"

"I'd love to, Frank. I'll get all the shoes brushed tonight. Listen, I'd like to bring a new customer along with me. At present he's only a prospect, but I think he might be big stuff."

"Bring him along, Alec. I gather he's got Bedelia B. behind him. Anyway, I'm looking forward to seeing you."

We both slept well that night. However one may laud the Super Chief, there is no escape from the symphony of the rails.

Next morning at nine o'clock we were in Frank Hulton's down-town apartment, I at least conscious of the esteem manifest in the invitation to his home, rather than to his busy office. Frank, a clean-living man of the highest principles who never had a contract with his clients beyond his given word, was devoted to his health, an idiosyncrasy typically exemplified in his choice of breakfast. When he had asked us what we wanted he rang down to the kitchen, gave the order and added: "The usual for me, please."

The 'usual', which came up with our coffee and rolls, was an inviting assortment of prepared raw vegetables: cut radishes, spring onions, dainty little carrots, hearts of lettuce, choice pieces of cauliflower, and fragrant strips of celery, all fresh that morning from the Farmers' Market. We agreed afterwards that we could well have forgone our excellent rolls and butter for such a mouth-watering spread.

Meanwhile, we talked, first of the chances of my book, then of Desmonde, whose dossier I reeled off while Frank listened intently.

"It's very apparent," he smiled at Desmonde, "that Bedelia B. is absolutely sold on you. And that, incidentally, is a rare bit of luck, for when Bedelia B. backs anyone or anything she usually sees it through. Mind you, she's not the Queen. That title belongs to Louella Parsons, a very different type and a great lady. But Bedelia is on the up and up, a sticker, who never lets a thing go, once she has her teeth in it. For days past she's been dropping hints, thick as a paperchase, mostly directed towards the young Caruso group. So the next move is up to her."

"What do you think this will be?" asked Desmonde.

"It's an easy guess. Bedelia has a terrific in with the really big movie people: Selznick, Sam Goldwyn, Meyer, particularly Sam. The next time one of them throws a big party, she'll have you there, Desmonde. My guess again is that she'll fix a real slam-bang opening for you. Take it, my boy, and you're in. And if you're in, don't sign any quick contracts or you'll bitterly regret it. I'll be here, waiting to help you make that first million."

When we left Frank some twenty minutes later, I felt that Desmonde had been impressed.

"You like him?"

"Who wouldn't?" He smiled drily. "And I rather fancied his breakfast."

"Frank has done me an awful lot of good. I don't mind what he eats."

Now there was nothing we could do but wait. And how pleasant, in that golden era, to idle in the garden of the Beverly Hills Hotel. The big blue pool was there for the early morning plunge, then the quick walk to the nearby resort of the faithful. How often, and always in vain, did I ask Desmonde to accompany me rather than watch me gloomily as I set off. He awaited me in the sun, studying me morosely when I returned.

"Got your sins forgiven?" he asked me sarcastically, one morning, when I was later than usual.

"No, Desmonde! But I had a good, and I hope useful, talk with Father Devis."

Fortunately, at that moment breakfast rolled in, crisp bread wrapped in a napkin, honey, coffee in the silver thermos and, best of all, the big pink grapefruits, halved and ready to be eaten.

On the fifth day of our stay, when I had begun to worry about the bill, we received a short yet momentous visit from Bedelia, who suddenly appeared as from thin air, pounced like an eagle upon Desmonde and, hooking him by the arm, walked him up and down, articulating rapidly into his ear. Intermittently Desmonde would nod in acquiescence. Finally, Bedelia returned him to the cottage where, with *empressement*, she produced a large and magnificently ornate card.

"Take care of this, Des, for although you'll wind up the star of the party, without it you'll never get in."

"What about my ticket, Delia B.?"

"Ah, Red," she said kindly, "you don't want no ticket. Sam's parties are big stuff. Authors definitely included out."

"Come on, D.B. Give. I'm entitled to see the fun. I'll sit like a mouse in one corner."

"Mice are out too, Red." Suddenly she laughed, handing over another ticket. "I guess you're due to be in on it. But see you clean yourself up nice, and don't even mention the word books, or you'll be chucked out on the spot."

On Delia B.'s departure, we examined the beautiful tickets: formal gold-edged, gold-inlaid invitations to a party to be given by Sam Goldwyn at his home in Beverly Hills, on the evening of June 12th. I looked at Desmonde. "Only four more days to wait!" After our big trip out, it seemed a very short time.

"Have you decided what to sing?" I asked. "The set piece, I suppose—the Prize Song?"

"Good God! Am I a school kid who has just learned up one bloody song? I'll sing whatever comes up my bloody back." After a pause he added: "I'm tired of that damn aria and I'm sure you are too. Let's not talk about it, Alec. We'll just go and see what happens."

The rule of silence was strictly observed, although the imminence of that fateful night weighed upon us. When, finally, it was upon us, we got ourselves, in the words of Delia B., cleaned up nice. I would never, on any occasion, look *soigné*, but Desmonde, bathed, shaved, in his dark suit and other new accoutrements, really looked smashing, a starlet's dream of delight. He was at his best a sensationally handsome man, and rest, sunshine, and the Beverly Hills good living had put a bloom on him.

When we were both ready we sat looking at each other in silence, since Delia B. had strictly enjoined Desmonde to arrive late, extremely late. Desmonde was calm, with that expression of complete indifference, now almost habitual. Had he, I wondered, taken a pill? If so I did not blame him. This was his moment of truth, the crux of a chequered career that might bring dazzling success or abysmal failure. Even for me, who mattered not at all, this waiting was hell.

At half-past ten, after several earlier false starts, sternly repressed, we passed through the hotel to a waiting taxi. The drive was short, too short, before we drew up at the large, brightly illuminated house. Our humble taxi was clearly suspect by the posse of police on duty at the entrance, but our tickets were eventually validated and we passed into the house where our hats were accepted by another detective, disguised as a butler, who showed us to the great drawing room of the house. On the threshold we looked at each other, took a deep breath, and went in.

The enormous room, brilliantly lit by two huge Venetian

chandeliers, furnished and decorated, carpeted and draped
with the taste and luxury that extreme wealth can command,
and sporting two Steinway grand pianos, one at either end,
was populated by perhaps forty human beings, the sexes
separated, according to American custom, so that the elegantly
gowned women chattered in a gay group on one side, while
the men, many immediately recognizable as international
stars, were scattered around self-consciously playing the role
of he-men on the other.

Between the two groups, on a somewhat elevated little
atrium, sat the inimitable Sam, master of all he surveyed,
surrounded by intimates amongst whom, beside a couple of
hard-faced men, and in full battle array, with a scarlet ostrich
feather in her hair, was Delia B. At one of the grand pianos
sat Richard Tauber, at the other, much to my relief, John
McCormack, and behind John, on a little settee, John's
wife. Both of these splendid people were my friends, so I
immediately made tracks across the room and sat down beside
Lily, who welcomed me with a smile. No finer or sweeter
woman ever set foot in Hollywood. Now she whispered:

"John tells me there's something cooking."

Desmonde alone, in the doorway, was naturally a con-
spicuous figure but, after surveying the room with complete
composure, he walked quietly to a deserted area of that
magnificent chamber, sat down in a Louis XVII gilt armchair,
crossed his legs, and with an air of remote interest, let his
eyes rest on a stupendous Andreo del Sarto on the opposite
wall, depicting in some detail The Rape of the Sabine Women.
Indeed, as Desmonde viewed it, a slight critical lift of his
left eyebrow seemed to indicate that in his considered opinion
it was not by the hand of the master, but rather by one of
his pupils, possibly Jacopo Fellini.

Was it my imagination, or was there a lull in the feline
chatter, almost a silence, as eyes were compelled towards
this elegant, imperturbable, solitary figure? Nothing attracts
women more in Hollywood than the attractive, when it is
unknown, and a man. Naturally, all the lovelies had their
beauteous optics trained on Desmonde. These were stars of
the silver screen, world famous, some without talent, but
drilled by clever directors into some semblance of the histrionic
art, performers who could be taught to mime the requisite

emotions upon request—I shall leave them nameless. But others there were, with magnificent talent. I could see Grace Moore, Carole Lombard, Jane Novak, Lila Lee and, sitting a little apart from the others, Ethel Barrymore and Norma Shearer.

There was, in fact, little else to attract. Tauber and John were playing little operatic snippets and tossing them across to one another, in a competitive kind of game. But the party had, in fact, dwindled to that mid-point in Hollywood parties when everyone is talked out, and waiting for something to happen before supper.

It was then that a woman detached herself from the group on the settee and, as every eye was turned upon her, slowly approached Desmonde. She was Grace Moore, young, slim, attractive, and already well-known as a singer. She paused and held out her hand as she reached Desmonde, who immediately stood up. At that moment Puccini took over, skilfully led in by John at the piano, and Grace, drawing near to Desmonde, began to sing that incomparable bridal aria from *Butterfly*.

> 'Quest' obi pomposa
> di sciolger mi tarda
> si vesta la sposa.'

Very beautifully she sang the first part of the love duet, then Desmonde broke in.

> 'Con moti di scoiattolo
> i nodi allenta e scioglie!
> Pensar che quel giocattolo
> è mia moglie . . .'

Let it be said, without further transcription, this beautiful and touching love duet was continued with appropriate amatory gestures. So unexpected, so gracefully accomplished, and with such restrained perfection of the male voice, there was immediate applause.

"Desmonde," said Grace, "that was delightful, I did enjoy it, so kind of you to keep yourself in check, and not drown me out. Now! You must sing for your supper, alone."

With a smile Grace disengaged herself and sat down.

Desmonde smiled too, but with assumed modesty. He was

I

off to a good start and was taking no risks: I knew it would be the set piece. He said:

"If it would not bore all the famous and distinguished people here I would like to offer a great aria, which as a boy I once heard sung by a voice infinitely greater than mine: the voice of Enrico Caruso."

It was a brilliant move. At the outset he had set himself up against the ultimate in perfection. A few suppressed female titters, followed by dead silence. Then with complete composure—that mood of uncaring unconcern that had lately possessed him—Desmonde began to sing. I had hoped he would play it safe and sing the Prize Song but he did not.

It was that last wild, heart-breaking aria of Cavaradossi in *Tosca*, as he is led to his execution.

> 'Amaro sol per te m'era il morire
> Da te prende la vita ogni splendore . . .'

I had heard that aria several times before, but never, never as Desmonde sang it now, with all the feeling, the bitterness that was in his heart.

There were no titters now, no whispers, scarcely a movement. Desmonde was really giving them the works. And when that final cry, 'Avrà sol da te voce e colore', hit the ceiling, the applause, for a party of this nature, was astounding. Everyone was standing, John stood up at the piano roaring: "Bravo! Bravissimo!" Tauber joined the tumult on the bass keys of the piano. Delia B. with cupped hands was trying to make herself heard. I was doing my bit with the full force of my lungs, but at the same time stealing towards the door. Desmonde had done it! Now I was no longer needed, a mere accessory to the fact. As I stood for a moment in the doorway I heard Delia B.'s voice come through:

"Now sing the Prize Song, Des."

"Yes, do, Desmonde," cried John. "But first, now that Cavaradossi is gone, let's have something simple and tender for the ladies. Sing 'Passing By'."

A silence fell while Desmonde seemed to reflect, then he smiled to John. I hoped it would be the Edward Purcell, the sweetest and most tender of them all. And so it was. Half turning to the ladies he raised his voice:

'There is a lady sweet and kind,
    Was never face so pleas'd my mind;
    I did but see her passing by,
    And yet I love her till I die!'

Nothing could have been more captivating, more intimate.
And so different from the *Tosca*. One glance at those rapt
listening faces assured me that it was a perfect choice.

Then, quietly, I took off.

VII

I CAME AWAY from that great beautiful, brilliant room,
my ears still resounding with the swelling acclamation of
all within, and set out at a hard pace for the Beverly Hills.
I knew I ran the risk of being picked up—night walkers are
criminally suspect in that choice district—yet it was only
a short way to the hotel and I felt I must violently exorcize
my inner turmoil.

Desmonde had done it, he had more than done it, he
had justified himself at last, and how rosy would be his future
from now on. And now, even as I exulted, I wanted only
one thing: to get home, as urgently, as speedily as train and
ship could take me. I had done what I set out to do, I had
helped my friend, at some inconvenience to myself, nothing
more was demanded of me. And oh, how overpowering was
the vision of my little country house and garden and of all
the dear people within. The raspberries and currants would
be in full swing, the Victoria plums and greengages coming
along, the roses in all splendour, at their best.

I reached the hotel in record time, and at the desk made
inquiry as to the means of sudden departure. I was not lucky
enough to catch a returning Super Chief, but the ordinary
Chicago train, non-sleeper, was due to leave at 6 a.m. this
very morning—it was now past 4 a.m. I immediately paid
the bill for the cottage to the end of the week, thus securing a
fuller co-operation from the night clerk, who rang Los Angeles
Station and booked me a first class reservation on the Chicago
train. We then studied the trans-Atlantic sailings from New

York. With luck I might be aboard the *Queen Mary*, leaving on the following Saturday. I then tipped the clerk, explaining that my friend would probably return later that day, and went through the hotel and garden to the cottage.

Here, I packed my belongings, sat down and wrote a note to Desmonde which I left on the desk. I then rang Frank and, surprisingly, his voice came over the wire at once.

"Frank," I said, "I know you hate being wakened, but this is Alec, and I absolutely had to call you."

"Don't worry, Alec. I've already been called four times in the last hour."

"Then you know he's made it. In a big way."

"I know, Alec. I'm just waiting on the early editions."

"Frank, I rang you to let you know I'm bowing out by the 6 a.m. train. I've done my little bit and now I'm relying on you to take care of the new star."

"I'll do that. Say, Alec, now you've done everything, double plus, for the guy, don't you want to stay and cash in on it?"

"I guess not, Frank. I've had an awful lot of Desmonde lately, I need a little rest, back home."

"I get you, Alec. Say, your book hits the bookstalls and libraries today. Rely on me to cash in on that."

"Thanks a lot, Frank. Good luck and goodbye."

"Same to you, Alec."

How easily one falls into the idiom of Hollywood. I hung up with a warm feeling round the pericardium and, as I was too bung full of impetus to rest, I went back to the desk and asked the clerk to call a taxi. This he did, the night porter brought my suitcase from the cottage, and I was off.

At the station I picked up and paid for my ticket at the booking office. My train was at Track 2, the engine, no Super Chief but a solid cross-country plodder, already with steam up, but I hung around waiting for the morning papers to come in. Just before we pulled out I managed to grab a copy of the *Hollywood Star*, and there it was, splashed across the front page:

'NEW STAR BLAZES INTO HOLLYWOOD SKY

'Last night at a splendid reception given by the King of Hollywood, our own beloved Sam Goldwyn, in the presence of all the top stars of his Kingdom, Desmonde Fitzgerald, a young man, admittedly of great personal attraction, one might even say beauty, but completely unknown, rescued from menial toil in Dublin, held his audience of stars, all experienced, worldly-wise, and talented in their own right, utterly spellbound for more than an hour by the magic of his voice, while he sang his way into their hearts with selections from Grand Opera, and in their own languages, arias of Italy and Germany, and above all, through repeated encores, the touching songs of his native Ireland.

'When at last, perforce, the recital was over, though all would have wished it to continue, every living being in that magnificent salon, not excepting our beloved Sam himself, stood up and took Desmonde to their hearts with a prolonged standing ovation. Not since Caruso took the U.S.A. by storm has such a voice been heard in America, the equal or, dare one say, yes one dares, the superior of the great Italian maestro.'

Lots more of this followed, lusher and lusher, and I read every word of it, forced to confess that as one horrendous superlative followed another, so did the warmth round my heart expand. Full credit to the little Trumpeter, but I had helped, in my own way, helped to rescue this splendid talent from despair and hopelessness.

We were now pounding over the metals at a steady pace. I wrapped myself in my coat and, as the seat in front of me was empty, I put up my feet and went to sleep.

This train was, in reality, a penance after the luxury of the Super Chief. But I have a strange masochistic streak which makes me welcome sufferings and tribulations, provided I have the ability to endure them: suffer in silence has, in my view, always been an admirable admonition.

I shall therefore pass over my journey to Chicago with no other comment than that I was delivered safely to the New York express, which sped me to Penn Station with just enough time to board the *Queen Mary*, in which accomplishment I must again extol the virtue of travelling 'light'.

My first action on board was to cleanse myself in a prolonged hot bath. I then asked the steward for the English papers. He brought me *The Times*, the *Daily Telegraph* and the *Daily Mail*. From this selection I must steel myself to endure the critiques of my new novel. But first I was burning to find out whether news of Desmonde had percolated. And there indeed, on the front page of the *Daily Mail*, was a passable photograph of Desmonde, and the following embarrassing screed:

'Young Irish tenor, Desmonde Fitzgerald, who, under the auspices of his friend, author Alec Shannon, hit Hollywood like a bomb last week, has now signed contracts to play the lead in *The Young Caruso* scheduled for immediate filming by Paramount. Only one slight snag: Fitzgerald reputedly sings better than Caruso!'

This was good news, in that it put the final hard, practical touch to our joint adventure. Frank Hulton would ensure that Desmonde's contract was gilt-edged, in Frank's terminology, a bonanza.

I did not feel like spoiling this good moment by turning directly to the literary pages. I thought, with despicable cowardice, that I would first take a little exercise. The windward side of the promenade deck was completely untenanted, the breeze blew fresh, and I set out to enjoy a fast walk. No ship was better fitted for such exercise than the beloved *Queen*—I cannot vouch for actual measurements, but the broad sweep of her promenade deck seemed almost as long as a football field.

The chief deck steward, in his cross-deck snuggery, had been watching me from time to time, with some amusement, and when I finally drew up beside him he said:

"You're a great walker, Mr. Shannon, sir. I remember you well from a couple of years back, on the outward trip. My mate said you practically walked your way to New York."

"It's because I'm nervous, steward."

He laughed. "Never saw a fitter man. By the way, sir, I think it might interest you to take a slow walk down the port side."

"How so?"

"We're fairly light this trip and it's not a sunny morning. But there's about thirty passengers on the deck-chairs, and believe it or not, they're nearly all reading the same book. Why not take a look?"

I took a look, moving slowly along the deck, and found that the steward was right. I walked back, to enjoy again a moment which, alone, was worth my long journey.

To the steward, who was smiling, I said sadly:

"It's hell! They've started giving them away already!"

Then I went down and, seated alone at my usual table, enjoyed a very excellent lunch. When I returned to my cabin I again turned, though reluctantly, to the papers. Suddenly, my eye was caught and held by a paragraph that put all thought of literary criticism out of my head.

'DOUBLE FATALITY ON THE GOTTHARD

'Early yesterday morning, an Italian couple, Signor and Signora Munzio, traversing the Gotthard Pass in a sports Alfa Romeo, were hurled to their deaths by a sudden freak ice-storm.

'Signor Munzio, well known on this route as a fast and skilful driver, was warned of the danger on the Swiss side and strongly advised to take the tunnel train. But as the barriers were not yet up he persisted in an attempt to beat the storm. Alas, without success. Both bodies have now been recovered. The car is a total wreck.'

VIII

THE NEWS OF Desmonde's meteoric career was fully conveyed to us through the public press. His first film, *The Young Caruso*, was a spectacular international success, followed almost immediately by an equally successful Hollywood adaptation of *Rigoletto*. Meanwhile came records, records of operatic gems, of Irish songs, of love songs, sending Desmonde's voice over the air and into a multitude of homes.

From Desmonde himself we heard only in short infrequent snatches, hurriedly written on postcards: '*Working hard, here on location, and hating it*', and again, '*After three retakes under Klieg lights, how dark the world seems. I am worn out, but resolved to stay the course.*'

I had begun to think that he had forgotten me and all that I had done for him when one afternoon, almost a year later, a huge metal-bound packing case was delivered to me at Mellington, the markings indicating that it had come from New York. With Dougal's help I opened it in the barn and there, after innumerable wrappings had been removed, was a breath-taking Degas, at least five feet by four, *Après le Bain*, immediately recognizable as the Master's late and best period, when he used colour unreservedly to offset the lovely nude female form stepping gracefully from her bath, an arm extended for the towel, handed by the maid.

Even Dougal was impressed as we both gazed at it in silence, my heart meanwhile beating like mad, with joy.

"It must have cost a pretty penny, sir," he said, at last.

"The earth, Dougal. It's priceless, really. Far beyond my purse. And just the one picture I needed for my collection."

"It's a beautiful thing, sir. Even I can tell that. But," he looked at me slyly, "what will the wee laddies say when you hing it up?"

"They'll just have to be educated up to it, Dougal." I laughed, fully aware of the comments that would be made in regard to the lady's beautiful bottom.

When we got it to the house I sat down and wrote Desmonde a long rapturous letter, thanking him for his most wonderful gift and begging him to take time to write me fully. We had all heard of his successes, yet we knew nothing of him. I then gave him all the news I thought might interest him. I had recently had a visit from Madame Donovan, and could assure him that all was well with his little daughter. But Canon Daly had been ill and was on sick leave from St. Teresa's. My sons had made another sortie on the wallflower bed. I had begun a new novel which Nan was busy typing. My wife was now better after a recent rather worrying attack.

I ended by again beseeching him to write to me unreservedly and soon.

I then sealed the letter and summoning Nan, who liked nothing better than a walk, we set off to the village to post it.

"What do you think of the new masterpiece, Nanno?"

She thought for a moment, then said:

"Very beautiful. But frankly, Maister, for me, it's a little bit much."

"You would have preferred a view of Sleaford Parish Church?"

"Yes, if painted by Utrillo."

We both laughed. I took her arm and said:

"Pictures apart, I'm terribly happy to have heard from Desmonde. Although I've a feeling that *he* is not happy."

"I'm sure he's not."

"Why not?"

"When he was a priest serving the Lord he *was* happy. Now he's merely a servant of the American Moving Pictures Industry."

"What a pity he ever met and loved that girl. I can't speak ill of her, now she's dead."

"The pity is that he was weak enough to fall for her. Love is quite a different cup of tea, Maister."

"Would you care to expound on the nature of that tender emotion, Professor?"

"Certainly. I love you, and I am happy to think that you love me. But we both have the virtue, the strength, and decency, quite apart from our love of dear Mum, to remain chaste. Desmonde, the weakling, did not have that. Now he's an outcast, blaming the Lord for what was entirely his own fault. He'll never find peace until he flings himself down on his pretty face and begs for forgiveness."

"That's exactly what an Italian padre said to me on the *Cristoforo Colombo* when I spoke to him of Desmonde."

Now we were in the village. I stamped and posted the letter.

"How about a coffee at the Copper Kettle? And one of these jolly good home-made gingerbread squares."

"Oh, good. And we'll bring Mum some. She's fond of that gingerbread."

We walked home by the Canon's walk, holding hands in silence.

My hope of an early reply from Desmonde was gradually dulled. I gathered from the popular weeklies that he was busy, beginning his third picture, and resigned myself to wait. And indeed, I heard nothing for a further three months, when I received the following long and extraordinary communication.

My dear Alec,

I have withheld my letters for so long simply because I have had nothing good to say. Indeed, my state of being has been so permanently depressed, troubled and unhappy that I have refrained from inflicting it upon you.

You know, I suppose, that the popular romantic conception

of Hollywood is a myth, fostered by those to whom glamour is the catchword for box office receipts. I can now assure you that the actual life in the studios is a hard, grinding, incomparably wearing business where, under blinding white lights, one repeats, often many times, a single piece of action or dialogue that forms a minute part of the completed film, or, in the final analysis, may even be cut out altogether. When not on the spot, under these blinding lights, one sits in the big draughty studio, watching drearily, awaiting one's turn to be called, or scanning the daily papers for news of the outside world. It is a dehumanizing existence which drives many of the actors, if I may so call the puppets controlled by a megaphoned director, to nightly excesses that hit the headlines, adding lustre to the popular notion of a glorious, gilded existence.

But enough, all this was borne in on me when I started work on my first picture. I then decided that I would endure this unnatural life, an existence utterly barren of all that I had previously enjoyed and loved, for three years and no more. I would then have fulfilled my three-picture contract and acquired a large fortune that would enable me to disappear, suddenly and forever, from this hollow city of glittering make-believe.

So far I have succeeded in pursuing my intention, and Frank Hulton, one of my few friends in this wilderness, has advised me well, and most admirably managed my affairs. Frank keeps urging me to take up some form of relaxation, to play golf at Bel Air, or to join the Racquet Club at Palm Springs. He has even suggested that I pick myself a nice girl from the flock of lovely starlets, poor little play-things, who hang around me, hoping and hoping to be noticed and taken up for the 'break' that would lead them to fame and fortune. Alas, they are out of luck with me. I have learned my lesson, and it was a bitter, bitter one. For this same reason I never, but never, go to parties.

How, then, do I spend such spare time as my overlords allow me? I live permanently in one of the Beverly Hills cottages, where everything is done for me and I am free of all housekeeping worries. On my free days, I drive out to Malibu in my unostentatious Rover, park, then walk, walk for miles on Malibu Beach, that great wide stretch of sand on which the

waves of the Pacific thunder endlessly. Few people use this
stretch, far from the swimming beach and bathing huts, and
I encounter only two regulars: Charles Chaplin, too enwrapped
in his own genius to be conscious of anyone but himself, and a
tall, strongly built man who walks slowly, reading, but who
occasionally nods and smiles to me as we pass. These apart,
one can find solitude, and here I walk, struggling with myself
and with my own unhappy thoughts.

You know, of course, that I have abandoned all my religious
beliefs, in the beginning from a sense of anger and resentment
at the unjust punishment meted out to me for a fault not
entirely my own. Now, anger fades after a time, so too does
resentment, and I will now confess to you that I have several
times, at first feebly and then more strongly, had the incentive
to seek the quiet of the Church in Beverly Hills, which you
yourself frequented, not for purposes of prayer but from a kind
of curiosity to see how it would affect me, or if indeed it would
in some way alleviate the inner ferment that churns, like a
live thing, in my breast.

Now mark this, Alec, and you know that I am not and
never have been, a liar. On three separate occasions when
I approached the Church and climbed the steps with the
intention of entering it, a frightful spasm took possession of
me, I trembled, felt deathly sick and thought I must vomit
but could not. Although unable to be physically sick, a stream
of words issued from my lips. You know that I have never
been addicted to the use of foul language. But these words
were unbelievably foul, blasphemous and obscene. So violent
were my spasms I thought I would have a fit, turned, and
stumbled down the steps. Only when my feet were on the
pavement of the public road did my agitation and vituperations
cease. I felt the blood course back to my arms, my legs, in
short, within a few moments I was myself again.

The first time this occurred I was not only alarmed, but
so shaken that I made up my mind never to risk a repetition
of the experience. Nevertheless, I was curious as to the nature
of my attack and presently came to the conclusion that I had
been the victim of a physical reaction, possibly cardiac in
origin.

To test this theory I drove out to the summit of Bel Air.
Here I parked the car, walked down hill for perhaps a hundred

yards, turned, and set myself to climb this steep incline at top speed. When I reached my car I was slightly blown but no more than I would normally have expected.

I drove back to my cottage, thoughtful and indeed worried. I was certainly the victim of some strange phobia, connected with the Church in Beverly Hills. You will remember that I refused to accompany you to this particular Church.

For the next few weeks I was busy in the studio, faking my way through the love scenes in the Hollywood version of *Aida*. But on my first free Saturday I drove through the city of Los Angeles to the big new Catholic Church, off Sunset Boulevard. I parked the car and, calmly facing the Church, assured myself that I was sound in mind, and body, I then set my teeth and began to walk up the steps of the great Church.

My God, Alec, how can I write you of my experience, worse, much worse than before, so violent that I fell down in a fit, rolled down the steps and came to myself in the centre of a crowd, with a policeman supporting my head.

Fortunately he knew me and fully realized that I was cold sober.

"You took a nasty toss, sir. And not the first here. They built these steps far too steep."

I got to my feet, thanked him, and assured him that I was not hurt. But as I drove back to Beverly Hills I was deeply and profoundly worried.

In this mood I reported for work at the studio where I went through some fatuous love scene retakes with the leading lady who has for weeks been trying to get off with me.

On the following day, Sunday, I drove out to Malibu, walked far along the strand, and sat down to examine my situation. Without doubt I was, under certain conditions, no longer master of myself or of my actions. A phrase from a poem learned in childhood came to mind. "He was the master of his soul." I was no longer master of my soul. And if so, what next was in store for me?

Crushed, and alarmed by this thought, I put my head between my hands, striving for self control. Without doubt I must seek advice. A doctor, a psychiatrist? I knew of no one.

At this moment I became aware that someone was speaking to me.

"Are you ill? Can I be of assistance to you?"

The tall man whom I had often passed was bending towards me.

"No . . . no, thank you. I'll be all right in a minute."

He looked at me doubtfully, then sat down beside me.

"You are Desmonde Fitzgerald, are you not? The film star."

I nodded silently. This was no beastly autograph hunter. He had a strong, lined, intellectual face. Suddenly I had a premonition that this was no chance encounter.

"I enjoyed your first film. Partly because I had often heard Caruso sing, in Italy. I found it difficult to decide which voice was superior, his or yours." He paused. "I believe you also have sung in Italy."

Now there was no doubt whatsoever. This man knew me. And from my earliest beginnings. Suddenly I had an impulse to unburden myself. I was in trouble. Perhaps he might help me. Then came the counter thought: don't make an ass of yourself with a total stranger. I got to my feet.

"I'll walk back now," I said.

"I'll come with you, if I may. I have often wished to speak with you, so often—forgive me—so often have I seen sadness and unhappiness written upon your face."

"Are you a doctor?"

"Of sorts."

"You seem to know of me rather intimately."

"Yes, I do," he answered simply. "I am the pastor of St. Bede's Church in Beverly Hills. Your friend, author and doctor, who brought you here, came to see me. He was anxious about you, worried by the complete change in your natural character and disposition. We had a long talk. Now, of course, I could not intervene, our meeting has been purely fortuitous, or should I say providential. I often come here to read my office and to get a breath of sea air. Now that we have met, come and sit with me, in my car, or yours, and let us have a little chat."

Resisting an impulse to tell him to go to hell, I sat with him in his old Ford and, compelled by the strength of his personality, I let him have the whole story. He heard me in silence.

"What's the matter with me? Am I possessed? Or merely going crazy?"

"Don't say another word," he commanded. "Get into your car and follow me."

I obeyed. Where was he taking me? To the yard of the presbytery of St. Bede's. Here we both got out. He came towards me, took my hand, and literally dragged me to the steps leading to the church. Then, before I could protest or resist, he lifted me bodily, bore me up the steps, then, with a final rush, into the church and up to the altar, where, suddenly, he relinquished me.

I fell flat on my face, literally writhing, in a series of convulsions, endlessly, the sweat pouring from my brow. At last, with a final spasm, I was still.

"Don't move, Desmonde."

He had a towel with which he wiped my lips, my brow, then raised me to sit beside him.

We sat in silence for perhaps five minutes, then he said:

"Desmonde, you are still weak. Nevertheless, I command you to go out of the church, and down the steps. You will then turn, and return to me here."

I went out of the church and down the steps. Then, without hesitation and with complete ease, I came back up the steps, into the church, and knelt down beside him.

Here the narrative broke off. And beneath, Desmonde had written:

I have to stop now, to go to the studio. I hope this long screed did not bore you. I simply had to write it to you, my dear, dear friend. Later on, I will continue.

When I had finished, I handed it to Nan to read. She was as deeply moved as I was. At last she said:

"What on earth? Was he really possessed?"

"Who can tell? Satan has many wiles. Yet it could be rationally explained. A long and powerful psychological build-up of hatred, following upon his unhappy marriage. Hatred and revulsion against the Church, against God."

"How terrible."

"Yes, but it can happen. I'm glad I spoke to Father Devis."

"That was a blessing."

"And now, we'll have to wait, and hope."

IX

ONCE AGAIN I was waiting for Desmonde, not at Euston but on this occasion at Victoria, and once again I was early. Rather than submit to the jostlings of porters and passengers already moving towards the P. and O. boat train, I went into the waiting room and began to re-read the amazing letter written with the old Desmonde sentimental and ebullient panache, which had brought me here and which, dated the week before, was incredibly headed, Seminary of St. Simeon, Torrijos, Spain.

My very dear Alec,
I am on my knees to you, begging absolution for my neglect, my unpardonable delay in advising you of all that has been happening to your old friend, of his trials and tribulations, and finally the wonderful solution, or say rather the Heaven inspired resolution which has raised his bowed head, fired him with new incentive, vigour and inspiration. Desmonde is himself again, looking forward to a new beginning, to an adventurous future dedicated to the service of suffering humanity and to the Lord. How can I adequately thank you, dear Alec, for your wisdom and foresight in alerting Fr. Devis to the fact that I should have need of him? He has brought me back to myself, as I was before, and although I have irretrievably lost my priestly privileges I am once again a practising and penitent member of the Church.
And how kindly and thoughtfully the good Fr. Devis has guided me into the channel that my life must now take, a course which, indeed, has been dormant within me ever since my arduous days at St. Simeon's. Yet who would have believed Fr. Hackett when he said: "I'll make a missionary of ye yet, Fitzgerald."
You must know that I could never be reinstated as a priest, and even if this were possible, what chance would I have of properly officiating in an Irish or an English parish, where my past would be a matter for scurrilous street corner gossip? Fr. Devis was emphatic on this point and so perforce was I. We decided that any work of expiation or atonement

which I might undertake must be in foreign fields. It was
then that Fr. Devis pronounced those fateful words: "You
must go to Father Hackett to see what he can do for you."

Of course, I agreed, for the same thought was in my mind.

I made my escape, with great difficulty, from the studios of
Hollywood, in which I never knew a single moment of
happiness. They tried hard to lasso me with a new contract,
but with Fr. Devis's help I escaped the noose, under the
pretext that my voice required rest. And so I went, as a
penitent, to St. Simeon's, bearing, as a gesture of propitiation
and submission, an exact replica of the Golden Chalice which,
for one short year, had been in the custody of the college.

I spare you, dear Alec, the moving sentiments and deep
emotions of my return to my alma mater. Needless to tell
you that I was profoundly affected, the more so since the
little monastic cell which I had once inhabited had been
prepared and allotted to me again.

Dear little Petitt, alas, is no more. I shed tears over his
grave. My enemy, the execrable Duff, has proved himself a
better man than I. He is now out in the Congo, not a particularly comfortable spot in which to lead the forces of Christian
endeavour.

Fr. Hackett is little changed, for a man almost continuously
afflicted by a recurrent fever; he is not only brave, but remarkably durable. He received me calmly and was greatly pleased
by my offering of the Chalice.

Once we got together on my problem he had little difficulty
in coming to a decision. He said, calmly and seriously:

"I know exactly, Desmonde, what I shall do with you.
Since you are no longer a priest you are useless in the general
field of missionary endeavour. In any case, you are not physically fitted for the jungles of Central Africa. However,"
here he paused, regarding me intently, "there is an opportunity
awaiting you, one eminently suitable, in India." He went on:
"You are aware, Desmonde, of the work I started in Madras,
amongst the children of the Untouchables, those little half-
naked beings, who clutter the pavements, even the gutters, of
the city, neglected, destitute and homeless. I had done something towards starting a dispensary and a school for them, and
when I was obliged to leave, this work was wonderfully
developed by an excellent American priest, Father Seeber. He

has done well, and now has a school of considerable size where many, many of these human waifs have been clothed, educated and transformed into happy and useful members of society. Some have even gone on to be teachers, priests, doctors.

"Now Father Seeber is no longer young. I know from his correspondence with me that he finds the work rather too much for him. He would welcome an assistant, particularly one who is fond of children and capable of dealing with them. What a blessing it would be if he could find the right person, who would help him to expand and develop his school, one especially who might assist him financially, for I assure you he is always in need of money." Father Hackett paused and looked at me significantly. "Would you wish me to cable him on your behalf?"

How can I describe, Alec, the arrow of joy that pierced my heart?

What a heaven sent opportunity! You know that I have always loved teaching children, and it was said at Kilbarrack that I 'had a way with them'. Now to have this chance to exercise my talent and in a foreign land, spiced with the savour of novelty and adventure. I immediately begged Fr. Hackett to cable.

He did so, and for all that day and most of the next I paced the grounds of the seminary in an agony of suspense. Then came the reply. I was accepted. I was to go at once! I went immediately to the Church and offered up a prayer of gratitude.

Then came the business of preparations for my departure, no easy matter, I assure you, Alec, since there was much demanding my attention. A P. & O. liner was due to leave Southampton for Bombay in six days' time and immediately, by cable, I booked my passage on this ship. In Madrid I would pick up some attire suitable for the tropics, and train direct to Paris, thence to London where I hope to meet with you. I thought it wiser not to break my journey in Ireland, but I shall return there one day when I have redeemed myself. So on to London where I shall be with you. And what a happy reunion this will be.

I should explain that my purgatorial period in Hollywood has not been entirely wasted, and under the judicious management of Frank Hulton a substantial fortune is wisely invested which supplies me with an annual income, adequate not only for the charitable needs in the adventurous future ahead of me, but for those personal obligations which it is my duty and pleasure to discharge.

You should know that an annuity has been settled on my daughter which will make her future safe and secure. I have also sent Madame Donovan a gift which I hope she will appreciate. This is a most adorable little antique silver statue of the Virgin, pure fifteenth century, not Benvenuto Cellini, of course, but by a comparable artificer, which I found in 57th Street, New York, before taking ship for Genoa. In the same street I chanced upon a delicious Mary Cassatt, a mother and child, of course, which I could not resist. This has been shipped to you, dear Alec, and I know you will love it. Nor did I forget Mrs. Mullen and Joe, who were so kind to me in Dublin. They have been well rewarded. Canon Daly was a more difficult proposition. I would have sent him "Dew" but I know he is well supplied with that commodity, so instead I sent him, with my love, some finely embroidered linens for his altar.

Oh, God, how it pains me to recollect these happy days at Kilbarrack, and the foretaste of Heaven that I threw away through my own folly. But I shall make reparation in the slums and stinking alleys of Madras. Already I have borrowed a Hindustani phrase book from Fr. Hackett!

But enough, Alec, I will cable you when I am due to arrive and where we may meet. Perhaps you will give shelter for a night to this happy pilgrim, your most loving friend.

I folded and pocketed this gushing, effusive, so typical screed, with the cable that had followed: DELAYED A FULL DAY BY YELLOW FEVER SHOTS IN PARIS. PLEASE MEET ME VICTORIA 10 AM FRIDAY FOR A FINAL FAREWELL DESMONDE. Train time was perilously near. Surely he must show up soon. I rose and went out of the waiting-room.

And there, suddenly, my eye was caught and held. Garbed in a pulled down black sombrero that had something of the cleric, but more of the bandit, a short black full-skirted coat, formidably belted at the waist by a four-inch leather strap, black trousers narrowed to ankle length, soft leather boots and striding with the serious air of a pioneer behind two porters, who staggered beneath a huge brass-studded cabin trunk. Yes, it was Desmonde, dressed up for his new part and playing it for all it was worth.

He saw me and immediately came towards me, holding out both his hands.

"My dear, dear Alec. How wonderful to see you again! And how sadly unfortunate that our meeting should be here. Those beastly yellow fever shots!" He looked at his large wrist-watch, which, peppered with the signs of the Zodiac, seemed also to be a compass. "Come! We have at least ten minutes." He drew me into the deserted waiting-room. "I've paid my bearers, they'll put my luggage in the van."

We sat down, looking at each other.

"You're just the same, Alec. You don't look a day older. It's these appalling cold baths. How do you find me?"

I saw that he was the identical Desmonde who had sent Fr. Beauchamp the birthday cake, but I answered:

"Vastly changed in the outward man."

He gave me a pleased smile. "I've been through the fires of hell, Alec, but now I'm a new man."

"You've had a great rush getting here. Have you had breakfast?"

"I had some *chota hazri* on the Dover train," he answered with affected indifference. "Breakfast, you know. By the way, did you get the Mary Cassatt?"

"I did, Desmonde, thank you immensely. It's lovely."

"I expect Miss Radleigh likes it."

"She does. And my wife too. It quite cheered her up. She's been not too well lately."

"I'm sorry, Alec." He had partly opened his coat, revealing, to my surprise, a formidable sheath knife, snugly holstered on his hip.

"You're armed, Desmonde."

"Dacoits," he murmured laconically. "They're around in the Madras area. One must be prepared. It's beastly uncomfortable, hurts rather, but I want to get used to wearing it." He paused. "Have you news from Ireland for me?"

"Yes, Desmonde. We see quite a bit of Madame Donovan these days. She has followed up our meeting in Switzerland, and when she's in London she comes to see my wife. They like each other very much. Very kindly, she has had me over to fish when the salmon were running in the Blackwater. I can report that she is well, that your little daughter is growing up bright and beautiful. And that the dear old Canon is still going strong."

He was silent, then said:

"Do let them know how you found me." He spoke with dramatic verve. "Sallying forth in my war paint, resolute and unafraid."

I found it difficult to repress a smile. This, indeed, was Desmonde, who would never, never grow up. How lucky he had been in Hollywood to have Frank Hulton, and Fr. Devis too. Otherwise, the wolves would have eaten him. He would do well, no doubt, in India, if there were an audience of sorts to watch and praise. Perhaps some youthful Maharanee might require enlightenment and instruction. But I cut the thought and said:

"You must go back to Ireland one day."

"Yes, Alec, when, like Clive, I have conquered India."

Now I looked at my wrist-watch, quite ornamental, but guaranteed pure nickel, at five bob a time.

"Don't you think, Desmonde . . . your train?"

"Ah, yes." He stood up. "Come with me to the barrier, dear Alec."

I complied, following as he strode on, like Cavaradossi to his execution. And there, under the startled eyes of a couple of ticket collectors, he embraced me, on both cheeks, before striding off, manfully, towards his compartment.

I felt I ought to play up to him by waiting to see his train pull out. But I was rather tired of waiting, my wife was ill, my new novel looked like being a flop, and, as I had come out without my *chota hazri*, I thought I would go home.

X

WE HAD FINISHED our usual Sunday lunch, quickly produced after church: green salad with toasted Gruyère cheese on Knäckebrot followed by fruit and coffee, and were seated at the big window of the sun room looking down the long garden at the distant Dents du Midi and Lake Leman far beneath. The sun shone in a blue sky, a cool wind flailed the light branches of the trees. And again I thought how blessed we had been five years ago to find this lovely little place, the low, beautifully designed house almost new, the garden already planted with choice shrubs and trees. Madame Donovan had heard of it and had enticed me to Switzerland.

"More coffee," Nan said. "Another cup, Maister, or you'll fall asleep."

"Quiet, child. You know I promised to trim the azaleas. If I don't, you'll get no blooms next year."

"I meant to tell you, Maister, I did them yesterday. But the peonies need weeding."

"My mind was firmly set on the azaleas, and you've done me out of them."

"Look! There's the darling little blue tit in my feeding box."

"Your darling will eat all the cherries, the little brute. And that fat blackbird you cherish, Mr. Pickwick, there he is, digging holes in the lawn."

Suddenly the front door bell buzzed.

"Damn it."

"I'll go," Nan said. "Gina's gone off for her afternoon."

"No, don't. It'll be some beastly intruder wanting to see round the garden. Don't answer and they'll go away."

The bell buzzed again.

"Two rings," I said. "They'll go now."

But after a short silence, the bell buzzed again, loud and prolonged.

"Now we must," said Nan and rising, hurried to the door. Almost at once a dialogue began which I could not distinctly hear, then Nan came back, looking troubled and uncertain.

"Maister," she said, in a low voice, "there's a strange little man out there, dressed in black, with a great bristling white beard. He wants to see you. I think he's a priest. His name is Father Keever."

"Keever?" Then I shot out of my chair and made for the door. "Could it be Seeber?"

And so it was! I would have known him anywhere, not only from Desmonde's frequent descriptions, but from the inset photo that always authenticated his delightfully amusing appeals for money.

"Do come in, Father," I said, offering my hand. "What a magnificent surprise!"

"I will, I will come in." He smiled. "But just to relieve your mind, I can't stay. I've been over in Cologne visiting my brother, but I couldn't go back without breaking my return journey to look you up."

"You simply must stay over with us."

"No, no, doctor, I cannot. My plane leaves Geneva at six-thirty."

"Then let me get you some lunch."

"No, doctor. I had a fair good feed on the plane from Cologne. But if you offer me a cup of your coffee I'll not say no."

Nan immediately poured a cup from the thermos flask. As he accepted it, he smiled.

"Miss Radleigh, is it not? I've heard of you from Desmonde. You don't like him?"

"Not him. Only his bowings, knee bendings, and hand kissing."

"You'll never shake him out of these." The little man laughed. "You haven't heard from him lately?"

"No. Not for ages. And we're thirsting for news."

"Well, you'll have it. But first, let's have news from you. You're both well?"

"Don't we look in fairly good form?"

"You do, you do. And your poor wife?"

"She is well too, physically. But . . . all else is gone. She does not know me now, nor her children. Yet she is happy and, I assure you, since she is prohibited from being at home, well cared for with two special nurses and her doctor in a beautiful country estate . . . the best clinic available for one in her condition."

"Oh dear, oh dear! What a pity!" He sighed, adding: "And what a fearful expense for you?"

This was an inquiry that required no answer. But it was my main reason for living in Switzerland.

There was a silence while our visitor studied us with wise kind eyes.

"And you two dear people, now you are quite alone here . . . You've been to church, of course, this morning?"

"Naturally, Father. In Vevey. Our churches are within one

hundred metres of each other . . . mine St. Teresa's, and for
Nan the nice little Church of England, All Saints."

"Good," he said. "So you are still keeping faith. The castle
has not fallen."

"Well, Father, the battlements have suffered some crushing
attacks, but the portcullis remains unbreached. Often when we
have spent a long heavenly day together and at night must
go to our separate rooms, I drool a little, and favour Nan
with that atrocious line from Tosti's 'Goodbye':

'Adieu the last sad moment, the parting hour is nigh.'"

He smiled. "Yes, it is hard. But you will both be the better
for it. And love the more. Besides, you have so much to be
grateful for, this lovely garden and house. Such peace too:
domus parva, magna quies." He glanced appreciatively round the
room, then exclaimed: "But where are your pictures? Desmonde speaks so often of your lovely Impressionists. I don't
see them."

"They have been removed by the Swiss police."

"Good heavens!" He sat up, startled. "For your debts?"

"No! There have been so many robberies lately of valuable
paintings that, as we go away often to visit my wife, I have
been constrained, almost compelled, to remove them to a
place of safety. They are now in the vaults of the Crédit
Suisse Bank where we may visit and view them as often as we
wish."

"Yes." After a moment's thought: "Undoubtedly a wise
precaution. But what a sad indictment of the world of today.
I must not tell Desmonde. He is proud of the pictures he gave
you."

"No, please don't tell him, Father. And certainly do not
tell him that the Mary Cassatt he sent me is not genuine."

"What! A fake!"

"A clever copy. Unrecorded. And of no provenance whatsoever."

"No, I must not tell. Or he would in atonement immediately
send you something extremely precious."

We both looked at him in surprise.

"You are joking, father?"

He shook his head, then smiled, and said:

"I see that you are burning to have news of Desmonde. Well,

I will tell you. So listen to what may be the grande finale of his varied and adventurous career." He paused, then began:

"When Desmonde came to me he was eager, ardent, overflowing with the resolution to prove himself, in every way, in short to redeem himself. He was tactfully persuaded to disarm himself—we assured him that his knife would not be needed, except in the kitchen where in fact it made an excellent ham slicer. Then we introduced him to his class. He immediately liked the little boys and it was evident that they were prepared to like him. Yet it was discouraging for him to discover that they were far from ready to be instructed, as he had hoped, in Greek and Latin. Instead, they must first be taught to spell, read and write. Another shock for Desmonde lay in our adequate yet admittedly plain dietary, which depends largely on the two varieties of millet: *ragi* and *varagu*, both food staples, but far from titivating to the sophisticated palate." Here Fr. Seeber broke off to indulge in a little private chuckle. "It was amusing to observe Desmonde's face when presented with these platters. But determinedly he got them down, a resolution ameliorated by the fact that on the Saturday holiday he would, at lunch time, be observed sidling off in the direction of the Commercial Hotel.

"Now, as you can imagine, Desmonde was not content to stop at 'c-a-t' spells 'cat' and 'two and two make four'. What did he do? He began, of course, to teach his little boys to sing. And how they loved it! Soon he had them carolling away sweetly at hymns and nursery rhymes. Was this enough? Not at all. Selecting eight boys with the best voices, he collared them after school and, teaching in the church or in the empty class room, he began to make a choir. And did he succeed? At our quarterly assembly in the big hall he produced his choir. It was, I assure you, a great, an immense success. God bless my soul! They even sang two of his favourite songs, 'Oft in the Stilly Night' and 'Passing By', and were cheered to the echo. Even I was moved, deeply moved by those pure, lovely young voices ascending in perfect harmony."

Fr. Seeber paused. We were both listening intently, aware that there was more to come.

"Go on, do go on," Nan exclaimed. "More coffee? It's still piping hot."

Another cup of coffee was poured and gratefully accepted.

"Yes," Fr. Seeber resumed. "As you've guessed, nothing could stop Desmonde now. Madras is a great city, but news travels fast. Word of Desmonde's choir got around and before long an invitation came for the choir to sing at an afternoon charity concert to be held at the Government's Art College. With my permission Desmonde accepted. Now, obviously, the little boys couldn't go in their poor, makeshift clothes. So Desmonde got busy, ordered and had made . . . you'll never guess what . . . eight little scarlet soutanes and eight red hats. His choir was now named the Little Cardinals."

One saw at once in this the expression of Desmonde's subconscious longing. We could scarcely wait till Fr. Seeber finished his coffee.

"Now, I'm not going to bore you with the success of the Little Cardinals. Early on we decided we must accept only the few invitations that were absolutely impeccable and select. In Madras, third city of India, where indescribable poverty exists, there is also indescribable wealth, manifest mainly in the great houses and estates congregated in the aristocratic district of Adayar. Many of these rich people are Christians, and not infrequently, when a society luncheon or garden party was given, the Little Cardinals were invoked to entertain the guests. They went, and Desmonde, their teacher, Cardinal *manqué*, went with them, not only to have them sing, but to look out that they were not spoiled with sweetmeats and caresses. Naturally, he stayed to lunch and was found to be charming, indeed even more beguiling than the little boys."

He paused, with a reminiscent air, half smiling.

"Oh, do stop teasing us, Father," I implored. "You're doing it deliberately."

Still smiling, he resumed.

"One of the Adayar hostesses who manifested the greatest and most persistent interest in the Little Cardinals was a Eurasian lady, Madame Louise Pernambur, Christian yet a veritable Ranee, widow of a Puisne Judge of the High Court of Madras, who had inherited an enormous fortune from her father whose cotton mills with many hundreds of looms had for years flourished in Calicut. Louise Pernambur, possessor of many things beyond her magnificent estate in Adayar and a house in Poona, whither she retired during the hot Madras summer, was at this time thirty-five years of age, admirably indolent, in figure tending slightly perhaps to a pleasing *embonpoint* and, as is often the way with Eurasian women, with her creamy complexion and dark languorous eyes inordinately attractive. But, as many potential suitors had quickly discovered, those dreamy eyes could also be hard. Madame Pernambur knew her value and would never be bought cheap.

"How surprising then, how commendable that this tough, superbly rich and beautiful woman should be so tenderly interested in eight little choir boys. So much so, indeed, that when the Little Cardinals were not permitted to come, their teacher was bidden to luncheon, even to supper, delicious food served on the garden terrace under a huge lustrous moon."

Suddenly Fr. Seeber paused and looked at his watch.

"Good heavens! Almost half-past three. The car will be coming for me, in fact I think I hear it on your drive. Now I can't tease you any more. There could be no doubt whatsoever. Although no words had yet been spoken, Louise had fallen deeply, extravagantly, in love.

"One Saturday afternoon when I was in Adayar visiting one of our patrons, I thought I would look in on Madame Pernambur. I knew that Desmonde had been invited there for tea and, as I was hot and thirsty, I hoped I might pick up a refreshing cup and a bun for myself.

"It was perhaps half-past three o'clock, the day a real Madras blazer, very different from the persistent rains and heavy floods devastating Bihar up north. As I am now familiar with the house, almost persona grata, I slipped in by the terrace door, along the passage, and on to the great lounge. Here I drew up, unobserved, in the shadow of the doorway.

"Seated side by side, on the great low settee, under the punka, rhythmically swung by one of the house boys, were Desmonde and his hostess: Madame in a lovely blue négligée of fine blue voile.

"Desmonde, to his credit, occupied the extreme end of the settee while Madame, as though by some process of gravitation, had drawn quite close to him and was looking fondly into his eyes. Suddenly, softly, she murmured a few words in his ear. He responded with a polite smile which, however, barely concealed an air of fatigue, one might even say boredom, whereupon she stretched an arm, and pressed a switch.

"I knew what was coming since recently an enormous electric organ had been imported from New York and, loaded with Desmonde's tapes, planted in a recess outside the lounge. And now, with a premonitory boom it launched into:

'You are my heart's delight,
And where you are I long to be . . .'

"As this incomparable young voice swelled through the room she drew still nearer to him. And if ever I saw matrimony in a woman's eyes, it was there, at that moment—I knew Louise well, and with her it could never be anything else.

"So I turned and tiptoed out by the way I had come, then made the circuit to the main entrance where I left a polite message with the butler."

As Fr. Seeber concluded, we gazed at him in silence, partially stunned by his recital.

"Well," I said at last, "trust Desmonde to make a soft landing. I hope he'll be happy."

"Wait, wait!" Fr. Seeber exclaimed. "Don't let us rush our fences. That evening, when Desmonde returned, rather earlier than usual, he went straight to his class room. Here his little pupils had gathered to await him. Immediately he entered he was greeted by a song which they had made up amongst themselves; childish rhymes of affection and praise, but which, sung by these sweet little voices, were really touching.

"Desmonde had moist eyes when he left the class room, and I noted that he went into the chapel. I knew then that he would come to me and indeed, half-an-hour later, he knocked at my study door.

"'Come in, Desmonde.'

"He entered and immediately knelt at my feet.

"'Father, I have something to tell you.'

"'Get up, you ass, and sit in that chair.'

"When, with reluctance, he obeyed, I went on: 'And you have no need to tell me. I already know, and you have only yourself to blame. With your hand kissing and knee bending, your long lingering glances from those big blue adoring eyes, you have made the poor woman think that you are hopelessly in love with her and too shy, too humble to declare yourself. So,' I paused, 'she has done it for you. Am I correct?'

"'Yes, father,' he said miserably. 'She wishes to take me to Poona for a quiet wedding.'

"'Do you wish to go?'

"He shook his head dolefully.

"'I don't want to end my miserable life in her boudoir. Besides,' the poor fool mumbled, 'I can't stand her smell.'"

Nan and I had an irresistible impulse to laugh, but a glance from Fr. Seeber restrained us.

"Desmonde was not quite himself. So very firmly I told him that if he wished to avoid further trouble he must clear out at once. They were yelling for helpers up in Bihar where the floods had created frightful havoc and the river had overflowed its banks, sweeping away an entire village. I told him to go and pack and to take a mattress, since it would be a long slow journey up the coast to Calcutta.

"'I don't want to leave my little boys, and you, Father.'

"'Then Madame will never let you be.'

"After a long moment he rose, silently went to his room, packed his bag and obediently brought down his mattress. At half-past ten that night I saw him board the north bound mail at Madras station."

A silence followed this long, and, for us, most interesting recital.

"Did he ever get to Bihar?" Nan asked.

"He did, and from reports coming back by wire, has conducted himself there with exceptional courage and resource."

"And Madame Pernambur?" Nan asked again.

"I have judged it expedient to pay a long-deferred visit to my brother," Father Seeber said mildly. "When I return she will be in Poona, to which lovely resort I shall direct a long, pleasingly adulatory, explanatory letter."

The car outside had now been hooting for some time. Fr. Seeber stood up.

"I wish I might stay longer. But now I must go. I'm glad to have found you both well and happy. And I shall tell Desmonde so."

As we escorted him to the door he took Nan's arm and, smiling, whispered in her ear. Then he shook hands, popped into the taxi and was gone.

"What a nice, wonderful little man," Nan said. "A perfect darling."

"He is indeed," I agreed warmly. "I must send him a decent cheque. But, my goodness, that Desmonde! Can you beat it! By the way, what did Father Seeber whisper to you?"

She lowered her eyes and murmured:

"Be good, sweet maid, and you will both continue to be happy."